FOURTH OF JULY MURDER

Lucy was pretty sure Pru was home because her car, an aged but impeccably maintained Dodge Shadow, was parked in its usual spot.

Lucy knew the wisest course of action would simply be to leave. She could leave a note, she could call later. She could stop by on her way home from work. The one thing she shouldn't do was start poking around in the hopes of finding Pru perched high on a ladder cleaning out the gutters or out behind the chicken coop.

On the other hand, she was here right now and she wanted to get this thing off her chest. She wanted to get it over with. It certainly couldn't hurt to peek around the hosue, where Pru kept a clothesline.

Lucy squared her shoulders and continued a few more paces down the drive, until she reached the corner of the house. There she had an unobstructed view of the turning area, where the driveway widened and where Wesley and Calvin parked their trucks. There were no trucks, today, but there was a crumpled pile of something blue, maybe laundry that had dropped off the line where several pairs of jeans were hanging heavily in the humid air.

Lucy went to investigate and as she drew closer she realized it wasn't a pair of blue jeans that had fallen at all. It was Pru, herself, lying in a heap.

Reaching the fallen woman, Lucy instinctively reached out and touched her shoulder, as if to wake her up. But Pru wasn't going to wake up. Pru was dead. Definitely dead . . .

Books by Leslie Meier

MISTLETOE MURDER

TIPPY TOE MURDER

TRICK OR TREAT MURDER

BACK TO SCHOOL MURDER

VALENTINE MURDER

CHRISTMAS COOKIE MURDER

TURKEY DAY MURDER

WEDDING DAY MURDER

BIRTHDAY PARTY MURDER

FATHER'S DAY MURDER

STAR SPANGLED MURDER

NEW YEAR'S EVE MURDER

BAKE SALE MURDER

CANDY CANE MURDER

ST. PATRICK'S DAY MURDER

MOTHER'S DAY MURDER

Published by Kensington Publishing Corporation

A Lucy Stone Mystery

STAR SPANGLED MURDER

Leslie Meier

KENSINGTON BOOKS
http://www.kensingtonbooks.com

KENSINGTON BOOKS are published by

Kensington Publishing Corp.
119 West 40th Street
New York, NY 10018

All Kensington titles, imprints, and distributed lines are available at special quantity discounts for bulk purchases for sales promotion, premiums, fund-raising, educational, or institutional use.

Special book excerpts or customized printings can also be created to fit specific needs. For details, write or phone the office of the Kensington Special Sales Manager: Attn.: Special Sales Department. Kensington Publishing Corp., 119 West 40th Street, New York, NY 10018. Phone: 1-800-221-2647.

Kensington and the K logo Reg. U.S. Pat. & TM Off.

ISBN-13: 978-0-7582-2898-7
ISBN-10: 0-7582-2898-8

First Kensington Books Hardcover Printing: June 2004
First Kensington Books Mass-Market Paperback Printing:
June 2005

10 9 8 7 6 5

Printed in the United States of America

For Daddy

Who enlisted in November 1941 and served in the Army Air Corps for "three years, nine months and sixteen days" in England, North Africa, and Italy.

Prologue

He'd killed before and he would kill again. He couldn't help himself. It was more than an addiction; he was programmed to do it. It was in his DNA. He loved the rush of excitement when he spotted his victim and the sense of power he felt when he'd mastered his prey. They were so stupid. Going about their daily business unaware of the eyes watching them. His eyes. They thought they had it all under control, but they didn't. They would live or die as he willed. As he desired.

He sighed and rolled over on the sorry excuse for a bed that his captors gave him. There would be no killing today. He stared at the thick wire mesh that confined him. It was nothing more than a pen, really, but there was no way out. He'd tried, of course. It was his major occupation, considering the small amount of exercise his captors allowed him. He'd examined every corner, looking for a gap, a loose screw, a flaw in the concrete. So far, he hadn't found any.

So he'd just have to bide his time until they made a mistake. He could wait. He was used to it. He'd had to get used to it. But that didn't mean he'd given up. Oh, no. He was simply waiting for an opportunity. Hearing a door slam, he looked up. Maybe this was his big chance.

The woman was coming towards him carrying a bowl. His dinner. He got to his feet and watched as she opened the door and carefully slid the bowl towards him. "Hungry?" she asked, in a high squeaky voice. What did she think? Of course he was hungry. And bored. Eating was the high point of his day. Even the slop they gave him. He licked his chops, turning his attention to his meal.

And then he heard it. A shriek. "Mom! Come quick!"

She whirled around, slamming the heavy gate and ran for the house. He waited until she disappeared inside, then gave the gate an experimental push. It opened. This had happened before. She'd slammed it too hard and it had bounced back without latching. Stupid woman. Would she never learn? In a moment he was outside, sniffing the air, feeling the warmth of the sun on his back. It was a fine day, a fine day for killing.

He gave himself a good shake, then he was off, tail held high. His bowl of kibble remained untouched. Kudo was in the mood for chicken.

Chapter One

Lucy Stone wasn't usually a clock watcher. Time didn't pass slowly for her; it galloped ahead of her. As a part-time reporter—not to mention feature writer, listings editor and occasional photographer—for the *Pennysaver*, the weekly newspaper in Tinker's Cove, Maine, and the mother of four, her life sometimes seemed to her an endless chase after a spare minute. She was always late: late for meetings she was supposed to cover, late for doctor's appointments, late for picking up the kids. But not today.

Today her eyes were fixed on the old electric kitchen clock with the dangling cord that hung on the wall behind the receptionist's desk in the *Pennysaver* office. If only she could stop the minute hand from lurching forward, if only she could stop time, then she wouldn't have to go to the Board of Selectmen's meeting at five o'clock.

"Is there something the matter with my hair?" asked Phyllis, whose various job descriptions included receptionist, telephone operator and advertising manager. She gingerly patted her tightly-permed tangerine do. "You keep staring at it."

"Your hair's fine," said Lucy. "I'm looking at the clock."

Phyllis peered over her rhinestone-trimmed cat's-eye glasses and narrowed her eyes. "Have you got the hots for Howard White? Can't wait to see him," she paused and smoothed her openwork white cardigan over her ample bosom, "wield his gavel?"

Howard White was the extremely dignified chairman of the Board of Selectmen, a retired executive who was well on in years.

Lucy laughed. "Howard's not my type," she said.

Phyllis raised an eyebrow, actually a thinly penciled orange line drawn where her eyebrows used to be. "Why not? He's not bad looking for an old guy, and he's rich."

"He also has a wife," said Lucy. "And I have a husband."

"Details." Phyllis waved a plump, manicured hand, nails polished in a bright coral hue.

"I don't want to go to the meeting. I wish Ted would cover the Board of Selectmen until this dog hearing is over."

Ted was the owner, publisher and editor-in-chief of the *Pennysaver*.

"Did I hear my name?" he inquired, sticking his head out of the morgue where the back issues going all the way back to the *Courier & Advertiser*s printed in the 1800s were stored.

"Ted? Do me a favor and cover the selectmen's meeting? Please?"

"Trouble at home?"

"You could say that," said Lucy. "It's Kudo. He's been going after Prudence Pratt's chickens and I got a summons yesterday for a dog hearing. I just feel so awkward trying to cover the meeting with this thing hanging over me."

"Is the hearing tonight?"

"Next meeting."

"Sorry, Lucy, but I don't see a conflict of interest tonight. I'll cover the next hearing though."

"Do you have to?" asked Lucy, picturing her name in the headline. That darned dog was such an embarrassment. She felt like a criminal. "Couldn't we just skip that meeting? Pretend it never happened?"

"No," said Ted, flatly. "And if you don't get a move on, you're going to be late for today's meeting. It's five, you know."

Lucy checked the clock. It was five minutes to five.

"They never start on time," she said, slowly gathering up her things. "And town hall's just across the street. There's no hurry, really."

"You better get a move on."

Lucy hoisted the faded African basket she used as a purse on her shoulder and drifted towards the door.

"I'm not going to miss anything. Bud Collins is never on time and they always have to wait for him."

Ted yanked the door open, making the little bell jangle. "Go!"

"See you tomorrow," said Lucy, walking as slowly as a convict beginning the last mile.

The door slammed behind her.

Selectmen's meetings were held in the basement hearing room of the town hall. The walls were concrete block painted beige, the floor was covered in gray industrial tile, and the seating was plastic chairs in assorted colors of green, blue and orange. One end of the room was slightly elevated and that's where the board members sat behind a long bench, similar to the judge's bench in a courtroom.

What with the flags in the corner and a table and chairs for petitioners, the room was quite similar to the district court, thought Lucy. It wasn't a comforting idea and she tried to put it out of her mind as she took her usual seat, smiling at the scattering of regulars who never missed a meeting. Scratch Hallett, a gruff old fellow who had a plumbing and heating business and was active in veteran's affairs, was a particular favorite. She also recognized Jonathan Franke, the former environmental radical who was now the respected executive director of the Association for the Preservation of Tinker's Cove, and several members of that organization. They were exchanging friendly nods when Lucy's attention was drawn to a newcomer. Tall and gaunt, with her skimpy red hair pulled back into a straggly ponytail, it was none other than her neighbor Prudence Pratt, dressed in her customary summer outfit of baggy blue jeans and a free Blue Seal T-shirt from the feed store.

Lucy's heart sank. She hoped Pru hadn't gotten the date wrong, and thought the dog hearing was today. Or maybe she wanted to file an additional complaint. Kudo had gotten loose again the other day, and had come trotting home with a chicken feather stuck in his teeth. The memory made Lucy wince. She was at her wit's end; she'd tried everything she could think of to restrain the dog but he was some sort of escape artist. And whenever he got out, he went after her neighbor's chickens.

Lucy tried to catch Pru's eye, hoping to start

some kind of dialog. Maybe if she apologized for the dog's behavior, or offered to pay for the damages, they could work something out and avoid the hearing. But Mrs. Pratt stared straight ahead, pointedly ignoring her.

A little flurry of activity announced the arrival of the board members, who filed into the room accompanied by their secretary, Bev Schmidt, who kept the minutes. They always came in the same order, with IGA owner Joe Marzetti going first. He was a bundle of energy, tightly focused on the task at hand.

He was followed by newly elected member Ellie Sykes, a dollmaker and member of the Metinnicut Indian tribe whom Lucy had gotten to know when Indian rights activist Curt Nolan was murdered a few years before. Kudo had actually been Curt's dog and Lucy had taken him off Ellie's hands when he'd begun raising Cain with her flock of chickens. Ellie gave her a big smile as she sat down and arranged her papers.

Next came board veteran Pete Crowley, whose crumpled face and world-weary attitude seemed to imply he'd seen it all in the twenty years or so he'd sat on the board and nothing would surprise him.

Chairman Howard White always took the center seat, and was the only board member to wear a sport coat. He invariably shot his sleeves when he sat down, as if he were chairing a high-level meeting of movers and shakers instead of this oddly assorted group of public-minded citizens.

Bud Collins always brought up the rear. A retired physical education teacher and coach, he seemed to have used up all his energy urging Tinker's Cove High School students to run faster and jump higher.

He often dozed off during meetings. Lucy would have made a point of it in one of her stories, except for the fact that she sometimes dozed off too, especially during presentations by the long-winded town accountant, who tended to drone on endlessly in a monotone.

"The meeting is called to order," said White, with a tap of his gavel. "As usual, we'll begin with our public comment session. This is the time we invite citizens to voice any concerns they might have, keeping in mind that once we begin the advertised agenda discussion will be limited to the issues under consideration."

Pru's hand shot up.

Lucy swallowed hard and sat up straighter.

"You have the floor," said White, with a courteous bow of his head. "Please state your name and address for the minutes."

"You know perfectly well who I am," she snapped, "and so does Bev Schmidt. Gracious, we were in school together."

Howard White was normally a stickler for detail, but after glancing at Bev and receiving a nod in reply, he decided to allow this breach of procedure. "Please continue," he said.

"Well, as you know, my property on Red Top Road goes back all the way to Blueberry Pond, which is owned by the town. It's conservation land, open to the public for swimming and fishing, duck hunting in the fall, and up 'til now there's been no problem."

"But now there is?" inquired White.

"I'll say there is. They're naked back there. Butt naked! It's a disgrace!" Pru was clearly outraged: her mouth seemed to disappear as she sucked in her lips and her pale blue eyes bugged out.

Lucy fought the urge to giggle in relief, concentrating instead on the board member's reactions. They also seemed to be struggling to keep straight faces.

"I think there has always been a certain amount of skinny-dipping at the pond," said Bud Collins. "The kids like to go there after practices, especially the baseball team. To cool off with a swim."

"I don't know who they are and I don't care. I don't like it and I want it stopped! Isn't there a law against this sort of thing?" demanded Mrs. Pratt.

White looked to the other board members, who shook their heads.

"I am not aware of any town bylaw that forbids nudity," said White.

"And a good thing, too," offered Joe Marzetti. "There's nothing the matter with a hard-working man stopping by the pond for a quick dip on his way home on a hot summer day. Or at lunchtime, for that matter. There's nobody there most of the time. What's the harm?"

"What's the harm?" Pru's eyes bugged out in outrage. "It's immoral, that's what. It's time this town took a stand and stood up for public decency!"

"You're welcome to write up a proposal and put it on the town warrant for a vote at the town meeting," said White.

"Town meeting! That's not until next April!"

"We could call a special town meeting, but you'd have to get signatures for that." White paused. "Bev, how many signatures would she need?"

"Two hundred and fifty registered voters," said Bev.

"Bear in mind that a special town meeting costs

money," said Marzetti. "It's not generally popular with taxpayers."

"We'll see about that," said Pru. "I'll be back, you can count on it."

"We'll look forward to it," said White, casting a baleful glance at Ellie, who was struggling to suppress a giggling fit.

Lucy knew her duty as a reporter, so she followed Pru out of the room, catching up with her in the parking lot.

"Do you have a minute? I'd just like to get your reaction to the board's decision for the paper. . . ."

"My reaction isn't fit to print," snarled Pru. "That board's a bunch of godless, lily-livered, corrupt scoundrels. They'll rot in hell and so will you, Lucy Stone, you and that dog of yours." With that she climbed into her aged little Dodge compact and slammed the door.

"Can I quote you on that?" yelled Lucy, as she rolled out of the parking lot.

When Lucy returned to the meeting, Jonathan Franke was making a presentation with the help of a laser pointer and a flip chart. He had certainly adopted all the accessories of success, thought Lucy, who remembered the days when he was usually seen holding up a sign protesting government inaction or big business profiteering and sporting an enormous head of curly hair.

"As this chart shows," he said, indicating a bar graph, "Tinker's Cove is blessed with one of the few surviving communities of purple-spotted lichen in the entire state. Once abundant, this complex life form has fallen victim to a sustained loss of environment due to development and pollution. It is now considered endangered and is protected under the state's environmental protection act. I'm here tonight, with other members of the Association for the Preservation of Tinker's Cove, to request that the town take all appropriate steps to protect our priceless legacy of purple-spotted lichen."

Judging from their pleased expressions, Lucy understood the board members were congratulating themselves on their good judgement and wise management of a resource they hadn't actually known they had. Whatever they'd been doing, it had apparently been the right thing, at least for purple-spotted lichen.

"And how do you suggest we continue to care for this rare and wonderful little plant?" asked Ellie.

"That brings me to my next illustration," said Franke, flipping to the next page on his chart, a map of the town with prime lichen areas indicated by purple patches of color.

"As you can clearly see," he said, making the little red laser dot dance over the map, "one area of particular concern is out on Quisset Point. This is actually the town's largest community of purple-spotted lichen, thanks to the abundance of ferrous rock."

The board members nodded, indicating their high level of interest in an issue that was surely noncontroversial and certain to resonate positively with voters.

"That is why our organization, the Association for the Preservation of Tinker's Cove, is here tonight to request the cancellation of the upcoming July Fourth fireworks display."

All five board members were stunned, even Bud Collins, who had been nodding off. They had certainly not expected this.

"I'd like a clarification," said White. "Did you say you want us to cancel the fireworks?"

"You mean call them off?" demanded Marzetti.

"No fireworks at all?" exclaimed Crowley. "Isn't that un-American?"

"Believe me, we are not making this request lightly," said Franke, looking very serious. "We wouldn't consider it except for these facts." He lifted a finger. "A: The lichen is severely endangered throughout the state. B: The lichen is extremely fragile and easily damaged by foot traffic. And C: The lichen is highly flammable and one errant spark could wipe out the entire Quisset Point colony."

"I get you," said Crowley. "What say we move the fireworks off the point? Onto a barge or something?"

"Once again I believe there would be substantial risk from sparks."

Crowley scratched his head. "Okay, you say this is the best colony in the entire state, right? Well how come, if we've had the fireworks out there every year since who knows when? I mean, maybe this pinky-spotted moss likes fireworks! Have you thought of that, hey?"

"Actually, we have, and we've concluded that the continuing success of this particular colony of purple-spotted lichen is nothing less than miraculous. We've been lucky so far, but it's far too dangerous to continue endangering this highly-stressed species."

The board was silent, considering this.

"Can I say something?"

Lucy turned and saw Scratch Hallett was on his feet, his VFW cap in his hand.

"Please do," invited White, desperate for an alternative to calling off the fireworks.

"This just don't seem right to me," began Hallett. "A lot of folks have fought and some have even made the supreme sacrifice to keep America the land of the free and the home of the brave. We celebrate that freedom on the Fourth of July, always have, ever since 1776, and I don't see what this purple-spotted stuff has got to do with it. We didn't know we had it, none of us did except these here environmentalists. I never noticed it myself, and I don't care about it. We defeated the Germans and the Japanese and just lately the Iraqis so we could enjoy freedom, and you're telling me we have to stop because of an itty-bitty little plant?"

"Mr. Franke, would you care to reply?" said White. "I think this gentleman has made an important point."

"Yes, yes he has," said Franke, beginning diplomatically. "And I and the other members of the Association value our American values and freedoms as much as anyone, and the sacrifices made by members of the Armed Forces. I want to assure you of that. But," he continued, his voice taking on a certain edge, "I'd also like to remind you that the purple-spotted lichen is on the list of endangered species in this state and is therefore subject to all the protections provided by the state's environmental protection statute, which includes substantial penalties to any person or agency judged to have caused harm to said species."

The board members looked miserable. If she hadn't known better, Lucy would have suspected they were all coming down with an intestinal virus.

"As much as I hate to cancel the fireworks, it seems to me we have a responsibility to preserve our environment," said Ellie.

"I think we have to look at the APTC track record," said Crowley. "They've been active in our town for a good while now, and Tinker's Cove is a better place for it. We've preserved open space, we've maintained our community character, I think we've got to give them the benefit of the doubt on this one."

"I don't know what community character you're talking about. It's things like the Fourth of July parade and the fireworks that give our town character. I refuse to vote against the fireworks," declared Marzetti, who had grown hot around the collar.

"Well said," drawled Bud Collins.

"Is this a vote?" Howard White seemed uncharacteristically confused.

The others nodded.

"Two for and two against. I guess it's up to me."

The room was silent.

"My inclination is to hold the fireworks. It's been a tradition in this town for as long as I've been here and I hate to see it end." White sighed. "But I truly believe it would be irresponsible and futile to ignore the state regulation. It would set a bad precedent and it would cost us dearly in the end. It's with great sorrow that I vote to discontinue the fireworks display."

He had hardly finished speaking when Scratch

Hallett was on his feet, marching out of the room. He paused at the door. "This isn't the end of this," he declared, as he set his VFW hat on his head. "We may have lost the battle, but we haven't lost the war!"

Chapter Two

The buzz of the alarm woke Lucy and she squinted, trying to make out the time. Five-thirty. There must be some mistake. Then reality gradually dawned and she remembered it was Wednesday, deadline day. It was no mistake. She had to get up.

With a groan she sat up and groped with her feet for her slippers. Then she slipped on her lightweight summer robe and headed downstairs to the kitchen to make a pot of coffee. While it dripped she made a quick stop in the downstairs powder room, then went outside and down the driveway to get the morning paper. Kudo greeted her with a wagging tail and she stopped by the kennel to stroke the big, yellow dog's long nose, which he poked through the heavy-duty wire mesh fencing. Then she went back inside to drink her first cup of coffee and check her horoscope. It didn't look good: only two stars out of a possible five. Not that she really believed that stuff. Not at all.

At six she climbed back upstairs with a cup of coffee for Bill and to wake Elizabeth, who had to be at work at the Queen Victoria Inn by seven.

Elizabeth liked to cut it close and sacrificed breakfast in favor of an extra half-hour of sleep before
starting work at her summer job as a chamber-
maid. Lucy knew she was counting the days until
she could go back to Chamberlain College in Boston
to begin her sophomore year. Toby, the oldest, was
already gone; he'd left the house well before four.
He was working for Chuck Swift on his lobster boat
this summer and had to be down at the harbor before dawn.

   While Bill enjoyed his coffee in bed, checking
out the sports pages, Lucy got dressed. Since she'd
be in the office all day and didn't have any interviews, she opted for comfort in a pair of khaki
shorts and a polo shirt. It was already warm and
there was every sign it would be a scorcher of a day.

   Elizabeth wasn't up yet, so she called her again.
"You're going to be late," she warned. Elizabeth
groaned in reply. Encouraged, Lucy went back
downstairs and popped an English muffin in the
toaster. She was sitting at the table, eating it, when
Elizabeth sped through the kitchen, the apron strings
of her uniform streaming behind her. Minutes later
she was back.

   "My car won't start."

   "You probably flooded it. Give it a minute and try
again."

   "A minute!" she shrieked. "I haven't got a minute!"

   "Shhh. You're going to wake up Sara and Zoe."
The youngest girls were still asleep; Friends of Animals day camp didn't start until eight-thirty. Since
she had to be at the *Pennysaver* as early as possible,
Bill would drop them off, starting a bit later than
usual on his current project, restoring an old one-

room schoolhouse that had been moved from New Hampshire to become a guest house for some wealthy summer people.

"Let me take your car, okay, Mom? Please?"

"But what if I can't start your car, either? Then I'll be stuck. Call and tell them you're running late. They'll understand."

"I've already been warned, Mom!" Elizabeth was close to hysterics. "They'll fire me."

"Well, whose fault is that?" grumbled Lucy. Maybe there was more to those horoscopes than she thought.

"I know. I know. I'll do better in the future I promise. If only you let me take the car this one time. Please. Pretty please."

Lucy knew she was making a big mistake.

"Okay," she said, handing over the keys. "But this is the last time."

"Thanks, Mom. You're the best."

When Lucy tried to start Elizabeth's car, the engine didn't sound right. "RRR," it droned. "RRR." After a few tries she gave up and went back into the house to get help from Bill.

"The battery's dead," said Bill, who had progressed to the breakfast table.

"Are you sure?" asked Lucy. "How can you tell?"

"I can tell," said Bill.

"Can't we jump it or something?"

"I doubt it'll hold a charge. You'd just stall out somewhere and get stuck," said Bill. "You'll have to ride with me."

"I'll be late," groaned Lucy. "On deadline day."

"Nothing you can do about it," said Bill, with a

shrug. "You might as well relax and have another cup of coffee."

At a quarter past eight, the girls were ready to go, but they didn't like the idea of cramming into the cab of the pickup truck along with their parents.

"Can't we ride in back?" asked Sara.

"Mom'll squish me," observed Zoe, smoothing her new summer outfit.

"It's way too hot in the truck," whined Sara.

"Get a move on," snapped Bill. "Time's a wasting."

"Bill," asked Lucy, as she struggled to get the seat belt around herself and Zoe, who was sitting on her lap. "Will you pick up a battery?"

"I will not."

"We've got to get that car back on the road. What will Elizabeth do?"

"She can damn well take care of it herself. It'll be good for her. Teach her a valuable lesson." He paused. "You're way too soft on that girl."

"Right," said Lucy, wondering why she couldn't take the same hard line that Bill did.

"You're late," said Ted, when she finally arrived at the *Pennysaver.*

"I know," said Lucy. "Car trouble."

"I don't want excuses. . . ."

"Not again. I've already been through this with Bill." Lucy practically growled at him. "You'll have your story. On time."

"Okay, okay." Ted held up his hands and turned to Phyllis. "Must be that time of the month."

"I wouldn't go there if I were you," warned Phyllis.

"I have proofs to check," said Ted. "I'll be in the morgue."

Good place for him, thought Lucy, as she booted up her computer. If only he could stay there permanently. With Bill. They could sit and congratulate themselves on issuing tough lines and demands and ultimatums while the women of the world conciliated and compromised and kept things going.

"Anything much happen at the meeting?' asked Phyllis. The little fan she'd set up on her desk didn't even ruffle her hair-sprayed hair.

Lucy stared out the plate glass window, through the old-fashioned wood venetian blinds. A few early tourists were cruising Main Street, looking for breakfast. Mostly older couples, the men sporting captain's caps and the women with straw sun hats.

"They canceled the Fourth of July fireworks," said Lucy.

Phyllis choked on her coffee. "What?"

Ted stuck his head out of the morgue. "What?"

"You heard me. They canceled the fireworks. 'Cause of this purple-spotted lichen. It's endangered. At least that's what Jonathan Franke and the APTC people say."

"Lichen?"

"A flowerless plant composed of algae and fungi in a symbiotic relationship," said Lucy, quoting from the dictionary open on her desk. "It grows on rocks. And there's a major colony growing on the rocks out at Quisset Point."

"So why can't they move the fireworks?" asked Phyllis, looking quite perturbed.

"That was suggested, but they'd have to be in the cove so people could see them and there's a danger of falling sparks."

"The board actually voted to cancel the fireworks?" asked Ted, incredulous.

"They weren't happy about it," said Lucy. "But I
think they figured it was that or face all kinds of
penalties from the state. This lichen is on the endangered species list. And Franke as much as threatened to take them to court and they're terrified of
spending taxpayer's money on legal fees."

"What does it look like?" asked Phyllis. "I never
heard of it."

"It's that patchy stuff on rocks and trees."

"Like barnacles?"

"Kind of. It's softer. Sort of fuzzy."

"With purple spots?"

"I guess so. It's called purple-spotted lichen. It
must have spots. Purple ones."

"We're going to need a picture," said Ted, reaching for his camera. "Quisset Point, you say?"

"Just look for the spotty stuff."

He left in a hurry, slamming the door behind
him and making the little bell fastened to the top
jangle.

"I wouldn't want to be one of those selectmen,"
said Phyllis. "This isn't going to be popular. Not at
all."

"The VFW's already declared war," said Lucy.

"I'm not surprised."

It wasn't the VFW who fired the first salvo, however. It was the Chamber of Commerce. When Ted
returned with his film he was accompanied by chamber president Corney Clark, who was toting a picnic
basket. Corney operated a successful catering business out of her stylish home on Smith Heights Road.

"I know it's deadline day and you all work under so much pressure, so I brought you some relaxing herb tea and some fresh-baked corn muffins with my homemade lavender-lemon marmalade," she cooed. "Lavender is sooo relaxing."

In a matter of moments Corney had spread a blue and white checked cloth on the reception counter and topped it with an artful arrangement including a basket of muffins, a crock of marmalade and a cute vase of pansies. A thermos held the tea, which Corney was pouring into blue and white striped mugs.

"Sugar?" she asked.

"Sure," said Lucy, absolutely amazed.

"Ted, would you like a muffin? With marmalade?"

"M-m-muffin," stammered Ted. "Thanks."

"This lavender marmalade isn't half bad," said Phyllis, talking with her mouth full. "I wouldn't have thought it, but it's very good."

"I'm so glad you like it," said Corney, taking a chair, crossing her legs and getting down to business. "Now, Ted, I have a letter to the editor here from the Chamber about the fireworks. It's very timely and I hope you can get it in this week's paper."

Lucy knew the editorial page was already set, ready to go to the printer.

"Sorry, but that's impossible," mumbled Ted, biting into a second muffin.

"It's extremely important," continued Corney. "I think we're all in favor of protecting endangered species, but the local economy is also something of an endangered species, especially if this fireworks ban isn't lifted. The Fourth of July celebration with the fireworks is traditionally the beginning of our summer tourist season, and Ted, I'm sure you know how much many local businesses rely on the tourists."

She flourished the letter, making Lucy wonder where she'd had it stashed. Was the woman a magician?

"Of course, this is all stated much better in the letter," continued Corney. "Joe Marzetti and I and some of the chamber members got together first thing this morning. We decided it would be best to simply ask the selectmen to reconsider the probable impact of canceling the fireworks."

"Great letter," said Ted. "But I'll have to run it next week."

"Now, Ted, I don't mean to tell you your business, but you're missing the boat here. This is a hot issue. Everybody's going to be waiting for their *Pennysaver* this week, believe me. You don't want to let your readers down."

Lucy found herself agreeing with Corney. "She's got a point, Ted. Why not run it in a little box, a sidebar to my story."

"Old news is no news," said Phyllis.

Ted knew when he was beat.

"Okay," he said. "I could use a little more of that tea."

"My pleasure," said Corney, reaching for the thermos. She paused before pouring, holding it in mid air. "No fireworks, and now Pru Pratt wants an anti-skinny-dipping bylaw!" She giggled. "What's the town coming to?"

Corney was just packing up her picnic basket when the contingent from the VFW arrived, dressed in their parade uniforms, already wilted from the heat. Scratch Hallett had brought reinforcements; he was accompanied by the post commander, Bill Bridges, and the chaplain, Rev. Clive Macintosh. They stood in a line, hats in hands, and saluted Ted.

"Good morning, gentlemen. What can I do for you?" he inquired.

"It's about the fireworks," began Bridges, removing his cap and mopping his forehead with a large red bandanna.

"We want you to write an editorial condemning this un-American action by the Board of Selectmen," continued Scratch. "The fireworks are an expression of American freedom, the right to pursue happiness. It's in the constitution."

"Actually, it's in the Declaration of Independence," said Ted.

"Well, wherever it is, it's a fundamental American right and we want to protect it," added the chaplain, uncharacteristically bellicose. "We're ready to fight!"

"I haven't really had time to form an opinion myself," said Ted, hedging. "But I'll certainly bear your thoughts in mind. In the meantime, if you want to write a letter to the editor, I'll be happy to run it."

"How soon do you need it? We can get it to you by twelve hundred hours."

Ted sighed. "That's fine, as long as it's not too long."

"Just one more thing," said Scratch. "In addition to our fundamental American freedoms, which must be preserved, we also need to bear in mind that the post, as well as other local organizations, counts on the fireworks for part of its operating budgets.

We run the parking, you know, at two dollars a car. The Ladies Aid Society has a big bake sale, and the Hat and Mitten Committee sells popcorn and glow sticks."

"He's right," said Phyllis. "I promised to make four-dozen brownies. The kind with cream cheese swirls."

"Most delicious," said the chaplain. "And the Ladies Aid Society does a great deal to help our less fortunate residents."

"Thanks for reminding me," said Ted. "That's a good point."

"I just can't understand people who think a plant's more important than people," said Scratch. He winked at Lucy, who was clacking away on her keyboard. "Gosh, she's fast, and in this heat, too." He chuckled. "Better make sure you keep your shirt on! You don't want to get Pru all upset."

Then Bill barked an order and the three made a neat about-face, encountering Jonathan Franke and Ellie Sykes. No words were exchanged, but Franke politely held the door open for the departing veterans.

"Let me guess," said Ted. "You're here about the fireworks."

Jonathan and Ellie looked at each other.

"The opposition's beat us to it?" asked Jonathan.

"Representatives from the VFW and the Chamber have already stopped by," said Ted. "They're pretty upset that there won't be any Fourth of July fireworks."

"We anticipated that reaction," said Jonathan. "That's why we're launching a public relations campaign, and we'd like you to help."

"It's called 'I Like Lichen,'" said Ellie, producing

a fact sheet. "This explains why lichen is important, it's vital role in the ecosystem, and the special properties of our own purple-spotted lichen. Did you know that researchers think it may offer a cure for cancer and other diseases?"

"They say that about every endangered plant," sniffed Phyllis. "But even if they do find some fabulous cure, who do you think is going to be able to afford it with drug prices the way the are? If you ask me, this is getting out of hand. Lichen, shmiken. Who cares?"

"That's exactly the problem," said Jonathan, pulling himself up to his full height and adopting an earnest tone. "Lichen's not glamorous, like the bald eagle or the moose, but it's every bit as important to the ecosystem." He gestured grandly with his arms. "It's a whole wonderful super-organism, and every species has a vital role to play. Lichen is a valuable winter food source for moose, you know. If the lichen goes, it's possible the moose won't have enough to eat and they'll disappear, too. Did you ever think of that?"

"I'm not all that keen on moose, if you want to know the truth," grumbled Phyllis. "My cousin Elfrida hit one last year on the highway and her car was a complete loss. Moose, shmoose."

Jonathan Franke's face was reddening, but Ellie put a cautionary hand on his arm.

"All we're asking, Ted, is that you consider this informational material. We know that you have a reputation for including all sides of an issue, so people can make up their own minds."

"Maybe we can run the information sheet along with the letters from the VFW and the Chamber," suggested Lucy.

"That's a great idea," said Ellie.

"Will you be writing an editorial?" asked Jonathan.

"Not this week," said Ted, with a sigh. He glanced at the clock. "I hate to push you out the door, but we've got a paper to put together."

"Thanks for your time," said Jonathan, extending his hand to Ted for a parting handshake.

"I just want a word with Lucy," said Ellie, seating herself on the extra chair next to Lucy's desk. "I'll catch up with you back at the office."

"I'm really in a hurry here," said Lucy.

"This will only take a minute. I know you have that dog hearing coming up and I'm sure you're worried about it."

"Do we have to talk about this now?" groaned Lucy.

Ellie smiled at her. "I just wanted you to know that I think you've done a good job with Kudo."

This wasn't what Lucy had expected her to say.

"Really?"

"I was so grateful when you took him after Curt died," she continued. "He was a handful, more than I could manage, that's for sure. He was constantly after my chickens. Curt never trained him, he had this idea that he was some sort of American wild dog and that training him would kill his spirit or something."

"He was doing pretty well," said Lucy, "until he discovered Mrs. Pratt's chickens. I try to keep him confined, I really do, but he's an escape artist."

"I know. I had the same problem with him going after my chickens. No matter what I did, I couldn't stop him. Fences, loud noises, nothing worked. Believe me, I tried." Ellie stood up. "I just wanted you to know that no matter how the hearing goes, the board members all respect you. They know you're a good person."

Lucy was appalled to discover she felt weepy. "Thanks."

"Well, I'm off," said Ellie, a naughty sparkle in her eye. "It's a pretty hot day, you know. I think I might stop by the pond for a quick dip . . . *au naturel.* Just don't tell Pru!"

"I wish I could join you," said Lucy, glancing over her shoulder at Ted. "But you know how he is." She pointed at the sign that hung above her desk: "It's not a guideline—it's a deadline."

Ted cleared his throat. "I need that story, Lucy. NOW."

Ellie scooted out the door, and Lucy bent over her keyboard. The little bell on the door gave a jangle or two, and then the only sound in the office was the steady clicking of three sets of fingers striking computer keyboards.

Chapter Three

By the time Lucy typed the final period and sent her story to Ted for editing, the digital thermometer outside the bank read an unseasonable ninety-four degrees. It wasn't much cooler inside the *Pennysaver* office, where the aged air conditioner wheezed and dripped.

"If you don't need me for anything else, I'm going to beat it," said Lucy, fanning herself with a sheaf of paper. "I'm hoping I can catch a ride home with Toby. They ought to be coming in around now."

"See you tomorrow, Lucy," said Ted, nodding his assent.

"Keep cool," advised Phyllis, lifting her brightly-printed Hawaiian shirt away from her skin so the little fan she kept on her desk could cool her. "This is awfully warm for this time of year. Must be that global warming."

Her words echoed in Lucy's mind when she stepped outside and was hit by a blast of hot air. The bright sunlight bounced off the concrete sidewalk, radiating heat, and shimmers rose from the black asphalt road, which felt sticky on her feet when she crossed the street. It wasn't much cooler at the harbor, either, but there was a faint breeze off the water. Chuck's boat hadn't come in yet, so Lucy found a shady spot and sat down to wait.

She didn't have to wait long. Pretty soon she heard the steady chug of an engine and spotted the distinctive red hull of the Carrie Ann, named after Chuck's wife, rounding Quisset Point. Lucy got up and slowly walked down to the floating dock to greet them.

"Hot enough for you?" she asked, watching as Toby tied the boat fast. Sweat was dripping down his face.

"Boy, it's a lot hotter here than it was out on the water."

"Phyllis thinks it's global warming."

"Maybe that explains it," said Chuck, hoisting a fish box onto the pier. He was already tanned from working outdoors and his hair was bleached by the sun. "I never saw such a small catch. This is piti-ful."

"Maybe the bugs are going deeper, to cooler water?" speculated Toby, using lobsterman's slang. "Or maybe it's that virus."

"Or maybe somebody's getting to the traps ahead of us," said Chuck.

"Poaching?" asked Lucy, unhappy at the idea. There hadn't been any poaching for some time, but she remembered the violence that rocked the waterfront years earlier, when Toby was just a baby. Accusations and suspicions had flown, and the body of a suspected poacher had been found float-ing face down, tangled in gear that didn't belong to him. He hadn't drowned; he'd been killed by a shotgun blast. "I hope not."

"Me, too," said Chuck, loading only two partly-filled boxes onto a barrow. "But I never saw so many traps come up absolutely empty. Usually there's females with eggs and undersized juveniles that you've got to throw back. Not this time."

"They're even taking the illegal lobsters?" Lucy was shocked.

"If they're stealing in the first place, Mom, they're not going to worry about breaking the rules," said Toby, who was hosing off the deck.

"I guess not," admitted Lucy, wiping her forehead with the back of her hand. "I need to ride home with you, and we have to get a battery for Elizabeth's car. Give me the keys and I'll open up your car, see if I can cool it off."

Toby tossed her the keys. "I'm almost through here." He laughed. "Promise you won't complain about the way I smell?"

"Wouldn't dream of it," said Lucy, reeling as she caught a heady whiff of lobster bait and honest sweat.

Bill was already home when they arrived, having quit early because of the heat. He was sitting on the back porch, freshly showered, drinking a beer.

"Too hot to work," he said, lifting the brown bottle that was beaded with moisture.

"You can say that again," agreed Lucy, collapsing onto the wicker settee beside him. Toby's rattle-trap Jeep wasn't air conditioned, and she'd spent a hot half-hour at the service station buying the battery. And then there was the matter of the way Toby smelled.

"I hope you're headed directly for the shower," said Lucy.

"You can't say I didn't warn you," said Toby. "It's too hot for a shower. I'm going for a swim at the pond."

"Good idea," said Bill. "Why don't we all go? In fact, why don't we have supper down there? It would save heating up the kitchen."

"I don't know," said Lucy, "maybe we should go to the beach instead. Mrs. Pratt was at the selectmen's meeting complaining about people misbehaving at the pond."

"Misbehaving?" Bill's eyebrows went up. "How?"

"Rowdiness, I guess." Lucy paused. "Skinny-dipping."

"Aw, Mom, everybody skinny-dips down there once in a while," protested Toby. "What's the big deal?"

"Not a big deal to me," said Lucy, looking up as Elizabeth whipped into the driveway in the Subaru wagon, with Zoe and Elizabeth in the back seat. "Since you're a filthy mess anyway, why don't you help your sister install that new battery?"

Once again Bill's eyebrows rose, but he didn't say anything.

"I'm going to change into my swimsuit," said Lucy. "Maybe you could start packing the cooler?"

"Can't I watch you change?" asked Bill, following her inside.

Lucy rolled her eyes. The man was impossible, she thought, smiling to herself.

An hour later the whole family had piled into Bill's truck and was bouncing down the old log-

STAR SPANGLED MURDER   39

ging trail that led to the pond. The kids were all
piled in the back, along with beach chairs, towels, a
cooler and a portable grill. Lucy and Bill were in
front, with the windows open. The radio was blaring out an oldies station and they were all singing
along to "She Wore an Itsy Bitsy Teeny Weeny Yellow
Polka Dot Bikini." Zoe was singing loudest of all,
delighted at this change in the usual routine.

When they came to the makeshift parking area
in a clearing near the pond, they found it was packed
with cars. It was full to overflowing and there wasn't
room for the truck, so Bill had to drive into the
underbrush in order to leave the road clear.

"Good thing it's old and has a few dings," said
Lucy. "I guess a lot of people had the same idea we
did."

"This heat's bringing 'em all out," grumbled
Bill, busying himself handing out all the picnic
paraphernalia. Toby and Elizabeth had run ahead
with the towels and chairs. "I'll take the grill, Lucy,
if you and Sara can tote the cooler. Zoe, is this bag
of charcoal too heavy for you?"

Zoe was offended. "I'm a big girl, Daddy."

"Do you think it's a church picnic or something?"
wondered Lucy. "I mean, only local people know
about the pond, and I can't believe the whole town
is here. I've never seen it this crowded before."

"High school reunion, maybe? Something like
that?" mused Bill.

"Could be. It's the right time of year."

Indeed, when they approached the pond they
saw that the large granite boulders surrounding it
were covered with people. Quite a few swimmers
were in the water, too. Music from portable radios

filled the air, and the inevitable cries of "Marco Polo" could be heard.

"Wow," said Bill. "The population boom is out of control."

"It's people like us," said Lucy. "We broke the zero population growth pledge. We have two extra children."

"Okay. We'll keep Sara and Zoe and eliminate the other two."

"Bill!" protested Lucy. "We can't do that! And we don't have to. Look, nobody's on our rock."

For as long as any of the Stones could remember, the family had always spread out their blanket and chairs on the same enormous rock.

The family formed a little procession, almost like a caravan, with Elizabeth and Toby leading the way. Toby was balancing a stack of folding aluminum beach chairs and Elizabeth had a canvas bag full of towels and sun lotion. Bill was next, toting the portable grill, followed by Zoe who was carrying the charcoal and a string bag containing some balls and frisbees. Lucy and Sara brought up the end, carrying the big red-and-white plastic cooler between them. It was heavy and Lucy was feeling a bit out of breath.

"Do you want to rest a minute, Mom?" asked Sara.

"Nnnnnh," said Lucy, distracted by Toby and Elizabeth's odd behavior.

They'd reached the rock and started putting down their stuff when they suddenly began laughing hysterically and bolted back down the trail to the rest of the family.

"Those people are tanning all over!" exclaimed Elizabeth.

"They're butt naked," added Toby.

"All of them?" asked Lucy, shading her eyes with her hand and taking a closer look.

Her chin dropped. It was true. Every single one of the people sunbathing at the pond was stark naked. Not a single person was wearing a stitch: not the babies, not the grandmothers, not the mommies and the daddies. Not even the very pink, corpulent man who was standing up and stretching.

Lucy dropped her side of the cooler and clapped her hands over Zoe's eyes.

"Back to the truck!" she barked.

"C'mon, Lucy, be a sport," teased Bill. "I'm game if you are."

"Well I'm not," said Lucy, dragging Zoe down the path.

"Mom!" protested Elizabeth. "I want to stay! Just think—no tan lines!"

"Me, too," agreed Toby. "There were some cute girls back there."

"And some really icky fat people," added Sara.

"You shouldn't have looked," said Lucy, primly. "We're not staying. We're going to the town beach, where they have regulations against this sort of thing. Chop-chop! In the truck, everybody."

Giggling, the kids obeyed and soon they were ready to leave.

"I can't believe it," mused Lucy, as Bill backed out and made a three-point turn. "This is Maine, for Pete's sake. Not the French Riviera."

"Don't you think maybe you're overreacting?" asked Bill.

"I don't think so," protested Lucy, but deep down she wondered if he didn't have a point. Even worse, she had to admit to herself that Pru Pratt was right. These were not casual skinny-dippers. The pond had been taken over by nudists.

Chapter Four

"Naked?"

The voice on the other end of the telephone line was incredulous. Sue Finch, Lucy's best friend, had never heard of anything so ridiculous.

"You mean without any clothes at all?"

"Not a stitch," said Lucy.

"But the swimsuits are so cute this year," said Sue, who had a lifetime subscription to *Vogue* magazine. "Little boy shorts, triangle top bikinis, though those aren't for me. I splurged on a wet-look halter number in black."

"You go swimming?" This was news to Lucy.

"It's not likely I'd actually get in the water," admitted Sue. "But I like to sunbathe on my deck. With plenty of sunscreen, of course."

"You don't get a tan that way," said Lucy.

"If you keep at it long enough, you do," said Sue. "You have to *work* at it."

"I thought the idea was to relax," said Lucy, who occasionally rolled her pants up to her knees in hope of tanning her legs when she was sprawled on a chaise lounge in the backyard. She usually fell asleep. And her legs usually kept that fish-belly look well into August, her tan developing just around the time the temperature started to drop and she had to start wearing long pants again.

"Well, within limits. I keep an eye on the time and turn over every ten minutes, and I make sure to drink a lot of water so I stay hydrated. And I'm aware of shadows and things like that. It makes a difference, it really does.

"And you don't worry about tan lines?"

"Not a problem. I wear the same suit all season."

"I'll suggest that to Elizabeth. She can't wait to join the crowd down at the pond. Says she doesn't want to have tan lines."

"Right." Sue sounded skeptical.

"Well, I can't imagine she's interested in anybody down there. They all seemed a bit the worse for wear, if you know what I mean." Lucy paused. "From what I saw, most of them could've benefitted from an article of clothing or two or ten."

Sue laughed.

The next caller was Pam Stillings, the wife of Lucy's boss, Ted, and the mother of Toby's friend Adam, who had a summer job mowing lawns and trimming hedges.

"Wow, news travels fast in this town," said Lucy, who hadn't been back from the beach for an hour.

"It's the heat. A lot of people had the same idea you did to go down to the pond for a swim. It's funny, but most of the folks around here don't like swimming in salt water. Anyway, I heard all about it from Adam. He went for a quick dip after work and got an eyeful."

"You can say that again."

"Oh, Lucy. You're so prim and proper. Didn't you go skinny-dipping when you were a kid. I did, all the time." She lowered her voice. "I even have photos of the whole gang."

"Photos? I'd get rid of them if I were you."

"No way. They bring back happy memories of the days before I had cellulite," said Pam. "But, you know, I grew up in North Carolina. It was a lot warmer there. I can't imagine why these folks think Tinker's Cove is such a great place that they put it on their Web site."

"What?"

"Yeah. They're an organized group. The American Naturist Society. Not nudist, *naturist*. That's what they want to be called. And they have a list of the ten best places for 'enjoying the natural world *au naturel*.' Their phrase, not mine. And little Blueberry Pond is number one."

"Well, I guess that explains why all those people were down there. There must've been at least a hundred."

"And this isn't the weekend, you know."

"Ohmigod," said Lucy. "There could be thousands."

"Not if this heat wave breaks," said Pam. "Don't forget the average high around here in June is something like fifty-eight degrees."

"We can only hope."

"And don't forget the black flies," said Pam, giggling. "This hot, still weather will bring them out. Reinforcements are on the way!"

* * *

Rachel Goodman didn't see anything funny about the black flies.

"Those poor people!" she exclaimed. "They don't have any idea what they're exposing themselves to."

"I think they know," said Lucy.

"They couldn't, or they wouldn't do it," said Rachel, who was a firm believer in the value of education. "The black flies are just the beginning. There's mosquitoes—they carry that West Nile virus. And I'm not at all convinced bug spray is safe for people. You have to figure that if it kills insects it must be full of toxins. And don't forget the wild animals—raccoons and all use that pond, too—and when they're rabid they lose their fear of people. And I know people like to swim there but I certainly wouldn't do it because I don't think that water is all that clean, what with the wildlife and all."

"I wonder what all those people are doing for toilets," mused Lucy.

"You know what they're doing—and it's filthy. You wouldn't catch me anywhere near the place."

"There were a lot of people. Children, too."

"Not children!" Rachel was outraged. "I hope they were wearing sunscreen!"

"Oh, I'm sure they were," said Lucy, not meaning to sound sarcastic at all.

"Oh, those poor babies," moaned Rachel. "They'll all get cancer and die. And their parents, too."

"Maybe before the weekend, if we're lucky."

"Lucy!"

When Lucy got to work Thursday morning there was no sign of Ted. But Phyllis, who was looking cool and comfortable in a brightly-printed green and blue muumuu, handed her a packet of print-outs from the American Naturist Society Web site.

"His Lordship wants you to look these over and then interview some of these naturists at Blueberry Pond. Find out if they've got a leader or something and talk to him," said Phyllis. Seeing Lucy's shocked expression she added, "Or her."

"You're kidding, right? This is a joke."

Phyllis pursed her Frosted Apricot lips and fanned herself with her hand. "I don't think so, honey. He wants you to get reaction to that proposed public decency bylaw."

"But those people are naked. I can't talk to naked people."

Phyllis was bent over, rummaging in her bottom drawer. "He wants photos, too."

"What did you say?"

Phyllis sat up and held out a box of candy. "Want one? These are really good. I'd go for the square ones, if I were you. They're usually caramels."

She waited until Lucy's mouth was full of gooey candy, then she repeated Ted's request. "I'm pretty sure you heard me, but I'll say it again. Ted wants photos of the nudists."

"Mmmph," said Lucy, plunking herself down at her desk and chewing furiously. She swallowed. "Absolutely not. I am not talking to naked people. I am not photographing them. If Ted wants this story so much he can get it himself. I've got another story. A bigger story. Lobster poaching."

Phyllis's brows rose above her rhinestone-trimmed half glasses. "You don't say." She examined her nails, which were painted bright blue, to coordinate with the muumuu. "That could get nasty."

"Exactly. I want to get on it before somebody gets hurt," said Lucy, scanning the printouts.

The American Naturist Society, she discovered, was indeed a national organization with thousands of members. Their purpose was to "promote and encourage the practices of healthful living including freeing the human body from restrictive and harmful clothing." While they insisted that all clothing was detrimental because it "smothered the pores" they were especially concerned about anything that changed the shape of the body such as high heel shoes or support garments like girdles and bras. In particular, they believed pantyhose to be especially harmful.

Lucy found herself agreeing with them.

"So they're not so crazy after all?" inquired Phyllis.

"They're death on pantyhose."

"Sensible group."

"They don't think much of elastic, either. They say it cuts off circulation."

"They're wrong there. The happiest day of my life was the day I discovered elastic-waist pants."

Lucy smiled and resumed reading, wondering why she'd had such a strong reaction to the presence of the naturists at Blueberry Pond. Now that she was reading about the group, they seemed pretty reasonable. Just regular folks who happened to dislike wearing clothing. Come to think of it, clothing was pretty unnatural. She remembered how she'd had to struggle to keep the kids clothed when they were little. They hated wearing snowsuits and even on the coldest days pulled off their hats and mittens. She remembered watching one of Toby's little sneakers floating downstream, after he'd pushed it off when Bill was carrying him across a bridge in a backpack when they were hiking on a nature trail. In fact, it had been difficult to keep that child in diapers; whenever she changed him he'd attempt a bare-bottomed dash for freedom. And the girls hadn't been much different, struggling and squirming whenever she tried to get them into their snow boots and protesting loudly when she tried to get them to trade their comfy overalls and sneakers for starched party dresses and Mary Janes.

When she finished reading the last page, Lucy leaned forward over her desk and propped her chin in her hand, asking herself what she found so offensive about the presence of naked people at the pond. She wasn't prudish, really she wasn't. She enjoyed a healthy sex life, she faithfully made appointments for annual physicals and mammograms, she'd given birth four times. She wasn't ashamed of her own body, she just didn't want to look at other peoples'.

Not that she didn't enjoy watching a steamy love scene in a movie, or looking at nude paintings and sculptures in a museum. She'd made a point of taking the kids to museums and introducing them to great art, with or without fig leaves. And she'd never objected to Bill's collection of *Playboy* magazines, they were fine with her. So what was the problem? Why was she so uncomfortable about these naturists?

Maybe, she decided, it was because they were practically in her backyard. Maybe it was because she could choose to look at a movie or a magazine or a work of art, but she had no control over the naturists. Now that they were around, they could pop up anywhere. What if they came to the house, asking for a Band-Aid or something? How could she talk to them? Where would she look? Not to mention the fact that the nudes in movies and works of art and even in magazines were carefully edited. They were presented attractively, even glorified. Imperfections were air-brushed away or edited out. Not like the folks at Blueberry Pond who were happy to let it all hang out.

Most of all, she decided, was the feeling she had that these people were depriving her of something she enjoyed by their presence. If she didn't want to see them, she couldn't go to the pond. Her pond. Well, it wasn't as if she actually owned it. It was conservation land, owned by the town. But Blueberry Pond was so close to the house, and the family went there so frequently, that they all felt a bit proprietary about it. If she saw litter, she picked it up and so did the kids. If somebody had dumped an old appliance or couch there, as sometimes happened, she made sure the town sent workers to pick it up. She loved the pond and the naturists had seized it. They might as well have marched in with an army and raised a flag, claiming it for their cause.

The bell on the door jangled, announcing Ted's arrival.

"What are you doing here, Lucy? I wanted you to go down to the pond and see what the naturists think about Pru Pratt's proposed bylaw."

"I'm pretty sure they won't like it, Ted. In fact, I think it's a foregone conclusion. There's something else I want to work on. Are you aware that there's lobster poaching going on? Chuck Swift told me."

"I hadn't heard anything about that, Lucy." Ted scratched his chin. "Are you sure?"

"I told you. Chuck says his traps are being poached."

"Anybody else?"

"That's what I want to find out. So I'll get right on it, okay?"

"No. The naturist story is top priority. This is big and you can bet it's going to get some regional, maybe even national attention. TV even." He waggled a finger at Lucy. "And we want to be the ones who break it."

"Not me," said Lucy. "I'm not interested. If you're interested, I think you should cover it yourself. I could get some more reaction to the fireworks cancellation. Or get a head start on the listings—there's a lot of holiday activities next week. We ought to play up the parade, for example, since there aren't going to be any fireworks."

"I would Lucy, except that's what I'm paying you to do. I'm the editor. I'm the one who makes the assignments. You're the reporter. You're the one who does the assignments." He gave her a hard look. "Do you understand?"

Lucy nodded and got to her feet. "If you're going to put it like that. . . ."

"I am."

She picked up her bag and checked to make sure she had her camera and a notebook.

"Well, I'm on my way." She stopped at Phyllis's desk. "If I die of embarrassment, let my family know that it was all Ted's fault. Promise?"

"If you ask me, honey, you're not the one who should be embarrassed."

* * *

Lucy tried to remember that as she approached the pond, camera in hand. She hoped to get some discreet long-distance shots first, before attempting any interviews. That was the plan, anyway. She really wasn't sure if she was going to be able to work up the courage to talk to any of the naturists.

But first she had to get to the pond, which was quite a hike. Recalling the lack of parking the previous day, she'd decided to leave the Subaru at home and walk. She wasn't going to risk having to park in the underbrush and scratching the finish on her relatively new station wagon. Walking also had the benefit of buying her some time, time to figure out a way of conducting the interviews.

She wasn't exactly marching along. She was dawdling her way down the trail, actually playing a little game of seeing how quietly she could walk. It was something she used to do when she was a little girl, pretending to be Lewis and Clark's famous Indian guide, Sacajawea. She was walking so quietly, in fact, that she surprised Calvin Pratt, Pru's husband, who was installing a wire fence along his property line.

"That's a good idea, Calvin," she said.

Calvin jumped a mile, dropping his hammer.

"I didn't mean to startle you," she said, smiling in a friendly manner.

Calvin looked like a deer caught in the headlights. He didn't say anything. He just stood there, a skinny fellow with a gaunt face sporting a stubble of beard in a pair of oversized farmer's overalls. He wasn't wearing a shirt and Lucy could see the ropey muscles in his arms and a tuft of gray hair sprouting from his hollow chest.

"Say, Calvin, I'm supposed to write a story for the *Pennysaver* about these naturists at the pond. Would you mind giving me a quote? How do you feel about having all these naked people so close to your property?"

Calvin didn't answer her. He bent down and picked up his hammer and, next thing Lucy knew, he was gone. He had vanished into the woods.

Lucy shrugged and continued down the path, wishing it would go on forever. It didn't, of course. It ended and she found herself in the cleared space bordering the pond. The rocks were once again full of people. It was still morning so there weren't quite as many people as there were the day before, but there were still quite a few naturists stretched out on blankets or sitting in beach chairs, enjoying the sunshine. It was a peaceful scene. Only one radio was playing and a few kids were splashing in the water. One serious swimmer was crossing the pond in a neat Australian crawl.

Lucy snapped a few shots of the general scene, figuring she was far enough away that the figures in the photo would be an indistinct jumble of arms and legs. No faces. No breasts. Maybe a round bottom or two, but no sex organs.

The thought froze her in her tracks. She wanted to flee, like Calvin. If only she could. But unlike Calvin, who had probably been forbidden by Pru to even glance at the pond, she was under orders to see everything she could.

Nothing ventured, nothing gained, she told herself, putting on her sunglasses. They would give her a bit of privacy, which she valued even if her subjects didn't. She took a few steps forward, scoping out the situation. Not so bad. The rock closest to her was occupied by a young woman, an attractive girl who reminded her of Elizabeth. She ought to be able to handle this, she told herself. Just pretend she was talking to her daughter.

Lucy took a few more steps. She looked closer. It *was* her daughter.

"Elizabeth!"

"Mom!"

"What are you doing here?"

"Getting a tan! It's great, Mom. You should try it."

"Put something on!"

"Relax, Mom. It's no big deal. Everybody's naked. It's cool."

Lucy didn't know what to say. Like Calvin, she was standing transfixed, with her mouth open. Like Calvin, she turned and ran for home. She was running pell-mell down the path, panting heavily, when she ran smack into somebody very solid. A naked somebody.

"I'm so sorry," she stammered, recognizing another neighbor, Mel Dunwoodie, who owned a nearby campground.

"Take it easy, Lucy," he said.

"I will," she said, continuing on her way at a brisk clip.

Thank goodness Mr. Dunwoodie had brought something to read.

Chapter Five

Ted was not amused when Lucy returned to the office empty-handed. He stared at her, incredulous. "You mean to tell me you didn't get any interviews? Any photos?"

"Sorry," said Lucy, slinking into her chair.

"Why the hell not?" he demanded, standing over her.

Lucy shrank into the chair, making herself as small as possible. "I got scared and ran away."

Ted scratched his chin. "Didn't you see any familiar faces down there? Wasn't there anybody you knew?"

Lucy spoke in a very small voice. "That was the problem."

Phyllis was intrigued. "Who? Who did you recognize?"

"Mel Dunwoodie, for one."

Phyllis let out a hoot. "Mel Dunwoodie! He must weigh two hundred and fifty pounds!"

"At least," agreed Lucy, who was trying to erase the image of all that naked flesh from her mind. She had an awful feeling the memory was going to stay with her for a long time.

"Anybody else?" asked Phyllis.

"Well, yes. In fact that's why I exposed my film."

"Who was it?"

"Elizabeth."

"No!"

"As much as it pains me to admit it, my own daughter was sunning herself in her birthday suit."

"I wish you hadn't done that, Lucy," muttered Ted, adding up potential sales that would not now be realized. "A nice, discreet shot of Elizabeth would have been perfect for the front page. Just think what it would have done for newsstand sales."

"That's exactly what I was thinking of, Ted," snapped Lucy, looking at him through a red haze. "There's no way my naked daughter's photo is going to appear in this paper. Not while I have breath in my body. No way."

"Well, I can understand that," he admitted, checking the film in his camera. "I guess I'll go down and see what I can do. You can make some phone calls."

Lucy was on her feet, shaking a finger angrily. "Ted, I'm warning you: Absolutely no photos of my daughter. Got it?" She paused. "I'll tell Pam."

"Don't worry," he grumbled as he left. "I won't even look at your daughter."

"I wish I believed him," said Lucy.

"Well, you don't honestly believe the little hussy's out there in broad daylight without a stitch on because she doesn't want people to look at her," said Phyllis.

"No, I don't," wailed Lucy, collapsing back into the chair. "That's the worst part. My daughter's an exhibitionist!"

* * *

Lucy was on the phone talking to Myra Dun-woodie—she'd caught her just as she was going out the door, on her way to join Mel at the pond—when the bell on the door jangled and she looked up to see Beetle Bickham entering the office with a piece of white paper in his huge hand.

"So how long have you and your husband been naturists?" asked Lucy.

She was having a tough time keeping her mind on the interview. She was curious about what had brought Beetle, who was head of the Lobstermen's Association, to the *Pennysaver*.

"Oh, forever," said Myra. "In fact, that's how we met. At a naturist camp in Pennsylvania. I fell in love with him during a game of volleyball. He had a fantastic spike, and his serve wasn't bad, either."

"Right," said Lucy. "Great spike."

"On second thought, don't put that in the paper," said Myra, giggling. "Someone might take it wrong."

"Right," said Lucy, who was dying to talk to Beetle. "Well, I shouldn't keep you any longer. I'm sure you don't want to miss this beautiful weather."

Hanging up the phone, she turned to Beetle, who was leaning on the counter and chatting with Phyllis. He was a terrific flirt, speaking with a faint hint of a Quebec accent, and Phyllis was all smiles, responding to his flattery.

"Anything I can do for you?" asked Lucy.

"Well, yes, Lucy, since you mention it." Beetle unfolded the paper and handed it to her. "This here's a letter to the editor I'd like you to print."

"What's it about?"

"Well," said Beetle, hitching up his waterproof yellow oilskin pants. "Some of the fellas are saying they think somebody's poaching their traps." He shrugged. "It's hard to tell seeing that the catch has been down lately and all. But there's signs. Some people, and I'm not naming names, seem to be doing better than others. A lot better than you'd expect, considering the amount of time they're putting in. Not to mention their history as kind of shiftless and not exactly hard workers."

"Could be luck," suggested Lucy. "Maybe they found a hot spot."

"Could be," admitted Beetle, sounding doubtful. "And that's why I worded this letter very carefully. It's just kind of a general plea to play fair, if you get my meaning."

"I get it," said Lucy, quickly perusing the letter. "But do you think the poachers will read it? And if they do, will they take it to heart?"

"I hope so, Lucy," said Beetle. "It'd be in their best interest, that's for sure. Lobstermen don't take kindly to poachers. Folks who mess with a man's livelihood have a way of turning up dead. It's happened before, and I don't want to see it happen again."

"Me, either," said Lucy. "I'll make sure Ted gets the letter."

"Thank you kindly, Lucy," he said, flashing her an irresistibly lopsided smile, "and have a nice day." He paused on his way out the door and winked at Phyllis. *"Au revoir, madame."*

Ted read the letter thoughtfully when he returned, but didn't say anything.

"I think we've really got to look into this," said Lucy. "Maybe we can help defuse the situation before there's any violence."

"We only report the news, Lucy," said Ted. "We can't change it."

"That's not exactly true, Ted. Take the school budget increase. That would never have passed except for our coverage, showing how Tinker's Cove students were doing worse on standardized exams than kids in towns with bigger budgets."

He read the letter again.

"Okay," he said, with a sigh. "I'll run the letter and budget space for a story in next week's issue. Okay?"

"Okay," said Lucy. She chewed her lip nervously. "So, did you get any good photos at the pond?"

"Sure did." Ted sounded awfully pleased with himself. "And interviews, too."

Lucy swallowed hard. "Elizabeth?"

"She wasn't there. She must've left."

Lucy gave a huge sigh of relief, but she knew it was only temporary. She wanted to stop Elizabeth's nude sunbathing but she wasn't sure how to do it. She couldn't lock her in the house, after all.

One of the things Lucy liked most about working at the *Pennysaver* was the flexible hours. Today, for example, she was finished by two o'clock which give her time to stop by the library to return her books. While she was there, she decided, she'd see if there were any books offering expert advice to parents of young adults. She could certainly use some help.

The library was only a few blocks down Main Street

so she decided to walk. She hadn't gotten very far, however, before she noticed a crowd of people gathered in front of town hall, where several tables had been set up. She was wondering what it was all about when a clipboard was shoved into her face.

"Would you like to sign our petition?"

"What's it for?" she asked the ponytailed girl holding the clipboard.

She was one of several college students dashing up and down the sidewalk accosting everyone. They were all wearing T-shirts printed with the APTC logo.

"It simply requests that the town take all necessary steps to protect the endangered purple-spotted lichen."

"Don't sign it, Lucy," yelled Scratch Hallett. He was seated at a flag-draped table with a couple of cronies from the VFW. "Sign ours, instead. We want to bring back the fireworks."

Lucy smiled and waved. "As a member of the press I have to remain impartial," she said.

"You can't avoid the day of judgement," warned a man with a familiar face whom Lucy couldn't identify. He was sitting at a third table with members of the Revelation Congregation, a fundamentalist Christian church that had grown steadily since its founding a few years ago. "Choose decency and godliness and support the anti-nudity bylaw."

Thinking of Elizabeth, Lucy was tempted.

"Sorry," she shrugged.

"Come on, Lucy," urged Jonathan Franke, who was supervising the APTC volunteers. "You're entitled to have opinions, especially since you live so close to Blueberry Pond."

"What's Blueberry Pond got to do with lichen?" she asked.

"It's a prime lichen environment and we're worried the increased use by naturists may have a negative impact."

Lucy reached for her notebook. "Does this mean APTC is supporting the anti-nudity bylaw?"

"Oh, no," he said, holding up his hands. "We're not *against* nudity, we're *for* lichen. Putting Blueberry Pond on the Web site has attracted large numbers of people, and people can be quite destructive to lichen. It's so small and blends into the rock so well that they may not even realize it's a life form."

"That's right," agreed the girl. "So will you sign?"

"I'll think about it," said Lucy. But what she was really thinking about as she continued on her way was how very strange it was that APTC was finding common ground with the Revelation Congregation.

Once inside the library, she shoved her books through the return slot and went to check out the new arrivals. There wasn't anything new about parenting, but there was a Family Medical Guide that had photographs illustrating skin cancer. Just the thing to put on Elizabeth's bedside table.

When Lucy pulled into the driveway, she noticed the kennel gate was swinging open once again. Kudo was gone and she had a good idea where she'd find him. She grabbed the leash and set off on foot along Red Top Road to her neighbors, the Pratts.

In contrast to her own yard, where the weeds and flowers and pea vines and lettuces all grew exuberantly and where bicycles and badminton racquets and volleyballs tended to sprout on the overgrown lawn, the Pratts' yard was extremely neat. A few clumps of hostas promised some pale and feeble blooms later in the summer, but nothing was flowering now, in late June, when almost every garden in town had at least one rambler rose in riotous bloom. The grass had been clipped to an inch of its life and was already turning brown in spots. Unless it rained soon, it would be entirely brown in a week or two, giving the yard a sere and dry look. Not that it was exactly lush and vibrant now. It was also empty; there was no sign of Kudo.

The house was a stark set of geometric shapes, a tall rectangle dotted with awkwardly placed square windows and topped with a rectangular roof. There was no chimney, no porch, no bushes to soften the harsh lines and angles.

Lucy knocked on the door and when she received no answer she went around back to check on the chickens. They were clucking and pecking at the ground in their run attached to the coop and seemed contented enough. There was no sign of any intrusion, no break in the fence. Even though she was relieved he hadn't attacked the chickens, Lucy was anxious about the dog's whereabouts. Where could he be? She decided to try the pond by following the path that wandered from the rear of the Pratts' yard and through their woods. Once behind their barn, however, her attention was drawn by the large amount of lobster gear that was haphazardly stacked there. It was funny to see traps stacked up this time of year, when they should be in the water. Lucy was taking a closer look when she was startled by Pru Pratt's voice.

"What do you think you're doing, Lucy Stone?"

Lucy jumped. "Hi," she said, forcing her mouth into a friendly smile. At least she hoped it was friendly and disarming. "I was just looking for my dog. You haven't seen him, have you?"

"No I haven't and I don't believe you, either. A pile of lobster traps is a mighty funny place to look for a dog."

"I thought he might've picked up the scent of the bait, you know," said Lucy, knowing it sounded lame. "Actually, I was on my way down to the pond. I thought he might have been attracted by all the activity there. I was just headed for the path."

"I'm not aware that my path has become a public right-of-way," said Pru, planting her feet firmly on her property and blocking Lucy's way.

"Ma! What's going on?"

It was the Pratt's son, Wesley. He was about Toby's age but the similarity ended there. Where Toby was relaxed, even lazy, Wesley seemed to be looking for a fight. He bounced on the balls of his feet and alternately flexed his fingers and balled them into a fist as if he were dying to take a punch at something, anything. He had inherited his mother's lean and wiry look; he even wore his dirty-blond hair long and pulled back in a ratty ponytail.

Lucy sensed it was time to beat a hasty retreat. "No problem. I'll go back along the road."

"And don't come back," snarled Wesley, as she trotted down the driveway.

Lucy wasted no time in getting back to the security of her own property, where she was relieved to see Toby's Jeep parked in the driveway.

"Those Pratts are something else!" she exclaimed when she found him in the kitchen, peering into the refrigerator. "I went over there looking for Kudo and they kicked me off their property! Like I was a bum or something."

"What do you expect? They've never exactly been friendly," said Toby, popping open a can of cola.

"I'm not trying to be best friends," said Lucy. "I'm just trying to be a good neighbor. A little co-operation wouldn't hurt, you know. I'm doing my best to control the dog and I could use a little help."

"I'll help," said Toby. "Do you want me to see if he's down at the pond?"

"That's awfully nice of you," said Lucy.

"No problem, Mom."

"I'll go, too," said Lucy. "Sometimes he comes if he hears my voice."

That wasn't the real reason. This was a rare opportunity to spend some time alone with her only son and she didn't want to miss it.

"You don't have to, Mom. I can handle it."

Lucy fingered the leash thoughtfully. "I get it. You want to check out the action down at the pond, and you don't want me along to cramp your style?"

Toby blushed. "That's not it. . . ."

"Okay then, let's go," said Lucy, resisting the urge to grab his hand as she used to do when he was small. Somehow it had never gone away, even though he now towered over her at six feet plus. "I just hope Elizabeth's not there."

"Elizabeth!" Toby was appalled. "What's she doing down there?"

"I don't know if she is or not, but I saw her there

this morning. It was really awkward, seeing her like that." Lucy sighed philosophically. "But if she's not going to wear clothes, I guess she doesn't mind people seeing her naked."

"It's not what she minds, it's what I mind. I don't want to see my sister naked."

"So it's okay to leer at other people, but not Elizabeth?"

"Yeah!"

"I see your point," said Lucy, as they walked past the garden and took the path through the woods. "Say, do you know anything about this lobster poaching? Beetle Bickham wrote a letter to the editor."

"Nah."

"But Chuck said he thought his traps had been poached, didn't he?"

"I guess."

"It's not just him. It's a lot of lobstermen, according to Beetle."

"Hmmm."

"Well, what are they saying down at the docks? People must be talking about it."

"Not really."

"Okay, okay. You obviously don't want to talk about it, so I won't ask you anymore," said Lucy. "But when I was over at the Pratts I noticed there was a lot of lobster gear piled up behind the barn. Isn't that odd, for this time of year?"

"Maybe he's got extra."

"Is that common?" asked Lucy.

"Sure," said Toby. "Like a spare tire, you know."

"Yeah," said Lucy. "But if it's all his gear, wouldn't it all have the same identification on it. The same license number?"

"Of course," said Toby, suddenly taking an interest. "Did his gear have a lot of different numbers?"

"I didn't really notice," lied Lucy, as they approached the pond. She sure didn't need any more trouble with the Pratts. "Do you see the dog?"

Toby scanned the sea of naked flesh stretched out before them. He shook his head.

"Damn," said Lucy, looking in vain for any sign of the dog. "We might as well go home. It's getting on for supper time and he never misses a meal. He'll probably show up soon."

"You go on back," said Toby. "I think I'll go for a dip myself."

"You, too?" She put her hands on her hips. "Where did I go wrong? Have you no shame?"

"Guess not," said Toby, pulling his T-shirt over his head.

Lucy turned around and headed for home as fast as she could.

Chapter Six

Kudo was back in his kennel, crouched on all fours with his chin resting on his front paws and a mournful expression on his face, when Lucy left for work on Friday morning. He'd come wandering into the yard after supper, when the girls were kicking a soccer ball around, and Lucy had coaxed him into the kennel with his bowl of kibble. He'd looked at her reproachfully when she slammed the gate shut, as if she'd played a dirty trick on him, and she was still battling a lingering sense of guilt as she drove off with Sara and Zoe in the back seat, ready to be dropped off at Friends of Animals day camp.

"Mom, Kudo looks so sad. Do we always have to keep him locked up?" asked Sara.

"It's like he's in jail or something," added Zoe, who had a flair for the dramatic. "A life sentence."

"I don't like it either," said Lucy, as she backed the Subaru wagon around in a three-point turn, "but he keeps getting in trouble. If we can't control him, the selectmen might decide to have him destroyed. That's a lot worse than a life sentence."

"You mean they could kill him?" asked Sara.

"No!" exclaimed Zoe.

"Yes. They could," said Lucy, as they tooled down Red Top Road. "That's why it's so important that you all help make sure he doesn't get out. If he kills any more of Mrs. Pratt's chickens we could lose him forever."

"That's not fair," whined Sara, resorting to the middle-school battle cry.

"It's not fair that he kills Mrs. Pratt's chickens either," said Lucy.

"Mrs. Pratt's a poop," said Zoe.

"Watch your tongue," admonished Lucy, as she turned into the camp driveway. "I don't want to hear any more of this talk. It's our responsibility to take care of Kudo and to make sure he doesn't do any harm." Under her breath, she added, "I only wish he'd make it a little bit easier."

Curious about the large flat-bed trailer that was taking up most of the parking lot, Lucy decided to have a chat with the camp director, Melanie Flowers, who was welcoming the kids as they arrived. Melanie was a petite woman with short, dark hair and a big, friendly smile.

"Hi, girls. Are you ready for a busy day?"

Sara and Zoe gave her the traditional camp high five and ran off to join their friends, leaving Lucy alone with Melanie.

"So what's with the rig?" she asked. "Are you going into the trucking business?"

"It's for the parade," said Melanie. "I know it doesn't look like much now, but it's going to be beautiful when we finish decorating it. The theme this year is 'With liberty and justice for all' and we think that includes animals."

"Are the kids going to be in the parade, too?"

"Sure thing. We're counting on their adorable little faces to win over the judges. Competition is especially keen this year. Since there are no fireworks the parade is going to be the centerpiece of the celebration. Everybody's entering floats: the Lions, Boy Scouts, Girl Scouts, the town band, the lumber yard, just about anybody you can think of." She lowered her voice. "Just between you and me, it's the garden center I'm most worried about. I think they'll give us a real run for the money."

"So what have you got planned?"

"Well, we're covering the base with a carpet of red, white and blue crepe paper flowers, you know the kind I mean. And then we're going to artistically arrange some small trees and flowers to make a sort of park-like setting, complete with a fire hydrant. Cute, don't you think? And there'll be the kids and some well-behaved pets . . . Zoe offered Kudo but I didn't think . . ."

"Understood," said Lucy. "He'd probably eat the other animals."

Melanie's eyes widened. "Well, anyway, the kids will wear Friends of Animals T-shirts with information lettered on the back: how many kittens a cat can produce if it isn't fixed, how many puppies are destroyed in shelters every year. Stuff like that. We'll also distribute flyers and cat and dog treats."

"Sounds like a winner to me."

"I hope so, but we have a long way to go." She turned to Lucy and placed a hand on her arm. "Say, Lucy. Do you think you and the girls could help out by making some of those crepe paper flowers? You know, while you're watching TV or something. We need an awful lot of them."

"How many?"

"I figure three or four thousand ought to do it."

"F-f-four thousand?" sputtered Lucy.

"Oh, goodness. I didn't mean for you to make all of them. Could you do, say, five hundred?"

"How soon do you need them?"

Melanie's voice was an apologetic squeak. "By Monday."

"We can try," said Lucy.

"Great. I'll send the crepe paper and pipe cleaners home with the girls."

"Thanks," said Lucy, wondering why she was saying it. Shouldn't Melanie be thanking her? No matter, Melanie was already on her knees, consoling a little boy who had tripped over his own feet, shod in brand-new sneakers with room to grow, and scraped his chin.

Next stop was the IGA, where Lucy had promised to pick up coffee and other supplies for the office. But when she tried to make the turn onto Main Street, her usual route, she encountered a police barrier. The yellow saw-horse was manned by Officer Barney Culpepper.

"What's going on?" she asked Barney.

Lucy and Barney were old friends, who had first met when they both served on the Cub Scout Pack Committee many years earlier when Toby and Barney's son, Eddie, were still in elementary school.

"Look for yourself, Lucy. It's them nudists. They're having a big demonstration against that public decency bylaw." Barney resembled a big old St. Bernard dog, and his jowls quivered as he pointed out the crowd of people gathered around the town hall steps.

"Do I dare?" asked Lucy, peeking through her fingers.

Barney roared with laughter. "You can relax. They're wearing clothes today."

Lucy dropped her hand and surveyed the crowd that was rapidly spilling out into the street in front of the town hall. There seemed to be hundreds of them, all decently covered and listening quietly to their leader, a middle-aged man with a pot belly and a bald spot.

"Where did all the Calvin Klein models go?" she asked Barney. "Do they all have to be middle-aged and paunchy?"

"They do seem to be a pretty well-upholstered bunch," said Barney, hitching his utility belt a bit higher on his pot belly. "Not that I'm much better, but at least I keep my clothes on, except when I'm showering. Their leader there, Mike Gold's his name, is a case in point. I can't see why he'd be in any hurry to strip down. Most guys his size would be happy to hide themselves inside a big old Hawaiian shirt."

The idea made Lucy grin. "Listen, you think it would be okay if I drove behind the plumbing supply place and through the bank parking lot to get to the IGA?"

"Fine with me," said Barney, holding up his huge hand to stop an oncoming VW and giving Lucy room to make her turn.

After she parked her car in the nearly empty lot in front of the IGA, Lucy paused to survey the scene. The naturists seemed extremely well-organized; this was no impromptu demonstration. They were carrying professionally printed signs, some of which had clever illustrations and sayings. "If people were meant to wear clothes, they'd be born that way!" proclaimed one placard. Another said: "Naturists have nothing to hide." "Wear a smile!," "Clothing is optional" and "Nudity is Natural" declared others, but the one that made her smile said, "Fig leaves belong on trees."

Most of the protesters were also wearing official American Naturist Society T-shirts. Lucy suspected that ANS headquarters had sent out a call for volunteers and this demonstration was the result. If they'd gone to all that trouble, she figured, they'd probably also alerted the media. After all, you didn't have a demonstration unless you wanted to get some attention.

Lucy considered pulling out her camera and getting a few photos for the *Pennysaver,* and some quotes, too, but changed her mind when she saw Ted working his way through the crowd, notebook in hand. He seemed to be the only reporter working the crowd, but Lucy figured it was just a matter of time before other media showed up. This was a story that TV news directors wouldn't be able to resist.

She turned and went inside the IGA, where a few locals were standing in front of the plate-glass windows, watching the show outside.

"My word," fumed one elderly lady, whose hair was shellacked into a permanent sixties-era flip. "I can't imagine wanting to go around with no clothes."

"I thought it was shocking when women stopped wearing girdles," confided her companion, wearing a tightly-buttoned twinset topped with a three-strand pearl necklace. "Mother always warned about girls who jiggled when they walked."

Amused by this exchange, Lucy was smiling to herself as she got a cart and headed for the paper goods aisle. There she bought jumbo packages of paper towels and toilet paper, which she balanced precariously on top of each other. She picked up a few basic cleaning supplies, then went on to the coffee aisle where she picked up a dozen cans of this week's special as well as a few jars of nondairy creamer. She never used the stuff herself but Phyllis loathed black coffee. A five-pound bag of sugar completed her purchases and she headed for the checkout where she found Miss Tilley and Rachel waiting in line.

Julia Ward Howe Tilley was the town's oldest resident and had reluctantly agreed to retire from her position as town librarian only a few years earlier. She was as strong-minded as ever and although a few telemarketers made the mistake of calling her by her first name, no one in town dreamed of doing so. She had always been Miss Tilley and always would be, even to Rachel, who helped her with daily tasks like shopping and preparing meals. Rachel's influence only went so far, however. Today Miss Tilley was wearing a track suit with racing stripes down the legs and the latest in high-tech athletic footwear.

Lucy greeted them with a smile. "What do you think of all these goings-on?" she asked.

"Not much," said Rachel. "I don't know how we're going to get out of the parking lot and home in time for lunch."

"Lunch can wait," said Miss Tilley, a naughty gleam in her bright blue eyes. "I'm hoping one of these protesters will strip—while it's still legal."

"She's been like this ever since she heard about Pru Pratt's proposed bylaw," said Rachel, clucking her tongue in disapproval.

"I'll never understand why people who claim to worship the good Lord and all his works find the human body so objectionable," said Miss Tilley, as Rachel began unloading their groceries onto the conveyor belt.

"You have a point," said Lucy. "What do you think about the fireworks?"

"I think Jonathan Franke is running out of projects. APTC got the town to set up a recycling center, they got that real estate surtax for buying up open space land, they've put up bluebird houses and poles for osprey nests all over town. Worthy projects all but not very exciting so he decided to make a big deal about the lichen, which seems to be doing fine without his help and despite the annual fireworks show." Miss Tilley snorted. "It's a lot of fuss over nothing, if you ask me."

"That'll be forty-seven dollars and fifty-six cents," said Dot Kirwan, the cashier.

They all waited patiently while Miss Tilley got out her rusty black purse and counted out the amount to the penny, then took her receipt and carefully folded it before tucking it into her purse. Then she and Rachel proceeded out to the parking lot at a stately pace, her silver sneakers giving off flashes of light with every step.

"Hi, Lucy," said Dot. "Big doings in town today."

"It all seems peaceful enough," said Lucy, unloading her cart onto the conveyor belt. "They're very well-organized."

"I haven't got any problem with them, as long as they stay out by the pond and don't go wandering around town in their birthday suits," said Dot, waving a can of coffee over the scanner. "And business has been up since they started coming. Joe says there's been a big jump in deli sales over last year. A lot of them take picnics out to the pond. Not to mention bug spray and suntan lotion." She raised an eyebrow. "Well, it figures, doesn't it? After all, some parts are more sensitive than others, if you get my drift."

"Are they mostly day-trippers, or do they stay around here?" asked Lucy.

"A lot of 'em are staying at Mel Dunwoodie's campground," volunteered Marge Culpepper, Barney's wife, who had taken the place behind Lucy in the check-out aisle. "He's got a big banner up that says, 'Nude is Not Lewd.' I almost went off the road when I saw it."

"I heard he's thinking of turning the campground into a nudist colony," said Dot. "That's what Jack Kimble said. He's in real estate, you know, and he said he's worried about property values."

"That's right in your neighborhood, Lucy," observed Marge. "You and the Pratts would be most directly affected. Are you worried?"

"I'm worried," admitted Lucy, thinking of Elizabeth. "But not about property values."

"I suppose you want this on account, like usual?" asked Dot.

"Righto," said Lucy, pushing her cart towards the exit. "Take care, now."

"Keep your clothes on!" said Dot, laughing. She leaned across the counter to Marge. "I used to say 'Have a nice day' but now I say 'Keep your clothes on'. The customers love it."

* * *

Outside in the parking lot, Lucy was interested to see that an impromptu counter-demonstration had formed. Members of the Revelation Congregation were out in force, making up for their lack of organization with righteous indignation. Their hand-lettered signs quoted Bible scripture, especially God's command to Adam and Eve to "cover their nakedness" when they were expelled from the Garden of Eden. The group's numbers were small, but they were doing their best to shout down the naturist speakers. One of the loudest was Pru Pratt.

"Sinners repent!" she shrieked, over and over, sounding like a crow.

Her husband, Calvin, was standing beside her. In contrast to his wife, Calvin looked abashed to be involved in a public display, and was practically hiding behind the sign he was holding. "Avoid the occasion for sin!" it proclaimed, in drippy red paint.

Not bad advice, thought Lucy, again thinking of Elizabeth as she wheeled the cart over to her car and unlatched the hatch. She tossed the giant package of paper towels into the back of the Subaru, then paused as she reached for the toilet paper. What was she thinking? She was once again agreeing with the Pratts. She needed her head examined.

Lucy was in the driver's seat, planning a route back to the paper that avoided Main Street, when she saw trouble looming on the horizon. A group of fishermen leaving the Bilge, their favorite hangout, had spotted the group from the Revelation Congregation. At first they were content to toss out a few ribald comments, and to laugh at the shocked reactions of the Revelation Congregation members.

They probably would have gotten bored and gone on their way soon enough, except for the fact that one of the more zealous demonstrators raised his sign and threatened the fishermen with it. That was all it took for them to charge into the crowd, seizing the signs and knocking several demonstrators to their knees.

Lucy grabbed her cell phone, intending to dial 911, but someone had beaten her to it. The wail of a siren was heard approaching and the fishermen quickly scattered. It was all over when the squad car came careening into the parking lot. Not far behind was a white van with a satellite dish on top. Tinker's Cove would make the TV evening news.

Chapter Seven

"This town's going to hell in a handbasket," announced Lucy, as she wrestled the giant package of paper towels through the back door at the *Pennysaver*. Traffic was still not allowed on Main Street and she'd had to wind her way through back streets and driveways to the grungy parking area behind the office. It was shared with other stores and businesses on Main Street and was primarily used for deliveries and as a place to store garbage cans and dumpsters.

"Want some help with those bundles?" asked Phyllis.

"No, I can manage," said Lucy.

She was out the door and back in a minute with the toilet paper. A third trip to get the bags of cleaning supplies and coffee completed her mission. Phyllis helped her unpack everything into the storage closet.

"Store-brand creamer?"

"You sound like my kids," said Lucy. "I don't think you appreciate what I went through to get this stuff. It's like a war zone out there, with the boys from the Bilge attacking the pious folk from the Revelation Congregation."

"Is that what happened? I heard the sirens and wondered what was going on." Phyllis was arranging cans of coffee on the shelf. "Anybody hurt?"

"I hope not." Lucy was picturing the encounter in her mind, wondering at the violence exhibited by the fishermen.

Phyllis voiced the same thought. "What do they have against the Revelation Congregation anyway?"

"I don't know," said Lucy. "Frankly, I'm kind of amazed that nudity is turning out to be so controversial. It's sure turned this town upside down."

"I wouldn't read too much into it," said Phyllis, with a knowing nod. "After a few boilermakers, those boys'll punch anything that moves."

"You've got a point," agreed Lucy, heading for the door. "See you Monday."

The hot weather held during the weekend and there was more traffic than usual on Red Top Road as naturists driving cars with license plates from all over New England and beyond gathered at the pond. Elizabeth spent every spare minute there, ignoring her parents' objections.

"You're asking for trouble," warned Bill, passing a platter of corn on the cob, the first of the season. They were all gathered around the picnic table for a barbecue dinner.

"Don't be ridiculous, Dad," replied Elizabeth. "The naturists are all polite and respectful."

"It's not the naturists I'm worried about," said Bill.

"Dad does have a point," said Toby. "A lot of the guys are going down to the pond to check on the action there."

"Well, I can't be responsible if they're pathetic and immature, can I?" countered Elizabeth.

"I hope you're using sunscreen," fretted Lucy. "Take it from me, sun can really damage your skin."

"You could get cancer," said Zoe.

"It's not fair," grumbled Sara, wiping her brow with a paper napkin. "Because of these nudists, we can't go swimming at the pond."

"Naturists," corrected Elizabeth. "And it isn't their fault. It's Mom's and Dad's. They're the ones who won't let you go."

"Well, maybe I don't want to go," snapped Sara, who was self-conscious about her developing body. "Maybe I'm not a show-off like you."

"That's enough, girls," said Lucy, determined to keep peace at the dinner table.

But keeping peace was no easy task, at the table or anywhere else for that matter, as the temperature soared and the humidity climbed. Frustrated by the unusual amount of traffic when he made his usual Sunday morning dump run, Bill finally slammed his hand on the horn and pulled into the road in front of a line of cars, prompting a flurry of honks in return. Toby made himself scarce, and when Lucy casually asked him what his plans were on Saturday night he was unusually evasive. There was no question about what Elizabeth was doing— she continued to go down to the pond and was so defensive about it that no one dared to say a word to her because she'd snap their heads off.

Finally, on Sunday afternoon, Lucy and the younger girls settled in the gazebo to make the crepe paper flowers. They occasionally caught a slight breeze off the ocean out there, and Lucy kept the lemonade pitcher filled as the piles of red, white and blue "carnations" grew around them. When they'd used up all the crepe paper they bundled the flowers into plastic garbage bags and stuffed them into the back of the Subaru to deliver on Monday morning.

Melanie was in her usual spot, greeting the campers, when Lucy pulled up. The girls hopped out of the car and unloaded the flowers, eager to show her how much they'd accomplished. While she oohed and aahed, Lucy went and parked the car. Today she was covering Officer Barney Culpepper's annual fireworks safety lesson. As community outreach officer, he was responsible for educating town children about the rules of the road for bicyclists, Halloween safety and the danger of fireworks. Lucy always looked forward to covering these events because she got cute quotes from the kids and adorable photographs.

Barney was just beginning his presentation when she arrived at the covered pavilion, positioning herself on the outside of the circle of children gathered around him.

"Who knows what this is?" he asked, holding up a sparkler.

Almost all the children raised their hands. He pointed to a little boy with red hair and a freckled nose.

"A sparkler," said the boy. "My dad gets 'em every year for the Fourth of July."

"Does your dad let you hold them?" asked Barney.

"Sure. It's fun."

"It's fun, but it's also dangerous," said Barney, lighting the sparkler he was holding and receiving a chorus of ohhhs. "Do you know how hot this is right now?"

The kids didn't know, but a few raised their hands anyway. Barney chose Zoe.

"Five hundred degrees," she said, making an educated guess. "That's the hottest the oven gets."

"More than one thousand degrees," said Barney, carefully inserting the spent sparkler into a large coffee can filled with sand.

The kids were impressed.

"If you were to touch a lighted sparkler, you'd get a very bad burn. It could also set your clothes on fire. Who can think of some safety rules for sparklers?"

"Don't have them," offered a little girl with glasses.

"That's the safest thing, absolutely," said Barney. "But what if you do have them?"

"When they're done, put them in sand like you did," suggested a serious looking little boy.

"That's excellent. Anything else?"

The group was stymied.

"Well, if you're holding a sparkler be very careful. Watch it. Keep it away from other people. Don't run with it. Hold it out, away from your clothes. Don't let it get near your face, and don't keep holding it after it burns out because the wire stays very hot. And always have a bucket of water nearby, just in case of fire. Okay?" Barney held up a string of firecrackers. "Who can tell me what these are?"

"Firecrackers!" chorused the kids.

"Anybody here ever set off any firecrackers?"

If they had, nobody was going to admit it.

Barney chuckled and winked at Lucy.

"Firecrackers make a lot of noise, right?" Barney had everyone step back and lit the string, which popped and crackled and banged and danced about on the ground. "They don't seem too dangerous, do they?"

"If you put one in a can it will make the can bounce," offered the boy with freckles.

"What do you do if you put a firecracker under a can and it doesn't go off?"

"You look and see if it's gone out."

"NO YOU DON'T!" yelled Barney. "If it goes off when you're looking, you could hurt your eyes. Even go blind."

Barney's expression became very serious. "Do you know how many people are injured by fireworks every year?"

"Millions?" guessed the boy with freckles. He looked so serious that Lucy couldn't resist snapping his photo.

"Not millions, thank goodness," said Barney. "It's around nine thousand, which is a lot of people. That's why firecrackers and most other fireworks are illegal in our state. They can get you in big trouble."

The children had grown very quiet. Lucy guessed some were probably thinking guiltily of the supplies of fireworks their families had at home, ready for the holiday. After all, they were sold legally in neighboring New Hampshire and Canada, too.

"Anybody here hungry? Anybody want some watermelon?" asked Barney, sensing it was time to liven things up.

He lifted a small, round watermelon out of a

box and held it up, prompting an enthusiastic reaction. The kids shrieked and clapped until he held up his hand for silence.

"Before we eat the watermelon, I want to try a little experiment. What do you think will happen if I put a little cherry bomb inside the melon and set it off?" He held up the little device. "It's pretty small, isn't it? It can't do much damage, can it?"

Lucy was surprised to see Zoe had her hand raised. She waited until Barney gave her a nod before posing her question.

"Officer Barney, isn't that cherry bomb illegal? You said only sparklers are legal, didn't you?"

"That's a very good question, Zoe," said Barney, adding a big humph. "This cherry bomb was confiscated from somebody who was trying to bring it into the country illegally from Canada. It was given to our department for demonstration purposes only." He paused, letting this information sink in, then pointed to a little girl with long braids. "I see we have another question."

"Will it make the watermelon taste funny?" she asked.

"It might," agreed Barney. "But we won't know unless we try. Everybody move back."

Once he had everyone gathered at one end of the pavilion, he took the melon to the other end, where he set it on a concrete block. Then he donned safety glasses before he dropped the cherry bomb into the melon and awkwardly scampered away. A minute later, the fireworks started popping and the melon exploded, spraying chunks of rind everywhere.

"Sorry, kids. I didn't expect that to happen. I

guess these firecrackers are more powerful than we thought, hunh?"

There were nods all round, as well as a few pouts.

"I want you to remember what happened to this watermelon if somebody asks you to play with fireworks on the Fourth of July, okay? They may look pretty, and you might think it would be fun to play with them, but they can be very dangerous They can really hurt you, and I don't want to visit you in the hospital."

The kids were clearly impressed, sitting silently with somber expressions.

"Well, lucky for you, I brought two watermelons." Barney bent over and hoisted an even larger melon out of the box.

The kids cheered.

Afterwards, when they were sitting side by side, chewing on half-moons of ripe, red watermelon, Lucy asked Barney about the scuffle on Friday afternoon.

"Just between you and me," he said, wiping his chin with his huge hand, "that whole brouhaha had nothing at all to do with the church. Those guys were after Calvin Pratt."

"Calvin?"

"Yeah. It's no secret that a lot of the fishermen suspect him and his son Wesley there of poaching their traps. He hasn't been very popular on the waterfront for some time."

"Really? I didn't know that."

Barney smiled slyly. "You should read those police logs you pick up every week."

"I would if I had time," said Lucy, defending herself. "Phyllis scans them into the computer."

Barney took a bite of watermelon. "We've saved his butt a coupla times, breaking up fights."

"No wonder he looked so miserable," said Lucy. "Pru probably dragged him there."

"I'll bet. He knew he was in big trouble if he was spotted."

"Did they hurt him?"

"Nah, he ran for his truck as soon as he saw them coming. A couple of the naturists got in the way, there were some bruises. No broken bones."

Lucy nodded. "You know, there's an awful lot of lobster gear on the Pratts' property, behind their barn. I went over there when the dog got out last week and it made me wonder because I figured they'd have all their pots in the water. But when I looked closer it seemed as if the stuff had a whole lot of different registration numbers on it. I think it was stolen." She paused. "Wouldn't that be evidence that they're poaching?"

"Not really. Fishing gear breaks off all the time. They could just say they found it floating around."

"Well shouldn't they return it?"

"They could say they've been too busy." Barney spit out a seed. "It's high season, you know."

"So a search is no good?"

"Gotta catch 'em in the act."

"How are you going to do that?" asked Lucy, who knew the town police department had limited manpower, stretched even thinner by the presence of the naturists in addition to the usual influx of summer visitors.

"We can't, but we've asked for help from the state natural resources people."

Lucy also knew the state was having budget problems, and had cut back many departments. Natural resources had been one of the hardest hit.

"You don't expect them anytime soon, do you?"

"Nope," said Barney, tossing his rind into the trash. "No I don't."

"Mind posing for some pictures?"

Barney grimaced. "I might break the camera."

She studied his homely, jowly face as he knelt down to show his portable radio to a little boy.

"I'll risk it. Handsome is as handsome does, Barney."

"Aw, Lucy." It was going to be a great photo, the big bear-like policeman and the adorable little boy, heads together over the radio. She snapped a couple of shots, just to be on the safe side.

"You'll look great on page one."

"Sales will drop, I'm warning you."

"Never fear. Ted's putting the naturists above the fold."

Chapter Eight

Back at the *Pennysaver*, deadline was approaching and Lucy could no longer ignore the pile of press releases that had been growing on her desk all week. A roast beef dinner at the VFW, a square dance in the Community Church basement, a meeting of the Ladies Aid Society, story hour at the library, bingo at the senior center, all these and more had to be added to the community calendar. Some, like the Drama Guild's upcoming production of "Our Town" merited more attention than a listing and Lucy had to write three or four inches of copy for a brief announcement.

"What can I write about 'Our Town'?" she wondered aloud. "Talk about an old chestnut."

"Don't you mean 'classic'?" corrected Ted, sounding a bit sarcastic. As deadline drew nearer he tended to grow increasingly caustic.

"If you say so, but that old thing has been performed by every amateur theatrical group on the coast," said Lucy. "The entire population must know it by heart."

"Okay, smarty-pants, do you know it by heart?"

"No, Ted, I don't. But that's only because I keep

my brain clear and uncluttered, so I can better concentrate on the intricate details of the bird club's walks. It's the conservation area on Sunday and Quisset Point on Tuesday and I wouldn't want to get them switched."

"Oh, I don't know," sighed Phyllis. "They've had the same schedule for years. You'd think anybody who's interested would know it by now."

"What about visitors? Or new residents?" snapped Ted. "Don't they deserve to know what's going on in Tinker's Cove?"

"Doesn't take long to figure that out," said Phyllis. "Not much."

The office scanner cackled just then, contradicting her observation. Something was indeed happening in town, something that required a response from the police or fire department. They all listened intently, but the only word they could make out was "waterfront," combined with a lot of garbled numbers, police codes for classifying incidents.

"Did you catch that?" asked Ted, screwing up his face.

"Funny, isn't it? When some old guy has difficulty breathing and needs an ambulance it's clear as a bell."

Ted was on his feet, checking his camera and making sure he had extra film.

"Do you get the feeling they don't want us there?" he asked, heading for the door.

"That would be my guess," said Lucy, slinging her bag over her shoulder and hurrying to catch up with him.

"I'll stay here and take the messages," said Phyllis, feeling sorry for herself. But nobody was there to listen.

* * *

The waterfront was only a couple of blocks from the *Pennysaver* office but Ted got in his car and started the engine. Lucy hopped into the passenger seat and they were off, chasing a police cruiser that was racing down Main Street with its siren blaring and its lights flashing.

The scanner in Ted's car was also cackling as the dispatcher reeled off numbers and called in units from the far ends of town. The sound of approaching sirens filled the air.

"I don't like this," said Lucy, who was growing nervous. "Fishing's so dangerous. I hope nobody's in trouble."

But when they careened into the harbor parking lot it was clear that this was no tragedy at sea. Instead, police officers were busy breaking up a brawl. And as they got closer and had a clearer view of things they discovered that Toby was in the center of the fray, locked in fisticuffs with Wesley Pratt. Lucy was shocked to see her normally peace-loving son grappling with Wesley, his face red and twisted with rage.

She winced as two burly police officers administered a liberal dose of pepper spray before grabbing the young men by their shirt collars and yanking them apart. Toby's eyes were tearing and he was coughing and sneezing but the officers ignored his distress as they clapped his wrists into handcuffs and bundled him into the back of a cruiser.

"He needs a doctor!" exclaimed Lucy, frantic with concern.

"He needs a lawyer," said Ted, busy snapping pictures of Wesley getting the same treatment.

"Where are they taking them?"

"The station for now. Court's in session today so they'll probably arraign them this afternoon."

"Arraignment?" Lucy was shocked.

"This is serious, Lucy. Toby's not going to get off easily. I meant what I said about getting a lawyer. Come on, I'll take you back to the office so you can make some calls." He paused. "You better let Bill know what's happened."

"I can't," said Lucy, as they climbed up the hill to the car. "He's over on the other side of the state, picking up some salvaged doors and windows."

"That's too bad." Ted was starting the car.

"Yeah," said Lucy, fastening her seatbelt. But she wasn't altogether convinced. It was probably better that Bill would learn about Toby's arrest after the fact, when things had settled down a bit.

When they got to the office Lucy immediately put in a call to Bob Goodman, her friend Rachel's husband, who was a lawyer. He promised to meet Lucy at the courthouse for the afternoon session which began at two o'clock.

The district court was located in Gilead, a good half-hour drive from Tinker's Cove and Lucy left early so she wouldn't miss anything. That meant she had to wait. She was too nervous to sit on the benches provided in the lobby, so she paced. A few other worried-looking people were also waiting, some sitting with slumped shoulders and grim expressions. Others could be seen through the glass doors, standing outside and puffing on cigarettes. Lucy had never smoked a cigarette in her life but she suddenly wanted one.

A bailiff opened the doors to the courtroom and people started to drift in. Lucy took a seat right up front. She wanted to know everything that happened. But where was Bob? Minutes ticked by, a few lawyers gathered in the front of the courtroom, chatting casually, but there was no sign of the judge. Or Toby. Where was he? What were they doing to him?

Bob Goodman slipped into the seat beside her and Lucy threw her arms around him. "I'm so glad you're here."

Bob made a reassuring figure, with his graying hair and rumpled suit. His shoes needed polishing and his briefcase was overflowing with papers, all evidence of his heavy caseload. He was one of the hardest working lawyers in the district with a reputation for fairness that attracted clients from his better-tailored competitors.

"Take it easy Lucy," he said, seeing her worried expression. "This is just routine. I'll ask for bail and we'll get it. Have you got cash?"

Lucy nodded. "I stopped at the bank."

"Here they come," said Bob, squeezing her hand. "I better get down front."

Lucy watched as the court officers led a straggly line of miscreants into the courtroom. Toby was there, along with Wesley and a few other fishermen. There were also faces she didn't recognize: an older man, a couple of young girls. They were all in handcuffs and looked disheveled and miserable. None of them made eye contact with anyone and a few attempted to cover their faces.

"All rise!" thundered the bailiff and the robed judge hurried in and took his place at the bench.

He pounded his gavel and announced that court was in session. The fishermen were the first item of business.

"These young men engaged in a brawl this morning on the docks at Tinker's Cove," began the assistant district attorney.

He was a clean-cut youth, apparently fresh out of law school, crisply dressed in a spotless summer suit. His sturdy black wingtips were polished until they gleamed and he wore a large, gold signet ring on his pinky finger. Lucy hated him. He'd probably never, ever done anything bad. Never made a mistake. Never got himself into trouble.

"Testimony from police officers who were called to the scene . . ." continued the prosecutor, "one Tobias Stone is charged with assault with a dangerous weapon: a shod foot . . . other charges include disorderly conduct, resisting arrest . . ."

"He didn't resist!" exclaimed Lucy, jumping to her feet. "He was pepper-sprayed. I was there. I saw it."

Everyone in the courtroom was looking at her, including the judge, who had a very stern expression on his face.

"You are out of order," he warned her. "If this happens again I will have you removed from the court." He leaned forward. "Do you understand?"

Abashed, Lucy nodded. "I'm sorry, your honor."

The judge turned to the prosecutor. "Do you have any objection to bail?"

"None, your honor."

"We'll set the pretrial conference for July 30 and schedule the trial for August 15. Is that agreeable to everyone?"

Both the prosecutor and Bob Goodman nodded.

"Bail is fifty dollars." The judge banged his gavel, then leveled his gaze at Toby.

"Young man, release on bail is conditional upon your continued good behavior. Bail can and will be revoked if there are any further problems. Do you understand?"

Toby nodded and mumbled something which Lucy didn't hear. A court officer removed his handcuffs and sent him over to the cashier, where Lucy joined him. She handed over the money, the cashier gave her a couple of sheets of paper. Silently, they left the courtroom, only to encounter Pru Pratt in the lobby.

For once, Lucy sympathized with her neighbor. After all, they were in the same position. They were both mothers intent on the defense of their sons. She greeted Pru with a little smile and a nod.

"Don't you smirk at me, Lucy Stone!" exclaimed Pru, obviously offended. "From what I hear it was your son who started the whole thing!"

Toby didn't linger, much to Lucy's relief, but went outside to wait for her.

"I guess the judge will have to sort that out," replied Lucy. "From what I saw, there's plenty of blame to go around."

Pru's eyes bulged and her face reddened. "You'd like that wouldn't you? Pin it all on somebody else while your kid goes scot-free. Well, your family's not so perfect as you think." She waved a long, bony finger in Lucy's face, practically spitting out the words. "And keep your kids and your dog off my property! This is the last time I'm warning you."

Pru brushed past her, marching straight for the courtroom, and Lucy ran after her.

"What do you mean?" she asked, breathlessly. "My kids?"

Pru whirled around to face her. "You know perfectly well. You sent those girls over to spy on me and don't pretend you didn't."

"My girls? On your property?" Lucy was stunned.

"Yes indeed and they've got no right to be there. I won't be responsible for what might happen if Wesley. . . ." This was one thought Pru decided she'd better not voice. "Well, anything could happen."

"I'm very sorry. It won't happen again," promised Lucy. "I'll talk to the girls the minute I get home."

"I've heard that before," said Pru, stalking off.

Lucy was wild with worry when she joined Toby in the car.

"Whatever were you thinking?" she demanded, when she slid behind the steering wheel. "You're in big trouble. And I don't even want to think about your father's reaction." She pounded the steering wheel. "I can't believe it. What did I do wrong? Did I raise you to beat up other people? To get in fights? Did I? Did I ever tell you that the best way to settle differences was with your fists? Did I?"

Toby hung his head.

"This is absolutely disgraceful. And it's going to be expensive. We're going to have to pay Bob to defend you, you know. I am so ashamed. So embarrassed I have to involve friends in this." A horrible thought struck her. "Your name will be in the newspaper! In the court report! I'm never going to

be able to show my face in town. It's absolutely out-
rageous." She glared at him, and waggled a finger.
"You're going to have to come up with the dough,
buddy. There's no way your father is going to pay
for this."

"I'll pay it, Mom. Every penny."

"What if you go to jail? Do you know you could
be going to jail? Did you think of that? My son a
convict! A criminal. Ohmigod. Jail!"

"Mr. Goodman said it would probably be a year's
probation."

"He can't be sure of that. What if the judge decides to make an example of you? What if Wesley
Pratt is his favorite nephew or something? You
could be in really big trouble."

"I don't think Wesley Pratt is anybody's favorite
anything," muttered Toby.

"Don't get wise with me!" snapped Lucy. "You're
in no position to start getting cocky."

"Well, your position isn't so hot, either, is it?" exclaimed Toby, finally exploding. "I mean, you've
got a court date, too, don't you? With the dog?"

Chagrined, Lucy bit her lip. "You're right. Who
am I to scold you? I'm in trouble, too." She chewed
her lip. "It's even worse than that. Mrs. Pratt said
she caught the girls on her property. What is going
on? When did we turn into a family of criminals?"

"We're not criminals, Mom. We're good people. Circumstances have been against us, that's
all, and we ended up on the wrong side of the
law."

"I know," said Lucy, wondering as she started
the car how something like this could happen to
such nice, decent people. And even worse, how
was she going to tell Bill?

* * *

Lucy made sure Toby was out of the house and the girls were upstairs, out of the way, when Bill finally came home towards eight o'clock. She warmed up his dinner in the microwave while he settled himself at the round golden oak kitchen table with a cold beer.

"How was your day?" she asked brightly, setting the plate of meatloaf and mashed potatoes in front of him and taking a seat.

"Good."

"Traffic bad?"

"Not really."

"Did you get what you wanted?"

"Pretty much."

"Did you get a good deal?"

Bill put down his fork. "Is something the matter, Lucy?"

"Why do you say that?"

"You seem unusually interested in my day. Plus, there's no sign of the kids. What's going on?"

"Brace yourself. I've got bad news."

Bill took a swallow of beer and carefully set the glass back down on the table.

"We're not at the hospital, so it can't be that bad. What is it?"

"Toby got in a fight and got arrested. He's out on bail but he has a trial in August. He's charged with disorderly conduct, resisting arrest and assault with a deadly weapon."

"Deadly weapon?"

"A shod foot."

"Oh," said Bill, spearing a piece of lettuce and chewing it slowly. "Who was he fighting with?"

"Wesley Pratt."

"Somehow I'm not surprised."

"It's not about the dog, if that's what you're thinking." Lucy sighed. "Not that Toby's saying much about it, but I think it's about poaching. Wesley and Calvin are the prime suspects."

"It would be a Pratt, wouldn't it?"

"Why do you say that?"

"I got a call from Mrs. Pratt the other day, when you were out. Apparently Sara and Zoe were over in her yard. She says if they come back she won't be responsible for what happens to them."

"Why didn't you tell me? I saw Pru at the courthouse and she lit into me." Lucy took a sip of Bill's beer. "What were they doing over there, anyway?"

Bill scraped his plate with his fork, getting the last bit of gravy and mashed potato. "They told me they're upset about the dog hearing and they wanted to get evidence that she mistreats her chickens." He chuckled. "They're their mother's daughters, that's for sure."

"And Toby's your son," replied Lucy.

"That's what you keep saying," said Bill, reaching into the refrigerator for another beer. "But personally, I have my doubts."

Chapter Nine

Bill was in a foul mood next morning and barely touched the bacon and eggs Lucy cooked up for him as a treat. Toby wasn't around and Lucy thought his early hours were one bright spot in a day that didn't look very promising.

"Don't forget we have the dog hearing tonight," she told him.

"It never rains but it pours," he said, adding a big sigh for emphasis.

"Oh, cheer up," said Lucy, who was consulting the horoscopes. "You've got a five-star day."

"What's mine?" asked Elizabeth, breezing into the kitchen and pouring herself a cup of coffee.

"Four. It says, 'Your adventurous nature can lead you in new and rewarding directions if you will trust yourself.' "

"I think she's been quite adventurous enough," said Bill, draining his coffee and standing up.

"What's that supposed to mean?" demanded Elizabeth, who was always ready to defend herself.

"You know very well what I mean, young lady," said Bill. "You've had your fling with this nudism but now it's time to stop, especially considering your brother's situation."

Elizabeth glared at him. "Are you saying I can't sun myself because *Toby* got himself in trouble? That makes no sense at all!"

"It makes plenty of sense," said Bill. "You've got to think about your reputation, and what your brother does affects that."

"What is this? A time warp?" Elizabeth rolled her eyes. "This isn't the fifties, Dad."

"Your father has a point," said Lucy. "This is a small town and people talk. They're going to start wondering what's going on with the Stone family." She looked out the window towards the kennel, where Kudo was stretched out with his chin on his paws. "We all need to keep a low profile for a while, until we drop off people's radar screens."

"This is nuts," said Elizabeth, throwing her hands up in exasperation. "I'm out of here. At least they're sane at the Queen Vic." She paused at the door. "And don't count on me for supper—I've got plans."

"What plans?" demanded Bill, but Elizabeth was out the door.

"You've got to do something about that girl," he said, picking up his lunch cooler. "She's out of control."

"Right. I'll do what I can," said Lucy, standing on tiptoe to give him a peck on the cheek. She stroked his arm. "Everything will be okay."

"I hope so," he said.

Lucy watched through the screen door as he trudged out to his truck, looking as if he had the weight of the world on his shoulders. She went back to the table and picked up the paper to check her horoscope—one star.

* * *

Like many other mothers, Lucy had discovered that the time she spent chauffeuring the kids was a good time to broach difficult subjects, so she decided to tackle Zoe and Sara about their trespassing on the Pratts' property when she drove them to day camp.

"You girls know better than to do something like that," she said. "What were you thinking?"

"Mrs. Pratt's mean," said Zoe.

"The whole family is mean," added Sara. "I'm glad Toby punched Wesley. And you know what? I bet if they hadn't broken up the fight he would have beat up Wesley."

Lucy couldn't believe her ears. "Sara! That's no way to talk. What Toby did was very wrong. There's no excuse for fighting. It doesn't solve anything. It just causes more problems."

"Well, I don't care," said Sara, stubbornly. "If I'd been there I would've helped him."

"Me, too," said Zoe.

"Well, I understand that you love Toby, but that doesn't mean he's perfect. He made a big mistake and he's going to have to pay for it."

"Will he go to jail, Mom?" Sara's voice was very small.

Lucy felt as if she'd been stabbed right in the heart. She pulled the car over and braked, turning so she could face both girls.

"I wish I could tell you that won't happen, but the truth is that there's a possibility, a very tiny one, that he might be sent to jail." She reached out and held their hands. "Remember when Melissa Knight had meningitis and they sent that letter home from school saying we had to watch for the symptoms? It's kind of like that. There was a chance that somebody else might have gotten sick, but nobody did, did they?" She smiled in what she hoped was a reassuring manner. "Well, Toby's not going to go to jail, either. He's going to be fine."

She turned around and restarted the car. "He's going to be fine," she told herself, repeating it like a mantra. "He's going to be fine."

By the time she got to work, Lucy felt as if she'd already completed a full day of hard labor. She had no energy for the pile of press releases that was waiting on her desk, no desire to check her phone messages and e-mails. All she wanted to do was crawl into a hole somewhere.

"Lucy, did you pick up the police log?" asked Phyllis. "I can't find it anywhere."

"I forgot," said Lucy, dropping her head onto her hand and shaking it.

Talk about a Freudian slip: she'd forgotten because she didn't want to see Toby's name included with the drunken drivers and wife beaters and marijuana smokers that filled the roster each week. Now she'd have to take time she didn't have to go over to the police station to get it. Leaving it out was unthinkable; the police log was one of the paper's most popular features. Or was it? Ted was just coming through the door. She might as well try.

"Ted," she began, greeting him with a big smile. "What's the space situation this week? Tight?"

"You bet," said Ted. "I'm considering adding some

extra pages, but I don't really have enough ads to justify it."

"Well, since there are so many big stories this week, what do you think about cutting some of the listings and notices, stuff like the gas prices and mortgage rates and maybe even the police log?"

"You forgot to get it, didn't you?" Ted seemed amused.

"Well, actually I did, and I have so much work to do. . . ."

"No problem," he said, and Lucy's hopes rose only to be dashed. "I'll go."

"That's not like him," observed Phyllis, after Ted had gone. "Do you think he's coming down with something?"

"Maybe," said Lucy, sounding so hopeful that Phyllis gave her a sharp look.

The day dragged on as Lucy struggled to concentrate on her work. Her mind kept wandering, going over and over the same worries, like one of those mule trains that went down into the Grand Canyon day after day, wearing a winding trail into the rocky soil. Once started she couldn't seem to stop and her anxiety about the dog hearing led to her worry about Toby and her disappointment with Elizabeth which brought her around to the younger girls' disturbing behavior and finally Bill's blood pressure which she thought he really should have checked because it was the "silent killer."

The clock alternately lurched forward and stopped in its tracks while Lucy struggled with her emotions. She wanted the day to end and she wanted it to last forever; she wanted to get the dog hearing over with and she wished it could be postponed.

That night she cooked a family favorite, spaghetti, but nobody seemed to enjoy it. There was little conversation and they all ate mechanically, going through the familiar rituals of passing the basket of Italian bread and grating the Parmesan cheese without quite realizing what they were doing, each lost in their own thoughts.

Finally, leaving the dirty dishes for the kids to wash, Lucy and Bill left for the dog hearing. But not before Lucy finished one last chore. She fixed Kudo's bowl of kibble, adding a leftover meatball, and carried it out to him. She shoved it through the gate and stood watching him eat, wolfing down his meal in a matter of seconds and licking the bowl clean. He then came to the gate, tail wagging, expecting his evening exercise.

"Sorry," she said, rubbing his nose. "Not tonight."

Chapter Ten

Lucy found it felt very strange to go to a meeting of the Board of Selectmen without her notebook and camera, and accompanied by Bill. They could hear voices as they descended the stairs to the basement hearing room, which didn't surprise Lucy. Between the naturists and the spotted lichen, plenty of people would want to voice their opinions. Worse luck for her and Bill that Kudo's fate would be decided on a night when so many people were at the meeting.

When they entered the crowded hall, Lucy was struck once again with how much the room resembled a courtroom. Just the other day she had been in court with Toby; now it was the dog. She was spending entirely too much time these days on uncomfortable seats in the halls of justice.

She picked up an agenda from the table at the back of the room and they made their way down front, where the rows of seats hadn't filled up yet. Once they were settled, she checked the schedule and discovered what she had feared had happened— they were the first item, after the public comment period. There were only a few other official items—

accepting the gift of a new flag from the VFW, granting family leave to a DPW worker, and a presentation by the Fourth of July parade committee—which meant that everybody was there for the public comment period.

"Do this many people usually come?" asked Bill, shifting uneasily in his chair.

"No," said Lucy. "Usually there's just a handful of interested citizens. Regulars."

She twisted in her seat, to see who else had showed up, and spotted Ted standing in the back, looking for a seat. There were still a few vacancies in their row, but she didn't wave to him. He was supposed to be impartial and inviting him to sit next to her didn't seem quite right. Ted apparently agreed, because she saw him making his way down the other side of the room. Her heart sank when she noticed Cathy Anderson, the dog officer, sitting nearby. Lucy had been harboring a faint hope that somehow the whole matter might be canceled or postponed, but that seemed a pipe dream now. When Pru Pratt arrived, looking as sour as ever, she knew she and Bill would finally have to face the music.

They watched glumly as the selectmen entered and took their seats. When Howard White called the meeting to order with a bang of his gavel, Bill placed his hand over Lucy's.

"We'll begin tonight as always with the public comment period, when the floor is open to one and all. Does anybody want to speak?"

A middle-aged gentleman in the Tinker's Cove summer uniform of khaki pants and a polo shirt raised his hand.

"Mr. Weatherby," said the chairman. "Please state your name and address for the record and tell us what's on your mind."

"Thank you. My name's Horace Weatherby and I have a summer home on Wequaquet Lane. The reason I'm here is that I'm very upset that the fireworks have been canceled and so are my neighbors."

A sizeable contingent had accompanied him to the meeting and they all nodded and murmured in support.

"In fact, I have a petition here with over one hundred signatures asking the board to reconsider the matter."

The contingent grew a little louder, joined by many others in the room.

"Hear! Hear!" boomed Scratch Hallett, waving a fist in the air.

Chairman Howard White banged his gavel and called for order.

"We'll have no more of that," he said, as if scolding a classroom of rowdy kindergarteners. "You'll all get to express your views, but you have to wait to be recognized by the chair, that's me." He pointed the gavel. "Reverend Macintosh."

"Clive Macintosh, I'm the chaplain for the VFW, and I want to express support for Mr. Weatherby's petition."

Heads nodded and hands shot up throughout the room.

"Am I correct in assuming you're all here because you want the fireworks restored?" asked Howard. "Just raise your hands."

Almost everyone in the room raised their hands.

Howard White sighed, and the other board members looked pained.

"Perhaps if I explain our vote," said Howard. "The problem is that this plant is protected by state law and the town could face an expensive court battle if the lichen is harmed. We really had no choice but to cancel the fireworks this year. But I'm willing to appoint a committee to look into alternatives for next year."

The other board members nodded in agreement.

"We don't want a committee!" yelled a shrill female voice. "We want fireworks!"

This was greeted with enthusiastic applause, prompting Howard to bang his gavel furiously.

"I don't want to have to clear the room," he warned. "We have a consensus, however, and the committee proposal will be put on the agenda for the next meeting."

This was met with grumbles and somebody called out, "We don't want a committee! We want fireworks!"

"That's not the way business is conducted in this town," said Howard, setting his jaw firmly. "Now, does anyone have any other matter to discuss beside the fireworks?"

"Hold on, Howard," said Joe Marzetti. "Maybe we should take another vote."

"That's impossible," snapped Howard, "and you know it. We can't vote on a matter unless it's placed on the agenda and duly advertised."

"Well, then, let's add it to next week's agenda," said Joe, speaking through clenched teeth.

"We can add it, but it will be too late. The next meeting is after July Fourth."

Joe's face was red with embarrassment at his mistake and fury at Howard's high-handed manner. He sat silently, drumming his fingers on the table.

Lucy was so caught up in the drama of the situation that she'd forgotten all about Kudo until Bill tapped her thigh a few times with his knee. "How long is this going to go on?" he whispered.

"I don't know," she said, looking around the room. Nobody seemed ready to leave and Howard was looking increasingly uncomfortable with the situation.

"Discussion on the fireworks issue is hereby closed," he said, adding a smack of the gavel for emphasis. "Does anyone wish to bring any other issue to the board's attention?"

If he had expected the crowd to pack up and leave, he was going to be disappointed, thought Lucy. Hands had shot up throughout the room. Howard gave the floor to Millicent Blood, a patrician woman who happened to be one of his neighbors. If he'd been seeking a conciliator, however, he'd made the wrong choice. Millicent's comments only fanned the flames of controversy.

"I would just like to say that I applaud the efforts of the Society for the Preservation of Tinker's Cove to preserve our natural heritage. . . ."

Millicent was drowned out by a chorus of boos. Seeking to restore order, Howard pointed his gavel at the first person he happened to see: Mike Gold.

The portly, frizzy-haired representative of the American Naturist Society had dressed for the meeting, albeit in sandals, rather short shorts and a tank-style T-shirt. Definitely not the sort of thing people wore in Tinker's Cove, thought Lucy, but at least he was decently, if minimally, covered.

"My name is Mike Gold and I'm here on behalf of the naturist community . . ."

If only she'd had a camera, thought Lucy, to capture Howard's horrified expression.

". . . and I'd like to express our appreciation to the people of Tinker's Cove for their tolerance and hospitality," continued Mike. "We'd like to apologize for any disruption we may have caused and ask for your patience. We understand naturism is controversial, not everyone approves, but we believe that if you get to know us, you'll find we're a pretty responsible group and we're eager to work out any problems that may come up in a constructive way. Thank you."

The next speaker, Mel Dunwoodie, wasn't quite as tactful. "Whether or not you like it, naturists have rights, too, and we intend to exercise our right to 'life, liberty and the pursuit of happiness' to the utmost," he said, turning to glare at Prudence Pratt. "I'd also like to add that this proposed bylaw against nudity is a bad idea for our town and urge everyone to vote against it."

The crowd was divided on this issue: some applauded while others grumbled. Hands shot up and Howard scanned the crowd until he found someone who was certain to say the right thing, whatever the occasion: Corney Clark.

Corney got to her feet gracefully and gave a little toss of her head, causing her blond hair to fall into place. Trust Corney to find a fabulous stylist, a genius with the shears.

"I just want to say," she began, in her well-modulated finishing school voice, "that in all the years I've lived here in Tinker's Cove I've never seen the town so divided. These are challenging times and we're faced with many difficult issues, but I want to remind everyone that we're all members of the same community and we all want what's best for our town. The days ahead will be much more pleasant if we treat each other as we would wish to be treated ourselves: with tolerance and respect."

For once, the crowd was silent. Howard White seized the moment, closed the public discussion period and moved the meeting forward onto the first item of business. He slumped in his chair, mopping his brow with his handkerchief, while dog officer Cathy Anderson came forward and arranged her papers.

Lucy, who'd been enjoying the meeting so much that she almost forgot about Kudo, clasped Bill's hand.

"I have received several complaints about Kudo, a mixed-breed dog owned by Lucy and Bill Stone, who live on Red Top Road. The dog has on several occasions attacked chickens, and I myself have witnessed him running loose in violation of the town's leash law. On at least two occasions these sightings have coincided with complaints about knocked-over garbage bins. When I contacted the owners, they were exceptionally cooperative, they even built a kennel to specifications I recommended, incurring considerable expense. Unfortunately, the dog continues to defy their best efforts and keeps getting out."

"Are the owners here tonight?" asked White.

"Yes," said Lucy, rasing her hand.

"Ah, Mrs. Stone, I didn't see you there. You're

not in your usual seat." He surveyed the audience. "Are any of the complainants here?"

"Yup. Right here," Prudence Pratt spoke out loudly.

"Well, I guess we better hear what you have to say, Mrs. Pratt."

Lucy found herself sinking lower in her chair as Pru strode to the front of the room, taking her place beside Cathy Anderson. Pru was much taller than Cathy, and in contrast to the dog officer's womanly figure, she looked mannish from behind. Her T-shirt and jeans hung loosely from her bony body. Cathy's blond hair was clean and shiny while Pru's was scraped back and clumped into a sticky-looking ponytail.

"Well," began Pru, "I've got a flock of about forty Rhode Island Reds. These are chickens I breed myself, and they regularly take the blue ribbon at the county fair. They're also good layers, I get a lot of double yolks. And when they stop laying they make a very tasty stew, if I say so myself. The problem is that this dog, here, keeps coming over and gets 'em all in a panic and, well, being chickens, eventually one of 'em will manage to flap its way over the fence and right into the beast's mouth. And then there's blood and gore and feathers all over the place." She snorted. "He doesn't even eat 'em, mind, just shakes 'em 'til they come apart."

There were a few groans from the audience and Lucy found herself wincing.

"You're saying he doesn't dig under the fence, or break it in some way?' asked Joe Marzetti.

"No, he's a crafty devil. He just keeps worrying

'em and worrying 'em until he gets one in a panic. He's a master at it."

"Have you asked the Stones to repay you for the lost chickens?" asked Ellie Sykes.

"Sure. They always pay, but what's the good of that? I can't replace the chickens. They're breeding stock, see. Last week he got one of my prize-winners, one I was planning to breed."

"Do we have any other witnesses?" asked White.

No one came forward, and Lucy had a little surge of hope. Then she was called to the front of the room. Bill squeezed her hand as she rose from her seat.

"All I can say," she began, looking each board member in the eye in turn, "is that we have done our very best to restrain the dog. As Cathy mentioned we built him a very sturdy kennel, but he is something of an escape artist. I would like to mention that he is not a vicious dog, except for chickens, and he's a much-loved family pet. My two youngest girls, especially, are very fond of him."

Again, she tried to make eye contact with the board members, but only Ellie Sykes met her gaze. The others looked away. Not a good sign.

Lucy went back to her seat when Howard White asked Cathy for her recommendation.

"This is a very difficult situation," she began in a tight voice, pausing to consult her notes. "As I mentioned, the Stones are responsible pet owners who have followed all my suggestions and recommendations. Unfortunately, they have been unable to control the dog and his problem behavior continues. This doesn't leave the board with too many options. You could banish the dog, which essentially means passing the problem on to some-one else, or you could vote to . . . ," she paused and swallowed hard, "destroy the dog."

Lucy actually felt her stomach drop.

"Is the dog a danger to people? To children?" inquired Ellie Sykes.

"I don't believe so," said Cathy.

From her seat, Pru Pratt snorted. "I wouldn't want to get between that dog and a chicken, that's for sure."

"That's definitely a factor to consider," said Joe Marzetti.

"I don't think we should concern ourselves with speculation," said Howard. "We should base this decision on the facts, on the dog's past history."

"The dog was before us a few years ago?" asked Marzetti, who was leafing through his information packet.

"Yes, when he was owned by Curt Nolan," said Cathy. "It was a similar complaint."

"I actually brought that complaint," said Ellie. "I keep chickens, too, and he did quite a lot of damage to my flock."

"I had a dog like that once," said Pete Crowley, "only he chased cats. He was always treeing the neighbor's cats."

"Do we have a motion?" asked Howard, cutting off Pete's reminiscences.

"I move we give the Stones one more chance," said Ellie. "We can continue the order that the dog be confined to their property with the condition that it will be destroyed if it gets loose again."

"Second," said Bud Collins, who Lucy had thought was asleep.

"All in favor?"

The vote was unanimous.

"Whew." Bill let out a huge sigh. "A reprieve."

"But he's still on death row," said Lucy, wondering how they were ever going to manage to keep Kudo confined, considering he'd overcome their best efforts to date.

Pru wasn't pleased with the decision. She was clearly in a huff as she went back to her seat.

"Our next order of business is a request from the July Fourth parade committee," said Howard. "Who speaks for the committee?"

"I do."

Lucy turned around and saw the speaker was Marge Culpepper, Barney's wife. She was a tall, plump woman who looked older than her years due to the curly, gray hair she refused to touch up with color. Lucy gave her an encouraging smile; she knew that Marge was terrified of speaking publicly.

"I'm here on behalf of the entire committee," stammered Marge, indicating four other people seated in the same row with her. They all raised their hands, to identify themselves. Marge stood up a bit straighter and swallowed hard. "We're here to request that the board cancel the Fourth of July parade."

There was a shocked silence in the room. Even the group from the VFW was too stunned to protest.

"What is the reason for this unusual request?" asked Howard.

"The problem is that the American Naturist

Society has applied for permission to march in the parade."

"So what?' asked Pete Crowley, scratching his chin.

"We're not confident they will be appropriately attired," said Marge, blushing furiously.

"You mean they might march naked?" asked Crowley.

"That's ridiculous . . ." protested Mike Gold, only to be silenced by a bang of the gavel. He and Mel Dunwoodie both raised their hands, but Howard ignored them.

"It's a concern," said Marge, nodding.

"So deny the application," said Marzetti.

"It's not that simple. Marching in the parade is an exercise of First Amendment rights. Free speech and all that. The application is just a formality, really. We can't turn away anybody who wants to march, unless they're breaking some law. It's a violation of their right to free speech."

"That's why we need a public decency bylaw," yelled Pru, from the audience.

"We'll open this up for public comment later," admonished Howard. "After the board has finished questioning Mrs. Culpepper."

"It sure doesn't make much sense to me to cancel the whole parade because of one group," said Joe. "Besides, the parade's a big tourist attraction."

"Folks with kids are going to leave town fast and never come back if we have naked people in the parade," said Pete.

"Have you expressed your concern to the naturists?" asked Ellie. "Perhaps you could get some sort of agreement from them in advance."

"We considered doing that, but when we checked

with town counsel he said we couldn't apply a restriction to one group that we didn't apply to all. And even if we did get some sort of informal promise, it wouldn't be binding. I don't think we can risk it."

"Whiskey?" Bud Collins opened one eye. "Where?"

"Not whiskey, risky," said Ellie.

Howard banged his gavel. "Any comment from the audience?"

Several hands shot up, joining Mike Gold's and Mel Dunwoodie's. Howard ignored them and chose the commander of the VFW post.

"Well, all I want to say is that Tinker's Cove doesn't seem to be interested in celebrating the Fourth of July anymore," asserted Bill Bridges, his dentures clicking furiously. "First it was the fireworks and now it's the parade. What next?"

"Yeah, I don't suppose you're even interested in this flag that we're giving you," said Scratch. "It flew over the Capitol, you know."

"I don't recall recognizing you," said Howard. "You only get the floor when I give it to you."

"Well, I don't want your floor," said Scratch, handing the flag to the commander. "I don't want anything to do with the lot of you. I think it's a sorry state of affairs when we can't even celebrate the founding of our country and I know who to blame, too." He pointed a finger, shaking with fury. "It's you, Pru Pratt. It's because of you and that stupid bylaw that these naturists want to be in the parade, instead of doing what they do over at the pond."

"Well, I never," said Pru, rising to her feet, ready to give Scratch a piece of her mind. But it was too late. He'd left the room.

Unwilling to court further controversy, Howard called for a vote and the board members agreed unanimously, albeit reluctantly, to cancel the parade. They had hardly completed the vote when people started leaving. Down in front, Ted was getting quotes from Gold and Dunwoodie, scribbling furiously into his notebook.

"Do you want to stay any longer?" asked Bill.

Lucy shook her head and they joined the throng leaving the room.

"It just doesn't seem right," she said. "No fireworks, no parade. It's not going to be much of a Fourth of July."

"You can say that again," agreed Bill.

"The parade's the least of it," muttered Mel. "Whatever happened to free speech in this town?"

Chapter Eleven

Lucy and Bill were both quiet on the ride home, thinking over the implications of the board's decision.

"It could have been worse," said Bill.

"How are we going to keep Kudo from getting loose?"

"I'm working on it," said Bill.

They fell silent.

It was almost midnight when they got to bed and Bill, unused to such late hours, fell asleep immediately. Lying beside him, Lucy's mind kept following the same worn track of worries, but now there were a few new twists. It seemed to her that the board hadn't really done them any favors—they'd already tried everything they could think of to keep the dog confined and he'd always managed to get loose. It was just a matter of time before they'd be back at another hearing, and this time the result was a foregone conclusion. What could they do?

It was an unanswerable question, but that didn't stop her from trying to think of something. She heard the grandfather clock in the hall downstairs chime two before she fell asleep and she didn't wake until Bill roused her an hour late in the morning.

"You shouldn't have let me sleep," she protested.

"I thought you could use the rest. Besides, you don't have to write up the meeting today."

"That's right," she said, relaxing back against the pillows. "No deadline for me today."

"I brought you some coffee."

"Thanks." She took the mug he held out to her and took a sip. "Coffee in bed—I could get used to this."

"Enjoy it while you can, Madame Pompadour. I'm off to work."

"Have a nice day," said Lucy, stretching luxuriously.

She had at least fifteen minutes before she had to wake the girls and she was determined to enjoy them. If only she could start every day like this, with time to organize her thoughts. She was glad she didn't have to make sense of last night's meeting for a story; she wouldn't know where to begin. She'd never had to cover such a divisive issue. People were angry enough about the fireworks and now the parade had been canceled, too. Once word got out, the selectmen could very well have a rebellion on their hands.

Lucy was thinking it was really time to get up when Sara and Zoe rushed into her room in their pajamas and climbed into bed with her.

"What happened at the meeting?" asked Sara.

"Can we keep Kudo?" asked Zoe.

"We can keep him as long as he doesn't get loose. If he gets loose, even once, they're going to put him to sleep."

"That's not fair!" protested Zoe, snuggling against her mother.

"He always gets out, no matter what we do," said Sara, who was sitting at the foot of the bed.

"I know, honey. We're going to have to try harder. That's all we can do." Seeing Sara's discouraged expression, she added, "Daddy's trying to think of something."

"Don't they understand he's an animal? He can't think like people can. He's just doing what his instincts tell him to do."

"I know." Lucy paused. "Maybe we should try obedience school."

"I know! We could send him to a trainer. There are people who specialize in difficult dogs. I can find out from Melanie."

"You can ask her for information, but I bet something like that is awfully expensive. I don't think we can afford it."

Zoe didn't want to hear it. "We have to save Kudo."

"We also have to pay college tuition for Elizabeth and the lawyer for Toby and groceries and taxes and the mortgage. . . ."

"But you said they'll put him to sleep."

Lucy looked down at Zoe's earnest little face and stroked her hair.

"We'll see what we can do," she said, deciding to change the subject. "So, tell me what you did in camp yesterday."

"We made T-shirts to wear in the parade," said Sara.

What a morning, thought Lucy. Was no subject safe?

"Mine's pink, with a kitty," said Zoe.

"Mine's blue, with a whale. A right whale because they're endangered. Did you know that whales are still hunted? For food?"

There was no point in letting them continue. She had to tell them.

"The shirts sound great, but I don't think you'll be wearing them in the parade."

"Why not?"

"The parade's been canceled."

For a moment the girls couldn't think of anything to say. This was something completely out of their experience. For as long as they could remember there'd always been a July Fourth parade.

"Are you joking?" asked Sara.

Zoe giggled with relief. "That's funny, Mom."

"It's no joke, it's the truth. They're afraid people will march naked," explained Lucy.

Zoe considered this. "I bet Elizabeth would."

Lucy couldn't help smiling. "Come on girls, we've got to start getting ready or you'll be late for camp."

By the time Lucy got herself dressed and the dog fed and the lunches made and got the girls into the car, she felt exhausted, as if she'd been swimming against the current. And resentful. Without the pressure of deadline, it was supposed to be a relaxed morning but it hadn't turned out that way. The car was hot, sweat was forming on her upper lip, and her clothes were sticking to her body. And it was going to get hotter: the sun was threatening to burn through the clouds.

"Turn on the AC, Mom," said Sara.

"It is on."

"I can't feel it back here. Can you feel it, Zoe?"

"It takes a while," said Lucy, turning onto Red Top Road. "Give it a chance."

She was beginning to pick up speed when she saw the unthinkable: Kudo was running through their yard heading straight for the Pratts' property. She immediately pulled to the side of the road and slammed on the brakes. Jumping out of the car, she called the dog.

He stopped, ears perked up and looked at her. Amazingly enough, he began to run towards her. Worried about a speeding car on the road, she began to cross, intending to meet the dog and grab him by the collar before he crossed the road.

This was really too much, she muttered to herself. That darned dog couldn't even stay out of trouble for twenty-four hours. What a nuisance. They would have to find another home for him, there was really nothing else to do. Not if they couldn't even keep him safe in his kennel for a single day.

Hearing the sound of an approaching engine, she turned her head and saw a pickup truck coming at high speed. She had no choice but to stop and wait for it to pass. To her horror, she saw that Kudo had a different idea. He was still coming, trying to outrace the truck.

"Stay! Stay!" she yelled.

But Kudo was intent on getting into the car and coming along for the ride. He kept on running straight into the path of the truck.

She watched, horrified, as the action unfolded in slow motion. The dog's happy, smiling face, tongue flapping in the breeze. The impact, and then his body flying into the air. A quick glimpse of the driver. The haze of smoke and the stink of rubber as Wesley Pratt slammed down the accelerator and sped off. The crumpled bundle of yellow fur lying in the grass by the side of the road.

Lucy ran to the dog and found he was breathing, just.

Sara was behind her, holding the blanket they kept in the back of the car.

"I know what to do, Mom. They taught us at camp. We'll slide the blanket under him and carry him to the car, okay? Zoe, open the back!"

Gently, trying to hurry because they knew moments counted, but afraid of hurting poor Kudo, they carried him to the Subaru wagon and placed him gently in the cargo area. Then Lucy drove as quickly as she dared to the veterinary hospital. Everybody there was nice as could be, rushing out to the car with a miniature stretcher and hurrying the dog into a examining room, but it was no good. The doctor was listening to his heartbeat and Lucy was gently stroking his head, whispering mindless words of encouragement when he breathed his last.

"I'm sorry," said the vet, removing his stethoscope.

To her horror, tears sprang to her eyes.

"It's just so sudden. I didn't expect this."

The vet handed her a tissue. "He didn't really suffer. He probably went into shock when he was hit."

"He was happy, he was smiling as he ran across the road." Lucy blew her nose. "I can't believe it."

"It takes time," said the vet. "Not to rush you, but how do you want to dispose of the body?"

Lucy didn't have a clue. "I guess we'll bury him in the backyard."

"Not advisable," said the vet. "He's a pretty big dog. I recommend cremation. Then you can bury the ashes."

"Oh," said Lucy. "I guess that would be better."

"We'll call you when the ashes are ready."

"Thanks." Lucy walked out to the waiting room, feeling like a robot.

The girls jumped up and ran to her. "Is he . . . ?"

She shook her head, and found herself bursting into uncontrollable sobs. The girls joined her. Together, holding hands, they went out to the car. Too upset to drive, Lucy sat behind the wheel, mopping her face and passing tissues to the girls.

"I don't know why I'm so upset," she wailed. "He was a terrible dog."

"I used to be afraid of him," admitted Zoe, "when I was little."

"He smelled pretty bad," said Sara.

"He was no end of trouble," said Lucy.

"I'm really going to miss him," said Zoe.

"Me, too."

"We all are."

Finally, automatically going through the motions without thinking, Lucy started the car and followed the familiar roads to Friends of Animals day camp. She drove slowly, wondering why driving faster seemed to take more energy. Whenever she was tired or upset, she found the car slowing, as if she couldn't summon the strength to press firmly on the gas pedal.

Melanie Flowers rushed out to meet them.

"I've been worried . . . I called the house but there was no answer. . . ."

"I'm sorry we're late," said Lucy. "We had to take our dog to the vet. He got hit by a car."

"Oh, how terrible." She held out her arms and embraced the girls, who were still a bit teary. "Did this happen just this morning? You must all still be in shock."

Seeing the girls' stricken expressions, Lucy wondered if she'd made a mistake bringing them to camp. "Maybe they'd be more comfortable at home. . . ." she began.

"Probably better to keep busy," advised Melanie. "Zoe's group is just about to go to arts and crafts." She gave the little girl a squeeze. "Maybe you'd like to make a drawing of your dog? Or a clay model?"

"That would be nice, Zoe," said Lucy, with an encouraging little smile.

"Okay," she said, giving a shaky little nod.

"Maybe you can walk her over," said Melanie, giving Sara a squeeze, too. "Janine's making dog biscuits with the Hummingbirds and I know she could use a hand. They're in the kitchen."

"Come on, Zoe," said Sara, taking her little sister by the hand.

Lucy watched as they walked off together.

"Sara was a big help," she told Melanie. "She knew just what to do."

"How did it happen?"

"The dog just ran in front of Wesley Pratt's truck. It wasn't his fault. There was nothing he could have done."

"That's a terrible feeling," said Melanie. "I hit a deer last fall—there was absolutely no way I could have avoided it. It just jumped from the side of the road right into my car. I was devastated."

"I can imagine." Lucy was remembering how

she'd seen Kudo heading for the road, but had been unable to stop him.

"And it made a terrible mess of my car, too." Melanie nodded solemnly. "It was in the body shop for weeks."

"Oh my gosh, I didn't think of that," said Lucy, wondering if Wesley's truck had been damaged.

"The insurance covered most of it, but I had a hefty deductible."

"Doesn't everybody," said Lucy, wondering what Wesley's deductible was, or if he even had insurance. "Well, I've got to get to work."

"Don't worry about the girls—I'll keep an eye on them."

"Thanks for everything," said Lucy, letting out a big sigh.

"Let me know if there's anything I can do," said Melanie.

"I might just take you up on that," said Lucy, "because I'm just about at the end of my rope."

Chapter Twelve

Back in the car, Lucy was alone with her emotions. She sat for a minute, trying to sort it all out. Shock and sadness, of course, but also a sense of relief. As much as she hated to admit it, a very difficult problem had been solved. She no longer had to worry about what to do about Kudo.

Of course, this wasn't the way she would have wished to solve it. It would have been better if their efforts to control the dog had worked. But the sad truth was, they hadn't. He'd been impossible. Nothing they tried seemed to work. Even Cathy Anderson had said they'd made every effort to restrain Kudo. No matter what they did, he continued to get loose, and once loose he generally went after Prudence Pratt's chickens.

He had truly been an awful dog, thought Lucy, feeling tears pricking her eyes. An awful, terrible, horrible dog, but she'd loved him. He was loyal, in his way. He always came home, eventually. And maybe she was fooling herself, but she thought Kudo had a special place in his doggy heart for her. When she was sad or depressed, he had a way of sensing it and would stay with her, often resting his chin on her knee.

Lucy sniffed and reached for her purse, she needed a tissue. How could she feel relieved that Kudo was gone? What kind of person was she? He'd been a good dog and here she was practically glad he was dead. She might as well start adding up how much she'd save on dog chow and anti-flea drops and annual checkups at the vet. Not to mention the additional coverage they'd had to get on their homeowner's insurance. They'd practically be millionaires now that the dog was gone, and they'd have better relations with their neighbors, too.

Or maybe not, thought Lucy, trying to remember if Wesley's truck had been damaged when it hit the dog. He had driven off so quickly, and she had been so concerned about the dog, that she hadn't really thought about it. But if there had been damage, she had to make it right. Things were tense enough with the Pratts, they certainly didn't need to give them any more grounds for grievance. She considered driving over to the Pratts and getting the matter resolved, but she was already late for work. It was true she didn't have to write the story about the Selectmen's meeting, but there were always a million last-minute tasks and Ted would want her to help with those. On the other hand, the noon deadline meant they always finished up early on Wednesdays. She could swing by the Pratts place after the paper was put to bed, in the early afternoon.

*   *   *

Ted was in a lather when she got to the office, struggling with the story about the meeting. He was hunched over his computer keyboard, alternately typing a few words and flipping through the pages of his notebook, looking for quotes. He was too involved in his work to notice that Lucy was nearly two hours late.

Phyllis gave her a conspiratorial wink. "I told him that he ought to appreciate you more, considering that you do this week after week," she said, fanning herself with a sheaf of papers. She was wearing a purple and green Mexican cotton dress today and was the brightest thing in the dingy office.

"It was a killer meeting," said Lucy. "Did he tell you about the parade?"

"He didn't have to. We've had a steady stream of irate citizens dropping off letters to the editor."

"Yeah, Lucy, could you edit them for me? We don't have room for them all, so pick a representative sample, okay?"

Lucy took the folder of letters from Phyllis, noticing with a shock that she'd polished her nails green to match her dress. She sat down at her desk and turned on the computer, waiting while it produced the usual clicks and groans. She felt the same way—it was hard to settle down to work.

"If you're writing about the dog part of the hearing I guess you ought to mention that Kudo's dead," she said.

Both Phyllis and Ted dropped what they were doing. It was as if she'd exploded a bombshell.

"Dead? How did that happen?" asked Ted.

"Wesley Pratt ran him over with his truck," said Lucy, surprised by the pricking in her eyes.

"I'm so sorry," said Phyllis, enveloping her in a huge billowing green and purple hug.

Now Lucy was really crying and furious with herself for losing control.

"It was horrible," she blubbered. "The girls were in the car."

"Oh, no!" Phyllis patted her hand.

"Did he do it on purpose?" asked Ted. "Was it some sort of retaliation for the fight?"

"Oh, no!" protested Lucy, eager to nip this misconception in the bud. "There was nothing he could do. The stupid dog ran right in front of his truck."

"Did he stop?" asked Ted.

"Well, no, but he's just a kid. I didn't really expect him to." Lucy dabbed at her eyes. "The truth is, I'm kind of worried that the impact may have damaged his truck."

"It doesn't take much," offered Phyllis. "My cousin Elfrida only grazed that moose and her car was a total loss. The insurance paid, of course, but they only paid the replacement value and considering she had a twelve-year-old Escort it wasn't much."

This was not encouraging news to Lucy.

"I guess I better follow up and let them know we'll take care of any damages," said Lucy.

Behind her, Ted's and Phyllis's eyes met.

"Oh, I don't know," said Ted, "from what I've seen of Pru she won't hesitate to let you know all about it."

"In fact," added Phyllis, "I'm surprised she hasn't called already."

"Maybe she's mellowing," said Lucy, opening the folder.

Phyllis snorted. "Mark my words, you'll hear from her before the day is out."

The rest of the morning passed uneventfully, however, with no word from Pru. A few people stopped in with letters to the editor about the parade or to buy last-minute classified ads and Mike Gold called to see if Ted needed any more information about the naturists, but that was all. They were able to wrap up the paper on time and Lucy was done for the day before one o'clock.

She decided to make good on her resolution to stop at the Pratts' on her way home. She didn't want to be worrying about this all day, she wanted to have it all settled before she told Bill and Toby about the dog's death. That way there would be no reason for them to have any contact with the Pratts, especially Wesley, and no chance that things would get out of control. Not that they would, she told herself, but it was better to be on the safe side.

As she drove, Lucy rehearsed what she would say. Keep it simple and direct, she told herself, the Pratts weren't much for small talk. It would be easier if Wesley was there because then she could just tell him there were no hard feelings about the dog and ask if there was any damage to the truck. If Wesley wasn't home, she'd have to explain the accident to his parents, and she'd have to make it very clear that she wasn't seeking redress. She understood full well that Wesley couldn't have avoided hitting the dog, and as for the fact that he left the scene of an accident, well, she herself was the mother of a twenty-one-year-old and she knew how irresponsible they could be. They tended to follow their first impulse, which was generally fight or flight, without taking time to think.

By the time she reached the Pratts' house Lucy was beginning to think that this might be an opportunity for some sort of reconciliation. She didn't like being at odds with her neighbors, and most of the animosity had been a direct result of Kudo's behavior. Now that he was gone, maybe things would be more relaxed and agreeable. She certainly hoped so.

She turned into the Pratts' driveway, struck once again with the bareness of their yard. Not even the weeds dared to sprout in the driveway, no bushes or flowers softened the stark angles of the house. Since she knew the Pratts didn't approve of trespassers she parked at the end of the drive and went straight for the back door, where she stood on the stoop and knocked.

When there was no answer, she called out, guessing that Pru might be out back, tending to her chickens, or her vegetable garden where the spinach and Swiss chard and onions all grew in straight lines with military precision. She was pretty sure Pru was home because her car, an aged but impeccably maintained Dodge Shadow, was parked in its usual spot.

Lucy knew the wisest course of action would simply be to leave. She could leave a note, she could call later. She could stop by on her way home from work. The one thing she shouldn't do was start poking around in hopes of finding Pru perched high on a ladder cleaning out the gutters or out behind the chicken coop wringing a chicken's neck.

On the other hand, however, she was here right now and she wanted to get this thing off her chest.

She didn't want it hanging over her, distracting her and causing her more worry. She wanted to get it over with. It certainly couldn't hurt to peek around behind the house, where Pru kept a clothesline. She wouldn't even have to step off the drive to do that. No reasonable person could call that trespassing. Not at all.

Lucy squared her shoulders and continued a few more paces down the drive, until she reached the corner of the house. There she had an unobstructed view of the turning area, where the driveway widened and where Wesley and Calvin parked their trucks. There were no trucks, today, but there was a crumpled pile of something blue, maybe laundry that had dropped off the line where several pairs of jeans were hanging heavily in the humid air.

Lucy went to investigate, and as she drew closer she realized it wasn't a pair of blue jeans that had fallen at all. It was Pru, herself, lying in a heap.

Reaching the fallen woman, Lucy instinctively reached out and touched her shoulder, as if to wake her. But Pru wasn't going to wake up. Pru was dead. Definitely dead.

Chapter Thirteen

Lucy's first reaction was utter disbelief. This was too much. First the dog, now Pru. Two deaths in one day. How could this happen? Especially to Pru. She had seemed invincible, a force to be reckoned with like the tides or the temperature. You couldn't change her, you had to deal with her. But now, it seemed, she had met a power greater than her own.

Recoiling, Lucy stood up and stepped back, studying the body. What could it have been, she wondered. What did she die of? From what she could see there was no sign of violence, no gunshot wound, no knife protruding from her body. Maybe it was a stroke or a heart attack. Something sudden and overwhelming like a burst aneurysm. Whatever it was, there was no clue in Pru's expression. Her eyes were slightly open, her jaw hung slack, her face was blank.

She hadn't been a beauty in life and death certainly didn't become her. The poor woman, thought Lucy, hurrying back to the car. She probably woke up this morning full of plans, never guessing what fate held in store for her. Reaching inside the car she pulled her cell phone from her shoulder bag and dialed 911 with trembling fingers.

It seemed to take a long time for help to arrive, and Lucy found herself going back to the body. She knew she hadn't imagined it but finding Pru dead like that seemed so incredible that she had to reassure herself that it had really happened. There was no doubt, however, when she rounded the corner of the house. You didn't have to be an expert to know that Pru was dead: her extremities were cold and she was beginning to stiffen up.

Lucy stood awkwardly a few feet from the body and looked around. As she had noticed earlier, Pru was lying in the turning area at the end of the driveway, behind the house. Her car was parked about ten feet away and was the only vehicle. The clothesline was next to the driveway and beyond that was the barn, a ramshackle affair that looked ready to fall down but didn't. It had been in pretty much the same condition for the twenty-plus years Lucy had lived next door, occasionally losing another cedar shingle or a pane of window glass. Beyond the barn Lucy could see the pointy tops of the dark green fir trees and she heard the distant caw of a crow. She felt very alone.

Where was everybody? The police, EMTs, somebody ought to be here by now. She listened, straining to hear the sound of sirens but all she heard was more crows, answering the first. She looked at the body once again, lying exactly as she'd found it. Of course it hadn't moved, what was she thinking? Dead bodies didn't move and they didn't see.

They didn't talk, either, so there was no way Pru could object if she looked around.

Shrugging off a guilty feeling that she was doing something she shouldn't, Lucy wandered across the yard, past the vegetable garden and the chicken house, where the sudden flapping of one of the hens startled her. She stared at the dozen or so hens in the pen and they stared back with reptilian yellow eyes, then resumed their pecking and scratching. Lucy continued on her way behind the barn, where she remembered seeing a jumbled pile of lobster traps, line and buoys that she suspected was evidence of Calvin and Wesley's poaching but it was gone. There was no sign of any of it, just a bare bit of dusty earth with a few clumps of crab grass.

Now, finally, she heard sirens, weak at first but growing stronger. She hurried across the yard and reached the driveway just as a small caravan of official vehicles arrived. She pointed out the body to the police officers and EMTs and waited for permission to leave. She was very hungry, she suddenly realized, and no wonder. She hadn't had anything to eat since breakfast.

Feeling a bit dizzy, she decided to sit in her car. She was digging in her purse for a mint or something, anything with a bit of sugar, when she remembered she hadn't called Ted. It was probably just as well, she decided. There was no way that Pru's death could be included in tomorrow's issue anyway and there was no sense in rushing to tell Ted the news because it would only make him miserable. Besides, it wasn't as if she'd been murdered or anything, it wasn't really a story. They'd probably just run an obituary.

"Mrs. Stone?"

Lucy looked up and met the serious eyes of a youthful police officer. She didn't recognize him, but she knew the department had hired additional help for the summer. A glance at his name tag told her she was speaking to Officer Blaine.

"Yes?"

"I understand you found the body?"

"Yes, I did. Can I go now? I'm not feeling very well."

"I'm sorry, but I have orders to keep you here. Lieutenant Horowitz wants to talk to you."

"Lieutenant Horowitz?" Lucy knew he was the state police officer who investigated serious crimes that were beyond the scope of the local department. "Why does he want to talk to me?"

The officer shrugged. "I'm just following orders, ma'am."

Lucy's stomach growled and she thought longingly of her well-stocked kitchen, just a few hundred feet down the road. What she'd like more than anything, she decided, was a peanut butter and jelly sandwich and a tall glass of milk. She had those things, they were all there, waiting for her.

"You know I just live in the next house. Couldn't the lieutenant talk to me there?"

"My orders are to keep you here," he said, squaring his shoulders and resting his hand on his holster.

"No problem," said Lucy, hoping she wouldn't die of hunger before the lieutenant arrived.

* * *

Lucy was feeling queasy and light-headed when Horowitz arrived in his state police cruiser, accompanied by the medical examiner's van and a couple of unmarked Suburbans from the state crime lab. They were emblazoned with the motto of the Maine State Police: "Integrity. Compassion. Fairness. Excellence." Quite a turnout, she thought, for an ordinary unattended death.

"Ah, Mrs. Stone," he said, approaching her car, "another body."

Lucy had investigated numerous crimes through the years and was well acquainted with Horowitz. He looked the same as ever, dressed in a lightweight gray suit that needed pressing. His pale hair was thinning, his eyes were gray and there was no sign of color in his face. Lucy doubted he got outdoors much. Something about his expression always reminded her of a rabbit. Not a scared bunny but a wise and wary old buck who'd learned to suspect everyone and everything.

"I'm afraid so."

"The victim's your neighbor, right?"

"Victim? What do you mean? This wasn't a crime, was it?"

"There's a definite possibility that Mrs. Pratt was murdered."

Lucy was glad she was sitting because she felt as if a rug had been pulled out from under her. Suddenly, everything was spinning and she was retching. Horowitz yanked her car door open and helped her turn and lower her head between her knees. When she felt better, she sat up.

"I'm sorry. I guess it's a delayed reaction."

"Quite understandable." He paused. "Although I am a little surprised that you, of all people, didn't suspect foul play."

"I thought she'd had a heart attack or something. How was she killed?"

"The medical examiner will determine the cause but we think she was run down by a car or truck."

Lucy didn't have time to absorb this information before he asked, "How long were you neighbors?"

The answer didn't come to her quickly. This upsetting news had confused her. "About twenty years. As long as we've lived here."

"Did you have any problems with her? Or her family?"

Lucy didn't like the direction Horowitz was taking.

"Everybody had problems with her."

"I didn't ask about everybody, I asked about you." There was a gleam in his eye. "You're the nearest neighbors. It's a legitimate question."

"We had a few problems. Our dog went after her chickens a few times, there was even a dog hearing. But the dog was hit by a car this morning. That's why I came over. I wanted to tell her there wouldn't be any more problems." Lucy knew she wasn't telling the whole story.

"Did you see the driver?"

Lucy sighed. "It was her son. Wesley."

Horowitz digested this information. "So you came over to have it out with her?"

"No! It was an accident. I saw the whole thing.

But the kid drove off and I was worried there might be some damage to his truck. I came to let her know there were no hard feelings and to offer to pay for any repairs." Lucy paused, watching the investigators gathered around Pru's body. "I was hoping to get on a better footing with her."

"So the dog was the problem?"

"Not exactly," said Lucy. She knew there was no sense trying to hide Toby's fight with Wesley because it was a matter of public record. "There was a fight down at the docks last week and my son took a swing at Wesley." Lucy felt her face reddening. "But he wasn't the only one. A lot of fishermen suspect Wesley and his father of poaching their lobster traps."

"So your son has an unruly conduct case pending in district court?"

Lucy's heart sank. "Actually, it's assault and battery."

Horowitz didn't show any reaction to this information. He stood in the driveway, getting the lay of the land. "There's a pond around here, isn't there?"

Lucy pointed to the woods behind the Pratts' barn. "Blueberry Pond."

"That's the one where the nudists like to gather?"

"Mrs. Pratt didn't like them much," offered Lucy. "She was trying to get an anti-nudity bylaw passed."

"Sounds like she had a real knack for riling people up," observed Horowitz. "I have a feeling we won't have too far to look for our murderer."

Lucy grimaced. If only she'd been convinced he'd been looking in the direction of the pond, instead of her property, when he said that.

"I don't think we need to keep you any longer, Mrs. Stone." Horowitz started to walk away, then turned to face Lucy. "After all, I know where you live."

Chapter Fourteen

Free to leave, Lucy had to exert every ounce of self-control she possessed to proceed at a sedate pace. All her instincts told her to floor the accelerator and get out of there as fast as she could. But that, she knew, would only make Horowitz wonder why she was in such a hurry to get home.

Home, that's where she wanted to be. It was a great relief when she turned into the driveway to the antique farmhouse, but her heart dropped when she saw the empty kennel. She firmly pushed thoughts of the dog from her mind and hurried up the porch steps and into the house. The slam of the screen door when she entered the kitchen seemed to assure her that everything bad was outside and she was safe inside. Her hands were shaking and she felt light-headed; she knew she had to get something into her stomach. She stood in front of the refrigerator and downed a glass of milk, then, feeling a little better she made herself the longed-for peanut butter and jelly sandwich and poured a second glass of milk. This was no time to count calories.

She wolfed down the sandwich and was considering making another when she remembered Ted. The fact that the police considered Pru's death a homicide changed everything. She had to let him know about it right away. Even if it was too late for the *Pennysaver,* he could sell it to the Portland and Boston papers as a stringer. She dialed his cell phone number, but he didn't answer and she had to leave a message. What was the point of the darn things, she wondered, if people left them lying about instead of keeping them with them?

She was rinsing out her glass when he called back.

"Pru Pratt was murdered," she told him. "The cops are there right now. Do you want me to go over?"

"Murdered? Are you sure?"

"Horowitz told me himself. I thought she'd had a heart attack or something."

"You thought?" Ted's voice was suspicious. "What do you have to do with it?"

"I found her body."

"Good grief."

"Do you want me to write it up? What should I do?"

"Hold on, Lucy. Don't do anything. I'll take care of it."

"Don't you want me to help? I was there, after all."

"That's the problem, Lucy. I think you may be a little too close to this one."

"What do you mean?"

"Just lay low, okay?"

"Okay."

Puzzled, Lucy ended the call. This had never happened before. Ted had never told her not to pursue a story. She couldn't figure it out. The story was right next door, for Pete's sake, and she wanted to follow it. It wasn't just a job, it was personal. She wanted to find out who had killed Pru. After all, maybe there was a homicidal maniac loose in the neighborhood. They had certainly been attracting a lot of attention lately, what with the arrival of the naturists. Could some wacko be on the loose? They lived right next door to Pru—were they in danger? If they were, what could they do to protect themselves, without even the dog to alert them.

Lucy was lost in thought when the screen door slammed, practically causing her to jump out of her skin. It was Bill, home from work a little early because of the heat.

"Ohmigod, you startled me," she said, sitting down and fanning herself with her hand.

"Sorry." He took a Coke out of the refrigerator. "What's going on next door?"

"You won't believe this. Pru Pratt is dead. The cops think she was run down in her own driveway. And that's not all. Kudo's dead, too. Wesley hit him with his truck this morning."

Bill sat down hard and popped the top on his soda, taking a long, long swallow that almost drained the can. "What did you say?"

"Kudo's dead. Wesley hit him with his truck. I don't think he did it on purpose. It was an accident. The dog ran in front of his truck. There was nothing he could do."

"Before that."

"Pru is also dead. I found her body when I went over after work to find out if there'd been any damage to the truck."

Bill finished the Coke and got up for another.

"And the cops say she was run over, too?" Bill sat down and opened the second can, taking a sip this time. "Doesn't that seem fishy to you?"

Lucy looked at him with wide, disbelieving eyes. "You think Wesley did it? He ran over his mother and was fleeing the scene when he hit Kudo?" Lucy fell silent, struggling with the idea. "His own mother? That's horrible."

"It happens," said Bill.

"I know," admitted Lucy. "But I don't like to think of it happening next door."

Bill stared at the table. "Well, I guess we won't be having any more trouble with the neighbors."

Lucy was appalled. "Is that all you can say?"

"Well, I am going to miss the dog," he continued.

"It's terrible, isn't it?" confessed Lucy. "I think I feel worse about the dog than I do about Pru."

"He was a big part of our lives."

"It's funny about dogs. The way they're just sort of there, all the time, but you don't really notice. If I was cooking, he was in the kitchen. When we sat down at the table, he was under it. A quiet evening in front of the TV, he'd be stretched out on the rug."

"He was a great companion."

"Not much of a talker. . . ."

"But a great listener."

"That's for sure. I really liked having him in the house if you were away for the night." Lucy shrugged.

"I know it's irrational but I'm always a little nervous when you're gone. But I knew I could count on Kudo to let me know if anything was amiss. If he was relaxed, I could relax."

Bill sighed. "I don't think there's going to be much relaxing until they figure out who killed Pru."

"I feel especially vulnerable without the dog," fretted Lucy. "With all the new people in town, all those naturists, how do we know one of them isn't a serial killer or something. We could be next."

"I don't think so, Lucy. People who get killed generally get killed for a reason." He stood up. "You know, from the back, Pru looked an awful lot like Wesley."

"I've noticed that," admitted Lucy.

"It could have something to do with the poaching. The killer could have mistaken Pru for Wesley."

Lucy looked out the window to the driveway. "I wonder where Toby is. Shouldn't he be home by now?"

Bill fingered his car keys. "It's time to get the girls, anyway. I'll pick them up. You've had enough excitement for one day."

Lucy watched as he went out the door. She would have bet the house that he'd detour past the harbor on his way to the camp, just to see if the Carrie Ann was in port.

She shook herself. She wasn't going to worry, she wasn't going to jump to conclusions. She was going to make supper. Something wholesome and comforting, that's what was called for. She began filling a pot with water and reached for a box of shells. If ever there was a night for pasta salad, this was it.

* * *

Despite the comforting food, Toby's absence cast a shadow of tension over the meal. Bill reported that the boat was sitting in its berth but he'd found no sign of Toby. He'd even checked the Bilge, where the fishermen hung out, but nobody there knew his whereabouts. Or if they did, they weren't telling.

Elizabeth took the news of the deaths coolly. She only considered things that directly affected her as real tragedies, like a late paycheck at the inn or getting her period early or discovering a big, ugly zit on her chin. Those were real disasters.

The younger girls, too, had little sympathy for the neighbor.

"Mrs. Pratt was mean to animals," said Zoe, spearing a noodle with her fork.

"She mistreated those chickens, you know," said Sara. "I think poor Kudo was only trying to liberate the chickens from their terrible conditions."

Lucy's and Bill's eyes met across the table.

"We all loved Kudo. . . ."

"Not me," insisted Elizabeth.

"As I was saying, I understand you want to remember the good things about Kudo, and there were lots of good things . . ."

Elizabeth snorted.

". . . but to him those chickens were an irresistible combination of fun and food," said Bill, finishing her sentence.

"Mrs. Pratt may have had her faults, but I think she took pretty good care of her chickens. She was always winning blue ribbons at the fair. She must have known what she was doing."

"That's not true!" exclaimed Sara. "You should have seen it. The chickens were in a little tiny space and there was tons of poop and they'd step right in it. It was disgusting! They'd even poop in their water dish."

"Well, that's chickens for you," said Bill.

"They're not the cleanest, or the brightest creatures on this good earth."

"That's no excuse to treat them badly!" exclaimed Sara.

"There were no toys, Mom," said Zoe. "Chickens can't read, they can't watch TV, so what are they supposed to do all day if they don't have any toys? Poor things. They must have been awfully bored."

Lucy was beginning to wonder if Zoe was getting the wrong idea about animals at Friends of Animals day camp. "As much as we love our pets, they're not people, you know. Animals are pretty much happy just being, they don't need to be entertained."

"Mrs. Pratt wasn't just mean to the chickens," said Sara. "She was mean to her own son."

Now this was interesting, thought Lucy. "How so?"

"We saw her yelling at him. Telling him he was a piece of . . . well, a lot of bad things. Worthless. Stupid. Lazy."

"You heard her say these things?" asked Bill.

"She was yelling. We couldn't help it," said Sara, self-righteously.

"You wouldn't have heard if you hadn't been snooping around," Lucy reminded her. "Mrs. Pratt didn't know she was being overheard."

"Mom, you always say we should be as polite to

each other at home as we'd be if we were visiting friends," said Zoe. "Mrs. Pratt was not polite to Wesley."

"Maybe he did something very wrong and that's why she was mad at him," said Lucy. "Sometimes that happens. Did Wesley yell back at his mother?"

"He did. He yelled some bad words at her and then he got in his truck and drove away very fast." Sara paused. "That's when Mrs. Pratt saw us, because we'd been hiding behind the truck."

"We ran as fast as we could," said Zoe. "She was chasing us."

"Let that be a lesson to you not to go trespassing," said Bill. "Just think what might have happened if you'd got caught."

"She might have put you in an oven and baked you, like in Hansel and Gretel," said Elizabeth.

Lucy was about to admonish her when Toby strode into the dining room and sat down at the table, reaching for the salad and piling it onto his plate.

"What is this?" demanded Bill. "No hello, no apologies for being late, you just march in and start eating?"

"Uh, sorry Dad. Great salad, Mom."

"Thanks," said Lucy. "What held you up?"

"Stuff."

"What stuff?" asked Bill.

"You know. Stuff."

"NO, I DON'T KNOW!" yelled Bill.

"We're all a little upset," said Lucy, hoping to lower the emotional temperature in the room. "Did you hear that Mrs. Pratt is dead?"

Toby was busy helping himself to seconds.

"Nah, I didn't hear that."

"And Wesley killed Kudo with his truck," said Sara, her voice trembling.

Toby stopped, holding the serving spoon in midair. "Wes Pratt killed the dog?"

"It was an accident," said Lucy. "I saw the whole thing."

Toby's face had hardened and Lucy could practically hear the gears grinding away in his head as he pushed the food on his plate around with his fork.

"We'd really feel a lot better if we knew what you were doing this afternoon," said Bill. "Considering your situation and all."

"What do you think?" Toby's face was crimson. "That I killed the old bag because of the dog? I didn't even care about that dog!" He threw down his fork and stood up, scraping his chair noisily on the wooden floor, and left the table.

The rest of the family sat at the table in a heavy silence. From outside they heard the engine in his Jeep roar to life, and the crunch of gravel as he sped down the driveway and took off down Red Top Road.

Chapter Fifteen

"He's up to something."

That had been Bill's final word on the subject, uttered just before he fell asleep. But while Bill slept, the sentence kept repeating in her mind like a mantra. Not soothing like a mantra was supposed to be, but a nagging reminder that these days she hardly seemed to know her son. He was constantly surprising her. She'd always thought he was a peaceable soul and she never would have expected him to get in a fight like he did with Wesley.

As she tossed and turned in bed she told herself that fundamentally he was a good person, she had to believe that. He'd been raised in a caring and loving home, he'd had plenty of advantages. But she had to admit to herself that he hadn't made the most of them—he'd dropped out of college after two years of miserable grades.

She certainly hadn't expected that. After all, he'd been one of the best students in his class at Tinker's Cove High School, ranking in the top ten percent. And he'd gotten a solid fourteen hundred on his SATs. What went wrong when he went to college?

And what was he involved in now? She agreed with Bill that he was up to something, and she prayed that it wasn't something that would get him into even more trouble. After all, he was in plenty of trouble already with an upcoming court date. And even if he seemed oblivious to his situation, Lucy was convinced that the police investigating Pru's death would be taking a long, hard look at Toby.

The thought made her heart race and she got out of bed and went downstairs, checking his room as she passed the door. He wasn't there, of course. Where was he? It was nearly one in the morning. She went downstairs and peeked out the window, hoping to see his headlights as he turned into the driveway, but there was only darkness.

She paced through the downstair's rooms, going from window to window. Realizing it was pointless, she poured herself a mug of milk, added a dash of vanilla extract and set it in the microwave to heat, then sat at the kitchen table sipping the warm liquid.

What could she do? Lecturing didn't work, neither did probing questions. Setting limits, demanding a certain level of behavior if he was to continue living in the house would only backfire because he'd move out. There were plenty of kids in town, living on their own in squalid, substandard housing. Old, worn-out trailers parked in the woods. Rooms above garages, storage sheds. She didn't like to think what went on in those places: unprotected sex, drug use, binge drinking. No, it was better to have him home, where she could at least keep an eye on him.

She didn't believe for one minute that he had anything to do with Pru's death, but she wasn't sure the police shared her view. They would be looking for a conviction and she knew that the court system was not infallible—thanks to DNA testing they were finding plenty of innocent people who'd been wrongly convicted and sent to jail.

That wasn't going to happen to Toby, she decided, setting down her empty mug. The best way, the only way she could protect him was by finding the real murderer. And starting first thing tomorrow, that was what she was going to do.

The hot and muggy weather continued the next morning, but that didn't faze Lucy. She was full of energy when she arrived at the *Pennysaver* office and eager to start working. Her job at the paper gave her an inside track, after all, and she wanted to find out everything she could about Pru's murder.

"Good morning," she sang, greeting Phyllis.

Phyllis, dressed in a dazzling shade of lime green, with eyeshadow to match, raised her finger to her lips in warning, tilting her head towards Ted.

Ted was hunched over his computer, pecking away at the keyboard.

"The *Globe* wants a firsthand account," said Phyllis.

"Great!" said Lucy, eagerly. "Anything I can do to help?"

"I've got it covered, Lucy," said Ted. "Phyllis needs help with the obits."

"Sure, I can do those," said Lucy, taking the sheaf of papers Phyllis handed her.

She sat down and turned on the computer, turning to Ted. "What's happening? Any new developments?"

"Still waiting for the ME's report," he said.

"So what angle are you taking? Community reaction? Small town stunned? Cantankerous neighbor gets a comeuppance?"

"I'm trying to work here, Lucy."

"Can I help? Can I make some phone calls for you? Just tell me what you want?"

"I want you to be quiet, okay?"

"Okay," said Lucy, sulking.

She looked to Phyllis for sympathy, but Phyllis was taking an uncharacteristically serious approach to her work this morning. Weird, thought Lucy. What was going on? The phone rang and she reached for it, but Ted beat her to it. That was odd. Ted hardly ever answered the phone.

Lucy looked over the announcements from the funeral home, but she wasn't really paying attention. She was listening to Ted's conversation.

"No comment, sorry. Wish I could help you," he said, quickly ending the call.

"You were kind of brusque, weren't you? Who was that?" she asked.

"TV news. They've been calling all morning. Too lazy to do their own footwork."

"TV?"

Phyllis nodded and the phone rang again. This time she grabbed it. "I wish I could help you," she said, "but we're very short-staffed. I'm sure you understand." There was a pause; the voice on the other end was apparently quite persuasive. "I'll check."

Phyllis looked at Ted. "It's 'Inside Edition,' Ted. They want to interview you."

Lucy's jaw dropped.

"I'll take it," he said. "Lucy, be a doll and run over to the Shack for me. I want a coupla plain donuts, get some for you and Phyllis, too." He picked up the receiver. "Take some money from petty cash."

Lucy took the five dollar bill Phyllis handed her and walked towards the door, uncomfortably aware that Ted was waiting for her to leave before he started talking. What was going on? Was she paranoid? Or was there some sort of conspiracy to keep her out of the loop?

She was walking down Main Street when she noticed a TV truck, a white van with the call letters of a Portland station painted on its side. It was parked in front of the police station.

There would probably be more, she decided, as she walked along. Big city media seemed to find crime in small towns irresistible, maybe they thought it went to prove that violence wasn't confined to urban areas. And thanks to the naturists, the media were already familiar with the town.

At Jake's Donut Shack she picked up a rumpled copy of the *Boston Globe* to read while she waited in line to place her order. The story, written by contributing writer Edward J. Stillings, was on the New England region section front. Good for Ted, she thought.

But when she started reading she could hardly believe what he'd written.

"Investigators are looking into the possibility that Pratt's strained relationship with her Red Top Road neighbors, may have played a part in her death. There had been disagreement about a dog owned by the Stone family which was apparently killed by Pratt's son, Wesley. Investigators

were also planning to question Toby Stone, 21, who has been charged with assault and battery against Wesley Pratt."

"Can I help you?" The kid behind the counter was clearly impatient.

"A half-dozen," she stammered. "Two plain and the rest assorted."

The kid rolled his eyes. "What do you mean assorted? Do you want cinnamon? Apple? You tell me."

"Make 'em all plain," gasped Lucy, feeling rather short of breath.

All she wanted to do was get out of there. She felt as if everyone in the place was looking at her. Suddenly she was the head of a criminal family, like Ma Barker or somebody. She felt like a marked woman.

When the kid handed her the bag of donuts she threw the five dollar bill at him and bolted for the door.

"Hey, lady! Don't you want your change?"

Lucy didn't want her change. She wanted to hide under a rock, or pull a paper bag over her head. She dashed across Main Street without looking and jumped back when somebody blasted a horn at her. Looking up, she was dismayed to see it was another TV truck. She waited for it to pass and ran straight for the *Pennysaver* office.

"I can't believe you did this!" she yelled at Ted, throwing the bag of donuts at him. "Is it true? Is Toby a suspect?"

Ted looked up from his desk with an expression of terrible sadness.

Lucy swallowed hard and struggled to hold back tears.

He stood up and put his arms around her and she started sobbing. Phyllis grabbed a box of tissues and hurried over.

"I'm sorry. I didn't have any choice," said Ted.

"Toby's really in trouble?" she asked, dabbing at her eyes.

"Not just him. They're looking at lots of people. Even Wesley and Calvin."

Lucy sniffed. "I guess that should make me feel better, but it doesn't." She straightened her shoulders and attempted a smile. "Well, let's get to work. We've got to keep the cops honest, right? Make sure they nail the real killer. Remind the DA that it's 'innocent until proven guilty.' "

There was an awkward pause.

"Lucy," Ted finally began, "I think it would be better if you didn't work on this story."

Lucy was stunned. "What?"

"I'd like you to help Phyllis with the listings and obits and classified. I'll handle the reporting."

"Why?"

"Because you're too close. How can you possibly remain objective?"

"You're kicking me off the story? To do obits?"

Ted nodded, and Phyllis put her hand on Lucy's shoulder. Furious with them both, Lucy shrugged it off.

"Well, no thanks." She spit out the words. "I quit."

"Lucy, don't . . ." began Ted, but Lucy didn't wait to hear the rest.

She was out of there as fast as her legs could carry her, making sure to give the door a good slam. The little bell jangled furiously, ringing in her ears as she marched down the sidewalk to her car. Her heart was pounding and her hands were trembling as she yanked open the door and sat behind the steering wheel. Automatically she started the car, then sat holding on to the steering wheel for dear life, wondering what on earth she was going to do next.

She could only think of one thing: she was going to find Bill.

It seemed to take forever, but finally she spotted the bell tower on the old schoolhouse poking up through the trees. She was almost there, she only had to cross the bridge and climb the hill and then she would be there. She was signaling, preparing to turn into the drive when she had to slam on the brakes to allow a police cruiser to clear the narrow track that was only wide enough for one vehicle. She studied the officer's face as he passed, but his expression revealed nothing.

She bounced down the drive, going as fast as she dared, driving right up to the steps of the old schoolhouse. Bill was standing in the doorway, a hammer in his hand.

"Why were the cops here?" she asked, afraid to know the answer.

Bill took one look at her and put the hammer down, enfolding her in his strong arms. She felt his bristly beard against her forehead and smelled his good, sweaty smell. He stroked her hair with his rough, calloused hand.

"Don't worry," he said. "It was all pretty routine. They wanted to know where I was yesterday."

"What did you say?"

"The truth. I don't have anything to hide. I was

here, working." He gave her a squeeze. "I expected it, really. We're her closest neighbors and there were problems, there's no use pretending there weren't."

"It was in the *Globe*. Ted wrote that the police are investigating the neighbors—that means us—and especially Toby. Because of that fight with Wesley."

Bill stepped back and looked at her. Then he spoke, slowly. "I was here alone, you know. The cop asked me if I saw anybody or talked to anybody and I had to say no. I can't prove that I was here."

"You don't have to," said Lucy. "They have to prove you weren't. That's how it works."

"Well, that's a relief," said Bill, sarcastically. "Now I feel a whole lot better."

"I'm really worried about Toby."

"If they questioned me, they're definitely going to talk to him." Bill looked at his watch. "He's on the boat with Chuck. I don't think they'll be back for an hour or so. I could call and warn him that the cops are likely to be waiting for him."

"He's innocent so he shouldn't have anything to worry about, right?"

"Right." Bill's voice was firm. "I think I'm going to head down to the harbor. I'd like to be there when Toby gets back."

Lucy watched Bill go, then started picking up his tools and putting them away in his toolbox. She knew he wouldn't want to leave his valuable tools lying about in the open. Then she found the broom and began sweeping up the sawdust and bits of wood that littered the wide old floorboards. She loved the smell of clean, new wood and sheetrock and the sense of emptiness in the nearly finished building. Soon enough it would be filled with rugs and furniture and all the owner's stuff, but now it was bare and fresh.

She remembered Toby as a little baby with unblemished, creamy skin and fine, curly hair and sweet round cheeks and tiny, tiny little toenails. He'd been an easygoing, bouncy baby who nursed enthusiastically and slept deeply. Full of energy, he'd walked and talked early. He'd been a delight and she'd been unprepared when colicky, cranky Elizabeth arrived on the scene.

Lucy brushed the floor sweepings into a dustpan and emptied it into a trash barrel, then propped the broom into the corner, tucking the dustpan behind it as she always did. She stood up. Toby hadn't killed Pru Pratt, she was sure of it. She wasn't sure what he was up to these days, there was a lot about him that she didn't know, but she knew in her heart that her sweet baby boy would never kill anybody. The problem was making sure the police believed it, too.

Chapter Sixteen

When Lucy got home, she found Elizabeth in the family room, watching TV and having a late lunch of diet soda and baby carrots.

"What are you doing here? I thought you'd be working on your tan."

"It's not so nice down there anymore, Mom," said Elizabeth, wrinkling her nose. "There's a lot of black flies and mosquitoes and there's litter. It's kind of icky."

"I'm surprised," said Lucy. "I thought the naturists were more responsible than that."

"I think Mike's organizing a clean-up party this weekend." Elizabeth chewed a carrot. "It's not just that, Mom. I've got a rash."

"It's probably a heat rash"

"No." Elizabeth held out her arm. "Look. It's gross." Her voice tightened. "Do you think it's skin cancer?"

Lucy felt a stab of guilt. Maybe she shouldn't have put that library book on Elizabeth's night table. She took a look at Elizabeth's arm and immediately recognized the honey-colored scabs. "Impetigo."

"What's that?" Elizabeth grimaced. "Is it bad?"

"It's stubborn, like you. You have to keep after it with antibiotic cream. It'll go away, but it'll take a while." Lucy couldn't resist adding, "You probably picked it up at the pond."

"Don't worry. I'm not going back there. Some of those people were kind of creepy."

Lucy didn't like the sound of this. "What do you mean?"

Elizabeth shrugged. "They weren't cool, you know. They'd stare."

"Sightseers?"

"You could say that."

Lucy went into the kitchen to make herself a sandwich. She felt better than she had all morning. At least something was working out, even if it took a dose of impetigo to convince Elizabeth to keep her clothes on. While she didn't like the idea of unsavory characters hanging around so close to her house their presence did open a promising avenue worth investigating. She was humming to herself and spreading mustard on a piece of bread when she heard Elizabeth shriek.

"Mom! Come here!"

Lucy ran into the family room, where Elizabeth was pointing at the TV. "It's Mrs. Pratt, Mom. On TV."

"Police are investigating whether a family feud in a small Maine town led to the death of a woman there," said Brad Hicks, the New England Cable News anchorman.

Lucy's jaw dropped as she watched the story unfold in pictures. First there was a shot of Pru, accepting a blue ribbon for her chickens at the county fair. It was the only time Lucy had ever seen her in a skirt and she looked rather attractive.

She'd even tied a bit of ribbon around her pony tail. Then there was rolling video of the Pratts' house with the driveway filled with police cars.

"Long-standing feud with neighbors Bill and Lucy Stone . . ." was illustrated with a shot of their house, ". . . culminated earlier this week in a dog hearing. Responding to complaints that the Stones' dog attacked the dead woman's chickens, town officials voted to destroy the dog if there were any further attacks."

"I can't believe this," muttered Elizabeth.

Lucy watched in horror as the screen filled with a familiar action shot of Toby playing lacrosse taken from his high school yearbook. His hair was matted with sweat, he had a streak of mud across his face and was grimacing with exertion. He was also attempting to whack the opposing player with his lacrosse stick. "The Stones' son Toby is currently under indictment for assault and battery against Prudence Pratt's son, Wesley."

Then Wesley's yearbook photo, picturing him in a shirt and tie with neatly combed hair, filled the screen. Lucy knew enough about public relations to know this was a disaster. Wesley was a neatly groomed "good" boy and her son was an aggressive hooligan.

That photo was replaced with a live shot of Brad Hicks, announcing breaking news in Tinker's Cove. She and Elizabeth watched, fascinated, as the camera panned the harbor parking lot, which was crowded with reporters, photographers and TV cameramen. The camera then settled on a young blond woman in a blue suit.

"Stacy Blake, reporting live from Tinker's Cove where police are awaiting the arrival of Toby Stone, a suspect in the murder of Prudence Pratt. Stone is believed to be aboard a lobster boat now approaching the dock."

The camera focused on Quisset Point, where the Carrie Ann could be seen steaming steadily towards its birth. A uniformed officer and a plainclothes detective were stationed on the gangway, where they were soon joined by Bill and Bob Goodman.

"Are they going to arrest Toby?" asked Elizabeth.

Lucy was perched on the sofa, wringing her hands. "I hope not." She could hardly believe what she was seeing: people and places she knew were actually on TV. Somehow it made everything seem unreal.

"As you can see," the reporter continued, "the lobster boat carrying suspect Toby Stone has now docked and police are boarding it. They appear to be questioning the two men on the boat, one of whom we believe is Toby Stone, but we cannot hear what they are saying."

"Tell me, Stacy," came Brad Hicks's voice, "can you tell our viewers why Toby Stone is considered a suspect."

"Yes, Brad, I can. Stone was arraigned in district court last week and charged with assault and battery against Wesley Pratt, the victim's son. The two apparently had some sort of altercation right here on the docks."

"Was Stone the only one charged?"

"No, Brad. As it happens, several other men were charged in connection with that altercation, including Wesley Pratt, the victim's son."

"Well, that is certainly interesting information Stacy. Can you tell us what's happening now?"

"The police appear to be continuing to question the men aboard the fishing boat, the Carrie Ann." Behind the reporter the police could be seen leaving the boat and climbing up the gangway. "No, I stand corrected. The officers appear to have completed their questioning and are now leaving the boat."

The scene at the harbor erupted into chaos as the pack of reporters surged in two directions. Some followed the police officers and others headed for the gangway. The camera wobbled, then settled on Bob Goodman. He stood patiently while microphones were thrust into his face.

"We have no statement at this time," he said.

"Who are you?" called out several reporters.

"I'm an attorney. Robert Goodman. I have offices here in town."

"Who are you representing?"

"I represent a lot of people in this town," said Bob. "Now I'm warning you that you're obstructing the right of these fishermen to conduct their business."

The feed from Tinker's Cove was abruptly disconnected and Brad Hicks was back on the screen. "In other news . . . ," he began.

Lucy and Elizabeth remained in place on the couch, in shock.

"This is crazy," said Elizabeth.

"I have a feeling it's going to get a whole lot crazier," said Lucy, as the phone began ringing.

She picked up the receiver, expecting it to be one of her girlfriends: Sue Finch or Rachel Goodman or Pam Stillings. It was NECN and she slammed the receiver down.

"Don't pick up unless it's somebody you know,"

she told Elizabeth. "We can use the answering machine to screen our calls."

Lucy grew increasingly nervous as the afternoon wore on and there was no sign of Toby or Bill. The constant ringing of the phone was an added irritation, especially since the callers were all reporters. The worst part, she decided, was that she really had no right to get indignant at this invasion of her privacy. How many times had she done the same thing, calling some troubled person for a reaction? How many times had she exposed someone to shame and censure, all in the cause of truth? And had she really discovered the truth or had she found a few facts and crafted them into a sensational story, just as the NECN reporters had done. Oh, it was all true, but it added up to a big lie. There was no family feud, or if there had been it had been on the Pratts' side. Finally, she heard Bob Goodman's familiar voice.

"Lucy, it's me, Bob," he said. "Pick up if you're there."

Lucy grabbed the receiver.

"What's happening? I saw it on TV. I've been so worried."

"That's why I called. Everything's okay. We went to the police station and I stayed with Toby when they questioned him and it turns out he's got a good alibi. He was out on the boat all day yesterday and Chuck can vouch for him."

"That's a relief," said Lucy. "Do they have a time of death?"

"Between ten and two, when you found her."

"Not earlier than ten?" asked Lucy.

"Nothing's definite, yet, but they seem to think that's the outside limit. Listen, Lucy, this is important. If you were watching TV you know the media is all over this case, the town is full of TV trucks. They're going to be after you, the kids, too. Don't talk to them. Don't let the kids talk to them. Try to ignore them, try to keep your expressions pleasantly neutral, if you can."

Lucy was getting the picture. "In case we're photographed?"

"Right. Try not to look guilty, okay?"

"That shouldn't be hard," said Lucy. "We're not guilty!"

"If only it were that easy," said Bob, with a sigh.

That evening Lucy and Bill held a family conference to clue the kids in on the situation. It soon became clear that Bob was right; it wasn't going to be easy at all. There was a lot of grumbling as they pulled the kids away from their various occupations but eventually everyone was gathered in the family room. The TV was off, and if Lucy had her way, it was going to stay off.

"Because of Mrs. Pratt's murder we might be getting some media attention," she began.

"It's like being the Osbournes," said Elizabeth. "Except they keep showing Toby and our house. Why don't they show me? I'm the most photogenic."

Lucy's jaw dropped and Bill was speechless.

"You wouldn't like it so much if they did show you," said Toby, scowling.

"Will we get paid millions of dollars, like the Osbournes?" asked Sara.

"When is it my turn?" asked Zoe. "I think I'll wear my new pink shirt tomorrow, just in case they want to film me."

"Maybe I'll get discovered and get a modeling contract," mused Elizabeth.

"Uh, guys, I think you've got the wrong idea," said Bill. "This isn't 'The Osbournes'. It's more like 'Inside Edition' and we're the bad guys."

Now it was the kids' turn to drop their jaws in disbelief.

"We're the bad guys? That's crazy!" exclaimed Sara.

"We're nice!" exclaimed Zoe.

"It's all Toby's fault," grumbled Elizabeth. "Because of him fighting with Wesley."

"You better mind your own business," said Toby. "I'm not guilty, yet, for your information, and last I heard there's no law against defending yourself."

"Enough!" barked Bill.

"We're in this together," said Lucy, "and we're going to get through it together. And the way we're going to do that is we're going to go about our business, we're going to stick to our routines, and we're not going to answer any of their questions. Like the president coming back to Camp David, we're just going to keep on walking. That's what we're going to do."

"But Mom, this could be my big chance. I could talk to them about the weather or something. Just to introduce myself to the nation," said Elizabeth.

"I'm warning you, Elizabeth. Even something you think is harmless can be used against you. 'Neighbor's Daughter Sheds No Tears for Poor Pru.' You think you're making polite chit-chat and they make you out as a callous monster. I've seen it happen."

"You're a reporter," accused Toby, "you've probably done it."

"Watch your tongue, Toby," said Bill.

"Actually, I'm not a reporter any more."

They all looked at her.

"I quit my job today and I'm glad I did. I don't want to be part of the media anymore."

Chapter Seventeen

Lucy's opinion of her profession wasn't improved the next morning when Bill left for work only to stomp angrily back into the house, instructing her to look out the window. She was shocked to see a couple of vans and a handful of reporters parked on the grassy verge opposite the driveway.

"I don't believe this," she said, but Bill was busy dialing the phone.

"This is Bill Stone on Red Top Road," he said. "I want to complain about some reporters parked on the road outside my house."

Lucy assumed he was calling the police department. She didn't think he'd get very far.

"Well, no, they're not obstructing the road," he said. "They're not trespassing on my property, either. But they've got no business to be here. They're harassing my family—we have no privacy." He listened, growing redder in the face by the minute, until he snapped. "It's great to see my tax dollars at work!" he snarled, slamming down the phone.

"There's nothing they can do, right?"

"The road's open to everyone, it's public property," said Bill. "They're not even going to send a cruiser. Apparently, there's media all over town and everybody's calling and complaining. They don't have the manpower, she says."

"Bob warned us this might happen. He said we should just ignore them, but try to keep a pleasant expression. Try not to look guilty."

Bill looked at her. It wasn't a pleasant expression. Then he left.

When it was her turn to leave the house to take the girls to day camp, she promised herself she would follow Bob's advice. She'd stay cool, she wouldn't get rattled as she ran the press gauntlet. When she braked at the end of the driveway and signaled her turn onto the road, several reporters approached the Subaru, snapping photos and shouting questions.

"Did you hate Prudence Pratt?" "Have the police questioned you?" "Has your son been arrested?" "Will you make a statement?" "Can I interview you? We'll pay."

Trying not to look flustered, Lucy drove carefully and deliberately until she'd worked her way free of the reporters. She was breathing a sigh of relief when she spotted a couple of cars following her. She was being tailed!

"I can't believe this," she muttered.

"Believe what?" asked Zoe.

"Nothing," said Lucy, keeping an eye on the rearview mirror.

At least they couldn't follow her onto the camp property, and the drop-off area was at the far end of the parking lot, blocked from the road by bushes. Nonetheless, she felt uneasy as she let the girls out.

"Remember, don't talk to strangers. If you see anybody who shouldn't be on the camp property be sure to tell Melanie right away."

"Okay, Mom," grumbled Sara. "We get it."

Driving home, Lucy was tempted to stop the car at the driveway and tell those reporters the real story. About the lobster poaching and the way Pru Pratt had made enemies of everyone in town. She'd like to give them a piece of her mind. Then she remembered Ted, cackling merrily when a controversial story prompted a flurry of irate letters to the editor.

"It's a win-win situation," he'd told her. "We get 'em mad and they write us letters which get more people mad so we get more letters."

Yeah, she thought bitterly, it was a win-win situation for the media, but a lose-lose situation for her family. The only thing that would end it would be the discovery of the real murderer. Then this supposed feud would be quickly forgotten. Yesterday's news. The faster the better, she decided, resolving to do everything she could to speed the investigation along. Even if she had to solve the murder herself.

But how was she going to do that, she wondered, when she got back to the house. Her home was under siege by the media and she was followed whenever she left. How could she possibly investigate if she couldn't get out of the house?

She was pondering this problem when the phone rang. It was Sue.

"It's so great to hear a friendly voice," said Lucy, feeling as if Sue had thrown her a lifeline.

"What do you mean?"

"Didn't you see the news last night?"

"I never watch the news. It's depressing and it gives me frown lines. I figure I may not be well-informed, but I'm saving a ton on Botox."

"Oh." Sue's attitude was a revelation to Lucy. "Really?"

"Really. So what was on the news?"

"Toby. They made him out like the prime suspect in Pru Pratt's murder."

"That's ridiculous," said Sue.

It was like a breath of fresh air to Lucy. "You don't know how much it means to me to hear you say that."

"Right," said Sue, not getting it. "Listen, I have to do some shopping today and I was wondering if you'd come along and help me."

"You need help shopping?" This time Lucy didn't get it.

"It's not that kind of shopping," said Sue. "I'm organizing a Fourth of July picnic and I need to buy paper plates and stuff like that. I'm going to that warehouse store. It's a drive but I figure the savings are worth it. So, want to come along? I'll buy you a hot dog for lunch."

"Uh, sure," said Lucy. "But I'm kind of stuck in the house. There's a bunch of reporters on the road and I don't want to face them."

"No problem. I'll pick you up. See you in ten."

Sue was as good as her word and came barreling up the drive minutes later in her huge black SUV. She was dressed for action in a jaunty baseball cap, black shades and a shorts outfit styled like a track suit. Her slender arms and legs were perfectly tanned and gleaming with moisturizer; all that work on the sun deck had paid off.

When Lucy took her place in the passenger seat, well-protected by the rhino guard, she began to see the advantages of the gas-guzzling monster. For one thing, the rabble of reporters stood back respectfully as Sue made the turn onto the road. A few cars did attempt to follow them, but Sue quickly lost them by turning off the paved road onto one of the old logging roads that criss-crossed the region. Lucy hung on to the grab bar above the door for dear life as they bounced through ruts and pot holes.

"Yee-ha!" yodeled Sue as they became momentarily airborne, going over one of the humps in the road Lucy called "thank-you-ma'ams."

They were definitely more fun when you were a kid, thought Lucy, and didn't have to worry about the fillings in your teeth shaking loose. There was no sign of the followers, however, when they picked up the town road a few miles from the interstate.

"This picnic sounds like a great idea. Who's invited?" she asked.

"The whole town."

"You're kidding, right? I mean, that's a whole lot of paper plates."

"I'm figuring on a thousand people."

"Wow," said Lucy. "How are you paying for it?"

"I talked to Marge and she got the parade committee to give me their money. If there's no parade, they don't need it, right?"

"But what about the naturists?"

"What about 'em?"

"What if they come?"

"I hope they do. The more the merrier," said Sue.

Maybe that old saying was right, thought Lucy. Ignorance was bliss. She knew entirely too much about the naturists, the environmentalists, the fishermen, the Revelation Congregation and others pushing the anti-nudity bylaw. In her view the town was splitting apart, driven by these warring factions. Sue, on the other hand, didn't see the problem. The Fourth of July was days away and they had to have a celebration. If there couldn't be a parade, and there couldn't be fireworks, there was jolly well going to be a picnic. And if anyone could pull it off, it would be Sue.

"So tell me, who do you think killed Pru?" asked Sue, swerving suddenly and accelerating up the ramp to the interstate.

"My favorite suspect is Wesley," said Lucy, checking that her seatbelt was fastened. "After all, he was driving hell for leather down the road when he hit Kudo."

"You mean he ran his mother down with the truck and fled the scene?" Sue was doubtful. "His own mother?"

"I don't think it was a happy family," said Lucy, taking a peek at the speedometer. The needle was hovering around eighty. "The girls were over there and they heard Pru calling Wesley all sorts of bad names. And Wesley gave it right back."

"What were your girls doing visiting the Pratts?" Sue was rapidly gaining on a Mini Cooper, but couldn't pass because a tractor-trailer truck was in the fast lane. She slammed on the brake and flashed her lights, but the driver of the Mini continued at a stately pace.

"They were uninvited guests. They were upset

about the dog hearing so they wanted to find evidence that Pru mistreated her chickens."

The tractor-trailer advanced and Sue shot into the passing lane, apparently oblivious to a second tractor-trailer that was making the same move. Now the SUV didn't seem quite so large, sandwiched between the two trucks.

"Ooh, they are their mother's daughters, aren't they?" The first truck moved into the traveling lane and Sue shot ahead.

This time Lucy didn't want to see the speedometer; she didn't want to know how fast they were going. "Sometimes the end justifies the means," she said, checking her seatbelt. "But in this case, I don't think it helps. The cops say Pru died after ten and Wesley was long gone by then."

"I wouldn't give up on him, yet," said Sue, switching on the radio and searching for a station. "Those times of death are always pretty approximate, aren't they?"

A road sign warned of a steep incline ahead and urged reducing speed.

"I'll do the radio," she offered, nervously. "You watch the road."

"Calm down, Lucy. If this baby can tame the Kalahari it can certainly handle the Maine Pike."

Sue had found her favorite oldies station and was tapping the steering wheel, singing along with the BeeGees. "Who else is on the list?"

"Well, Cal, of course. Poor guy was probably the original hen-pecked husband."

"I know the husband's always the first suspect, but Cal? You've got to be kidding. He's afraid of his own shadow."

Sue was now weaving between lanes. Lucy wrapped her hand around the grab bar and tried to think of an appropriate prayer.

"They're the ones to watch out for," said Lucy, deciding to say something. "Are we in a big hurry or something? You're going awfully fast."

"It just seems like that," said Sue, hitting the brakes to avoid slamming into a horse trailer. "I don't know why they let these things on the road. And campers! Gosh, I hate those things! They're supposed to be seeing the country, but I don't think most of them ever get more than fifty miles from home, and it must take them two weeks considering how slow they go."

Well, she'd tried, thought Lucy, as Sue hit the accelerator and passed, only to swing abruptly onto the exit ramp.

"There was no love lost between Pru and the naturists. I suppose one of them could have done her in," speculated Lucy. "If they got rid of Pru they wouldn't have to worry about the bylaw. Chances are it would die with her."

"Are you serious? They seem pretty peace-loving to me."

"I'm not saying they did it as a group or anything like that. All it takes is one loony, somebody who feels threatened by the bylaw. And then there's the folks they attract. I've heard there have been some suspicious characters hanging around the pond."

"That's just local prejudice," exclaimed Sue, tapping the brake at the stop sign at the end of the exit ramp and zooming in front of a battered pickup truck. "Who else?"

"I have a theory," began Lucy. "You've heard about the lobster poaching, right? How everybody is convinced it's Calvin and Wesley?"

Sue nodded.

"Well, I have noticed that Pru and Wesley look an awful lot alike, especially from behind. If one of the fishermen came to even things up with Wesley he might have gone after Pru by mistake."

"That makes sense to me," said Sue, cutting off an oncoming station wagon and turning into the superstore parking lot. "Those fishermen have a code of their own when it comes to poaching. Whoever it was might have only wanted to scare Wesley, figuring he could jump out of the way, but Pru wasn't so quick and agile. It could have been some sort of tragic mistake."

"You don't like to admit that there could be a cold-blooded killer among us, do you?"

"No, I don't." Sue was cruising the lot, looking for a parking spot.

"What about Mel Dunwoodie? The guy with the campground? He had a lot to lose financially if Pru's bylaw went through. Maybe he did it."

"I don't think so," protested Sue, spotting a woman pushing a cart full of bags walking down one of the aisles between cars. Intent on her prey, she turned the SUV around and began a slow stalk.

"I'm adding him to the list. So far we've got Wesley Pratt, Calvin Pratt, a crazed naturist, an angry lobsterman and Mel Dunwoodie. Anybody else?"

"I can't think of anyone," said Sue, letting the car idle as she watched the woman load the shopping bags into her car. When she finished, she pushed the cart to one side and got in, taking her time starting the car. Sue drummed her fingers on the wheel impatiently.

"Finally!" she exclaimed when the woman backed out at a speed roughly that of a fresh bottle of ketchup. "Could she move any slower?"

When the car finally drove off, Sue hit the gas and promptly collided with the cart, which had rolled into the space.

"Shit!"

Lucy bit her lip and didn't say anything.

They'd just finished filling every inch of space inside the SUV with blocky cardboard boxes of paper goods and bags of red, white and blue party decorations when Sue suddenly asked, "What do we do now?"

"Try to get home alive so we can do this all over again and unload the stuff," said Lucy, pushing the cart back to the corral.

"No, silly. I mean about the murder," said Sue, following with the second cart. "How are you going to find out who did it?"

"Start asking questions," said Lucy, adding her cart to the line of linked carriages. "See what I can find out. I only wish there was some way I could find out more about the Pratt family. If they had some friends I could talk to them, but I don't think they had any."

"Pru belonged to the Revelation Congregation," said Sue, giving her cart a final little shove. "And so do my neighbors, the Wilsons. I could talk to them."

"That's a good idea."

"You'll have to pay me, though."

Trust Sue to extract her pound of flesh, thought Lucy. "Whatever you say."

"Ten pounds of potato salad, for the picnic."

"No problem." Lucy considered. "You've told Ted, right?"

"He's giving it front page coverage."

"That's good." For a minute Lucy wished she was back at the *Pennysaver*, writing up the story.

"His story won't be half as good as what you would have written," said Sue, patting her hand.

"You're right. He's probably missing me like crazy."

As she said it, Lucy was aware that she was voicing her own thoughts, not Ted's. She was already missing her job. She climbed up into the passenger seat and began fastening the seat belt. It didn't seem quite adequate; she wanted something sturdier for the trip home, like the harnesses they used in stunt aircraft. An ejection seat would be nice, too.

"Ready?" asked Sue, starting the engine and shifting into reverse.

"As ready as I'll ever be," said Lucy, resigned to her fate.

Chapter Eighteen

Lucy pondered her next move when Sue dropped her off at the house. Amazingly enough she was in one piece, but somewhat rattled by Sue's aggressive driving. She took a couple of aspirin for her tension headache and stood at the kitchen sink, drinking a glass of water and watching the watchers.

They were still there, which surprised her. You would think they would have something better to do than sit for hours in front of an empty house. Maybe, she thought, she could give them some help. Fearful that her Dutch courage would desert her, she placed her glass in the sink and marched out of the house and down the driveway, stopping at the road. Predictably, the reporters gathered around.

"This is off the record," she began, trying to ignore the cameras. "But I'm afraid you're missing the big story."

Now that she was actually face-to-face with them, the reporters looked very young. They were probably rookies, assigned to watch the house while their more experienced colleagues were attending news conferences and interviewing officials.

"What do you mean?" asked one, a freckle-faced kid with a crew cut.

"Well, you know, Blueberry Pond is just a bit down the road."

"So? What's Blueberry Pond?" This poor girl was camera-ready in a pastel polyester suit and Lucy knew she must be cooking in the heat.

"Haven't you heard about the nudists?" Lucy kept her voice neutral.

"Nudists?"

"Well, they prefer to be called naturists." Lucy dangled the bait. They were nibbling, but would they bite?

"Around here?" The kid with the crew cut was wary, sensing a trick.

"At Blueberry Pond. Some days there are hundreds over there. Sunning themselves and swimming. It's an official hot spot on the naturist Web site."

"That is interesting," began the girl, "but what's that got to do with the murder?"

"Oh, didn't you know? Prudence Pratt was very upset about all those naked people practically in her backyard. She was trying to get the town to pass an anti-nudity bylaw."

"At the very least it would be a photo op," said the photographer.

"And it might tie into the murder," said the girl.

"Thanks. Thanks a lot," said the kid with the crew cut.

"No problem," said Lucy, turning and strolling up the driveway. She turned back to look when she reached the porch and saw that the little caravan was departing.

Wasting no time she grabbed her purse and started the Subaru. Which way to go? She ran through her list of suspects and decided to head for the harbor, the scene of the most recent violence before the murder. She wanted to find out more about the lobster poaching and this was her chance, but only if the time and tide were right for the lobstermen to return to port.

Her heart sank when she turned into the harbor parking lot and discovered nearly all the berths were empty. If everybody was out fishing there wouldn't be anyone to talk to. Even the harbormaster's little shack was shut tight, with a handwritten sign indicating he would be back in two hours. Lucy wandered from one end of the pier to the other, looking for signs of life. All she found were seagulls perched on pilings, waiting for the boats to return with their dinner of bait bits and fish scraps.

She was about to give up when she heard a string of oaths, delivered by a gruff voice, coming from the Reine Marie, Beetle Bickham's boat. She went closer to investigate and noticed the hatch was open. She heard a series of clangs, followed by more profanity. Beetle was in the hold, working on his engine.

"Hi, down there!" she yelled.

"Hi, Lucy." Beetle's sweaty, red face appeared in the opening. "What's up?"

"Nothing much," she said, shrugging. "Do you have a minute to talk?"

"Sure. I'll be glad to take a break from this stubborn, hard-hearted old bitch of an engine. There's Cokes in the cooler."

He pulled himself up easily through the hatch with his powerful arms, strong from years of raising heavy lobster traps from the deep, and seated himself beside her on the locker. Lucy handed him a frosty can and he popped the top, downing most of the contents in one gulp.

"That is thirsty work." He looked down ruefully at his grease-stained hands and shirt.

"Sure is," said Lucy, sipping her drink. "Have you missed many days of fishing?"

"Naw. She just started acting up yesterday, when I was coming back in. And I made my quota anyway this week."

"Already?" Lucy was surprised since she'd heard that catches were low.

Beetle shrugged his shoulders. "Yeah. It's pretty good, much better than it was for a while there."

Lucy noticed that Calvin and Wesley's boat, Second Chance, was tied up at the dock, too.

"So you think the poachers have been busy with something else?"

His black eyes twinkled. "That might just be it."

Lucy took another sip. "You know, I've been wondering if whoever killed Pru Pratt might have mistaken her for Wesley. From the back, they looked a lot alike, you know?"

"She was a good woman, very religious, but not a womanly woman. You understand what I'm saying?" Beetle's hands were in motion, this was a subject he felt strongly about. "I used to make a little joke about her, eh? I'd sing that old song about skin and bones and a hank of hair. That's all she was." He paused, perhaps thinking of his own amply endowed wife and his curvaceous daughters, who had all inherited his sparkling black eyes. "But I heard she was a good cook, especially her chicken fricassee." He shook his head, pondering this incongruity.

"So do you think one of the lobstermen might have killed her by mistake, thinking she was Wesley? Were tempers running that high around here? Over the poaching, I mean?"

"It's hard to say," said Beetle. "Men get upset over a lot of things: women, money, politics. Lobsters, too." He glanced at the ramshackle Bilge, perched precariously on the hill overlooking the harbor. "Especially if they drink a little too much Pete's Wicked Ale, no?"

Lucy looked at him sharply. "Does anybody like that come to mind?"

Beetle raised his hands. "No, no. Nobody in particular. But the Bilge is a popular place. A lot of guys go there and drink, all night sometimes."

"All night? That's illegal," began Lucy, prompting a world-weary chuckle from Beetle. "Okay, I admit the Bilge is a law unto itself. So can you think of anybody who was especially upset by the poaching?"

"I'm sorry, Lucy, but I have to get back to work."

"I thought you said there was no rush."

"I need a part and I just remembered the boatyard closes early today."

Lucy didn't believe it for a minute. She suspected Beetle didn't like the direction her questions were taking.

"Oh, I'm sorry." Lucy said slowly. "I didn't mean to keep you."

"No problem. You know I wish the best for Toby. He's a good kid."

"This has been hell for him, for all of us. If you could give me something to go on I'd be so grateful."

"I wish I could help you, Lucy." Beetle shook his head. "Say thanks to Ted for me, will you? I saw my letter in the paper."

She had to expect this, she realized. People didn't know she'd quit.

"I don't work there anymore."

"No?" Beetle's black eyebrows shot up in amazement.

"No. Ted says I can't be in the news and report it, too."

"He fired you? There was nothing else you could do there?"

"There was nothing I wanted to do, so I quit."

"Well, maybe you'll go back when this is all over."

Lucy gave him a tight little smile. "Maybe."

Maybe he was right, she thought, as she drove home. Maybe she would go back to the *Pennysaver* when this was all over. But right now it didn't seem as if it would ever be over unless Pru's killer was found. And that seemed extremely unlikely unless somebody talked. But if her conversation with Beetle was any indication, it wasn't going to be one of the lobstermen. They followed an unwritten code of loyalty, grown out of necessity. They depended on each other to help them if they ran into trouble on the water; it was expected that they would risk their own lives to save a fellow lobsterman.

The problem was that while most of the lobstermen were hard working and followed the law, a handful took advantage of the code of silence to supplement their incomes by scrubbing female lobsters of their eggs, a practice forbidden by law, or even to use their boats to smuggle illegal drugs, even cigarettes now that they were so highly taxed. If one of the lobstermen had killed Pru Pratt, it would be extremely difficult for her, or the police for that matter, to finger the culprit.

Lucy was thinking over this discouraging truth, when she spotted Ellie Sykes's "Fresh Eggs" sign. Remembering the ten pounds of potato salad she'd promised Sue, she slammed on the brakes, spun the Subaru into Ellie's driveway, bounced down the rutted dirt track and braked by the house.

The eggs were set out on a card table, underneath a huge shady maple tree, packed in recycled cartons from the supermarket. Lucy opened one of the boxes—these beauties were a far cry from supermarket eggs. The shells shone as if they'd been polished, gleaming globes of brown and blue and green, some even speckled. They were varying sizes, too, big jumbos for daddy and extra larges for mommy and even a few itty-bitty pullet eggs for baby.

Lucy was trying to decide how many dozen she needed when Ellie came out of the house.

"Can I help you?" she asked in her official egg-lady voice.

"I'm fine," said Lucy. "I'm just dithering, trying to decide how many to take."

"Hi, Lucy, I didn't realize it was you. The sun's in my eyes and you're in the shade."

"These are such beautiful eggs. I forgot how wonderful homegrown ones are, I've been buying those poor excuses the supermarket sells. I guess I got in the habit over the winter."

"My hens only lay enough for me in the winter," said Ellie, in a matter-of-fact voice. "I don't have enough to sell, so folks have to go to the store. It takes a while for people to find me again in the spring."

"Well, I'm glad I saw your sign. I need them for some potato salad I'm making for the town Fourth of July picnic. I guess you heard about it?"

"I think it's a great idea. Something to bring the whole town together."

"Not like the anti-nudity bylaw," ventured Lucy. "Do you think there's any hope for that now?"

Ellie shrugged. "Pru had drummed up quite a lot of support, before she was killed. I know the Revelation Congregation came out in force to demonstrate and I guess they'll carry on the fight." Ellie drew her brows together. "You know, these are yesterday's eggs. I can get you some fresher ones if you like. You can gather 'em yourself, for that matter."

"Really?" Lucy felt like a little kid. "From the hens?"

"Sure." Ellie grabbed a basket that was hanging on a handy hook. "Follow me."

They walked together to Ellie's chicken house, a neat little shed situated behind her house. An old apple tree partially shaded the fenced-in run, where a small flock of plump hens were busily engaged in preening their feathers and scratching at the pebbly soil.

"They're very handsome birds," said Lucy. "They look so healthy."

"Thanks," said Ellie. "Maybe this will be my big year, now that Pru's out of the picture."

"What do you mean?"

Ellie's nut-brown face reddened, and she looked embarrassed. "I didn't mean it the way it sounded. I'm sorry Pru is dead. Nobody should die like that. But the fact remains that she always got the blue ribbon at the county fair. Bitsy Parsons and I took turns getting second and third."

"Bitsy?"

"You know her. She has that little flower and egg stand on Newcomb Road."

Lucy nodded. "The snapdragon lady."

"And cosmos and zinnias and coneflowers and I don't know what all. She can make anything grow, claims it's the chicken manure. She's the sweetest thing, too, always giving away extra plants." Ellie waved a hand at the flowering border that ran along the front of her porch. "Most of my flowers came from her garden."

"I suppose the competition will be cutthroat now," said Lucy, entering the chicken house as Ellie held the door open for her.

"Not likely," laughed Ellie. "So what do you want? Colors? Jumbos? I bet we've got some double yolkers here."

Lucy reached into one of the straw-lined nesting boxes and found a warm egg. She liked the way it felt in her hand, she liked the smooth texture and the way it fit into her palm, and lifted it to her cheek.

"Don't you peck me," said Ellie, reaching under a sitting hen who glared at her with disapproving black-bead eyes.

"She wants to keep her eggs," said Lucy.

"Well, she's not going to," laughed Ellie. "If she gets a clutch and goes all broody, she'll stop laying."

"Do you eat them when they stop laying?" asked Lucy, tucking her egg into Ellie's basket.

"I do. It seems more respectful somehow, to me at least. Continuing the cycle of life."

Lucy knew that Ellie was part Metinnicut Indian and had a deep reverence for living things. She was certain that Ellie's chickens met a quick and merciful end on their way to the stew pot.

"So how many eggs do you want?' asked Ellie, breaking into her thoughts.

"Three dozen, I guess. And if I run out, I'll be back for more."

It was amazing, thought Lucy, how a simple change from the ordinary routine could make such a difference. You wouldn't think homegrown eggs would be that different from supermarket eggs, but somehow they were. She'd seen and touched the chickens and heard their throaty clucking, she'd gathered the eggs herself from their strawy nests, and she'd spoken with the woman who raised the chickens. It was a whole different experience from pushing a wire cart around a sterile supermarket and plucking a Styrofoam container from a chilly cooler. From now on, she decided, she was going to make a stop at Ellie's to buy eggs a regular part of her routine.

The route home took her past Mel Dunwoodie's campground where the "Nude is Not Lewd" banner was still flying high above the entrance. Workers were busy installing a stockade fence along the property line and Lucy wondered if Mel really intended to convert his campground into a nudist colony. It would be interesting to hear what the town's Planning Board would have to say about that, she thought, as she parked the car outside the office.

She hesitated for a moment outside the office, remembering her encounter with Mel at Blueberry Pond. She fervently hoped he would be wearing clothes, and breathed a sigh of relief when she saw him standing behind the counter. He was wearing a shirt, and although she couldn't see his lower half she assumed it was also decently covered.

"What brings you here?" he said, scowling at her.

"Are you upset with me about something?"

"I just don't need any more newspaper types nosing around here," he said.

"Well, you're safe from me. I'm not working for the *Pennysaver* anymore. And if there's any significance to that fence you're building, I could care less. I'm here to talk about Pru Pratt."

"Can't help you," said Mel. "You're not supposed to speak ill of the dead."

Lucy smiled at him. "I wasn't exactly a fan myself, and the police have been taking a very close look at my family, so I'd really appreciate any help you can give me. The sooner I can figure out who killed her the sooner we can all get back to normal."

"So you want to finger me?"

"No way," said Lucy. "I just thought you might be able to give me some leads. You must have gotten to know her pretty well. You were neighbors, for one thing. And you were on opposite sides of the bylaw issue, that would have brought you into contact at least."

"She was a sick woman," said Mel. "She said she was against nudity but she couldn't keep herself away from the pond. I think she was obsessed or something."

"You know, that doesn't surprise me," said Lucy. "I think a lot of people who vehemently reject some sort of behavior—say homosexuality for example—are actually fascinated by it. Sometimes they really are latent homosexuals themselves."

"I don't think she wanted to take off her clothes, but she didn't mind spying on people who did," said Mel, warming to his subject. "She'd sit there in a folding chair with binoculars and a paper and pencil, observing everyone and writing things down."

"She was observing and taking notes?"

"There's not much to observe, in spite of what her son said."

"Wesley? What did he say?"

"He tried to pick a fight with two of the guys one day. Claimed he'd seen them getting up to something in the woods."

"Does that happen?"

"No more than at a regular beach. I mean, I'm not gonna say it never happens. People have a way of. . . ." Mel shrugged. "You know. Sometimes they pair off. Sometimes something happens. It's normal human behavior." He scratched his chin. "Considering the situation here, with all the media and the bylaw and all, I think there's been very little of that sort of thing. Most of the naturists I've talked with feel a little bit uncomfortable, a little pressured."

Lucy nodded sympathetically. "I can relate to that." She paused. "Could you give me the names of the men who had the confrontation with Wesley?'

Mel shook his head. "I don't think so."

"It would be such a help."

"Sorry."

Lucy sighed. "Oh, well. Thanks anyway for taking time to talk to me. I know you must be very busy." She paused. "What time do you open in the morning? It must be pretty early, right?"

Mel grinned at her. "I suppose you want to know if I was here the morning Prudish Pru was killed?"

"You got me. I would like to know."

"Just like I told the cops, I was right here, checking out a family from Montreal. I've got the charge slips and paperwork to prove it."

"Lucky you," said Lucy.

Lucky for Mel, but a bad break for her. Not that she exactly wanted Mel to be guilty of murder, but she would like to feel she was making some progress on the case. But now as she headed for home she didn't feel any closer to figuring out who killed Pru than she had when she started. And if that weren't bad enough, when she passed the Pratts' place she noticed the press pack was back, with reinforcements, encamped opposite her driveway.

* * *

They were still there when Bill brought the girls home from day camp. When they went upstairs to wash up, he placed a small cardboard box on the kitchen table.

"Kudo's ashes," he said, in answer to Lucy's inquiring glance. "Shall I just bury them or . . . ?"

"I guess we should have some sort of ceremony," said Lucy. "He was a big part of our family for a long time."

After supper, Bill and Toby went out to dig a grave while she and the girls cleaned up the dinner dishes. Then they all gathered at the grave site underneath a gnarled old apple tree.

"Who will begin?" asked Lucy.

"I will," said Bill, kneeling down and carefully placing the box in the hole. He tossed a bone-shaped dog treat on top of it. "I had my differences with Kudo, but he won my respect when I saw him chase off a coyote one day when Zoe was playing outside all alone. He was absolutely fearless when it came to protecting her. I realized he wanted to protect my family just as much as I do. He was one tough dog and I hope they have room for him in doggy heaven."

"I'm sure he'll go to doggy heaven," said Zoe, "and there will be lots of rabbits to chase and big bowls of dog food and no fleas at all. Kudo deserves to go there because he saved me from the coyote, and he always warned us when somebody came to the house. He made me feel safe."

"He made me feel safe, too," said Lucy. "Especially if I was home alone at night. As long as he was snoozing I knew everything was okay. I think he knew when I needed a little extra security, because he always stuck very close to me when I was here alone. He kept me company, he was a good friend."

"I didn't like Kudo when Mom first brought him home," said Sara. "I thought he was smelly and scary and I was afraid of him. But after he'd been here awhile, one day he saw me and my friends playing soccer and he joined in. He was a really good soccer player; you couldn't get the ball past him."

The others all nodded, remembering.

"People at school who'd never noticed me before all wanted to come over and see my amazing dog. All of a sudden, I was popular, all because of my dog." She tossed a little plush dog toy shaped like a soccer ball into the grave. "Thanks, Kudo."

"I never told anybody this before," said Elizabeth, "but one time I came home from a date and it was a beautiful night and the guy suggested we lie down on the grass and look at the stars. We did that for a while but then the guy got a little pushy, if you know what I mean. He wanted me to do things I didn't want to do."

Lucy's and Bill's eyes met.

"He wouldn't stop and I started pushing him away and he started holding me tighter. I was really struggling when the door opened and Kudo came bounding out. He stuck his nose between me and this guy so I got a chance to break loose. Kudo didn't let the guy up, though. He put his paws on his chest and started growling at him. He did this for a minute or two and the guy started acting real scared, yelling at me to call the dog off.

I was on the porch then, so I called him and very slowly he backed away and came up and stood by me."

"What happened to the guy?' asked Sara.

Elizabeth smiled. "He ran away and I never heard from him again."

Lucy breathed a huge sigh.

Elizabeth tossed an old shoe into the grave. "Here you go, Kudo. You already chewed up one, now you can have the other."

Everybody laughed.

"What about you Toby?" asked Zoe. "Do you have a story about Kudo?"

Toby cleared his throat. "Kudo taught me an important lesson, that I've never forgotten. When I was in high school, there were a couple of guys that everyone was kind of scared of. They'd walk down the hall and everybody'd get out of their way, you kind of wanted to stay clear of them, didn't want to end up alone in a bathroom with them or anything like that. Sometimes I'd see 'em coming towards me and I'd almost feel sick. Sometimes I even dreamed about them. It was pretty weird. Anyway, one day I was in the yard, mowing the grass, and a couple of enormous German shepherds came down the driveway. Kudo had been sleeping under the apple tree, but he immediately woke up. He didn't stop to think or anything, he just started barking and headed straight for these dogs, teeth bared, hair on his back all bristly, he was ready for business. It was awesome, and the two German shepherds thought so, too, because they just turned tail and ran away as fast as they could, even though they were a lot bigger and probably could've beat him up pretty bad. So after that, whenever I saw those two bullies, I'd just stand up straight and stick my chest out and kind of show my teeth in a sort of half-smile and look those guys straight in the eye and walk right by them." He smiled and tossed two tiny ceramic figurines of German shepherd dogs into the grave, figures that Lucy had often seen on Toby's desk. "They never bothered me, ever again."

For a long minute they all stood silently, staring at the grave. Finally, Bill spoke.

"Good-bye, old pal," he said.

"Good-bye, old pal," they chorused in response.

"This service is now concluded," said Bill, pulling the shovel out of the mound of dirt and starting to fill in the grave.

Zoe was beginning to sniffle, so Lucy took her hand and led her away, towards the house.

"It's time for your bath," she said, "would you like to use some of my bubble bath?"

"Okay." Zoe wiped away her tears with the back of her hand.

"You know, it's really nice to know Kudo meant so much to all of us," said Lucy, as they walked through the firefly-lit twilight and mounted the porch steps. The screen door creaked as she pulled it open and they stepped inside. It was a comforting sound.

But later, as she filled the tub and watched the bubbles grow, Lucy felt prickings of worry. Bill's words about how Kudo protected the family played in her mind, as did Toby's story about learning to stand up for himself. Valuable lessons and laudable values, true enough, but they could be taken too far. She understood Toby's need for independence, but she wished he didn't have to be quite so private. She'd sure feel a lot better if she knew what he was up to these days.

Chapter Nineteen

Lucy was frying up some bacon and eggs for breakfast when the phone rang. It was Sue.

"Are you busy? Can you talk?"

"Talk away. I'm just cooking up some bacon and eggs."

"Are you trying to kill your family? Haven't you heard of cholesterol?"

"Oh, shut up. I haven't cooked a real breakfast for them in years. But now that I'm not working I have time to make things that take a little time and fussing. I think Sara was still in diapers the last time I made pancakes."

"Pancakes!"

"Tomorrow. If you're gonna do it, you might as well go all the way."

"That's the advice you give Elizabeth?"

"Not quite, but she doesn't listen to me anyway."

Sue chuckled. "That's so true. When Sidra was in college she'd smile and nod and agree with me...."

"And then she'd go and do the exact opposite."

"Right!"

"Well, everything worked out for her," said Lucy. Sidra had a promising career in television in New York City and was happily married to her high school sweetheart, Geoff Dunford, who was a science teacher at the Bronx High School of Science.

"It will work out for Elizabeth, too," said Sue. "Listen, I had that talk with the Wilsons."

Lucy poked at the bacon with a fork, turning over a few pieces. "That's fast work. Did you learn anything?"

"Yes. It seems that, unfortunately, I am doomed to hell because I have not been born again."

"But you're such a nice person and you give lovely parties. I'm sure they'd love to have you in heaven."

"That's what I thought, too, but I was wrong. The important thing is being born again. You can be absolutely rotten, stinking with sin, but if you find Jesus and repent, you get to go to heaven."

"You mean heaven is full of crooks and thieves and murderers?"

"Reformed ones."

"They're the worst kind," said Lucy. "I'm not sure I want to go now. Especially if you're not going."

"Don't worry. Wherever we end up, we'll stick together."

"Good." Lucy lifted a piece of bacon with her fork and set it on a paper towel to drain. "There'll be all the fried chicken you want and you never gain any weight."

"Whipped cream?"

"Of course. The clouds are made of it." Lucy

smiled. "In Bill's heaven, the clouds will be made of beer foam."

"You're not going to be together?"

"Not all the time. How about you and Sid?"

"Well, you know how he hates shopping and there would have to be shopping, right?"

"Absolutely. Of course, maybe that would be your particular hell. Endless shopping, at full price, with your husband tagging along and complaining."

"Enough theology. I called to tell you what the Wilsons said about the Pratts." Sue paused for breath. "Apparently, many of the Revelation Congregation members considered Pru their cross to bear, if you know what I mean."

"Even those pious folk didn't like her?"

"Not much. She made a habit of pointing out other people's deficiencies, for example, she told Mrs. Wilson that her cakes were flat because she didn't have enough faith."

"Her baking powder's probably old."

"That's what I told her and it came as a great relief. Apparently Pru's accusation touched a nerve, because she was pretty upset about it. She also accused Mr. Wilson of lusting after other women because she saw him buying a *Playboy* at the Quik-Stop, but he insists it was only a gag gift for a friend at work."

"Likely story," scoffed Lucy.

"Well, whoever he was buying it for really wasn't any of Pru's business. She sounds like a real bully. Telling everyone how they ought to behave and pointing out their shortcomings. Especially Calvin's. The Wilsons said everybody felt sorry for him. She was constantly nagging him and belittling him in front of other people. It was painful to watch, they said. Everybody was waiting for the day when Calvin would stick up for himself." Sue paused. "Do you think he finally did? Maybe he snapped and ran her down. You can just picture it: She's standing in the driveway, giving him what for about buying a *Playboy* or leaving the toilet seat up or not cleaning out the gutters and he impulsively slams his foot down on the gas. It's over before he has time for a second thought."

"You think Calvin did it?" Lucy remembered her encounter with him in the woods near Blueberry Pond. Rather than speak to her, he had run away, vanished into the woods. "He's afraid of his own shadow."

"Those are the ones, Lucy. The quiet ones. Isn't that what the neighbors of the murderer always say. 'He was so quiet. He always kept to himself.' "

"I still think Wesley's a better candidate. He's hot tempered, and then there's the incident with Kudo. He was definitely running away from something that morning." She took the last pieces of bacon out of the pan and flipped the eggs. "Whichever one it was, it's going to be awfully hard to prove. If it were a stranger, there might be a footprint or some kind of physical evidence. But Wesley and Calvin live there."

"What about damage to the truck?"

"He hit the dog right after. He could say the dog caused the damage. If only I could talk to Calvin I bet he would fold pretty quickly," said Lucy. "But I'd have to catch him when Wesley isn't home, when no reporters are around. We'll probably have a solar eclipse before that happens."

"I have an idea," said Sue. "I could go to Pru's funeral. The Wilsons actually asked me if I was going."

"That's a great idea. Will you do it?"

"For you, sure. But in the meantime, since you're home anyway and enjoy cooking so much, do you think you could make *twenty* pounds of potato salad?"

Lucy's heart was bursting with gratitude. "Absolutely."

"And one other little thing?"

Lucy's grateful heart was shrinking; she was beginning to think the price of this particular favor was getting rather high. But what was she going to do? She couldn't go to the funeral herself without causing a scandal. "Whatever you say."

"Bake six dozen red, white and blue cupcakes. You don't have to make them from scratch—you can use a mix if you want."

"That's big of you," said Lucy.

"I know. I can't believe I'm not going to heaven."

"I can," said Lucy.

Lucy didn't really mind baking the cupcakes; she didn't really know what to do with herself now that she didn't have to go to work at the *Pennysaver*. She had a couple of boxes of cake mix in the pantry and it only took a few minutes to mix up a batch. While they were baking, she stirred up some brownies using her favorite recipe. She hadn't made it in a long time, and it reminded her of the days when the kids were small and she turned out a steady stream of baked goods for their lunch boxes and after-school snacks. Whatever happened to that recipe for peanut-butter bars, she wondered. That had been a favorite, with a thin coating of chocolate frosting.

She smiled when she took the cupcakes out of the oven, admiring the festive paper cups decorated with red and blue stars. She had found them in the pantry, tucked away with cupcake papers for every conceivable holiday: hearts for Valentine's Day, pastels for Easter, red and green bells for Christmas, little green shamrocks for Saint Patrick's Day. No holiday had gone unremarked when the kids were small.

Once she'd started working, however, that had changed. Dinner had to be something she could throw together quickly, and instead of baking treats she usually grabbed something from the store. These days they all seemed to be watching their weight anyway. More often than not they had fruit or frozen yogurt for dessert.

She sniffed the rich chocolate scent of the brownies baking in the oven and sighed. All that butter and sugar, not to mention the walnuts, they had to have tons of calories. But it would be worth it, just this once. A chocolate extravagance.

Maybe a bit too extravagant, she decided, taking the pan out of the oven and setting it on a rack to cool. It was a big recipe, making at least four dozen brownies. Elizabeth and Sara wouldn't touch them, Toby was hardly ever home, and Zoe shouldn't eat too many. Neither should she and Bill, considering their ongoing battle with middle-age spread.

She touched the brownies, waiting for the magic moment when they would be just the right temperature to cut. Too soon and she'd end up with a mess. Wait too long, and they'd be tough. She tapped the side of the pan with her knife.

Maybe she could take a few brownies into the *Pennysaver.* Phyllis loved her brownies and Ted would wolf down any food that came his way. It would be a good way to show there were no hard feelings, and maybe she'd even pick up some information about the murder investigation. She sank the knife into the brownies and drew it towards her in a straight line. Perfect.

Lucy was a bit surprised to see the little encampment opposite the driveway had disappeared when she left the house that afternoon. Maybe they were all at the funeral, or maybe they were busy chasing down nudists. Maybe the family feud was old news. She certainly hoped so. It felt great to go about her business unobserved.

The *Pennysaver* office hadn't changed a bit, she discovered, when she arrived carrying her plate of brownies, carefully covered with plastic wrap. The little bell on the door still jangled, the motes of dust danced in the sunlight that streamed through the venetian blinds, and Phyllis was still sitting behind the reception desk.

"Howdy, stranger," said Phyllis, beaming at her through her half-glasses. The rhinestones were gone, replaced by a pair with a garish abstract design inspired by Jackson Pollack.

"I like your glasses," said Lucy. "Wild."

"That's what I thought," said Phyllis, peering at the plate. "What have you got there?"

"Brownies. They're for you and Ted. Is he around?"

"Nope. He's covering the funeral." Phyllis picked

the largest brownie off the plate and took a bite, closing her eyes and moaning with pleasure. "These are fantastic. You really shouldn't have."

"I've got a lot of time on my hands these days."

"Ted doesn't, that's for sure," said Phyllis, her shoulders shaking with laughter. "I think he really misses you."

"Good," said Lucy. "You can tell him I'm enjoying this little vacation."

"I will." Phyllis eyed the plate. "I guess I better save some for him," she said, choosing a second brownie.

"It would be nice." Lucy glanced at her desk, which was covered with papers. "Whatcha doing?"

"Letters to the Editor." Phyllis sighed. "Between the nudists and the Fourth of July and the lichen, we're getting an awful lot of mail these days. Everybody's got something to say."

"Ted must be in seventh heaven," said Lucy, picking up a letter. "This one says the environmentalists are in league with the Communists."

"We've gotten a couple of those."

"This lady says she's glad there won't be any fireworks because they always used to upset her dog."

"Listen to this," said Phyllis, waving a sheet of paper with an impressive letterhead. "It's from the VFW. They say they've voted to oppose the anti-nudity bylaw because, and I quote, they 'fought for freedom, not for some petty-minded prudes to start telling people what they could do.' "

"Wow," said Lucy, taking the letter and examining it. "It gets better: 'A ridiculous attempt to legislate morality by a sexually repressed and unfulfilled woman who is attempting to impose her extreme religious beliefs on an entire town.' "

Phyllis raised an eyebrow. "Pretty strong language, especially about a dead woman."

Lucy checked the date. "It's dated the day she died."

"I'm behind in the mail," admitted Phyllis. "Who wrote it? The whole VFW?"

"It says they all voted on it, but the letter's written by Scratch Hallett."

"Sounds to me like he got a little personally involved."

The bell on the door jangled and Ted came in, accompanied by Mike Gold.

"Hi, Lucy!" he exclaimed, cheerfully. "Don't tell me you've reconsidered and you're here to help with the mail?"

"Not on your life, Ted," said Lucy, smiling sweetly. "But I did bring you some brownies, to help you keep your strength up."

"Your brownies? Your fabulous brownies?" Ted took one from the plate and passed it to Mike Gold. "You've got to try one. These are fabulous."

Lucy would have liked to ask Ted about the investigation but she knew she wouldn't get much out of him while Mike was around. Or even if he left, for that matter. She knew Ted well enough to know that he often used high spirits and jollity to block questions he didn't want to answer.

Mike had taken a brownie and was smiling as he bit into it. "Mmm. Real butter. You can always tell."

"Ah, so you're a connoisseur," said Lucy, wondering if he would be a better bet.

"More of a consumer, I'm afraid," said Gold,

patting his ample belly. He turned to Ted. "Do you have any more questions for me? I don't mean to rush you, but I've got another appointment. You said I could have some back issues. . . ."

"Oh, right." Ted disappeared into the morgue for a minute, returning with a handful of papers. "Here you go. Thanks for the interview."

"No problem. It was a pleasure," said Mike, opening the door.

"I'm going, too," said Lucy. "Mind if I walk with you?"

Ted's eyebrows shot up, but she was through the door before he could say anything.

"I'm Lucy Stone, by the way," she said, introducing herself.

"I know. I've seen you on TV." Gold's eyes twinkled mischievously.

Lucy rolled her eyes. "You can't believe everything you see on TV."

"You're telling me?"

They laughed together, walking down the street and stopping in front of the storefront the ANS was using as a temporary headquarters.

"I guess you're used to all the media attention," said Lucy.

"It's a constant battle for the organization," said Gold. "All we want is responsible, fair reporting but as soon as they realize who we are, they start to sensationalize our position. Basically, all we want is to be left alone to take our clothes off."

Lucy smiled sympathetically. "All I want is to find out who killed Pru Pratt so my family and I can get on with our lives." She sighed. "Do you mind if I ask you a few quick questions?"

Gold checked his watch. "Gotta be quick. I don't want to keep 'Inside Edition' waiting."

"Trust me, they'll wait for you," said Lucy. "I'm just curious about my neighbor, Mel Dunwoodie. Has he been involved with ANS for long?"

"Dunwoodie? The guy with the trailer park?"

Lucy nodded.

"I know he's a dues-paying member, and he's been real helpful to the organization. He's a member of the task force we organized to deal with the anti-nudity bylaw issue, but I don't really know anything about him personally." He paused. "He seems nice enough. He's a real hard worker."

"What about his relations with . . ."

"Sorry," said Gold, cutting her off. "I've got to go."

Lucy watched as one of the big white trucks with a satellite dish on top rolled up to the curb, then put on her sunglasses and quickly turned and walked down the street. She didn't want to risk any more media attention. Back in the car she considered her next step and decided she'd like to have a little chat with Scratch Hallett.

Driving through town to Hallett Plumbing & Heating, she remembered how angry he'd been at the selectmen's meetings when first the fireworks and then the parade had been cancelled. He'd been particularly angry about the parade, even blaming Pru for raising such a fuss over the nudists that organizers felt the parade had to be canceled. She wondered where all this anger was coming from, and if there was some long-standing grudge behind it.

Hallett Plumbing & Heating was located behind

Scratch's modest clapboard house, in a garage that had been enlarged throughout the years as the business grew. Scratch now employed five or six mechanics, and a small fleet of blue and white vans was parked every night on the blacktop outside the shop. Now, of course, the vans were gone as the crew of plumbers were out turning on the water in summer homes, repairing leaky faucets and replacing busted water heaters.

Lucy parked in the area reserved for customers and went in the office, pausing to admire a Rube Goldberg-like assemblage of pipes and plumbing fittings that was displayed in the window. Scratch himself was seated at an enormous gray steel desk dating from the fifties. A pinup calendar from a tool company, featuring a busty girl in a skimpy bikini holding a very large monkey wrench hung on the wall behind him.

"Lucy Stone! Are you here to interview me for the *Pennysaver?*"

"You know, I should. You're a real success story. What did you start with? A station wagon?"

"That's right. Back in '45. I got home from the war, married Mrs. Hallett and started the business, all in a couple of weeks. Didn't have time to waste after spending four years overseas in the Army Air Corps. Wasn't the Air Force then, it was still part of the Army."

"I guess you saw a lot of the world."

"I sure did. I crossed over on the *Queen Mary,* she was converted into a troop ship you know. We were stacked in bunks four or five high, and when your shift was done somebody else got your spot.

We was in England for a good while, then they sent us on to North Africa. I ended up in Italy, in Naples."

Lucy felt a twinge of envy; she'd never been to Europe. "Have you ever considered going back and visiting those places?"

"Nope. Once was enough," said Scratch. "So what can I do for you? I see you're not writing any of this down."

"No. I'm on a forced vacation. Ted says I'm too involved to work at the paper until this Pru Pratt thing is over."

Scratch raised an eyebrow. " 'Cause of the dog?"

"Well, that, and being neighbors and having differences with the Pratts. The whole package, I guess. The paper is supposed to be impartial and Ted's not convinced I can be objective," Lucy paused. "So I decided the sooner this thing is over, the sooner I can get back to work. The cops don't seem to be making much progress so I'm investigating on my own."

"Good for you!" said Scratch, leaning back in his chair and lighting his pipe. "So how's it going?"

"Not very well," admitted Lucy. "When you get right down to it, there are a whole lot of people who didn't like Pru Pratt."

"I suppose I'm one of 'em," said Scratch, pulling at his eyebrow. They had grown extremely bushy, as some men's do when they age. His were impressive, as was the white and wiry hair sprouting from his ears. "You probably think I could be the one who did the evil deed."

Lucy blushed. "I doubt that very much. But you've lived here your whole life. I bet you know a thing or two about the Pratts. For instance, was Pru always religious?"

Scratch laughed. "She was a real devil in high school. She was a couple of years ahead of my oldest and he used to say she was fast. Her father was a real mean one, rumor was he used to beat her." Scratch raised an eyebrow. "Mebbe even more, if you get my drift."

"Incest?"

"That's what some said. I don't put much stock in gossip meself, though."

"When did she change?"

"When that Revelation Congregation started, she was one of the first to sign up."

"Repenting for her sins?"

"That's prob'ly what she thought, but you ask me, those folks just replace their old sins with new ones. They're not fornicating so somehow that entitles 'em to go all intolerant. See what I mean? They start thinking they're better than everybody else."

"Pru was like that, that's for sure." Lucy paused. "What about Calvin? Did he grow up here?"

"Cowardly Calvin!" snorted Scratch. "That's what we used to call him. He kinda disappeared for a while during the Vietnam War, said he had business in Canada." He nodded at her. "When he came back, he came around here looking for work. I told him no way. No way I was going to hire a draft dodger. Not after what I saw in the war."

"I can understand that," said Lucy.

"A man's gotta do his duty," said Scratch. "It's the American way."

"The price of freedom," murmured Lucy.

Scratch was gazing into the distance. She wondered what he saw, what memories came to him.

"The *Queen Mary* hit a smaller ship when we
made the crossing, you know. It felt like a bump,
like she'd hit a log or something. Later I found out
over three hundred British sailors died, went down
in the cold dark Atlantic." He turned his bright blue
eyes on her. "Beats me why Calvin Pratt thought his
skinny little ass was worth more than those poor
fellows' lives. They didn't try to get out of serving,
most of 'em enlisted. That's what we did back then."

"I know," said Lucy, thinking of the dwindling
ranks of veterans who showed up for Memorial Day
and Veterans' Day observances. She could never
get through one of those ceremonies without crying when the trumpeter played "Taps." "People
forget. They can't even be bothered to vote."

"Not us vets," said Scratch. "We've got long memories."

"I bet you do," said Lucy, standing up. "It's been
nice talking to you. Have a good day."

Going back to the car, Lucy felt terribly sad.
Scratch had survived the war and come home to
his sweetheart, but so many of the young men who
had marched off to war with him never returned.
She'd seen the photos of military cemeteries in
Europe, row upon row of white crosses. And then
there were the ones whose bodies were never even
found, the missing in action. The prisoners of war.
And the shell-shocked, who hadn't been able to
forget the horrors they'd seen. The concentration
camp liberators who turned to drink to get through
the rest of their lives; the hollow-eyed survivors of
the Bataan death march and D-Day invaders, who
saw their comrades sink into the sea beside them.

She wondered about Scratch's wartime experiences. What had he seen? What had he done? She wondered if he'd been in battle, if he'd killed enemy soldiers. It was frightening to think of this white-haired old man taking a life, but she didn't doubt for a minute that he would have done his duty as a soldier. The question was whether he was still fighting the war, his own private war.

Chapter Twenty

Lost in her thoughts as she drove away from Scratch's, Lucy didn't notice the TV news van that was following her until she braked for a stop sign and checked her rear-view mirror. Curious to see if it was following her, she flipped on her turn signal. So did the van.

She'd enjoyed the break but she might as well face it: they were back. Noticing that several more vehicles had joined the line behind her, she decided that Pru Pratt's funeral must be over and the newshounds were sniffing out any possible leads. She decided to follow their example and head over to Sue's house to get a report on the funeral.

"I see the gang's all here," commented Sue, when she opened the door to Lucy.

Lucy paused and looked over her shoulder, straight into the lenses of several cameras.

"Darn!" she exclaimed, ducking into the shelter of the house. "I should know better by now. I suppose I'll look all furtive and guilty."

"Too bad your shirt is all scrunched up," said Sue, observing her coolly. "It makes your bum look bigger than it is. Of course, the baggy khaki shorts don't help."

"I didn't know I was going to be a cover girl when I got dressed this morning, now did I?" demanded Lucy.

"I think you should assume that somebody's going to be snapping your picture," said Sue. "I'd wear black if I were you. Maybe capris, they're slimming."

"Thanks for the fashion tip." Lucy's voice was dripping with sarcasm. "Like I've got time to go shopping. I'll put it on the 'to do' list, right after 'solve murder.'"

"Oooh, you are touchy, aren't you," said Sue, leading the way to the kitchen. "Would you like a glass of iced tea?"

"Yes, please," said Lucy, feeling like a scolded child. "It's just that I really thought the media had turned their attention elsewhere. I didn't think I was going to have to cope with this any more."

"I know," said Sue, setting a tall frosty glass in front of her. "It stinks. Lemon?"

"Please."

Lucy squeezed her lemon wedge into the tea and stirred it, then took a big swallow. "So how was the funeral?"

"Dry."

Lucy was puzzled. "Was rain forecast?"

Sue gave her a sharp look. "There was no booze. Not a drop. Not even that disgusting sweet sherry."

"What did you expect? The Revelation Congregation doesn't approve of alcohol."

Sue was doubtful. "Really?"

"Really. No drinking, no dancing, no card playing, no gambling."

"What do they do for fun?"

"I don't think they believe in it."

"That explains a lot," said Sue. "It was very somber. Definitely not Finnegan's wake."

"Who was there?"

"The entire congregation, I guess. There was a good turnout, but I didn't really know anybody, except my neighbors, the Wilsons. The hymns were all weird, too. I didn't know them, but everybody else did. They were in great voice, they sounded much better than the Methodists."

Considering that the Methodist congregation consisted of a handful of aged ladies, Lucy wasn't surprised.

"Did they have a reception afterwards?"

"In the church hall, not at the house." Sue considered. "The food was pretty good. They had little tiny egg-salad sandwiches with the crusts cut off, chicken salad, too. And cake and homemade cookies and deviled eggs and little cherry tomatoes stuffed with egg salad."

"You actually ate this stuff?" Lucy was doubtful; Sue was a career dieter.

"I did. There was nobody to talk to except my neighbors and they were busy with the food, and nothing to drink, so I ate." Sue patted her flat tummy. "I'll skip supper."

"You can send Sid over to my house—I'm grilling pizzas on the barbecue."

"Thanks, Lucy, but he's on duty at the fire station tonight."

Lucy nodded. She knew Sid was a volunteer fireman. "Did you overhear any interesting conversations?" she asked. "And how come they had so many egg dishes?"

Sue fluttered her beautifully manicured hand for emphasis. "I'm glad the great detective finally asked. That's a very interesting point. I asked Mrs. Wilson the very same question and she said all the eggs were donated by Bitsy Parsons, who apparently has been carrying a torch for Calvin. She thought it was very odd indeed that Bitsy wasn't there to comfort him in his time of trouble."

"And to remind him that she would be available to comfort him in the future?"

"Yes."

"It does seem funny that she would pass up the funeral," mused Lucy. "Maybe she didn't feel well."

"Maybe she was exhausted from cooking up all those eggs." Sue wrinkled her nose. "Faint from sulphur fumes."

"Maybe she was home, waiting, arranged attractively on the divan in hopes Calvin would show up after the funeral?"

"If she thought that, she miscalculated. I overheard Wesley saying that he and his dad were going fishing after the funeral. He said it's the only place they find any comfort."

"That's kind of fishy, isn't it? I mean, right after the funeral?"

"No puns allowed."

"Sorry. But they must have a reason for going out today, like they're meeting somebody or something."

"Like drug smugglers?'

"Or handing off poached lobsters." The wheels

were turning in Lucy's head. "I wish there was some way we could find out what they're doing."

"We could follow them in Pam's boat. She won't mind. She leaves it down at the harbor, you know."

"That's not a bad idea. What kind of boat is it?"

Sue was nonchalant. "A boat boat. I don't know. It floats."

Lucy got up and walked through the living room to the front window, where she peeked out through the blinds. "There's more of them now. How are we going to get down to the waterfront without being followed?"

Sue joined her and peered through the slats. "Good God! Don't they have anything better to do?"

"Apparently not."

"I could just go out and tell them you're not that interesting," offered Sue. "And certainly not a murderer."

"It's kind of you to offer, but they'd never believe you." Lucy tossed her hair. "I've become notorious."

"You know, J. Lo, I've got an idea. I bet Sid would drive down the street with his siren going and his light flashing."

"They'd all follow him! That's brilliant."

"I'll call."

Ten minutes later, Sue and Lucy heard Sid approaching, siren blaring. They watched out the window as he sped down the street in his shiny red pickup truck, with the light flashing. The reporters, who had been lounging against their vehicles, chatting in small groups, scattered and ran for their cars. They were all gone within seconds.

Minutes later, Lucy and Sue arrived unnoticed at the harbor, just in time to see Wesley and Calvin heading out to sea in their boat, Second Chance. They lost precious moments parking the SUV, then Sue led the way to the farthest end of the float where Pam's little runabout was bobbing in the water.

Lucy wasn't impressed with the little aluminum boat's seaworthiness.

"Pam doesn't go out of the cove in that thing, does she?" she asked.

"Sure." Sue eased herself into the boat and started fiddling with the engine. "Hop in! We're going to lose them."

"We'll never catch them in this thing," said Lucy, carefully lowering herself into the tippy little craft. In the distance she could see Second Chance rounding the point and heading out to the open sea.

"That's okay. We don't have to. We just want to keep an eye on her. The idea is to look like we're just out for some sun and fun on the water."

"You're wearing a little black dress," said Lucy.

"Perfect for any occasion," said Sue, slipping off her black slingbacks and rummaging in her over-sized designer purse. "Aha!" she exulted, producing a pair of miniature binoculars. "I knew they were in here."

"I'm not even going to ask," said Lucy, amazed.

"You keep an eye on them while I steer," ordered Sue, bringing the little boat neatly around the point.

"Aye-aye, Captain." Lucy squinted through the eye piece and fiddled with the adjustment knob. "I can barely make them out."

"You're looking through the wrong end."

"Oh." Lucy flipped the binoculars around. "That's

better. Oh no it isn't. They're looking right at us. They know we're following them."

"You're right. They're speeding up." Sue shaded her eyes with one hand, the other remained on the tiller. "That's a serious engine in that boat. Look how fast it's going."

"Especially considering how low it's sitting in the water. That boat is loaded with something."

"As long as we can keep them in sight, we're okay," said Sue, relaxing a bit. "Slow but steady wins the race, you know."

"It's a nice day for boating," said Lucy, settling in for the ride.

And truth be told, it was a nice day to be out on the water. The sun was strong and hot, but a gentle breeze cooled them. The sky was bright blue, broken only by the occasional soaring gull. The water was deep, deep blue and glassy with only the occasional little wave to lift them up and then gently set them back down.

"Too bad we don't have fishing rods," said Lucy.

Sue immediately began searching in her purse.

"Don't tell me you have a fishing rod in there?"

Sue raised her head. "No. Sunscreen. Put some on."

"Thanks." Lucy eyed the purse. "How about a sandwich? Or a candy bar?"

"Breath mints."

"I'll take one."

Lucy was placidly sucking on her mint when the engine sputtered.

"Oops."

"Don't panic. It's probably air in the line or something."

The engine sputtered again, then went dead.

"No big deal, right? It'll start right up."

"No." Sue was squinting at a little gauge. "We're out of gas."

"But there's a gas can, right?"

"I don't see one."

"You've got to be kidding."

"We were in a hurry, right? I didn't think to check."

"You've got your cell phone, though. We can call for help."

"No. It's on the kitchen counter, recharging. It's time to row."

At least the oars were in the boat, thought Lucy, as Sue moved from the rear of the boat to join her on the middle seat. They each took an oar.

"This is kind of like Girl Scout camp," said Sue, giggling.

"Yeah, except we're not in the middle of Lake Tiorati. We're in the middle of the North Atlantic."

"Not the middle, we're not even near Greenland, and there are no icebergs in sight," said Sue. "So don't start getting all dramatic on me."

"Well, how far do you think we are from shore?"

"Maybe a mile, certainly less than two."

Lucy looked around doubtfully. There was no sign of land. "We were going at a pretty good clip, you know. And I don't see land."

"That's 'cause of the fog," said Sue, rubbing her bare arms. "It's getting chilly."

"The sun's gone."

"It's definitely clouded over."

"Oh, shit. We could be rowing in the wrong direction."

"Don't panic," said Sue, her voice tight with nerves. "We'll put on life jackets and just sit tight. Somebody's bound to come along."

"That's the best thing," agreed Lucy, whose arms were tired from rowing. "And there's an air horn, right? We can let off a blast every five minutes or something."

"No air horn," admitted Sue, passing her a very small life jacket. "We'll have to yell."

"What is this thing?" demanded Lucy, who was having trouble fastening the straps.

"It's a kiddie-size. It was probably Adam's," said Sue, who was putting on an old-fashioned orange life preserver. "I'd give you this one, but it's pretty mildewed. It stinks."

"I can't believe this," said Lucy, her teeth chattering. "Doesn't Pam pay any attention to Coast Guard regulations? You're supposed to have . . ."

"I know. I know," snapped Sue, cutting her off. "But she's a free spirit. And all she uses the boat for is to putter around in the cove. I bet she never goes past the point."

"Still," fumed Lucy. "It's awfully irresponsible."

"She probably didn't realize we'd be borrowing her boat," said Sue, wrapping her arms around Lucy in an effort to stay warm.

"I know," said Lucy, slipping her arms around Sue's waist. "We'll be okay."

"I'm freezing." Sue's teeth were chattering.

"Me, too."

"We'll yell, on the count of three. Ahoy. Okay?"

They yelled, and then they listened. There was no sound except the lapping of the water against the side of the boat.

"At least it's calm," said Sue.

"There is that," agreed Lucy, shivering. "I'm starving. I didn't eat any lunch."

"Let's yell again," suggested Sue.

They yelled, but all around them there was nothing but silence. Lucy thought of the old sailor's prayer that was often printed on little wooden plaques and sold in gift shops: "Lord, thy sea is so great and my boat is so small . . ."

"I hear something," said Sue. "Listen!"

Lucy listened, then shook her head.

"No, really. It's a hum. A definite hum. Like an engine."

"Ahoy!!" yelled Lucy. "Mayday! Mayday!"

"Together!" ordered Sue, and they yelled together, at the top of their lungs. Lucy was starting to get hoarse when she finally heard the motor.

"It's coming closer!"

"We have to keep yelling." Sue counted off three on her fingers, and they both screamed.

Through the fog, they could just make out a dark shape.

"We see you!" yelled Sue.

The engine noise immediately grew quieter, as the boat cut its speed. Even so, it seemed to be coming awfully fast and the two women held on to their oars tightly, prepared to move quickly if they had to. There was no need, however, as the huge shape became clearer and glided towards them. It was the Carrie Ann.

"Mom!" exclaimed Toby. "What are you doing out here?"

Chuck maneuvered the larger boat carefully, bringing it close enough so that Toby could throw them a rope. Once the rowboat was tied fast, he helped them scramble aboard the larger lobster boat, where they were immediately wrapped in blankets and given hot coffee.

"Fog sneak up on you?" asked Chuck.

"You could say that," replied Sue.

"This is a real pea souper. You were lucky we found you."

Shivering, Lucy clutched her coffee in shaking hands. She didn't want to think about what might have been, but Toby wasn't going to let her off the hook.

"What were you thinking?" he demanded. "That's not a regulation life jacket. And where was your fog horn? What about a compass? Don't you have any navigational equipment?"

Sue pulled herself up to her full height and glared at him. "We had sunscreen," she said.

"That's something, I guess," grumbled Toby, reaching for the thermos and refilling their cups.

It was only when they were safely docked and alighting from the boat that Chuck mentioned Sue's outfit.

"Were you on your way to a funeral or something?" he asked.

"Actually," she said, "I went to one this morning." She paused. "Boy, that seems like a lifetime ago."

"Well, next time you take your boat out, make sure you've got the proper equipment. This could've been *your* funeral."

"I will," said Sue. "Thanks for everything." She turned to Lucy. "Are you coming?"

"No, I'll catch a ride with Toby," she said.

Toby didn't seem pleased with that idea. "It'll be a while, Mom," he said. "We've got a lot of work to do."

"I want to help," said Lucy, determined to make amends for her foolishness. "Just tell me what to do."

Chuck and Toby glanced at each other.

"Really," insisted Lucy. "I'm strong and capable. What do you want me to do?"

"Okay," said Chuck. "You can hose off the deck. There's a pipe stand and hose about halfway down the dock."

While Lucy went to get the hose, Chuck and Toby busied themselves unloading their haul. Each heavy box was hoisted out of the hold and onto the pier, then placed on a wheelbarrow to be taken to Chuck's pickup truck. Once the truck was full, he drove the short distance across the parking lot to the cooperative's refrigerated truck. When the day's catch was in, the truck took it to the fish markets in Boston and New York.

"Good haul?" she asked, as she began hosing down the fiberglass deck.

"Pretty good," said Chuck, grunting with the effort of lifting a plastic fish box filled with lobsters. "The catch has been up last few days."

"You know, I saw the Pratts' boat heading out to sea. It was sitting very low in the water."

Toby ducked and turned, suddenly very interested in getting the cover fastened tight on one of the plastic fish boxes.

"Maybe they haven't cleaned out the bilge for a

while," said Chuck, a smile curving his lips. "All it takes is a little leak, or maybe the pump's not working the way it should, and you can take on quite a bit of water. It's gradual, so you might not notice."

"Especially if you're kind of lazy to start with," added Toby, his shoulders shaking with suppressed laughter.

"Yeah," mused Chuck. "They're not exactly poster boys for good seamanship."

"Or maybe they've got a hold full of something they shouldn't have, like other people's lobsters," said Lucy.

"Or bales of marijuana," said Chuck, laughing. "It's been known to happen."

"Do you think that's what they're doing?"

"I don't know what they're doing and I don't care," said Chuck. He put his hands on his hips and surveyed the boat. "Nice job, Lucy. Thanks."

"No problem," said Lucy.

Chuck slapped Toby on the shoulder. "See you tomorrow, buddy."

"Right."

In Toby's Jeep, with the hot, asphalt-scented breeze whipping through the torn fabric roof and doors, Lucy soon discovered the tables had turned. This time it was her turn to get a scolding.

"Is that what you were doing? Following the Pratts? Why would you do that? Don't you know I've got this pretrial hearing coming up? This is the last thing I need. Believe me, I'm staying as clear of Wesley as I can and you should, too. For all I care, he can steal the whole damn town. I'm not saying a word."

"That's crazy, Toby. If he is doing something illegal and you knew about it and fought with him to get him to stop, well, that would be a mitigating circumstance."

"I'm listening to Mr. Goodman, Mom, and he said to mind my own business and stay out of trouble. And that's what I'm going to do." He gunned the motor as he turned onto Sue's street and parked behind Lucy's car. "And I wish you would, too."

"C'mon Toby, I know you've been up to something. You're never home. Where are you spending all your time?"

"Can't a guy have any privacy?"

Lucy exploded. "Sure, you can have all the privacy you want when you move into your own place. But while you're living in my house, I think I deserve some basic courtesy. Especially considering the fact you've got a court date coming up." Her voice softened. "Don't you understand? I worry about you."

Toby shifted in his seat and sighed. "Okay, Mom. You don't have to worry. I've been seeing somebody."

"Seeing somebody? Who?"

"A girl."

Lucy's jaw dropped. "Oh."

"Yeah."

"Do I know her?"

"Sure. It's Molly Moskowitz." He paused. "She's really cool."

"I'm sure she is," said Lucy, opening the car door and getting out. She leaned in through the window. "You should bring her around sometime, for dinner, maybe, so we can all meet her."

"Yeah, Mom." He tapped the accelerator, making the engine roar, and Lucy stepped back as he drove off.

So Toby had a girlfriend. That was a relief, she thought, as she started the Subaru. Or was it?

Chapter Twenty-one

When Lucy got home, she found trouble waiting in the form of a police cruiser parked in the driveway. Its arrival had not gone unnoticed by the newshounds, and the encampment had sprouted once again on the opposite side of the road, like a weed that had been pulled only to reappear a few days later, sturdier than ever.

As Lucy made her way down the driveway she saw Toby getting out of his Jeep. The waiting officer also got out of his cruiser and Lucy was relieved to recognize Barney. She hoped he was making a social call. Something to do with the picnic, maybe. She hurried to join them.

"Hi!" she greeted him with a big smile. "What brings you here?"

Barney's face was serious; he looked more than ever like a bloodhound, and Lucy's heart sank.

"Actually, Lucy, I'd like to have a word with Toby."

Lucy felt her back stiffen. "I'll call Bob Goodman. I don't think Toby should say anything without Bob."

"It's okay, Mom."

"Don't be foolish, Toby. You've got a lawyer, you should follow his advice."

"Let me find out what it's about before you go all hysterical," said Toby.

"I'm not hysterical," said Lucy, in a very controlled voice. "But there's no way I'm going to let him coax you into some kind of admission. . . ."

Barney looked hurt. "Lucy, you know me better than that."

Lucy immediately felt ashamed of her outburst. "I'm sorry, Barney. I'm a little irrational, I admit it. I've had a tough day."

"That's okay, then. Listen, both of you. The lab tests have come up clean on all your vehicles."

"That's a relief," said Lucy, stifling her impulse to hug Toby and do a little dance with him in the driveway.

"Same with Wesley Pratt's truck, too. They didn't find any human blood, just blood from the dog."

"So Wesley's in the clear?" Lucy tried not to sound disappointed.

"Looks that way." Barney's jowls quivered. "Calvin, too."

"So where's the investigation headed?"

"Nowhere fast," said Barney. "But there is something else I'd like to talk to Toby about." He gave Lucy a meaningful look.

"Right. I can take a hint. I've got to get supper started anyway," she muttered, heading for the house.

Once inside, she couldn't resist watching through the glass panel in the kitchen door. But they seemed to be having nothing more than a friendly chat. They even laughed together, before shaking hands and separating. Barney went back to his cruiser and drove sedately off; Toby came in the house, whistling.

"Did you tell him what he wanted to know?" she demanded, as soon as he was through the door.

"I did. And Barney said he'd be sure to put in a word for me with the DA's office."

"Really? Well, that's all right then," said Lucy, who was making a salad. "By the way, you don't need to mention my little adventure today to anyone, okay?"

Toby popped the top on a can of soda. "You mean Dad?" he asked, grinning mischievously.

"Dad, or anyone, for that matter."

"Okay, Mom." He took a long drink. "You don't need to mention that stuff I told you about Molly, either. Okay?"

He didn't wait for an answer but bounded up the stairs to his room, where he slammed the door.

After supper, Lucy and Bill settled down in the family room with their coffee to watch the news. "It's been more than a week since Prudence Pratt's lifeless body was found in her Tinker's Cove driveway and police are no closer to solving the mystery," began the announcer.

His face was bland and expressionless; it was all the same to him whether he was pitching Barbara Walter's next celebrity interview or announcing the end of the world. The report began with footage of the funeral, then turned to the "feud" between the two families. The network reran the same footage of the Stone family that had been aired so many times, ending with a new shot of the police cruiser in the driveway and Toby and Barney's conversation. In this context it didn't look like a friendly chat at all; the camera stopped running long before Barney and Toby laughed and shook hands.

Without saying a word, Bill got up and left the room.

Lucy reached for the remote, clicked off the TV and went into the kitchen. She had twenty pounds of potatoes to peel.

She set the bag on the floor next to the sink and rinsed off a few potatoes. She scraped furiously, making little bits of peel fly every which way. It just wasn't fair. Toby was no longer a suspect, the lab tests had cleared him, but that important piece of information hadn't made it into the evening news report. Probably because the police hadn't bothered to issue a statement to the press. And the media was so enraptured with the family feud story that they'd already convicted Toby without giving him the benefit of a trial.

She was so angry that the sink was filling fast with soaking potatoes. She transferred them to a pot to cook, and drained the sink, refilling it with fresh water. She was standing there, wishing the murderer's name would magically form in the water, when the phone rang.

It was Rachel Goodman, Bob's wife.

"Are you okay, Lucy? Sue told me what happened today. You two are lucky you made it home safely." She lowered her voice. "I can't believe Pam didn't have any safety equipment on that boat."

"She had life jackets."

"Come on, Lucy. Sue told me how you had to wear Adam's old kiddie-jacket."

Lucy groaned. She was never going to live this

down. "It wasn't Pam's fault. We were really stupid," she admitted. "I don't know what we were thinking. I haven't even told Bill."

"Is that wise? He's sure to find out anyway. Somebody's sure to tell him."

"The timing's not right. Bill's pretty upset about the TV news tonight. It showed Barney questioning Toby. It looked pretty incriminating."

"Oh, nobody pays attention to TV," said Rachel. "Don't let it upset you. You could try meditation, or yoga, to clear your mind."

"Actually, I'm peeling twenty pounds of potatoes. It's remarkably soothing."

"Twenty pounds! Whatever for?"

"The picnic. Sue asked me to make twenty pounds of potato salad."

"That's a lot."

"I know. I never made so much before."

"You'll need to be very careful, you know. Did you hear about that church in Gilead? Practically the whole congregation got food poisoning at a potluck supper. It was traced back to some strawberries that weren't properly washed."

Lucy glanced at the stove where two kettles full of potatoes were bubbling merrily.

"Mayonnaise," she said, groaning.

"If I were you, I'd make sure the potatoes were good and cold before I added the mayo. The eggs, too. And keep it in flat pans in the refrigerator, instead of a bowl. That way it will stay colder. And make sure it's kept on ice at the picnic."

"I will," promised Lucy. "Thanks for the advice. We don't want any more deaths in Tinker's Cove."

Chapter Twenty-two

After thinking over Rachel's warning, Lucy decided the safest course of action would be to cook the potatoes, slice them, toss them with a bit of olive oil and vinegar and chill them thoroughly in the refrigerator in a couple of plastic containers she'd bought just for the purpose. She would add the mayonnaise and hard-boiled eggs at the last minute. It would mean leaving the ball game and dashing home just before the picnic, but she wasn't going to risk the possibility of contamination. As it was, she planned to set the trays of potato salad in a bed of ice, considering the forecast of sunny skies and ninety degree temperatures.

The cupcakes were another matter. They were so full of sugar and cake-mix preservatives that she didn't have to worry about them spoiling. She brought them along when the family arrived at the softball field behind the Tinker's Cove High School. The others went ahead while she took the cupcakes over to the long tables covered with red-and-white check tablecloths set up in the shade of the building and she added them to the mouth-watering array of brownies and cookies. Several large watermelons were cooling in a tub of ice water.

Members of the volunteer fire department were already firing up the huge grills constructed out of fifty-five-gallon steel drums and the sharp chemical scent of charcoal starter filled the air. A small refrigerator had been set up temporarily behind the tables to hold hot dogs and hamburgers but there was no room for salads. A cluster of Crock-Pots filled with fragrant molasses-baked beans were connected to a power source by a spider's web of extension cords. It was going to be quite a feast.

"Where's your potato salad?" demanded Sue, planting herself in front of Lucy.

"At home. I'll get it at the top of the ninth, I promise," said Lucy, aware that she was babbling. "Rachel's got me terrified about food poisoning."

"I didn't know you murder suspects were so picky," said Sue. She was dressed for the occasion in a red-and-white striped T-shirt and a blue denim mini skirt and had added a red, white and blue ribbon to her straw hat.

"Ha, ha," replied Lucy, scowling. "I was going to tell you what a fantastic job you've done organizing all this but now I don't think I will."

"It's pretty amazing, if I do say so myself," said Sue. "I've even arranged for some surprises."

"Like what?"

"Wait and see," said Sue.

The sun was shining, balloons were bobbing in the breeze and the discordant notes of the high school band tuning their instruments were heard as Lucy made her way to the packed bleachers where Bill was saving a seat for her. Some of the players, including Toby, were out on the field, warming up, stretching their muscles and tossing balls back and forth. Groups of teenage girls clustered near the dugouts, arranging themselves to advantage in the midriff-baring outfits that were currently the rage. Younger kids were chasing each other, playing endless games of tag. The very youngest, the babies, were tucked in backpacks and strollers, or were napping on blankets spread out on the grass under the trees. It looked to Lucy like a Norman Rockwell painting.

"Who's got the best team?" she asked Bill, taking her seat beside him. "Should I root for the Bait Buckets or the Nail Bangers?"

"It's hard to say," he said, watching the Bait Bucket's pitcher warming up. "Jeff Sprague was named to the state all-star team when he was in high school, but the Nail Bangers have some solid hitters."

"I guess I'll cheer for everybody," she said, shifting over to make room for Elizabeth, who had climbed up the bleachers to join them.

"Don't bother, Mom," she said. "I'm sitting with Molly. I just want to use your sunscreen. Did you bring any?"

"Sunscreen?" This was the last thing Lucy had expected.

"Yeah, Mom. You can't be too careful. Sun causes wrinkles, you know, and I sure don't want to end up looking like you."

"Heaven forbid," said Lucy, rummaging in her bag. "Isn't Molly the girl that Toby's seeing?"

"Yeah. That's her talking to him."

Lucy abandoned her task and checked the field, where a petite blond in a pink halter top was standing beside Toby. She was shifting her weight from one side to the other, moving her hips provocatively, and had her hand on his arm.

"I work with her at the inn," continued Elizabeth. "They hooked up a few weeks ago."

"Hooked up?"

"Yeah, you know, Mom. They're, uh, a couple now."

Lucy looked at Bill, who was nodding approvingly at his son's choice. He was also smirking.

"Do you mean they're . . . ?" Lucy's eyebrows shot up. "Is that where he's been spending the night?"

"Yeah, Mom. He's twenty-one, you know."

Lucy watched as Toby and Molly parted with a kiss, he to join his teammates in the dugout and she taking a seat in the stands.

"Sunscreen, Mom?"

"Oh, right." A bit dazed, Lucy resumed her search and found the tube.

"Thanks, Mom."

Elizabeth skipped down the bleacher steps and Lucy turned to Bill.

"Did you know about this? What do you think? Isn't he awfully young?"

"Had to happen sooner or later." He shrugged philosophically and stood up as the VFW color guard began marching onto the field.

Lucy was watching Molly, but she couldn't really learn much from the back of the girl's head. She turned instead to the color guard, who looked especially sharp as they went through their paces, following Scratch Hallett's barked orders. The high school band took their places behind the color guard and then a group of singers filed onto the field.

"Who are they?' asked the woman next to Lucy. "I don't recognize them."

"Oh my goodness," said Lucy, recognizing Mike Gold's curly head of hair. "I think it's the naturists."

"At least they're wearing clothes," fumed the woman.

"They are indeed," said Lucy, placing her hand over her heart as they began singing the National Anthem.

As she sang, Lucy's eyes drifted over the scene: the brightly colored flags snapping in the breeze, the aged members of the color guard standing at attention, the red faces of the high school band members whose uniforms were too warm for the weather and the earnest faces of the chorus. Tears sprang to her eyes as they always did when she heard the Star-Spangled Banner and she was glad she was wearing sunglasses.

The singers belted out the last words of the song—"and the home of the free"—and everyone cheered and clapped and whistled as the town's oldest resident, Miss Julia Ward Howe Tilley, was driven onto the field in a red mustang convertible. The car circled the playing field and Miss Tilley waved to everyone, her pleasantly pink face wreathed with an aureole of fluffy white hair. The car stopped at home plate and she was helped from the back seat and led to a spot about fifteen feet from home plate. There Howard White presented her with a brand new ball.

"This ought to be good," muttered Bill. "I'll bet she can't throw it four feet."

"You might be in for a surprise," said Lucy.

Miss Tilley bounced the ball a few times in her age-spotted hands, leaned forward, winked at the pitcher and hurled it straight into the glove.

Everyone cheered and clapped enthusiastically as she made her way to the seat of honor behind home plate.

"Play ball!" yelled the umpire, and the game began.

First up to bat for the Nail Bangers was Eddie Culpepper, Barney's son. He was the same age as Toby and Lucy remembered the days when they were on the same Little League team. Quite a few players from that team were playing today: Tim Robbins was playing, as well as Ted's son Adam. Not Richie Goodman, he was spending the summer in Greece studying ancient ceramics. And come to think of it, Wesley Pratt had been a member of that team, too, though Lucy remembered he rarely showed up for practices. She scanned the field and the bench, but there was no sign of him.

Hearing a solid thwack she looked up just in time to see Eddie send up a high fly, which was neatly caught by Chuck Swift. That's how the first half of the inning went, with the Nail Bangers getting some promising hits, but no runs thanks to the Bait Buckets' competent fielding. After the third out the Nail Bangers took the field, with Eddie pitching. He had quite an arm, but Tim Robbins had been an all-star player when he was in high school. He sent the ball speeding through first and second base and past the fence, rounding the bases to applause and groans.

After a while Lucy lost interest in the game, simply enjoying sitting in the sun and people watching. Maybe she was crazy, but it looked to her as if folks were a little more prosperous these days. A lot of the kids had new summer clothes instead of thrift shop shorts and tees, she'd noticed some new trucks in the parking lot, and a lot of the young wives had frosted their hair—at ten dollars a foil, that was something that tended to get skipped when money was tight.

"Those naturists have really given the local economy a boost," she said.

"Why do you say that?" asked Bill.

"People have got money again. Just look around. And it can't be the lobsters, so it must be the influx of naturists."

"That, or the fireworks," said Bill, groaning as Toby hit a low ball directly to the first baseman who easily caught it.

"But there aren't any fireworks," said Lucy, puzzled.

"I mean the smuggling."

"Smuggling?"

"A lot of the lobstermen have been buying fireworks in Canada and New Hampshire and taking them down to Massachusetts. They're illegal there, they don't sell them in stores and people will pay a lot of money for them."

Lucy was horrified. "They should be illegal everywhere, you know. They're dangerous. Are Chuck and Toby doing that?"

"Have to ask them," said Bill, narrowing his eyes

and watching closely as the next runner made it to first, by a hair.

"I will," said Lucy, her eyes returning to a certain blond head of hair, "I have a lot of questions for Toby. But first I have to go get the potato salad."

Bill was on his feet, cheering as Tim Robbins whacked another homer high above the scoreboard.

Driving home, Lucy's emotions were in turmoil. Her little boy wasn't a little boy any more. He was practically setting up housekeeping with that girl. And smuggling! She hoped he wasn't involved with that. She remembered the blown-out watermelon, she believed fireworks were dangerous, you didn't have to convince her. How many people would get hurt because of the illegal fireworks the fishermen were smuggling? Kids could lose fingers, even eyes, or be horribly burned, but that didn't dissuade these fishermen from making a quick buck.

Though she had to admit, fireworks were legal in lots of places. And to be fair to the fishermen, they worked hard trying to make an honest living, but were constantly frustrated by fisheries' regulations, unpredictable weather and dramatic fluctuations in fish and shellfish populations due to disease, pollution and even natural causes. There was also a long tradition in Tinker's Cove of making money whenever and however you could, dating back to eighteenth-century mooncussers.

No wonder she couldn't make much headway in this murder investigation. Folks in this town were slippery and devious. They all had secrets. Here she'd lived next to the Pratts for years and she had no idea what their family life was really like. Had Calvin lived in terror of Pru? Had Wesley grown up simmering with resentment, even hatred for his mother? It certainly seemed likely, but she hadn't known about it. But the more she thought about it, the surer she was that Pru had been killed by either her husband or her son, or perhaps both of them working together. Just how she was going to prove this, though, was one detail she hadn't worked out yet.

Checking her watch, Lucy discovered it had only taken five minutes to make the drive from town. She'd be back in plenty of time for the picnic. She hurried into the house and went straight to the refrigerator, taking out the trays of cooked potatoes, the jars of mayonnaise and, well, where were those eggs?

She'd left an entire dozen, hard-boiled, in a bowl with a little note on top that said "NO!" in capital letters. Such notes had been Lucy's solution to the problem of snacking husbands and children, who were continually on the watch for anything edible. They had learned over the years to respect these notes, or risk incurring Lucy's wrath. That wrath was building, as she scrabbled around the shelves, shoving pickle jars and plastic containers aside in a frantic search for the eggs. All she turned up, was the note, which had landed on top of the crisper.

What was she going to do? She was known for her potato salad, everybody loved it. And it always had eggs. The eggs gave it a lovely golden tint, and added a nice flavor note. Damn it! She wanted the eggs.

She looked at the clock. She had time, if she hurried. But where could she get eggs? The stores were closed for the holiday, everybody was at the game, including Ellie. But not Bitsy Parsons, she realized. Members of the Revelation Congregation didn't celebrate holidays. Maybe she could call Bitsy and ask her to get a dozen eggs cooking. They'd probably be almost done by the time she got there. It was worth a try, she thought, consulting the phone book. But when she dialed, there was no answer.

No matter, she decided. Bitsy was probably outside tending to her little flower and egg stand. She'd leave a message. It was worth a try, anyway, she decided, packing up the trays of undressed potato salad. If worse came to worst, she could serve one tray plain while she cooked up the eggs in the home ec room at the school and dressed the second tray.

She was not going to get frantic about this, she told herself as she headed over to Bitsy's. It was only potato salad. It wasn't a life and death situation. And the drive to Bitsy's was beautiful, taking her along Shore Road with its incredible ocean views. Bitsy had certainly lucked out when she came into possession of the family property. It was perched on a rocky bluff high above the water and she had been heard to joke that on a clear day she could see straight to England. She couldn't, of course, but on certain crystal-clear days it seemed a distinct possibility.

Lucy took a deep breath of the ozone-scented air when she got out of the car, then leaned back in and honked the horn.

"Coming, coming!" called Bitsy, hurrying out of the house and drying her hands on a dish towel. She stopped in her tracks when she saw Lucy.

"Did you get my message?" asked Lucy, running towards her.

Bitsy stepped back. "Message?"

"On your answering machine," said Lucy, impatiently.

"No. I didn't notice," said Bitsy, blinking nervously.

"Well, I need eggs and I need 'em fast. Any chance you could hard-boil a dozen for me, while I wait?"

Bitsy looked puzzled. "Are you really here for eggs, Lucy Stone?"

"Of course," said Lucy, growing frustrated at Bitsy's dallying. "Why do you think I came all the way out here on the Fourth of July?" Then Lucy remembered that Bitsy was reputed to have a crush on Calvin Pratt. Could he possibly be paying her a call? Is that why Bitsy seemed so nervous? "Listen," said Lucy, "I know all about . . ."

"I'll get the water started," said Bitsy, cutting her off. "You go on and get the eggs."

That was all Lucy had to hear, she was off and running for the hen house. She yanked the door open, startling a few chickens who rushed out the little door for the safety of the run. Only one or two stubbornly broody hens remained on their nests and Lucy decided she would avoid them. There were plenty of eggs in the other nesting boxes. One on the bottom, in fact, seemed to have nearly a dozen. She bent down, not looking up when she heard Bitsy enter.

"Are you finding enough?" asked Bitsy.

Lucy turned to answer, but never had a chance to speak. She was out like a light before she knew what hit her.

Chapter Twenty-three

Lucy didn't want to wake up, so she kept her eyes screwed tight shut. She had a pounding headache and if she could only go back to sleep she wouldn't have to deal with it. Or the pain in her shoulders and arms. The arm she was lying on was asleep and if she moved it, if she rolled over onto her other side, she might be able to get back to sleep. But she couldn't move her arms. That's when she realized she was tied up.

Eyes wide open, she discovered she was lying in the sawdust litter on the floor of Bitsy's chicken house. The chickens didn't seem to mind this strange creature in their midst; one was perching on her foot. Lucy shook her foot as well as she could, considering a rope was neatly looped around both ankles and dislodged the bird, who ruffled its feathers in protest before hopping up onto a perch. The occasional clucks of the chickens had an oddly soothing effect, but Lucy didn't want to be soothed. She needed to get out of there before whoever did this to her came back to finish the job.

Who had done it? Had Bitsy conked her on the head and tied her up? It seemed impossible. Bitsy was a little homebody who loved her chickens. She was a faithful member of the Revelation Congregation, a sect that Lucy did not necessarily agree with on doctrinal points but which held its members to the highest standards of conduct. Members didn't smoke, drink, dance or play cards, but they apparently did conk people on the head and tie them up. Lucy couldn't believe it. Just thinking about it made her headache worse.

She had to get out of here and figure out what was going on. Maybe it wasn't Bitsy who had tied her up; maybe it was Calvin or Wesley, or some maniacal stranger who might also have attacked Bitsy. Who might even be doing awful things to Bitsy at this very moment. And who might be saving her for last.

Lucy struggled against the ropes, straining against them in hopes of loosening the knots. She couldn't tie a knot to save her soul, not one that would actually hold against persistent pressure, and she hoped whoever had trussed her up like this was similarly challenged. It hurt her sore muscles to tense them and her efforts to twist loose from the ropes around her wrists seemed only to have the opposite effect of tightening them, and rubbing her skin raw. She let out a huge sigh of frustration and realized her mistake when a cloud of sawdust rose and settled back on her face, causing her to sneeze furiously. She knew she had to get control of herself, so she concentrated on her breathing and gradually her heart stopped racing and the sneezing was replaced with persistently running eyes and nose she could do nothing about.

When she heard the door opening her heart began pounding with fear, a reaction that didn't subside when she recognized Bitsy, holding an evil little hatchet. It was so sharp that the edge gleamed, despite the deepening gloom. How long had she been here, she wondered. From the lengthening shadows she guessed it must be close to seven o'clock.

"Oh, dear," said Bitsy, standing before her and waving the hatchet. "Oh, dear. Oh, dear."

"Could you do something for me?" asked Lucy, struggling to keep her voice conversational. "Could you untie me?"

"Oh, silly me," exlaimed Bitsy. "What was I thinking?"

She immediately fell to her knees and began sawing away at the ropes. Lucy sat up, wiggling her toes and turning her feet in circles to restore the circulation and gently rubbing her tender wrists. She wanted to question Bitsy about what happened but hesitated for fear of setting off some sort of psychological fit. She was beginning to doubt Bitsy's sanity. And she still had that hatchet.

"I'm terribly sorry, Lucy. This was a terrible thing to do," said Bitsy. "I just panicked when I saw you, but now I see the error of my ways. I spent the afternoon praying and God has told me what I must do."

"And what's that?" asked Lucy in a small voice, keeping a wary eye on that hatchet.

"I have to accept responsibility for what I did. I have to go to the police and confess. Will you take me, Lucy?"

"Take you to the police station? That's not necessary, Bitsy," babbled Lucy, giddy with relief. "We all make mistakes. I'm perfectly happy to forget about this. I don't want to press charges."

"You didn't know?" asked Bitsy, looking down at the blade. "You didn't figure it out?"

"I just came for some eggs," said Lucy. "Figure what out?"

"That I killed Prudence Pratt."

The confession hit Lucy like a sledgehammer.

"*You* killed Pru?" she stammered.

Bitsy fell to her knees, facing Lucy, and letting the hatchet drop to the floor beside her. "If only I could do it over and take it all back," she said, sobbing. "I just lost my temper—I literally saw red—and when it was over, Prudence was lying there in the driveway. Dead."

Lucy reached out and patted her hand. "I'm sure it wasn't entirely your fault. Pru had a way of upsetting people."

"Oh, I was upset. I've struggled with this for years, you know, and I've struggled to forgive her. Sometimes I even thought I was making progress. I'd see her and Calvin sitting together in church and I'd say to myself, well she's the one he chose. He married her, not me, and that's the way it is. There was absolutely nothing I could do about it, even though it was very painful to see the way she treated him. But he chose her and they were married and marriage is forever in the sight of the Lord and that's all there is to it. So I prayed and prayed for acceptance and to make my life worthy in other ways. Without Calvin. And one day when I was praying it came to me, a revelation, that I should raise chickens. I should forget about pining for Calvin who I could never have and raise chickens instead. So I did. I took all the love I had for Calvin and poured it out into my chickens. My beautiful chickens."

Bitsy gestured with her hand and oddly enough, Lucy saw that at least half a dozen of the birds had gathered around Bitsy, as if listening to every word.

"They're amazing chickens," said Lucy.

"Oh, thank you, Lucy. I certainly think so." Bitsy patted the nearest chicken on the head, and stroked its feathery breast. "People tend to underrate chickens, but I've found that my birds are quite intelligent and, well, empathetic. They seem to sense when I'm troubled and try to comfort me. They'll lay extra big eggs, for example. And that clucking noise they make is so lovely. I've tape recorded it and play it when I have trouble sleeping."

"What a good idea," said Lucy, utterly convinced that Bitsy had lost her marbles. Every single one.

"I've always fed my chickens extremely well. Not just feed from the store but cracked grains for variety and lots of greens. They love them and it makes the egg yolks so yellow, and keeps the birds healthy, too. Some friends told me I should enter them in the county fair, so a few years ago, I did. And one of my birds won second place. And I really tried to be happy with second place even though Prudence's chicken won first place. I know envy is wrong, we're not supposed to covet our neighbor's chickens and I didn't. I honestly didn't because Pru's chickens are mean and don't have the same loving personalities that my chickens have. And I'd rather have a sensitive second-place chicken than a mean first-place chicken that pecks at all the other chickens."

"Absolutely right," agreed Lucy, observing the

little group of chickens that were clustered around Bitsy. A couple were even sitting in her lap.

"Then last year, one of my hens produced a clutch of chicks, and one of them was really eye-catching right from the beginning. She was a Buff Orpington, and that's a handsome breed to start with. They're kind of strawberry blond. Very pretty chickies. And this one was really kind of a Miss America of chickens. Just perfect. Everything you want in a Buff Orpington. Breasty and fluffy and pretty, with clear, bright eyes and a curvaceous beak and a coquettish little comb. So pretty. I named her Mildred, after my cousin who was a Miss Maine runner-up in 1982."

Lucy looked around the hen house, trying to identify Mildred, but in the growing gloom all the chickens looked pretty much the same to her.

"Now I know that saying about not counting your chickens before they're hatched and I believe it, I mean, there's a lot that can happen to a chicken. Dogs. Skunks. Raccoons. Disease. But I must say that Mildred seemed to thrive. She was a delight, and I was beginning to hope that she'd win the blue ribbon at the fair. I was just hoping, you understand, and taking good care of her. And praying. Not that she would win, because that would be wrong, but only that she'd have a happy, fulfilling life."

"Which one is Mildred?" asked Lucy.

"Bitsy's face whitened and she pressed her lips together. "She's gone."

"I'm so sorry," said Lucy.

"Prudence stole her. I didn't notice she was gone right away, because I was out all morning getting names on the petition about those nudists and then I stayed in town for the noontime prayer service. I had some nice salad greens for the hens—Dot Kirwan has the produce man at the market save them for me—so I went out to give them their treat and that's when I discovered Mildred was gone. I went over to my neighbors to ask if she'd seen anyone and she described Prudence's car, and then I remembered she left the petition drive when I got there and she wasn't at noontime prayer either. So I went over to her house and challenged her and she didn't even bother to deny it. She just looked at me in that mean way she has and asked if I'd like to have some lunch. She'd just cooked up some chicken fricassee, she said, and I knew she was referring to Mildred."

"Oh, dear."

"That's when I saw red. Everything went red. And I got in my truck and she was standing there in front of me, smacking her lips over the chicken hash and I just put my foot down on the pedal and the truck vroomed ahead and she was there and then she wasn't."

Lucy didn't know what to say so she simply reached out her hand to pat Bitsy's knee.

"Will you take me to the police station now, Lucy?"

"Whenever you're ready."

"I'm ready," said Bitsy.

Chapter Twenty-four

Bitsy seemed perfectly at peace sitting in the passenger seat but Lucy's mind was a whirl of ifs, buts and maybes. Maybe Bitsy didn't really kill Pru, maybe it had all been an insane delusion. Perhaps she'd wished so hard for it to happen that she'd actually convinced herself she'd done it. Some sort of guilt process. Lucy didn't know much about psychology but she knew even the soundest mind could play tricks. And she wasn't convinced that Bitsy was actually sane. Maybe she could plead insanity and go away for a nice, long rest somewhere.

It was amazing the stuff a good lawyer could come up with. She'd have to make sure Bitsy had a lawyer. Somebody who'd really fight for her. Who knows, maybe she could avoid a trial altogether by pleading guilty to a reduced charge of manslaughter? Or maybe she could get off entirely by arguing that it was justifiable homicide, considering the callous way Pru had murdered Mildred. It was just one of many mean things Pru had done and there were plenty of people in town who could testify to similar incidents. Bitsy was popular, too, and could certainly produce plenty of character witnesses.

"Try not to worry," said Lucy. "I'm sure things will work out."

"I'm not worried," said Bitsy. "I know that whatever happens the good Lord will take care of me. I'm truly sorry for what I did and I know he'll forgive me and that's all that really matters."

"Right," said Lucy, wondering if Bitsy had actually ever seen the inside of the women's wing at the county jail and if she knew what was in store for here. Lucy had visited on several occasions and she'd found the experience difficult. There was something terrifying about the way everyone was treated so impersonally. "Processed" they called it, whether you were being admitted as an inmate or a visitor. Though it was infinitely better to be processed as a visitor because that only involved a quick pat down, a walk through a scanner and a handbag search instead of a humiliating full-body examination. That and the fact that even though all the doors closed with a final-sounding clang, you knew you'd be able to leave.

Lucy felt absolutely horrible when they reached the police station and she turned into the parking lot. She hoped Bitsy wouldn't have to spend time in the county jail—maybe they would release her on bail or even her own personal recognizance. She was certainly no threat to the community and wasn't a flight risk, either. On the contrary, she seemed eager to confess and receive her punishment.

"Thank you, Lucy," she said, her face radiant in the glow of the street lamp. "I'm sorry for any distress I caused you and I want you to know that today you were truly God's instrument."

Somehow that didn't make Lucy feel any better

as she accompanied Bitsy into the police station lobby. A uniformed officer she didn't recognize was sitting behind a counter, protected by a thick sheet of Plexiglas with a small opening that allowed a visitor to present documents or identification. The only access from the lobby to the offices beyond was through a forbidding, metal-plated door. It had always irritated Lucy, who wondered exactly what threat the Tinker's Cove police department believed required such an extreme level of security.

"What can I do for you ladies?" asked the officer, speaking through a microphone. His voice echoed.

"I'm here to make a confession," whispered Bitsy. "I murdered Prudence Pratt."

"You'll have to speak up," said the officer, looking like a goldfish in a tank.

"I murdered Prudence Pratt," yelled Bitsy. "I want to turn myself in."

"Sure you do," said the officer, looking extremely doubtful. "Tell you what, we're kind of busy right now with some holiday merry-makers, so why don't you go on home and come back tomorrow?"

"I'm a murderer," said Bitsy, indignantly. "I'm not leaving until I talk to somebody. I should be locked up."

"If you say so," replied the officer, yawning. "You can take a seat on the bench there but I can't guarantee anybody will get to you anytime soon."

"That's all right," said Bitsy. "We'll wait."

Once they sat down, however, Bitsy's resolve seemed to crumple. She began crying quietly, carrying on a whispered, prayerful dialog with God. Lucy felt excluded and useless, unable to offer comfort, but didn't want to leave Bitsy all alone, either. She shifted restlessly on her chair, worried that Bill and the kids would be missing her. She checked the clock on the wall and discovered with a shock that it was almost eight o'clock. Poor Bill must be frantic with worry. She wanted to get out of there and rejoin her family.

Suddenly ashamed of her selfishness, she patted Bitsy's hand.

"Do you have someone to take care of your chickens? Do you want me to do it?"

"That's sweet of you, Lucy, but Ellie Sykes said she'd do it."

"Ellie? When did you talk to Ellie?"

"It was the last thing I did before I went out to the coop and untied you." Bitsy paused. "I know I apologized before, but I'm so sorry I hit you on the head like that. There was no excuse for it, truly. I don't know what I was thinking. And tying you up like that. It must have been horribly uncomfortable. And the hatchet. I can understand why you were so frightened, though of course I only intended to use it to cut the ropes. I never meant to harm you."

Lucy happened to glance at the officer, noticing his surprised expression. He was talking on the phone.

"I think the detective is free to talk to you now," he said. "Come on through."

A buzzer sounded and Lucy was able to open the heavy metal door leading to the bowels of the station. The officer met them on the other side.

"One at a time," he said, pointing to Lucy. "You can wait outside."

Then, before she could even wish Bitsy luck, the door slammed in her face.

Lucy hesitated a minute, standing uncertainly in the lobby, then decided to make her escape while she could. If the cops wanted to talk to her they knew where she lived. She was going to salvage what she could of the holiday.

A pungent smell assailed her when she opened the car doors—the potatoes. Sitting in the hot car at Bitsy's, not to mention the long wait at the police station, hadn't done them a bit of good. There was nothing to do but throw them out, all twenty pounds. Lucy drove the car over to the dumpster and chucked them in, then opened all the doors and windows to let the car air out. While she waited she called home on her cell phone. There was no answer—everyone must still be at the picnic.

The party was still going strong when Lucy arrived at the field overlooking the harbor. A local rock group was in the bandstand playing oldies. Some people were dancing, especially the kids, while others sat on lawn chairs and blankets listening to the music. Lucy spotted Bill chatting with Rachel and Bob, but before she could join them she was confronted by Sue.

"Lucy Stone, you promised me twenty pounds of potato salad. What happened?"

"I got tied up, solving the murder," said Lucy. "It was Bitsy."

"Right," laughed Sue. "Tell me another."

"Later," said Lucy, spotting Bill coming towards her. "I've got some explaining to do to my husband."

She ran up to Bill and threw her arms around him, practically knocking him off his feet.

"Whoa, Lucy," he said. "What's this all about."

"I'm safe. Everything's okay."

Bill looked at her sideways. "Of course you are."

"Don't tell me you didn't realize I was gone?"

"I thought you were helping out in the kitchen."

Lucy was indignant. "I was held captive in a chicken coop."

Bill was starting to speak when a huge explosion seemed to rock the very earth they were standing on. It was followed by shrieking rockets that soared high into the sky before exploding into streams of shimmering light. Shock quickly turned to delight and everyone cheered as dazzling chrysanthemum bursts of red and yellow filled the sky. They oohed and aahed as showers of whirling pinwheels danced high above their heads. The explosions came faster and faster, filling the sky with one beautiful display after another. It was the best fireworks show anyone had ever seen. It was incredible and it went on and on until Lucy began to wonder if it would ever stop.

"I didn't think they were going to have fireworks this year," said Bill, when the last rocket fizzled out and the sky was once again dark.

"They weren't," said Lucy, wondering exactly who had set them off and what the repercussions would be.

It wouldn't take long—police sirens could already be heard.

Chapter Twenty-five

The phone was ringing when they got home and Lucy was pretty sure she knew who it was. Her hunch was confirmed when she picked up the receiver.

"This is Lieutenant Horowitz," began the deep voice at the other end of the line. "I understand you were the victim of an assault earlier today and I'd like to talk to you about it as soon as possible, preferably tonight."

"Uh, sure," began Lucy, aware of her civic duty.

"I can be there in ten minutes."

"Uh, I don't think so," said Lucy, having second thoughts. She didn't want to add to Bitsy's woes. "I don't want to be interviewed."

"Bitsy Howell has confessed to assaulting you in her chicken coop."

"There must be some misunderstanding," said Lucy, firmly. "There was no assault."

"Ms. Howell claims she hit you on the head with a feed bucket rendering you unconscious. She then proceeded to tie you up and left you unattended for several hours, according to her statement, given willingly and freely and under no duress whatsoever."

"I can't imagine why she's saying that."

"Mrs. Stone, I'd like to remind you that it is your duty as a citizen to report a crime to the proper authorities."

"I understand that."

"If you refuse to press charges we will be unable to prosecute this case. Have you thought of that?"

"Actually, I have."

"Am I to understand that you are refusing to press charges?"

"That's right," said Lucy, smiling as she hung up the receiver.

The phone rang again almost immediately. It was Ted.

"Lucy, can you come back to the paper and write a first-hand account of how you solved the murder? And don't forget to include Bitsy's attack in the chicken house."

Lucy considered. She wanted to get back to work, but there was no way she was going to go public about the episode in the chicken house. She knew all too well what it was like to be the subject of media scrutiny and she wasn't going to inflict that on Bitsy. She didn't want to add fuel to the prosecutor's case, either. She wouldn't lie under oath, if it came to that, but she wasn't going to volunteer damaging information. Pru Pratt had caused enough grief in Tinker's Cove and Lucy was determined to end it.

"I'll come back, but I won't write about Bitsy."

There was a long pause.

"That's okay," said Ted, "There's plenty of other

stuff you can work on like the big fireworks explosion on Calvin's boat."

"The fireworks were from Calvin's boat?"

"Yeah," said Ted, chuckling. "He was desperate to get them to Massachusetts before the holiday so he and Wesley left yesterday as soon as the funeral was over. They only got a few miles before the bilge pump conked out and the engine was flooded. The current was pretty strong and pushed them back towards the cove, which was the last thing they wanted, of course. They were trying to solder a connection in the pump when they set off the fireworks by mistake. It was a heck of a show."

"People were saying it was the best they'd ever seen," said Lucy.

"Well, it looks as if they wiped out the purple-spotted lichen. The boat was just off the point when the fireworks started going off. Calvin and Wesley are in big trouble. The state environmental police are pressing charges and I'll bet Franke and the APTC are going to sue them, too."

"That doesn't seem fair. A lot of people are probably going to be grateful to Calvin and Wesley."

"What do you mean?"

"Well, if the lichen's gone, there's no reason the town can't have fireworks next year."

"That's right," said Ted.

"It gets better," said Lucy. "If the Quisset Point colony is gone, that means the only remaining lichen is at Blueberry Pond, and that means APTC will be making sure the naturists don't disturb it. At this rate, Calvin and Wesley will probably be named grand marshalls of the parade next year."

"I wouldn't count on that, Lucy. Don't forget

Wesley is still facing assault charges and Calvin has confessed to killing his wife."

"Calvin's confessed? But what about Bitsy?"

"That's exactly it. Barney told me that when Calvin heard about Bitsy's confession he went crazy, jumping up and down and screaming that he did it. And people say chivalry is dead."

"So who are they going to charge?"

"It's anybody's guess right now. But I can tell you that Horowitz is fit to be tied. It doesn't look as if he's going to be able to make a case against either of them." Ted paused. "There's a lot going on Lucy. I really need you. Will you come back?"

"See you tomorrow, Ted," she said.

"Don't be late."

Lucy smiled to herself. Some things never changed.

She was rinsing off the glasses and mugs that had collected in the kitchen sink when Toby came in the kitchen and opened the refrigerator, looking for a snack.

"Toby, I heard Calvin and Wesley had some trouble with their bilge pump. Do you know anything about it?"

"Poor maintenance, Mom," he said, lips twitching as he reached for the orange juice. "It's amazing how something like that can blow up in your face."

"Very funny," said Lucy, shaking her head.

She went into the family room to join Bill, who was watching the holiday shows on TV with Sara and Zoe. They were all sitting on the couch, and Lucy squeezed in between the girls just as the Boston Pops began playing the final section of the "1812 Overture" complete with church bells ringing and howitzers firing. The music ended and the fireworks were beginning when Elizabeth came in the room.

"Shut off the TV," she said. "I've got a surprise."

Bill clicked the remote and the TV fell silent.

"Promise you'll keep your voices low and soft. No shrieking, okay? He's little and his ears are sensitive."

"Whose ears?" asked Lucy, but Elizabeth had dashed out of the room.

When she returned she was accompanied by Toby and Molly. Molly was holding a squirming bundle wrapped in a towel.

"Mom, Dad, everybody," said Toby, "this is Molly. She's got something for you."

Molly placed the towel in Lucy's lap and unfolded it, revealing a wiggly little chocolate lab puppy.

"My dog had puppies a couple of months ago. When I heard about Kudo I told Toby you could have one, if you want it that is."

"We made sure it was a boy, like Kudo," said Elizabeth. "We thought you'd like that best."

"He's adorable," cooed Lucy as the puppy squirmed against her and licked her face. "What a cutie. Of course we want him."

"That's a cute puppy, sure enough," said Bill, "but it's no he."

Lucy lifted the dog up to see for herself. Bill was right.

"Goodness, Elizabeth. All the time you've been spending down at the pond with the naturists, and you still can't tell the difference?"

Epilogue

Things hadn't been going well on the home-front, that was for sure. For one thing, Mom just hadn't been her sweet self lately. Instead of settling down with the family and opening the milk bar, the way she used to, she'd suddenly become restless. Up and down. A pup would no sooner find her spot and start snacking when Mom would be up and on the move, leaving her and the others to dangle hopefully for a minute or two before tumbling to the floor with a thud. And there'd been no restorative, healing licks, either. Mom was too busy pawing at the door, demanding freedom, to attend to the puppies' needs.

It was nothing at all like those first blissful days when they all curled up together for endless naps and cuddles with plenty of rich, warm milk to drink. Now, even if Mom did decide to catch a rare nap things had suddenly gotten very crowded indeed. And the competition was fierce with everybody pushing and shoving and nipping at each other. No, things had definitely changed.

In some ways, it was probably better. It was fun to chase her own tail and even more fun to chase somebody else's tail. And then there was wrestling, rolling around with her brothers and sisters and attempting to pin the other one down. Though even if she succeeded she only had the advantage for a moment before they were off and running again.

She'd finally gotten used to the routine—naps and meals and playtime—when it all changed again. She was plucked out of the pen, taken away from the gang. Without any warning, she found herself held tightly by one of those large, noisy, pink creatures. Its voice was so loud and piercing it hurt her ears. And then she was stuck in a box, all by herself. It was very upsetting and she'd started to cry.

That's when they had all descended on her—a whole litter of the huge, hairless beasts. All talking and passing her back and forth like she was a hot potato. And when she'd had that little accident, oh, the shrieks! All she wanted was to go back to Mom and the gang.

She was resigned to misery when she was picked up again and carried to one of the enormous creatures. This one was different. She felt soft, kind of like Mom. And her voice was quiet. She didn't shriek. Maybe there'd be milk, she thought, licking hopefully at the creature's face. There wasn't, but it was all right. Suddenly tired, she yawned, then curled up in the creature's lap and went to sleep.

Libby, Liberty, had found her new home.

Please turn the page for
an exciting sneak peek of
Leslie Meier's
NEW YEAR'S EVE MURDER!

Chapter 1

WIN A WINTER MAKE-OVER for YOU and YOUR MOM!

A solid month of baking and chasing bargains and wrapping and decorating and secret keeping and it all came down to this: a pile of torn wrapping paper under the Christmas tree, holiday plates scattered with crumbs and half-eaten cookies, punch cups filmed with egg nog, and sitting on one end table, a candy dish holding a pristine and untouched pyramid of ribbon candy. And then there was that awful letter. Why did it have to come on Christmas Eve, just in time to cast a pall over the holiday?

Lucy Stone shook out a plastic trash bag and bent down to scoop up the torn paper, only to discover the family's pet puppy, Libby, had made herself a nest of Christmas wrap and was curled up, sound asleep. No wonder. With all the excitement of opening presents, tantalizing cooking smells, and people coming and going, it had been an exhausting day for her.

Lucy stroked the little Lab's silky head and decided to leave the mess a bit longer. Best to let sleeping dogs lie, especially if the sleeping dog in question happened to be seven months old and increasingly given to bouts of manic activity, which included chewing shoes and furniture. She turned instead to the coffee table and started stacking plates and cups, then sat down on the sofa as a wave of exhaustion overtook her. It had been a long day. Zoe, her youngest at only eight years old, had awoken early and roused the rest of the house. Sara, fourteen, hadn't minded, but their older sister, Elizabeth, protested the early hour. She was home for Christmas break from Chamberlain College in Boston, where she was a sophomore, and had stayed out late on Christmas Eve catching up with her old high school friends.

She had finally given in and gotten out of bed after a half-hour of coaxing, and the Christmas morning orgy of exchanging presents had begun. What had they been thinking, wondered Lucy, dreading the credit card bills that would arrive as certainly as snow in January. She and Bill had really gone overboard this year, buying skis for Elizabeth and high-tech ice skates for Sara and Zoe. When their oldest child, Toby, arrived later in the day with his fiancée Molly, they had presented him with a snow board and her with a luxurious cashmere sweater. And those were only the big presents. There had been all the budget-busting books, CDs, video games, sweaters, and pajamas, right on down to the chocolate oranges and lip balm tucked in the toe of each bulging Christmas stocking.

It all must have cost a fortune, guessed Lucy, who had lost track of the actual total sometime around December 18. Oh, sure, it had been great fun for the hour or two it took to open all the presents, but those credit card balances would linger for months. And what was she going to do about the letter? It was from the financial aid office at Chamberlain College advising her that they had reviewed the family's finances and had cut Elizabeth's aid package by ten thousand dollars. That meant they had to come up with the money or Elizabeth would have to leave school.

She guiltily fingered the diamond studs Bill had surprised her with, saying they were a reward for all the Christmases he was only able to give her a handmade coupon book of promises after they finished buying presents for the kids. It was a lovely gesture, but she knew they couldn't really afford it. She wasn't even sure he had work lined up for the winter. The economy was supposed to be recovering, but like many in the little town of Tinker's Cove, Maine, Bill was self-employed. Over the years he had built a solid reputation as a restoration carpenter, renovating rundown older homes for city folks who wanted a vacation home by the store. Last year, when the stock market was soaring he had made plenty of money, which was probably why the financial aid office had decided they could afford to pay more. But even last year, Bill's best year ever, they had struggled to meet Elizabeth's college expenses. Now that the Dow was hovering well below its former dizzying heights, Bill's earnings had dropped dramatically. The economists called it a "correction" but it had been a disaster for vacation communities like Tinker's Cove as the big city lawyers and bankers and stockbrokers who were the mainstay of the second home market found themselves without the fat bonus checks they were counting on.

The sensible course would be to return the earrings to the store for a refund, but that was out of the question. She remembered how excited Bill had been when he gave her the little box and how pleased he'd been at her surprised reaction when she opened it and found the sparkling earrings. All she'd hoped for, really, was a new flannel nightgown. But now she had diamond earrings. He'd also written a private note, apologizing for all the years he'd taken her for granted, like one of the kids. But they had surprised her, too, with their presents. Toby and Molly had given her a pair of buttery soft kid gloves, Elizabeth had presented her with a jar of luxurious lavender body lotion from a trendy Newbury Street shop, Sara had put together a tape of her favorite songs to play in the car and Zoe had found a calendar with photos of Labrador puppies—all presents that had delighted her because they showed a lot of thought.

So how was she repaying them for all their love and thoughtfulness? In just a short while she was going off to New York City with Elizabeth and leaving the rest of the family to fend for themselves. Really abandoning them for their entire Christmas vacation. The bags were packed and standing ready in the hallway; they would leave as soon as Elizabeth returned from saying good-bye to her friends.

She had been thrilled when Elizabeth announced she had entered a *Jolie* magazine contest and won winter makeovers for herself and her mother. Not only was she enormously proud of her clever daughter but at first she was excited at the prospect of the makeover itself. What working mother wouldn't enjoy a few days of luxurious pampering? But now she wished she could convert the prize into cash. Besides, how would Bill manage without her? What would Zoe and Sara do all day? Watch TV? That was no way to spend a week-long holiday from school.

Also, worried Lucy, checking to make sure the earrings were still firmly in place, what if the supposedly "all-expense paid" makeover wasn't quite as "all-expense paid" as promised? Traveling was expensive—there were always those little incidentals, like tips and magazines and mints and even airplane meals now that you had to buy them, that added up. What if it turned out to be like those "free" facials at the make-up counter where the sales associates pressured you to buy a lot of expensive products that you would never use again?

Lucy sighed. To tell the truth, she was a little uneasy about the whole concept of being made-over. There was nothing the matter with her. She stood up and looked at her reflection in the mirror that hung over the couch. She looked fine. Not perfect, of course. She was getting a few crow's-feet, there were a few gray hairs and that stubborn five pounds she couldn't seem to lose, but she was neat and trim and could still fit in the sparkly Christmas sweatshirt the kids had given her years ago. And since she only wore it a few times a year it still looked as festive as ever.

Now that she was actually giving it a critical eye, she could understand why her friend Sue always teased her about the sweatshirt. It was boxy and didn't do a thing for her figure. Furthermore, it was the height of kitsch, featuring a bright green Christmas tree decorated with sequins, beads, and bows. Not the least bit sophisticated.

She sighed. She hadn't always been a country mouse; she'd grown up in a suburb of the city and had made frequent forays with her mother, and later with her friends, to shop, see a show, or visit a museum. It would be fun to go back to New York, especially since she hadn't been in years. And she was looking forward to a reunion with her old college buddy, Samantha Blackwell. They had been faithful correspondents through the years, apparently both stuck in the days when people wrote letters, but had never gotten in the habit of telephoning each other. Caught in busy lives with numerous responsibilities, they'd never been able to visit each other, despite numerous attempts. Lucy had married right out of college and moved to Maine, where she started a family and worked as a part-time reporter for the local weekly newspaper. Sam had been one of a handful of pioneering women accepted to study for the ministry at Union Theological Seminary and had promptly fulfilled the reluctant admission officer's misgivings by promptly dropping out when she met her lawyer husband, Brad. She now worked for the International AIDS Foundation, and Lucy couldn't wait to see her and renew their friendship.

Which reminded her, she hadn't had a chance yet today to call her friends to wish them a Merry Christmas. That was one holiday tradition she really enjoyed. She sat back down on the couch and reached for the phone, dialing Sue Finch's number.

"Are you all ready for the trip?" asked Sue, after they'd gotten the formalities out.

"All packed and ready to go."

"I hope you left room in your suitcase so you can take advantage of the after-Christmas sales. Sidra says they're fabulous." Sidra, Sue's daughter, lived in New York with her husband, Geoff Rumford, and was an assistant producer of the *Norah!* TV show.

"No sales for me." Lucy didn't want the whole town to know about the family's finances, so she prevaricated. "I think I'll be too busy."

"They can't keep you busy every minute."

"I think they intend to. We're catching the ten o'clock flight out of Portland tonight so we can make a fashion show breakfast first thing tomorrow morning, then there are numerous expert consultations, a spa afternoon, photo sessions and interviews, I'm worried I won't even have time to see Sam." She paused. "And if I do have some free time, I'm planning to visit some museums like the Met and MOMA. . . ."

Sue, who lived to shop, couldn't believe this heresy. "But what about Bloomingdale's?"

"I've spent quite enough on Christmas as it is," said Lucy. "I've got to economize."

"Sure," acknowledged Sue, "but you have to spend money to save it."

It was exactly this sort of logic that had led her into spending too much on Christmas in the first place, thought Lucy, but she wasn't about to argue. "If you say so," she laughed. "I've got to go. Someone's on call waiting."

It was Rachel Goodman, another member of the group of four that met for breakfast each week at Jake's Donut Shack.

"Did Santa bring you anything special?" asked Rachel.

Something in her tone made Lucy suspicious. "How did you know?"

"Bill asked me to help pick them out. Do you like them?"

"I love them, but he shouldn't have spent so much."

"I told him you'd be happy with pearls," said Rachel, "but he insisted on the diamonds. He was really cute about it. He said he wanted you to wear them in New York."

This was a whole new side of Bill that Lucy wasn't familiar with. She wasn't sure she could get used to this sensitive, considerate Bill. She wondered fleetingly if he was having some sort of midlife crisis.

"Aw, gee, you know I'm really having second thoughts about this trip."

"Of course you are."

Lucy wondered if Rachel knew more than she was letting on. "What do you mean?"

"Haven't you heard? There's this awful flu going around."

"What flu?"

"It's an epidemic. I read about it in the *New York Times*. They're advising everyone to avoid crowds and wash their hands frequently."

"How do you avoid crowds in a city?"

"I don't know, but I think you should try. Flu can be serious. It kills thousands of people every year."

"That was 1918," scoffed Lucy.

"Laugh if you want. I'm only trying to help."

Lucy immediately felt terrible for hurting Rachel's feelings. "I know, and I appreciate it. I really do."

"Promise you'll take precautions?"

"Sure. And thanks for the warning."

She was wondering whether she should buy some disinfectant wipes as she dialed Pam's number. Pam, also a member of the breakfast group, was married to Lucy's boss at the newspaper, Ted

Stillings, and was a great believer in natural remedies.

"Disinfectant wipes? Are you crazy? That sort of thing just weakens your immune system."

"Rachel says there's a flu epidemic and I have to watch out for germs."

"How are you supposed to do that? The world is full of millions, billions, zillions of germs that are invisible to the human eye. If Mother Nature intended us to watch out for them, don't you think she would have made them bigger, like mosquitoes or spiders?"

It was a frightening picture. "I never thought of that."

"Well, trust me, Mother Nature did. She gave you a fabulous immune system to protect the Good Body." That's how Pam pronounced it, with capital letter emphasis. "Your immune system worries about the germs so you don't have to."

"If that's true, how come so many people get sick?"

"People get sick because they abuse their bodies. They pollute their Good Bodies with empty calories and preservatives instead of natural whole foods, they don't get enough sleep, they don't take care of themselves." Pam huffed. "You have to help Mother Nature. She can't do it all, you know."

"Okay. How do I help her?"

"One thing you can do is take vitamin C. It gives the immune system a boost. That's what I'd do if I were you, especially since you're going into a new environment that might stress your organic equilibrium."

Lucy was picturing a dusty brown bottle in the back of the medicine cabinet. "You know, I think

I've got some. Now I just have to remember to take it. It looks like we're going to be pretty busy with this makeover."

"Don't let them go crazy with eye shadow and stuff," advised Pam.

"Is it bad for you?"

"It's probably a germ farm, especially if they use it on more than one person, but that isn't what I was thinking about." She paused, choosing her words. "You're beautiful already. You don't need that stuff."

"Why, thanks, Pam," said Lucy, surprised at the compliment.

"I mean it. Beauty comes from inside. It doesn't come from lipstick and stuff."

"That's the way it ought to be," said Lucy, "but lately I've been noticing some wrinkles and gray hairs, and I don't like them. Maybe they'll have some ideas that can help."

"Those things are signs of character. You've earned those wrinkles and gray hairs!"

"And the mommy tummy, too, but I'm not crazy about it."

"Don't even think about liposuction," warned Pam, horrified. "Promise?"

"Believe me, it's not an option," said Lucy, hearing Bill's footsteps in the kitchen. "I've got to go."

When she looked up he was standing in the doorway, dressed in his Christmas red plaid flannel shirt and new corduroy pants. He was holding a small box wrapped with a red bow, and her heart sank. "Not another present!"

"It's something special I picked up for you."

Lucy couldn't hide her dismay. "But we've spent so much already. We'll be lucky to get this year's bills paid off before next Christmas!" She paused, considering. There was no sense in putting it off any longer. "And Elizabeth's tuition bill came yesterday. Chamberlain College wants sixteen thousand dollars by January 6. That's ten thousand more than we were expecting to pay. Ten thousand more than we have."

He sat down next to her on the couch. "It's not the end of the world, Lucy. She can take a year off and work."

"At what? There are no good jobs around here."

"She could work in Boston."

"She'd be lucky to earn enough to cover her rent! She'd never be able to save."

Bill sighed. "I know giving the kids college educations is important to you, Lucy, but I don't see what it did for us. I'm not convinced it really is a good investment—not at these prices."

Lucy had heard him say the same thing many times, and it always made her angry.

"That's a cop-out, and you know it. It's our responsibility as parents to give our kids every opportunity we can." She sighed. "I admit it doesn't always work out. Toby hated college; it wasn't for him. And that's okay. But Elizabeth's been doing so well. It makes me sick to think she'll have to drop out."

Bill put his arm around her shoulder. "We'll figure something out . . . or we won't. There's nothing we can do about it right now. Open your present."

Lucy's eyes met his, and something inside her began to melt. She reached up and stroked his beard. "You've given me too much already."

"It's all right, really," said Bill, placing the little box in her hand. "Trust me."

"Okay." Lucy prepared herself to accept another lavish gift, promising herself that she would quietly return it for a refund when she got back from New York. What could it be? A diamond pendant to match the earrings? A gold bangle? What had he gone and done? She set the box in her lap and pulled the ends of the red satin bow. She took a deep breath and lifted the top, then pushed the cotton batting aside.

"Oh my goodness," she said, discovering a bright red plastic watch wrapped in cellophane. "It's got lobster hands."

"That's because it's a lobster watch," said Bill. "They gave them out at the hardware store. Do you like it?"

"Like it? I love it," she said. "I think it makes quite a fashion statement."

"And it tells time," said Bill, pulling her close.

Lucy took a second look at the watch. "Was it really free?"

"Absolutely. Positively. Completely."

"I'll wear it the whole time I'm away," said Lucy. "I'll be counting the minutes until I get home."

"That's the idea," said Bill, nuzzling her neck.

The wrapping paper underneath the tree crinkled and rustled as Libby rolled over. Instinctively, just as they had when they'd briefly shared their bedroom with the newest baby, they held their breaths, afraid she would wake up. They waited until she let out a big doggy sigh and her breathing became deep and regular, then they tiptoed out of the living room.

As they joined Sara and Zoe in the family room, where they were watching a "A Christmas Story,"

Lucy resolved to enjoy the few remaining hours of Christmas. She'd have plenty of time on the plane to break the news to Elizabeth and to try to come up with a solution. A ten thousand dollar solution.

ABOUT THE AUTHOR

Leslie Meier lives with her family in Rhode Island. Her newest Lucy Stone mystery, MOTHER'S DAY MURDER, will be published in hardcover in April 2009. Leslie loves to hear from her readers and you may write to her c/o Kensington Publishing. Please include a self-addressed stamped envelope if you wish a response.

Grab These
Kensington Mysteries

Mischief, Murder &
Mayhem – Grab These
Kensington Mysteries

More Mischief, Murder
& Mayhem in These
Kensington Mysteries

Star Trek: The Next Generation

Star Trek: Deep Space Nine

Star Trek: Voyager

STAR TREK®
VOYAGER™

GHOST OF A CHANCE

MARK A. GARLAND
&
CHARLES G. McGRAW

POCKET BOOKS

New York   London   Toronto   Sydney   Tokyo   Singapore

This book is a work of fiction. Names, characters, places and incidents are products of the author's imagination or are used fictitiously. Any resemblance to actual events or locales or persons, living or dead, is entirely coincidental.

An *Original* Publication of POCKET BOOKS

POCKET BOOKS, a division of Simon & Schuster Inc.
1230 Avenue of the Americas, New York, NY 10020

Copyright © 1996 by Paramount Pictures. All Rights Reserved.

A VIACOM COMPANY

STAR TREK is a Registered Trademark of Paramount Pictures.

This book is published by Pocket Books, a division of Simon & Schuster Inc., under exclusive license from Paramount Pictures.

ISBN: 0-671-56798-5

First Pocket Books printing April 1996

10 9 8 7 6 5 4 3 2 1

POCKET and colophon are registered trademarks of Simon & Schuster Inc.

Printed in the U.S.A.

To my wife, Genevieve,
Who makes all the difference

M.A.G.

With love and thanks to the women who have shaped my
life—
Elizabeth, Nancy, Nora
Mother, wife, daughter

C.G.M.

With thanks to Tyya Turner and John Ordover,
For the chance to join the Voyager on its odyssey

and special thanks to Angela Frey,
for helping to polish all the rough spots

GHOST OF A CHANCE

CHAPTER
1

COMMANDER CHAKOTAY'S SPIRIT GUIDE HAD VISITED HIM many times in his dreams. Unlike the often arbitrary or chaotic dreams of others, the spirit guide brought clarity through visions that helped explain the world outside as well as the world within. But it was not the guide that came into the mind of the commander tonight, finding him as he slipped deeper into his dreams. It was a ghost. . . .

The entity had no true form, though like a strong, cool wind it made itself known. It drew closer, touching his unconscious fleetingly at first, as if unsure, or unwilling. But this seemed to last only a moment. The ghost began to change, enriched by the encounter somehow, and Chakotay sensed a certain . . . excitement. Suddenly he saw into the ghost's mind.

The images were less alien than the ghost that

brought them. A beautiful world full of life, and graced with a vast, thriving wilderness. The world moved, passing his mind's eye too quickly. When the images settled again, they revealed a huge village nestled among the trees, a place populated by a vibrant primitive culture. He found details difficult to distinguish, but there were many things familiar about these people and their community, and Chakotay could not help but compare them to his own people, of perhaps a thousand years ago.

Their homes were fashioned from the materials they found all around them, as were their clothes, and he saw no signs of suffering or war. But this vision too lasted only for a short while. New images of death and destruction rushed into the dream. A different place, perhaps, or a different time?

He saw the land split, saw oceans turn to steam and mountains spewing the planet's molten interior upward into the smoke-filled skies. The world seemed bent on destroying itself and all that lived on it in a frenzy of earthquakes and fire. Then the ghost and the images were fading from the dreams, but they were replaced by a clearly understood message, one that echoed through the commander's mind until it brought him shuddering into consciousness. As he sat up, the fateful pleas of the ghost seemed to radiate outward through his skull until they reverberated off the walls of his cabin. It was a desperate cry for help.

Chakotay looked directly at Harry Kim in the Ops bay as he entered *Voyager*'s bridge. The hiss of the turbolift doors caused the young ensign to look up from his operations and communications panels. Kim was the youngest, greenest member of the bridge crew. *Voyager*'s mission to the Badlands had been his first assignment, but he had already proven himself under fire.

"Status?" Chakotay asked him.

"We will arrive at the Drenar system in eleven minutes," Kim reported. Another ensign, who was carrying a PADD containing the updated Ops report, moved away from Kim, then handed the report to the commander. Chakotay glanced briefly at the data. As he looked around the bridge, his gaze lingered only twice. Tom Paris, the young human lieutenant at the helm, regarded Chakotay with his characteristic, only slightly arrogant smile. Though he came from a family full of admirals, his expression was born of talent and experience, not ego.

Lieutenant Tuvok, the only Vulcan on the bridge, stood in the tactical bay to Chakotay's right, and was at this moment paying strict attention to the screens and displays at his station—something he apparently believed had a higher priority than idle greetings. Which suited the first officer just fine. Because *Voyager* was always in unknown, uncharted space, its tactical station was perhaps the most important on the ship.

Chakotay took a deep breath and decided all seemed to be in order, reassuringly so just now. He slowly exhaled, letting the lingering tension flow out of him. The dreams and visions of the night before still flickered in his mind, too real to let go of, yet clearly not real at all, and not worth dwelling on for now. Only a dream, he told himself yet again, trying to shake off the images.

He had half expected to find some tangible evidence of his strange visions as he joined the day shift, so real were the images. He had already gone over most of the duty and sensor logs from the previous shifts, reviewing everything that had happened while he slept, but nothing out of the ordinary had turned up.

Chakotay stepped forward and down, then walked slowly about the bridge's main, lower level, letting the dreams quiet themselves, absorbing the gray-and-black reality of the walls and railings, the strangely comforting electronic glow of many lit panels at the engineering and science stations.

"Six minutes, Commander," Kim said.

"Very well. Captain to the bridge," Chakotay called out, raising his voice to engage the intercom system. It was a routine stop, but one that Kathryn Janeway, captain of the *Starship Voyager,* had been looking forward to. She and Tuvok had devised a method of replenishing the impulse engines' deuterium tanks, at least in theory. In just a few minutes they were going to put those ideas into practice.

A few moments later Captain Janeway strode smartly onto the bridge, followed closely by the Talaxian, Neelix. She wore her uniform trim and proper, her hair tucked up into a neat bun on the back of her head, no strand or thread or movement out of place. She stood in stark contrast to Neelix, whose short frame, oddly spotted face, scruffy wisps of orange hair, and bright, multicolored tunic made him seem somewhat clownlike in her presence.

They made an effective team, however: the eager, ardent and decidedly capricious alien was *Voyager*'s only guide in this part of the galaxy, and Janeway's straightforward discipline, along with a certain measure of insight, allowed her to make good use of Neelix's counsel.

Janeway, like her first officer, made a quick visual inspection as she stepped down and stood at ease near the center of the bridge, beside Chakotay. She folded her arms with a look of satisfaction. "Report," she said.

"Three minutes to arrival," Kim responded.

"It's right where Neelix said it would be." Paris glanced back, raising an affable eyebrow to the alien.

"Thank you," Neelix replied cheerily, bowing briefly from the waist. He smiled at the captain. "I think you'll find the Drenarian system will provide the perfect opportunity to test your ideas. The system contains several gas giants, most with an assortment of moons that should make any captain happy as can be."

"Thank you, Neelix," Janeway answered him, adding a crisp nod. She let half a grin slip before turning away. "Bridge to Engineering."

The voice of B'Elanna Torres, *Voyager*'s half-human, half-Klingon chief engineer came instantly back, "Yes, Captain."

"How are we doing?"

"We're all set down here. Whenever you're ready."

"You haven't explained exactly what it is you're going to do," Neelix said, tipping his head to one side almost birdlike as he awaited Janeway's reply.

She hadn't explained the details of the plan to anyone, really. She had been a scientist long before becoming an officer, and she had a habit of forgetting that many of those around her did not possess those same credentials.

"We're going to use the Bussard ramscoops to draw raw material from a suitable moon around one of Drenar's largest gas giants. We're hoping several of them will have rich hydrogen-methane atmospheres. We should then be able to convert the collected material into usable deuterium slush—at least that's what Torres and I have in mind."

"A full description of the conversion process is available in the computer, should anyone wish to examine it," Tuvok noted. "I can supply you with the file location."

Neelix, for his part, made no immediate request.

"We have reached the coordinates," Kim reported.

"Go to impulse," Chakotay ordered.

"Disengaging main drive," Lieutenant Paris said, touching points on the panel before him. The instant the ship dropped out of warp it slammed into a wall.

Captain Janeway found herself momentarily pinned beneath her first officer as the two of them tumbled to their left and were slammed down onto the deck. The ship lurched to the right then and shuddered violently, setting off alarms. The impulse engines howled as the lights dimmed and systems began to go down.

The captain's head bounced off the gray-carpeted deck plates, and she felt her teeth bite into her tongue, tasted blood. She looked up into Chakotay's eyes as he tried to regain his bearings and attempted to roll off her. Paris was clinging to his station, fighting to regain control of the helm. Behind her she could hear Tuvok wheeze as he thudded against something hard.

The ship lurched to the left once more, sending everyone tumbling yet again. Janeway managed to grab hold of the deck rail and steady herself briefly. She craned her neck and saw Tuvok still at his post, every bit as tenacious as Lieutenant Paris.

"Mr. Tuvok, report!" she shouted over the wail of the emergency klaxon and the onerous groan of the engines.

"We are caught in an intense gravitational field. I am attempting to determine the source."

"That would be a help."

"Captain," Tuvok came back almost at once. "There seems to be a star, a small brown dwarf, dead ahead."

"I'm attempting to compensate," Paris called back. "It's really got a hold of us."

"There was no brown dwarf here before, I'm sure of it!" Neelix cried from the heap he had tumbled into just in front of the captain's chair. "And it's only been a few years."

Janeway looked at the main viewscreen, but even at this distance there was almost nothing to see. Yet as she looked more closely she began to notice the star's outline, an apparent hole in space where the brown dwarf's dark sphere blocked out the stars behind it.

"Transferring all available power to the impulse engines," Kim said, following procedure perfectly.

"Engines at full," Paris acknowledged. "It's having an effect, but we're still not breaking free." He sat up, rigid in his chair, bracing himself as the lurching ceased—only to be replaced by a steady and rapid shaking that quickly threatened to rattle the starship apart.

"Systems failure reports coming in from all over the ship," Kim reported, even before Janeway could ask.

The captain worked her way along the railing, hand over hand, toward her command chair. "Injuries?"

"Numerous, but all minor so far," Tuvok replied.

"We're too close. The star's gravity is too strong," Paris said, his voice straining in sympathy with the engines.

Janeway lifted her head and shouted at the ceiling. "Engineering, can we go to warp? We have to get out of here."

"Yes, Captain," B'Elanna replied. "The upper matter-constriction segments shut down briefly. I'm reinitializing now. Just give me a minute."

"We don't have a minute."

No one said a word for several very long seconds. The shaking grew worse, or it seemed to, as Janeway stood bent-kneed on the trembling deck.

"That should do it, Captain," B'Elanna announced, sooner than expected.

"Mr. Paris!" Janeway snapped.

"Warp drives engaged," Paris said, as the deck again suddenly tilted beneath their feet. Janeway's grip tightened on the deck rail as Chakotay grabbed the chair behind him. On the viewscreen the dark circle began to move, but it did not go way.

"It's still no good, Captain," Lieutenant Paris said, glancing frantically over his shoulder. "We just aren't pulling away."

"Engineering, we need more power!" Janeway demanded.

"You've got everything we have," Torres came back, her voice nearly lost in the background roar of the engine room.

Janeway turned to her officers. "Tuvok, Kim, divert

everything to the engines, including life-support, do it now!"

In an instant the bridge went nearly dark, lit only by the dim glow of red emergency lighting. The ship pitched and shook again as yet another surge made itself felt. Janeway watched intently as the stars off the bow began to move, taking the dark circle with them. Again, they did not go far.

"We still can't break free. We're holding position, but we can't keep that up for long," Paris informed the captain, paying frantic attention to his console.

"Captain." It was Torres in Engineering again. "I have a suggestion."

Janeway's eyes went wide, then narrowed as her mind came around to what was very likely the same idea. "Emergency flight rules," she said.

"Yes," B'Elanna answered. "We can add a minute amount of antimatter to the impulse reaction chamber. That might give us the extra power we need."

"If it doesn't blow us all up," Chakotay added.

Janeway looked at him, one eyebrow going up.

He shrugged, guileless. "Don't let that stop you," he said.

"Do it!" Janeway commanded.

For a long moment the howl of the engines and the bone-jarring tremors that swept the ship continued unchanged, then B'Elanna spoke again, "Transferring antimatter . . . *now.*"

Voyager surged like a boat swept up on a passing wave.

"Hull stress climbing beyond maximum design levels," Tuvok reported calmly.

Janeway looked at him only briefly. "Keep it coming, Mr. Paris."

"Aye, Captain."

"We're pulling away!" Kim shouted, just as Janeway felt it happen, felt the ship abruptly move much farther than before as their momentum shifted decidedly away from the darkened star.

"We've lost the warp engines," Paris announced. Even as he spoke, entire panels on the bridge erupted in a series of bright flashes followed by curling smoke and a flicker of flames. The smell of burned circuits filled the stagnant air. The fire-suppression systems quickly detected and snuffed out the flames while the bridge crew scrambled to the extinguishers, then held them at ready until it was clear they would not be needed.

"The impulse engines have dropped back to within normal levels, and are still on-line," Paris informed the captain, then added, "For the moment."

"Proceed in-system at half impulse," Janeway ordered. "Let me know if the engines get any worse."

"Transferring power back to life-support systems," Kim said, working swiftly. As life-support came back on-line, the computer automatically began to rid the room of the smoke and fumes. Full lighting was restored to the bridge.

Janeway sat back in her chair and asked for damage reports as *Voyager* finally began to settle down. Judging by the bridge, she expected the worst. As it turned out, she was not surprised.

"Almost everything is off-line," B'Elanna reported from Engineering, confirming the bad news Tuvok had already begun relating. "The main computer detected stresses high enough to trigger an automatic warp core shutdown. Warp drive, phasers, transporters, anything that uses a lot of power, is gone for the moment. I'm using everything we've got to keep the main computer up and the impulse engines and life-support running. I won't know how bad it is until we can run complete level four diagnostics."

The captain frowned. A long strand of thick dark blond hair had been pulled free from the top of her head; it hung in her face now, as if intent on adding annoyance to catastrophe. She brushed it straight back, only to have it fall again. "At least we're not dead in the water."

"No, Captain," B'Elanna said, "but go easy on the impulse engines. After that last jolt, I don't know what shape they're in."

"Helm?"

"Sluggish but responding, Captain," Paris came back.

"Understood." She turned slightly to her right. "Mr. Neelix, I'd like another word with you."

The alien appeared to be quite shaken, as he stood straightening his colorful tunic, his narrow fingers shaking noticeably. "Captain," he said, "I must go to Medical and see that Kes is all right."

"Of course, but first I'd like to know anything you can tell me about that brown dwarf. Anything at all."

"Which would be nothing, Captain, as I said. It's as much a surprise to me as it is to you. Had I only known—"

"Understood." The Talaxian was not a liar. The captain was going to have to figure this one out on her own. "Very well, you may go."

Neelix turned and rushed through the open door of the turbolift. Nothing happened.

"It seems you will be staying on the bridge a while longer," Tuvok said with a dry Vulcan finality that Neelix was apparently not inclined to emulate.

For the first time in several minutes Janeway smiled. She let it fade. "Mr. Tuvok, contact Medical, find out how Kes has fared and let Neelix know. The rest of you, get to work on restoring these systems. Mr. Paris, set a course for the system's largest gas giant. I don't see any reason just to sit here and sulk. Mr. Kim, I'll want full sensor sweeps, the best you can give me. Start with that brown dwarf, and then scan the entire Drenar system. I want to know everything. Transfer all available data to my ready room. I need to figure out just what the hell is going on."

CHAPTER

2

As her officers acknowledged her commands and went to work, Janeway breathed a heavy sigh. She gazed at the viewscreen once more. The Drenar system contained a G-class star and eleven planets, and appeared quite ordinary in most respects. Clearly it had never been a binary system, the positioning of its planets was indication enough of that. With luck, the system would provide some interesting astrophysical data, and with a little more luck, they would be under way again in a few days' time. But in truth, just at this moment she didn't feel very lucky.

She left Chakotay on the bridge and headed for her ready room.

For now Janeway's only hope, and *Voyager*'s, was that her crew was equal to the task of getting the starship up and running again, or at least in a condition that would set them once more on their journey home. There would be other star systems, places where at least some aid might be found, where proper supplies could be procured—Neelix had assured her of that. But with nothing but a badly crippled ship between the crew and the harsh, endless night waiting all around them, none of those tentative safe oases mattered.

Out here there was no hope of assistance from anyone familiar, no starbases to turn to, nowhere to run. It was a truth everyone onboard tried not to think about very often, though just lately such thoughts had become impossible to avoid.

Janeway blinked the darkness from her thoughts and went back to concentrating on the data displayed before her on the ready room terminal. The brown dwarf was moving through space undisturbed, and its trajectory was easy to mark, a path that had taken it through the middle of the Drenar system. Its effect on *Voyager* had been profound, and she was just beginning to explore the more serious consequences that its preceding path implied. She was still deep into the exact calculations when the door chime sounded. She glanced up. "Come in."

The door slid aside, and Commander Chakotay stepped into the opening. "We are in orbit around the largest moon of the sixth planet, Captain," he said. "The impulse engines seem to be holding their own, and we still need fuel—more than ever, in fact. I don't see any reason why we shouldn't go ahead with your original plan. With your permission, Tuvok and Kim would like to begin collection procedures."

"Agreed, and thank you," she said. She had intended to discuss that very possibility with her senior officers; it pleased her to find them way ahead of her. "I'll be right there."

"Have you seen the casualty reports?"

Janeway held her breath. "No."

"Nothing serious, mostly bumps and bruises. We did have one broken arm, though. Fortunately it happened in Sickbay."

"Ah, good." Janeway nodded, glancing down at her screen again.

"The bad news is, it was Kes."

Janeway's head snapped up again. Kes was an Ocampa, a species that had a life span of only nine years; at just over one, Kes was already an adult, but she was still young enough to heal very quickly. No doubt she was in better shape than Neelix so far.

Chakotay shrugged. "At least we managed to get the turbolifts working again, so Neelix is with her instead of with us."

Janeway touched her comm badge. "Captain to Sickbay. How is Kes doing?"

"Quite well, as a matter of fact," the holographic doctor said. "Though I'm sure the other patients would be happier if she were able to assist me again. I can tend to only one patient at a time. She is a great help. I . . ."

Janeway waited, exchanging a glance with her first officer in the unexpected silence.

"I understand," Janeway said. "She is remarkable."

"She'll be back to work tomorrow. A little stiff, perhaps, but otherwise . . ."

Janeway found herself waiting again.

He sounded cheerful enough, which was almost unusual. The holographic medical assistant program that had been pressed into service as *Voyager*'s only doctor was doing a splendid job, and Janeway couldn't have been more pleased, but his attitude and bedside manner were sometimes difficult to manage.

"Yes?" she prodded.

"Captain," the doctor replied, his voice just **ab**ove a whisper, "if you could please find something for Mr. Neelix to do, and someplace else for him to do it, I would be extremely . . . grateful."

"We'll see what we can do," she replied, suppressing a chuckle, then signing off.

"I'll add that to my list," Chakotay said. He was grinning as he left the ready room.

Janeway stayed at her panel for a moment, working with the ship's main computer, completing her reconstruction of the rogue star's recent path. The brown dwarf had passed close enough to Drenar nearly to make this a new binary system. An interesting place to study, given sufficient time, which was something *Voyager* simply could not afford to spend.

Still, enough raw data could be collected to provide for countless hours of analysis in the months, or years, to come. After another moment she shook her head. She didn't need to be here right now. She told the computer to continue, then rose and followed Chakotay out.

"Mr. Tuvok," she said, stepping onto the bridge.

"Ready, Captain," the Vulcan answered. "The main deflector has been reconfigured, and approximate calculations have been completed."

Kim nodded confirmation from behind the Ops consoles. "Thrusters are at station-keeping," he said. "I've diverted just enough impulse power to do the job."

Janeway took to her captain's chair, then rested two fingers gently against her chin. "Then let's begin."

"Activating Bussard ramscoop fields," Tuvok said. Janeway watched on her own monitor as the electromagnetic fields, designed to be used for emergency collection of interstellar hydrogen during warp travel, began to expand outward, stretching in front of the ship from both of the warp nacelles.

"Deflector field wrap initiated," Kim said, working at his own console.

"Field overlay achieved, Mr. Kim," Tuvok said. "You may begin bending them downward."

"Commencing . . . now."

On the display, the captain witnessed the results as the two EM fields wrapped themselves around each other to form a tighter, more cohesive funnel, one that began to bend down and away from *Voyager* at nearly a forty-five-degree angle, an energy funnel theoretically capable of channeling the hydrogen-rich material of the moon's upper atmosphere back toward the collectors located in the warp nacelle caps.

"Take us in a little closer, Mr. Paris," Chakotay told the helmsman, and *Voyager* slowly, gently descended.

Gradually the mouth of the funnel began to fill with tenuous clouds of hydrogen-methane as the twin fields skimmed the atmosphere's surface, drawing in material the way a draft drew smoke from a room. Paris brought the ship down another hundred kilometers, as close as he dared to get while using the thrusters almost exclusively, but within seconds the ram fields started to collapse as the increased volume of gases leaked through.

"Too much," Janeway told him. "Back us off a bit."

As the ship slowly rose again, the fields reestablished themselves.

"The process seems successful on a limited scale," Tuvok reported.

"Thank you," B'Elanna Torres's voice said over the intercom.

Janeway looked up from her monitor and smiled. "I think we can live with that. B'Elanna, how long can we sustain the fields at this level?"

"Approximately twenty-seven minutes."

"Good. We might try this again later. Meanwhile, as soon as we're finished here I'd like to complete our preliminary scan of the rest of the system. The astrophysical data I've seen so far are quite remarkable, but I know there's more."

"Agreed, Captain," Chakotay said. "Actually, some of the early data would suggest the need for a more thorough survey as well. The fourth planet appears to have an extremely rich biosphere. It could even provide a good source of food. And . . ." He stopped himself, then shook his head.

"What?"

"Nothing," he said.

She sensed there was definitely something more. She stood silent for a moment, studying her first officer and feeling more certain. "You're not telling me something."

"May I have a word with you in private?" Chakotay said, suddenly pensive.

A rare mood for this man, Janeway thought. She nodded once. "Tuvok, you have the bridge," she said. Then she turned. "Commander, my ready room.

"All right, what's going on?" she asked evenly, once the door slid closed behind them.

"I had a vision last night," Chakotay said, focusing on many things in the room before finally looking at Janeway. "Or a premonition. I'm not sure which, but it was unlike anything I've ever experienced. I was visited by . . . by a ghost."

Janeway crossed the small room and sat on the sofa along the opposite wall. "A ghost?" she asked, after giving them both a moment. She tried to get Chakotay to sit as well, but instead, the commander began pacing as he told her about the beautiful world and its people, then about the destruction he had seen, and the final desperate cry.

"If it's real," he concluded, "if these things I saw are true, then their plea for help was, too.

"And you think we can help these people, whoever they are?"

"I don't know. But I'd like to look into it, at least."

"And there's a possibility that they are on the fourth planet in this system?" Janeway said, proceeding.

"Nothing else fits. In fact, that planet may well be inhabited, and early spectral analysis of the atmosphere is consistent with a volcanically active planet. And something else, Captain. I checked with the doctor in Sickbay. Several other crew members have complained to the doctor about nightmares, about seeing things. Visions, you could say."

"Like yours?"

"Two specifically mentioned seeing ghosts."

Janeway looked at him with narrowed eyes. "Are you saying *Voyager* is haunted?"

"I really don't know."

Janeway couldn't help frowning. "As if we didn't have enough problems."

Chakotay raised both eyebrows, compressing the Indian tattoo on the left side of his forehead. "I know," he said. "But I thought . . . well, as long as we're in the neighborhood . . ."

"We'll look into this more." Janeway nodded. "I have a certain fascination with this system myself. I'd like a detailed survey, including the fourth planet, which should certainly include any effect the passing of that brown dwarf may have had on indigenous populations, if they exist. We'll go through with it. But understand, if we find any pre-technological civilizations living here—"

"We'll keep our distance. I continue to be aware of Starfleet's precious Prime Directive," Chakotay cut in, making sure his tone indicated his mild dissatisfaction.

"The Prime—" The door chime interrupted her. "Come," she said, and Tuvok entered the room.

"We have nearly completed refueling, Captain. The impulse engines are now functioning at nearly eighty percent, but Lieutenant Torres estimates repairs to the rest of the damaged systems, including repairing and restarting the warp core, will take several days."

"Days?" Chakotay said, beating Janeway to it.

"It seems we will be in the neighborhood for some time," Janeway said, glancing at her first officer. She had an urge to go over everything one more time, restate all of the possible repercussions—a step that she, perhaps more than any other currently active Federation captain, felt always compelled to take—but she was also learning to define the line between prudence and paranoia.

"Very well. Mr. Tuvok, we will conduct a complete

analysis of this sytem, but I won't promise anything beyond that." She rose and stood in front of Chakotay, eye to eye. "We still don't belong in this part of the galaxy. I respect your instincts and your beliefs, as well as your apparent desire to look into these visions of yours, but *Voyager* can't go running off, tossing away the Prime Directive every time the spirits move you, or anyone else aboard."

"Understood, but if an alien race contacts us, in whatever fashion, we are already involved," Chakotay answered quickly, taking up the argument yet again, the same one they had been having ever since encountering the Caretaker and his Array, and the Ocampa.

"I would point out that the consequences of our actions and, logically, our inactions, are potentially equal," Tuvok interjected. "Either way, we might theoretically be accountable."

"But accountable to the present, or to the future?" Janeway countered.

"Both," Chakotay replied. He leaned toward Janeway, a calm yet discerning look in his eyes. "But we can only live one day at a time."

"If we find a population on Drenar Four, and if I am convinced that they have never seen a spacecraft or an alien being before, there will be no contact of any kind," Janeway stated flatly. "We will proceed according to the Prime Directive. Is that completely clear?"

"Yes, it is, Captain," Chakotay answered, a somewhat forced but adequate grin finding the corners of his mouth.

"When the refueling is completed we'll head for

Drenar Four at half impulse and survey as we go," Janeway told both officers. "Keep each other updated. And tell everyone to stay out of Torres's way. Dismissed."

She watched them leave, then sat back down, this time at her desk. At half impulse it would take *Voyager* until noon the next day to reach the vicinity of Drenar Four. The captain knew she should get some sleep for now and let tomorrow deal with itself. She decided she would at least try. One day at a time, she repeated to herself, shaking her head as she made her way back to her quarters.

She rested for several hours, but did not get very much sleep. After what seemed like forever, Captain Janeway got up and pulled her uniform back on. A few minutes later she sat once more in her ready room, facing the data console, reviewing the latest data.

The Drenar system was easily old enough to have produced sentient life-forms, and Drenar Four in particular had all the earmarks of a lush, habitable world. It boasted three very large moons as well, which was most unusual for a planet so near its sun.

As *Voyager* approached the planet, more data became available. There was no evidence of an industrial society, just as Janeway had suspected. The upper atmosphere lacked industrial gases such as hydrocarbons, and no unnatural radiation sources had yet been detected. But as the dark side of this world came under scrutiny, fires too small and too numerous to be of natural origin were clearly evident on the largest continent.

Janeway sat back, nodding to herself. From the

looks of things, Chakotay would not be happy. She rubbed her eyes, then sat back from the console and felt a chill sweep through her body, as if a door had just been opened, letting in the cold of space itself. She shuddered and looked up, and was suddenly aware that she was not alone.

CHAPTER
3

THE PRESENCE THAT HOVERED JUST ABOVE THE CARPETED deck was insubstantial, nearly formless, but it was there nonetheless, shimmering as if lit from within, changing as if moved by unseen currents. Like a spirit, like . . . a ghost.

Captain Janeway stood up slowly, examining the strange blends of transparent colors as they gelled slightly, further defining the entity. She opened her mouth to speak, but instead, the visitor began to speak to her, not in words, but with images, at first no more substantial than the ghost itself, though they quickly began to clarify.

In her mind she saw what could only have been the same images Chakotay had described—a people dying as their world shook their houses down around them and split their fields apart, as their sky filled with smoke and fire and their lands turned gray as they were covered with ash and soot. But there was more.

The visions darkened, then came to light again revealing a vast, grassy clearing. On the ground dozens of unfamiliar but quite humanoid aliens lay motionless, most of them still clutching crude weapons—knives and crossbows, axes and slings. Their bodies and simple clothing were marked by terrible burn wounds of a sort Janeway found disturbingly familiar. . . .

Again the visions grew dark, replaced this time by a message that needed no images or words at all. As if through an instinct or a strong emotion, Janeway understood that the ghost was conveying a clear and desperate plea for help.

Once more the presence faded from her mind, allowing her conscious senses to come back to the fore. She saw the ghostly form of her unknown visitor fading from her eyes as well, replaced by the familiar sight of her ready room. Janeway felt a surge of fatigue move through her as the ghost's last traces vanished. She tried to rise and nearly fell. She put her hands on her desk, steadying herself, eyes closed, taking deep breaths, and let the feeling pass. When she had recovered sufficiently, she cleared her throat, straightened her uniform, and headed for the bridge.

"What is our position?" she asked, striding as briskly as she could through the doorway, avoiding her officers' eyes for the moment.

"We're entering a high scanning orbit around Drenar Four, Captain," Paris answered, looking up from his consoles.

"We've just begun detailed scans of the planet," Chakotay added. "We should be seeing some results in a few minutes."

"Good," she said, standing in front of the commander's chair. She noticed that Chakotay seemed to be considering her more carefully.

"Everything all right, Captain?" he asked.

"Yes."

The two of them stared at the main viewscreen. Drenar Four was a beautiful world, Janeway noted: blue oceans, white clouds, one very large continent on the day side covered by thick forests and trailing mountain ranges. Even from here, though, she could see clear evidence of heavy volcanic activity along several mountain chains. Long plumes of smoke and ash painted dark lines across the stratosphere.

"You're sure?" Chakotay persisted.

"What?"

"Sure everything is . . . all right?"

"No," Janeway said.

Chakotay looked at her. "Captain?"

She dropped the pretense. She leaned close to his ear. "I'd like to talk with you for a moment, Commander, about those visions you had."

Chakotay nodded. "Of course."

"There are some things about this planet that already don't make sense," she whispered.

"Like what?"

"For starters, it's gorgeous. The sort of prize that would have been colonized by any number of races if it were in Federation space. Unless someone was keeping it as a resort of some kind, a possibility that is rare but not unprecedented. In such places there are usually maintenance facilities or visitor centers, something easily detectable. I am surprised to find such a world still in so pristine a condition."

"There is apparently someone down there," Chakotay said.

"Yes, the numerous small fires seem to indicate that," she said.

"Mr. Tuvok," the first officer said loudly, "please report."

"We are registering hundreds of humanoid life-forms," Tuvok told her, examining the gray-and-orange images on his sensor displays. "A pre-technological society, mostly agricultural. I am still gathering data."

"We're also picking up a lot of seismic activity down there," Kim said, glancing first at Tuvok, then at Chakotay. "Well beyond anything I would have expected."

"What about that, Mr. Tuvok?" Janeway asked, though her gaze had already settled back on the main screen. Her thoughts were still full of ghosts. She tried to push them aside.

"Confirmed, Captain," the Vulcan said, "and on a potentially cataclysmic scale. I am reading numerous earthquakes moving through the planet's crust. Radiant shock waves are registering everywhere. Volcanic eruptions are extremely abundant. The overall level of geothermic activity is unprecedented on a planet of this apparent age."

"Certainly worth looking into, wouldn't you say, Captain?" Chakotay offered, though his tone implied he did not expect a rebuttal. "Especially since this is precisely what I thought we would find."

The visions the ghostly entity had brought her were still strikingly fresh in the captain's mind, as were

Chakotay's descriptions of his own encounter. "Yes, Commander," she said, still eyeing the planet below. "I'd say it is." She blinked and tried to shake the fog of images from her mind. "Mr. Tuvok, would you agree that the indigenous population may be in considerable danger, under such circumstances?"

"There is every reason to believe so," Tuvok said. "I should point out, however, that any attempt by *Voyager* to aid them in any way would be a violation of the Prime Directive."

"She knows, Tuvok," Chakotay said.

Janeway looked at them both, then let a sigh pass her lips. "Yes, I do know," she said. "But thank you, Mr. Tuvok, for reminding me. Continue scanning, and let's learn everything we can. I'm not rushing in anywhere, not yet. Just looking at the options. It's difficult to explain, but a few minutes ago—"

"Captain, alien vessel detected," Tuvok said abruptly, his hands working quickly at the tactical station as a small warning klaxon sounded repeatedly. "In close proximity."

Janeway attended him at once. "What kind of ship?"

"Unknown configuration. It appears to be in a very high orbit, just slightly below ours, and is presently moving to put the horizon between us again."

"So they're trying to stay hidden," Janeway said.

"I suspect that is the case," Tuvok agreed.

"Stay with them, Mr. Paris," Janeway ordered the helm. "Why didn't we detect them earlier?"

"A cloaking device?" Kim suggested.

Janeway shook her head. "Then why aren't they using it now?"

"If they had such a device, it could be malfunctioning, but I find that line of reasoning highly speculative," Tuvok said.

Janeway nodded agreement. "Open a hailing frequency."

Ensign Kim worked to comply. "No response, Captain."

"We can get a little closer," Paris offered.

Janeway took two slow steps toward the main viewscreen, on which the distant image of the alien ship appeared as a dim spot poised between the darkness of space and the wash of reflected sunlight from the planet below. "Do it, Mr. Paris."

The helmsman responded, and *Voyager* began to close the gap.

"Mr. Neelix, this is the captain. Please report to the bridge at—"

"Captain," Neelix's voice came back almost at once, a ready bit of woe already present. "I trust everything is fine."

"No. I need you up here right away."

"But I can't leave Kes. Surely—"

"Captain," the doctor cut in, "Kes is resting nicely. When she wakes up, she should be almost as good as new. The only problem I can foresee is Neelix waking her up."

His tone had grown noticeably more terse with each word.

"On the double, Mr. Neelix," Captain Janeway said.

"Captain," Tuvok interrupted, "the alien ship is scanning us. They're powering up their weapons systems."

"Damn," Janeway muttered, placing her hands on her hips. "Go to red alert. Engineering, can we raise our shields?"

"Not yet, Captain," Torres replied over the intercom. "I've had to take them completely off-line."

Janeway felt a familiar knot form in her gut—something she had learned to live with in times past, something no good captain could afford to be without. The best remedy was to take positive action, though there were times, like this one, when no path seemed to present itself. "Mr. Paris, evasive maneuvers, but let's try not to provoke them. Kim, keep trying to hail them. Tuvok, arm the photon torpedoes . . . if we can do that."

"The photon firing systems appear to be inoperative at this time," Tuvok replied, much too calmly.

"Engineering, I need some options," Janeway snapped.

"They're still not responding," Kim said.

"Alien vessel opening fire," Tuvok said.

On the screen a brilliant yellow-tinged energy beam instantly crossed the distance between the two ships, narrowly missing *Voyager* as Paris frantically reacted. The image on the main viewscreen reeled as he continued to move the ship in anticipation of the alien's next shot.

"Phaser-type weapons, Captain," Tuvok reported, analyzing. "However, sensors indicate enemy beam strength at less than five hundred megawatts." He paused, waiting. "Four hundred forty-four point seven-two-three megawatts, to be precise."

"That's only half of *Voyager*'s upper phaser array's strength," Chakotay said. "Do you think they're holding back?"

"Approximately forty-three point six percent," Tuvok corrected. "And it is possible."

"Even at that strength, without our shields, they can still do a lot of damage," Ensign Kim said, a twinge of anxiety in his voice. Despite the tone, Janeway knew his remark was largely an observation. And an accurate one.

The turbolift door hissed open and Lieutenant Torres rushed out onto the bridge. She went immediately to the engineering bay, where she tapped frantically at panels as they came quickly to life.

"Captain," she said, still working, talking half over her shoulder. "We have two photon torpedoes ready to launch, we'll just have to do it manually. And I think the phasers are back on-line, but—" She finished working with her hands, then looked straight at Janeway. "But I haven't tested anything yet. I'm just getting the plasma-distribution manifolds aligned now."

"Good work!" Janeway exclaimed, allowing herself a brief lapse in composure. She glanced up in time to see another beam strike out through space just as Tuvok announced the fact. This time the beam struck a glancing blow, shaking the ship, though most of it seemed to miss *Voyager*.

"Minor damage to the outer hull," Tuvok reported. "Three casualties, apparently none serious."

The turbolift deposited Neelix on the bridge. He went immediately to Janeway's right side, opposite Chakotay. "Everything all right?" he said, his tone a combination of sarcasm and fright.

"That shot was too close," Janeway remarked.

"I predict the next one will be a direct hit," Tuvok informed her.

"Thanks for the vote of confidence," Paris said.

"I simply meant," Tuvok began, "that—"

"I know," Paris said, grinning momentarily.

"Ready phasers," Janeway said. "I want to discourage them from trying that again."

"Was there something in particular you needed me for?" Neelix asked, obviously nervous. "You seem quite busy at the moment, and I really would like to be with my beloved—"

"There," Janeway said, pointing at the screen. The alien vessel was visible in some detail now, a great gray wedge shape with several long appendages. "Do you recognize them?"

"Ready, Captain," Torres said, her head snapping around.

Janeway narrowed her gaze as if sighting down the barrel of a phaser rifle, something she simply couldn't help. "Upper forward array, full burst. Fire."

Voyager's return fire was noticeably brighter than that of the alien vessel, and more precise, the captain was pleased to note, as Lieutenant Kim announced a direct hit. The words had barely left his lips when *Voyager*'s lights suddenly dimmed, followed by a bright flash that erupted from the engineering station. Janeway saw Torres draw back, then wave a small waft of smoke away with her hand.

"The target's rear shields have collapsed completely," Tuvok reported. "I am reading some apparent damage to their stern."

"Torres, what happened?" Janeway asked, temporarily ignoring Tuvok's good news.

B'Elanna looked outraged, as if her Klingon blood were about to boil over. She hammered the consoles with both fists, then seemed to regain control, though her chin did not rise. Her hair hung in her face, partially obscuring her expression. "We've lost the phasers again, Captain." Her voice shook—too much adrenaline, worry, or pressure, Janeway couldn't be sure.

"Can you get them back?"

"I . . . I don't think so, Captain. It's a little more serious this time. I'm sorry."

"Do what you can," Janeway said in response. "None of us are having a very good day."

Janeway closed her eyes. She needed to think of something. Their best option was to attempt a quiet retreat. Now that the aliens knew that *Voyager* was superior, there was at least a chance they would not attack again. If they did, and if nothing else changed, she could guess how this might end. She had to assume the other ship was capable of warp speeds.

"Captain, the alien vessel is hailing," Kim announced, interrupting Janeway's train of thought.

She looked up. "On screen," she said.

"We have audio only," Kim replied.

"That's curious," Chakotay said, stepping closer to Janeway, as if to lend further support. "And more than a little suspicious."

"Perhaps," Janeway said, seeing any contact as an opportunity. They were in a tight spot, yet all of her crew members were doing their jobs, trusting in themselves, in their ship, in their captain and first officer. Things could be worse, she told herself, feeling the knot still there, though loosened just a bit. The aliens could have any number of reasons, from security to cultural taboos, for wanting to conceal their faces. "Maybe they're just shy," she said. Then she smiled just a bit. She could feel the slight release of tension in the room as the other officers blinked, then nodded to her.

"Proceed," she said.

"Channel open," Kim announced.

"This is Captain Kathryn Janeway of the Federation starship *Voyager*. We mean you no—"

"This is Third Director Gantel of the Televek." The alien's voice was low and dry, though quite humanoid by any measure. "You are ordered to move away from this planet, or you will be destroyed."

"We mean no harm," Janeway finished.

"You do harm by being here."

Janeway tipped her head. "How?"

"Why are you here?" the voice of the alien asked after a moment. Janeway felt a slight but growing relief in this exchange of dialogue instead of phasers.

"One moment, please," she said. She signaled Kim to mute the channel, and he quickly complied. "Torres," she said, hardly turning her head, "get back to work on those shields and weapons systems. And the warp drive. Whatever you can do will certainly be appreciated. Keep Mr. Tuvok informed."

"Yes, Captain," B'Elanna answered. She shut down the bridge's engineering station and headed back toward the lift. Janeway signaled, then accepted Kim's nod once more.

"We are making numerous minor repairs to our ship," she said to the alien, "and we intend to move on when they are completed. They should not take long. Again, we have no quarrel with you, or with anyone in this quadrant. The repairs are necessary, however, and already under way." She stopped short of apologizing for possible territorial infringement: she was fairly certain the alien vessel was not from the Drenar system, and never had been.

She waited as a long silence followed. After a moment she decided to try again, the other way around. "Why are you in orbit around this planet?" she asked the aliens. "And why have you fired on us?"

Yet another pause, then: "We are curious as to why you have chosen this planet in particular as the place to complete your repairs."

"I won't bore you with particulars, but in part we are interested in replenishing our organic supplies—foods, seeds perhaps, and several raw materials. We were also attempting to determine whether the population below is in any danger due to the extreme seismic activity our sensors have detected. But you haven't answered my questions."

It was worth a try, she thought. These aliens had to know something about what was going on down on that planet, and they had to know she was aware that they knew.

She waited for their reaction. The wait was a long one. Janeway began to pace a few steps away from Chakotay, followed closely by Neelix, whose continued silence was for him commendable. Then she turned, waited for Neelix to get out of her way, and walked back.

"Captain," Neelix said softly, "I was going to say—"

"It was just a matter of time, Mr. Neelix," Janeway said. "Now, do you know anything about them?"

"I think so."

"Captain," the alien voice said at last. "You bring up an interesting point. That is, in fact, precisely what we are here for as well, to investigate the planet's unusual geologic disturbances and possibly to offer aid to the planet's inhabitants . . . if necessary. We only fired upon you because we thought you were going to attack us. We've never seen a ship like yours."

"Understood," Janeway said. "Please stand by." Again she signaled the channel mute. "Finish what you were going to say, Mr. Neelix," she told the short alien still beside her.

"I have been trying to do just that," Neelix said with minor indignation. "They are a very old race, these Televek. A rather . . . hmm, unsavory lot, you might say."

"Go on," Chakotay urged him.

"Their past endeavors have included slave trading and piracy, and worse, I'm told. Though in more recent times they have become very well known in this quadrant as weapons brokers. Dealers in death."

"Parasites that feed off hostilities among others," Janeway said, characterizing them.

"And encouraging them, I believe," Neelix added. "Good for business."

"The truth is, their kind are often necessary," Chakotay suggested. "Where do you think outlaw resistance fighters like the Maquis got most of their weapons from?"

"These particular traders are not known for their scruples, Commander," Neelix went on. "They frequently sell to both sides in a conflict, or to all sides, raising the level of weapons technology little by little, and usually escalating the death toll in the process."

"Until their customers annihilate themselves completely," Paris said, shaking his head.

"Those practices could indeed generate many enemies," Tuvok suggested.

"Which might make them a little touchy," Janeway agreed.

"They are known to be very secretive," Neelix said. "I have never actually met one of their kind, or done business with them, I assure you. But as I understand it, they normally deal only through specially trained advocates."

"Captain," Tuvok said, "if I may make a suggestion."

Janeway nodded.

"Lieutenant Torres has just informed me that an EPS submaster flow regulator will be needed to restore the phasers. It will be extremely difficult to fabricate one from scratch. Since the Televek are apparently arms and technology merchants, and since they obviously have phaser technology, it is possible they may be able to assist us."

Captain Janeway had long relied on Tuvok for sage advice in all manner of situations. He had a knack for determining the most reasonable means to proceed, even when there seemed to be none. Again she found herself looking at him with rapt regard. His idea was extraordinary at first take, but intriguing nonetheless.

"So you're suggesting we try to do business with them?" Chakotay said, eyeing the Vulcan curiously.

"We need what they likely have," Tuvok said. "It is logical, and possibly in everyone's best interest, to assume a replacement valve could be procured from them and then modified to fit our systems."

"I like it," Janeway said, thumbing her chin as she

considered it further. "But what would we have to trade?"

"Maybe they could think of something," Chakotay suggested.

"From what I've heard, they are quite good at that, Captain," Neelix said. "But I don't recommend you bargain in good faith."

"No?" Chakotay asked.

"No. How can you be sure that they will?"

Janeway nodded at this. "Point taken, Mr. Neelix." She signaled Tuvok to open the channel once more. "Director Gantel, we may be able to work together," she said. "Help each other. An exchange of some kind, a mutually beneficial trade. Would you be willing to discuss such an idea?"

Once again the wait was a long one.

"Perhaps," came Gantel's reply. "We are a reasonable people. What do you suggest?"

"Captain, we have significant new data on the planet," Tuvok said, leaving it at that, letting Janeway decide whether she wanted to hear it now.

"A moment, again, please," she told Gantel. She made a slashing gesture with her hand, and Kim muted the communication link. "Go ahead," she said to Tuvok.

"Drenar Four is coming apart," Tuvok replied. "The seismic activity is increasing steadily. At the present rate Drenar Four probably will not survive as we know it, and the end will come relatively soon. I've noticed a considerable change in the stability of the planet's magnetic fields as well. They appear to be reorienting themselves."

"If the molten core of the planet is moving about, it would have that effect," Janeway said. She nodded to

Kim. The link opened again. "We should be able to agree on one thing at least," Janeway told the Televek director. "The populations on Drenar Four are in grave danger, and we are both concerned about them. That might be a starting point. What can you tell us about them?"

"Tell you?" Gantel's voice came back.

"Yes. We are reading numerous primitive villages, some large enough to be cities, but we know nothing at all about the inhabitants. Have you made contact with them?"

"Why, no, Captain, we have not. We also know very little about them."

"I see." She paced a moment, then looked up, wishing she had a face to talk to.

"We would like to discuss terms," Janeway told him. "We are hoping you can help us obtain some hardware we require. I'm sure that, in return, we can help you with any relief or rescue operations you are conducting here on Drenar Four."

"Of course, Captain, we commend you for suggesting the idea. You seem a shrewd and reasonable people indeed. But we suggest a meeting to discuss this in more detail. On your own magnificent vessel, if you like. I'm sure there exists a variety of terms we can agree on. We can send a small team of representatives over in an unarmed pod. Will you agree to this? And will you guarantee their safety?"

Janeway looked to Chakotay, found her first officer looking back at her. They both shrugged at the same time.

"We aren't getting anywhere just sitting here," the commander whispered.

That was obvious. "Very well," Janeway said. "We will be waiting, and you have my assurance that your people will not be harmed."

"Mr. Chakotay, you have the bridge," Janeway said as soon as the aliens had signed off.

"Captain," Kim said, then waited for Janeway to look directly at him. The ensign had not served with her very long, but she had no trouble reading the subtle concern in his expression.

"What is it?"

"There is something else, Captain. I ran it twice to be sure; the interference is pretty bad."

"Go on," Janeway said.

"We've detected a highly advanced stationary power source located several kilometers beneath the planet's surface. It does not match any known configurations."

Janeway quickly made her way to Kim's station and began examining the data for herself. This time Neelix stayed put, apparently content to remain with Chakotay.

"Where?" she asked the ensign. "Display, please."

"On the main continent, under a ridge of foothills just east of one of the largest villages." He showed her the spot on the monitor. She turned to face the aft deck. "Mr. Tuvok, what do you make of that?"

"I have no idea yet, Captain, but I am also picking up numerous energy signatures that are smaller but nonetheless similar to the main source. Most appear to be mobile." He paused, touching points on the panel before him. "There does not seem to be an organizational pattern, however. They appear and move at random in the area, and for random periods."

"I've been watching the primary signature for a while," Kim went on. "The power levels tend to spike downward, then slowly recover, also at random intervals. I don't know whether there is any correlation yet. In general, though, the median level is slowly declining."

"I'll bet our Televek friends over there will say they don't know anything about that, either," Chakotay remarked.

"It is odd the Televek didn't mention it," Tuvok said.

"I agree." Janeway pursed her lips, still looking over the data. The magnetic field fluctuations seemed to be playing havoc with the sensors, making it difficult to get good readings. Still, she was certain Kim was right. The power source was real, considerable, and unlike anything she had ever seen before. Then suddenly she saw something else in the readings, a faint shadow on the surface of the planet that faded from the sensors as quickly as it had appeared. "Did you see that, Mr. Tuvok?"

"Yes, Captain. A brief sensor reflection."

"What could cause something like that?"

"Processed alloy metals?" Kim offered.

"That is the likely explanation," Tuvok replied.

"So . . . a metal structure," Janeway postulated. "Or . . . another ship."

"Possibly," Tuvok said.

"I told you they couldn't be trusted," Neelix reminded one and all, hands clutched tightly against his chest. "Will you be needing me any longer, Captain?"

"Your advice is well taken," the captain assured him. "We may need more of it."

Neelix made a face that Janeway found unreadable.

"But if we know not to trust them, can't we use that knowledge to our advantage?" Paris asked. "I mean, they're the only game in town. We can't change that, but it doesn't necessarily mean we have to let them make all the rules."

"Agreed," Janeway said, "but asking the Televek for assistance or bartering for it would surely necessitate a transfer of knowledge and technologies. I don't want to give away any of *Voyager*'s secrets to a race that probably shouldn't have them—perhaps this race more than most."

"Of course not," Paris said, "but information, to some extent, would have to flow both ways, wouldn't it?"

"The lieutenant makes an excellent point, Captain," Chakotay noted. "As it stands, we are at a severe disadvantage, and it will only be a matter of time before the Televek fully realize that."

Despite the weight of the situation, Janeway felt a slight swell of satisfaction as she listened to this exchange between the members of her strange crew. Thrown together by fate and circumstance, seventy-five million light-years from home, their ship lacking half of its major systems, and hostile aliens hanging in orbit off the bow, and still they functioned well—as well as any captain could expect. Far too many of her decisions in this quadrant were difficult ones, but it helped to know she had the people to back them up.

"If we are to help anyone on Drenar Four, or help ourselves, it seems dealing with the Televek on some level is the only logical course," she said, acknowledging Tuvok with a nod.

"Couldn't we just leave the system?" Neelix asked.

"No, not yet," Janeway said. She stood silent for a

long moment. Then: "Mr. Tuvok, you will see to security arrangements. We don't want to appear unfriendly, but I'd rather not take any chances. I'll be stopping off at Engineering if you need me. Let me know when they arrive. Mr. Kim," she added, turning to the younger officer, considering him a moment, "you're with me. I want you to go down to the shuttle bay. I may have a job for you."

She turned on her heel and headed for the turbolift with the ensign close behind.

CHAPTER
4

B'ELANNA TORRES HELD HER LOWER LIP BETWEEN HER teeth as her eyes scanned the data on the main engineering console. "Lieutenant Carey, how are those magnetic constrictor coils coming?" she shouted. He was on the upper level, somewhere out of sight. She saw him peek down at her through the railing, a look of exasperation on his face.

"They're coming."

B'Elanna took a deep breath, then nodded to him. Her greatest regret was that she couldn't do everything herself, but Carey was a good man, as were the others working with him to get the warp drive back on-line. Let some of it go, she told herself.

But she had to keep everyone pushing hard right now, including herself. Partly because the captain required it, partly because she couldn't help it. Not with so many systems so badly damaged. Not when at any moment *Voyager*'s survival might well depend upon the work they were doing here. Still, there were limits, and some of them applied to everyone.

She bent over the panel and began touching keypads. Schematics flashed one after another on the dark glass screens above the console. She had so many people crawling in conduits that she'd lost track of some of them. Then there was the crew assigned to the transporter subsystems, all of which needed work and none of which seemed to be improving according to the red indicators on the display she was looking at right now. She'd been after them on the intercom not ten minutes ago, but she hadn't gone up there and personally . . . *inspired* them. Not yet, anyway.

Another grid appeared as she touched the control. More red flags. "The captain isn't going to like this," she muttered, thinking out loud.

"Like what?" Janeway said.

B'Elanna looked around to see the captain standing just behind her. She made a sour face. "Plenty."

"Tell me what's going on."

B'Elanna took a deep breath, tried to think of a good place to begin, decided there wasn't one. "I've got Carey working on the warp drives; that's our number-one priority right now. Life-support is stable. The transporters are still down, but we're making progress there. The impulse engines are running at eighty-five percent, maybe eighty-six. That's the good news. The phasers . . . well, I'm sorry, Captain, but I'm afraid they aren't—"

"I know, Tuvok told me. At least the Televek don't know about it yet. Not specifically. At least I don't think they do. We're working on the phaser problem from another angle."

B'Elanna looked at her. "What's that?"

"The Televek may have the hardware we need, if you think you can adapt their technology to ours. It's possible they'll want to cooperate. It seems they are merchants first and whatever else second, and from the looks of things, we are certainly potential customers. They're coming over for a visit."

"I'm more than willing to try," Torres said. "I'd use rubber bands right now if I thought they'd help, but do you think we can trust the Televek to help us rearm?"

"No." Janeway grinned, which seemed to put B'Elanna somewhat at ease. "That's the tricky part. But I'm willing to try, as long as we proceed cautiously. I would like my chief engineer to be there when we talk to them. Can we spare you down here for a little while?"

B'Elanna looked around, making a quick evaluation. She saw several sweaty brows flash in her direction and couldn't help a little smile of her own. "I think everyone here would welcome that idea," she answered.

"Good."

"Bridge to Captain Janeway," Tuvok hailed. The captain raised her voice to engage the intercom. "Yes, Mr. Tuvok?"

"The Televek are aboard. They are unarmed."

"Escort them to the briefing room. We're on our way."

No two first contact situations were ever the same, but Captain Janeway had seen enough of them to know that there were often similarities and that certain rules of engagement always applied. She was prepared to give her visitors the benefit of the doubt from the start, but she was equally prepared to give them nothing more, unless they earned it.

"Welcome aboard *Voyager*," Janeway began, introducing herself after Tuvok had presented the three aliens. Of the three Jonal was the only male, an elegant, strangely handsome figure slightly older than his two companions, who were both stunningly beautiful by any definition. All were physically impressive, a fact well demonstrated by the cut of their colorful two-sectioned tunics, with allowed much of their finely sculpted arms and legs to show. Like Jonal, Mila and Tassay had skin that was bronze in color, and each possessed a pair of ridges that grew from either side of her forehead, beginning just behind her bright green eyes and sweeping back under her long stark-white hair.

Janeway turned to the others of her crew. "This is my first officer, Commander Chakotay, Mr. Paris is our helmsman, Mr. Neelix, our . . . liaison officer, and B'Elanna Torres our chief engineer."

The aliens nodded and held their hands out, palms up, an apparent gesture of goodwill. Janeway returned the gesture, reassured by the knowledge that their transport pod and their persons had been thoroughly scanned for weapons and implants, and nothing had turned up.

"We are not Televek," Jonal said. "We are Drosary."

"We are advocates," Mila, the shorter of the two women, explained. "We are here on behalf of our benefactors."

The other female, Tassay, remained silent as everyone was seated around the conference table.

"Why won't the Televek come themselves?" Janeway asked.

"It is their way," Jonal answered.

"We are only too happy to provide this service, as it benefits all," Mila said, with an affable air that seemed natural in her and her two companions.

Jonal seemed especially attentive, Janeway noticed, particularly to her. And as she looked around, she decided Tassay's regard had already centered on Chakotay. With this in mind, she began to notice that Paris's visual scrutiny of Mila seemed to be reciprocal as well.

These three Drosary were apparently quite friendly, but Neelix's less flattering comments concerning their sponsors were still fresh in Janeway's mind. "What can you tell us about the Televek as a people?" she probed, leaning slightly forward. "We hear . . . disturbing reports."

"Many of which are not true, or we would not be here," Tassay said, speaking for the first time. Hers was another soft voice, even softer than the others', perhaps.

"The Televek are often misunderstood, Captain," Jonal said.

"I have never been fond of misunderstandings," Janeway assured them. "Please enlighten us."

"We were found on a war-ravaged world, a world that was not our own," Jonal explained without hesitation. "A place where our people had tried to set up a colony. We were among the thousands who sought to escape the tyranny and genocide that were destroying our home. But the wars that had brutalized our people for so long seemed to follow us, and many of the other colonies as well, involving other races as they went. Soon we became the target of brutal raids carried out by a neighboring world. We were no match for them. Our people were being victimized."

"Our own government would not help us," Tassay added, speaking directly to Chakotay, it seemed. "They claimed we were outside the primary realms. We were left to fend for ourselves. You can't know what it was like."

"Oh, I don't know," Chakotay said, glancing at B'Elanna Torres, the only other Maquis present. "I think some of us probably do."

Janeway let it pass.

"The Televek rescued a few of us from the ashes, and offered to train us as advocates," Mila said "They have been kind to us. We know them as few others do."

"That's quite a testimonial," Chakotay said, "but—"

"But they attacked my ship," Janeway pointed out.

"The Televek are somewhat . . . nervous at times, Captain," Jonal explained. "It is a consequence of circumstance. When confronted, they have a tendency to shoot first, and often with very good reason. You must understand, the Televek deal in the finest, and often the newest, technologies in many a sector, especially defensive technologies. Therefore—"

"And these are offensive technologies, perhaps?" Neelix said, apparently unwilling to let this last pass unchallenged.

"As the premier merchants in their field, the Televek offer a full range of merchandise," Jonal said in answer.

"And why shouldn't they?" Mila proposed, using an almost pleading tone. "What right does anyone have, after all, in a universe such as this, to pass judgment on others without true knowledge of their circumstances?"

"Agreed," Chakotay said, seeming eager to hear the rest. "Please go on."

"Yes, please," Janeway concurred, leaning forward.

"Their position makes them the focus of many races' attention, and for many reasons—from all manner of agreements and disagreements to outright piracy," Jonal said. "This can produce complications. Not everyone is willing to pay a fair price, for example."

"Yes," Tassay added, folding her slender hands almost prayerlike in front of her. "You see, some races will stop at nothing to get the technologies they desire."

"Furthermore, each time the Televek honor a contract, they make friends, and enemies," Mila said. "Some enemies have been known to carry a grudge. It happens often enough."

"So I hear," Neelix remarked, not quite under his breath. All three of the advocates stared silently at him.

"This is very interesting," Janeway said honestly, "but I still find their aggression toward this ship, a vessel they admit was unknown to them, a bit disturbing. I might be willing to overlook it, but I would like to know more about what the Televek are doing here, in orbit around Drenar Four. If their only purpose is to help the primitive population below, then I am curious as to what interested them in this planet, or those people, in the first place."

"We'd also like to know what other terms Gantel

had in mind," Chakotay added, watching the visitors carefully.

"We want only what is best, of course," Jonal replied.

"And reasonable," Tassay said, again speaking to Chakotay. The two of them sat looking at each other for a moment, as if the conversation had momentarily ceased to matter.

A passionate people, Janeway thought, not at all certain she liked the idea, though she found it harder to object to Jonal's apparent fascination with her.

"We understand your concerns," Jonal assured her. "We would be happy to answer all of your questions, and then we hope you will answer some of ours. The Televek can supply your people with almost anything they might need to get you up and running again, I am sure. And you may have a great deal to bargain with. At the same time, your ship and your technologies are new to them and, frankly, quite fascinating."

"Our technologies," Janeway repeated.

At that Jonal seemed to stop in spite of himself. "Of course," he went on, as he glanced about the room. "I'm sure you can understand. After all, your vessel is unique in the Televek's experience. It is along those lines that they are most interested in what you intend to offer them."

Janeway had been waiting for this. They seemed a sincere and malleable bunch, these Drosary, but she had the distinct impression she was about to haggle with a polished salesman, perhaps a team of them. She didn't have a great deal of experience in that field, but nearly all negotiations, like first contacts, were based on a number of common principles, and she had read more than one period novel that dealt with the subject. The best approach to such a dilemma was to carry very little currency in any one pocket—but to bring plenty of pockets.

"We can offer you certain medical techniques and technologies that I'm sure you would find most valuable," Janeway said.

"We have excellent medical science," Mila responded, a flat statement of fact.

"We can also arrange to let you download most of the contents of our library," Janeway continued, smiling broadly for emphasis, "which is filled with texts and data from hundreds of peoples in our own part of the galaxy, peoples you have never encountered. Some of our greatest works of literature and—"

"We find it hard enough to keep up with the many cultures and politics in our own quadrant, Captain," Jonal said. "I hesitate to mention the size of my current reading list. But I will make a note of this. Certainly there is a measure of value there. What else?"

"What else?" Chakotay asked, mildly indignant.

"As I indicated to Gantel," Janeway said more sternly, "we are also willing to do whatever we can to help you render aid to the people on the planet below, as that is your stated mission here. The medical and library data are being offered as an added consideration."

"Yes, of course," Jonal said quite agreeably, though he seemed less than enthusiastic. Then he looked at Janeway as though he had known her for a very long time, as if they had shared, or were about to share, some profound secret together, some defining knowledge. "May we make yet another suggestion?"

Janeway leaned back. "Please do."

"The Televek deal frequently in weapons, Captain, that is no secret, and to be blunt, yours are quite impressive. To be more precise, my employers would be most interested in learning how you've managed to get your phasers to operate at such incredibly high power levels, all while maintaining such extraordinary accuracy. Also, their sensors indicate that your warp drive nacelles are not fixed, but are—"

"No," Janeway said, a flat statement of her own. A troubled voice was calling to her from the back of her mind, one she had been listening to since her days at the Academy. She purposely took her eyes off the Drosary, especially Jonal, and focused instead on the relief sculpture of *Voyager* that hung on the wall. The euphoria that had begun to dominate the meeting seemed to have ebbed slightly, and her inner voice was growing louder. "Under no circumstances will we give Federation weapons technologies to the Televek, or to anyone else. That is simply out of the question."

"We are sorry to hear that, Captain," Mila replied, looking at her two companions. They seemed to reach a silent accord of some kind, almost as if they could communicate without speech. Janeway didn't think they were telepathic, but she found herself wishing Kes were here. The Ocampa had demonstrated some mild telepathic tendencies; she would likely be the best judge of these new visitors in that regard. Still, that wouldn't change the facts.

We're running out of pockets, Janeway thought, still avoiding Jonal's bright green eyes. *Voyager*'s variable geometry folding wing nacelle configuration, which tended to minimize the negative effects of warp fields on the subspace continuum and on habitable worlds, was no doubt a curiosity to the aliens. In fact, their own ships appeared to operate on a more primitive reactor technology. She might agree to discuss that, at least. In a pinch.

She said as much.

"My dearest Captain," Jonal replied, as if greatly saddened, and perhaps a bit ill as well. "I will certainly convey all of this, I promise you, and in the best possible light, but I do not think these . . . these preferred arrangements you mention will be enough. I know our patrons are particularly interested in phaser performance. I understand your concerns, but the Televek already possess phaser technology, after all. It is simply an area in which you seem to have made some rather significant improvements."

"Our sensor scans indicate you have two warp-powered payload-type weapons trained on the Televek cruiser," Mila said, tipping her head, letting a thick mane of long white hair drape itself across one dark-skinned shoulder, yet keeping her eyes on Paris the whole time. "The Televek might be interested in discussing those. I know they are curious as to why these weapons remain armed even though the Televek have powered down all their weapons."

"They're photon torpedoes," Paris explained, gazing back at Mila. "They're very efficient, too."

"Captain to Ensign Rollins," Janeway said, tapping her badge. "Secure photon torpedoes. Maintain yellow alert." She looked at Mila as the Drosary glanced in her direction. The two women smiled politely at each other.

"Ah, of course," Tassay said, finally speaking again. "This is encouraging. The Televek have weapons of that type as well, and of comparable strength, I believe, but they use a pulse generator. A comparison to your systems would likely be of minor interest, but perhaps some equity could be found there."

"I'd say that is also unlikely," Chakotay responded, glancing candidly at the captain, and she knew that, like her, he was not totally convinced of anything yet.

"Please try to be reasonable," Jonal said, clearly addressing Janeway. "It is in your own best interest, after all, to cooperate as fully as possible."

Janeway sat considering her visitors a moment, particularly Jonal, who seemed as pleasant and straightforward as any diplomat in the captain's memory. And utterly attentive toward her, she noted. And they were right, of course. But so was she.

It was the Televek she was ultimately dealing with, after all, not these people. How could she know that something painted here in black and white would not turn gray once it got over there? How could she even trust these three Drosary, no matter how reasonable a choice that seemed to be?

Still, her own options were quite limited, while theirs were not. She was clearly the one under pressure to compromise. But not just yet. She still had a vest pocket remaining. . . .

"Will you excuse us while we talk this over," Janeway said, not really making it a question. "Perhaps you would like to discuss it as well. I need to evaluate our protocols, among other things."

"Of course," Tassay said graciously.

"I'm not certain how long our discussion will take. You are welcome to stay aboard, of course. We will try to make you comfortable, and then see if we can reach some sort of agreement."

"Entirely understandable, Captain," Jonal said,

showing Janeway a smile full of fellowship. Mila and Tassay joined him in a genial nod.

"Thank you," Janeway said. She signaled the two security officers standing near the door, and they gently escorted the aliens out.

"Wait a few minutes—as long as you can—then bring them back in," she told Chakotay when they were alone. "Keep them talking until I get back. You have the conn, and you have full authority to make a deal if you can persuade them on our original terms, but I have a feeling nothing like that will happen. Despite their overtures, these Drosary, or our friends the Televek, or whoever it is we're dealing with, don't seem terribly interested in anything other than their own terms."

"Can I ask where you are going?" the first officer asked, clearly perplexed.

"The more I try, the harder it is to get all of this to fit together. If the Televek are involved in some kind of rescue operation, they don't seem very eager to get it under way; I've seen no evidence to indicate it has begun. And when I brought it up, the Drosary virtually ignored the topic."

"They do seem to present a one-track agenda," B'Elanna said, speaking for the first time since the meeting had begun. "I don't think I'd like the idea of them probing around in our weapons and propulsion systems, even if I was standing right there. And I would be, no matter what. I don't know what this feeling is based on, but something about them gives me the creeps." She looked around the table, apparently searching for confirmation.

"I didn't notice anything quite like that," Chakotay said.

"I definitely didn't," Paris said.

B'Elanna only frowned at this.

"It's not the Televek's style, all this sharing, I assure you," Neelix said, finally giving B'Elanna what she wanted. "If you ask me, they're up to something. You are right not to trust them, Captain. The stories I've heard are enough to make your skin crawl. Why, I once had a very profitable agreement arranged with some Idsepians, not fifty light-years from here, until it turned out they were also having a rather nasty argument with the Tethoeen, who occupied a neighboring solar system, and before I could get my assets—"

"Thank you, Mr. Neelix," Janeway interrupted. "I do appreciate your input. And I quite agree, at least in principle. We can't afford to trust them implicitly, even if we'd like to. We don't know enough, and there is too much at stake."

"Agreed," Chakotay said.

Janeway felt a dull pang of exasperation, something that had haunted her since *Voyager*'s nearly fatal encounter with the brown dwarf—a niggling feeling that things were only getting worse. Being on the losing end of any situation was something Janeway could not abide, even in the best of circumstances, and these were anything but. She took a deep breath; she was determined not to let anything else go wrong.

"I have to know what's going on down there on Drenar Four," she said. "Since our sensors can't tell me, and since the Televek don't seem interested in discussing it, I'm going to have a quiet look around for myself."

"I'll go with you," Chakotay offered immediately.

Janeway shook her head. "No. I need you here. Mr. Tuvok, you're with me."

"Captain," Chakotay said. "I—"

"Don't worry," Janeway told him, "at least not any more than you have to." Her first officer nodded wordlessly. She bade the others good-bye, and then the Vulcan followed her out.

They walked in silence most of the way, until they had nearly reached their destination.

"What is it you expect to find?" Tuvok asked as they entered the shuttle bay. Harry Kim stood waiting beside the open hatch of one of *Voyager*'s two main shuttlecraft.

"I don't know," she told Tuvok. "People. Volcanoes. Earthquakes, perhaps. Other than that, nothing, I hope. Though I'm beginning to doubt it."

"Ready to launch, Captain," Kim reported as Janeway acknowledged him.

"Excellent, Mr. Kim." The three of them boarded the shuttle and secured the hatch, then waited for the bay door to open. At the sound of the all-clear, Kim increased the small craft's power levels while Janeway guided them through the opening, into space.

"Bring our visitors back in," Chakotay said, touching his comm badge. He thought it would serve no purpose to keep the Drosary waiting around indefinitely, and in truth he felt eager to continue, to try. The two security officers reappeared once more in the briefing room, flanking the three envoys. Once everyone was seated again, Chakotay explained that the captain was conducting her reviews and hoped to rejoin them shortly. He tried to pick up where they had left off.

"I thought we might talk a little more about sensor

technologies," he said. "I believe we have a slight advantage in that area."

The three advocates regarded one another with mildly enlightened expressions. "Perhaps," Tassay finally said, glancing admiringly at Chakotay.

"We would have to determine whether there is any real benefit for the Televek," Jonal said. "But I do see the sensors as a step in the right direction. We are not talking about the sale of empires here, only token exchanges. You needn't be afraid of us, or of the Televek, Commander. They know what they're doing. You must tell this to your captain, help me convince her."

Chakotay couldn't help grinning. "I'm afraid I won't be much help there."

"Commander to the bridge!" the voice of Lieutenant Rollins shouted over the intercom.

"Chakotay here. What is it?"

"Commander, the Televek have fired on the shuttle," Rollins answered. Paris was already up and heading out the door as Chakotay sprang to his feet. "What's their status?"

"The shuttle has taken a direct hit. We've lost contact. They're descending out of control."

"The three of you will remain here," the commander told the Drosary. "See to it," he ordered the guards, who quickly raised their hand phasers and trained them on the three aliens.

"But, Commander," Jonal said, despondent, "I assure you, this is—"

"Not now," Chakotay said, moving past them.

"Wait, Chakotay, please," Tassay said, reaching for him. "You must let us—"

"No!" Chakotay replied coldly, avoiding her hand. He vanished into the hall at a jog.

Kim's shout of warning came at the same instant the energy beam flashed from the Televek cruiser. The shuttle rocked, then began to spin. As the cabin lights went out, the flash and sizzle of burning systems illuminated the darkness. Then the red emergency lighting brought grim clarity to Kim's eyes once more. Janeway and Tuvok scrambled up from the deck and dragged themselves into position over part of the shuttle's main console. The spin continued. Kim felt the fear fill his chest, a tightness that threatened to steal his breath. He forced his lungs full of air several times and tried to work past the fright. "We've lost power in the port nacelle," he reported, hauling himself up among the others, working quickly to evaluate the rush of data displayed before him.

"That is not all," Tuvok said, sounding somewhat shaken as well, a rarity in any Vulcan, and no comfort to Kim.

"We've got to pull out of this spin or we don't stand a chance," Janeway said, struggling with the controls. "Mr. Kim, see what you can do with those starboard stabilizers."

Telemetry readings glowed next to a screen displaying the shuttle's position relative to the horizon. Kim rerouted the stabilizer controls while Janeway and Tuvok regained minimal control, then began to ease the shuttle into a more shallow dive. Momentarily the rate of descent started to slow, and the planet's surface, bathed in daylight, rotated into view.

"We might just make it, Captain," Kim said, feeling

a need to say something as he realized survival was now a possibility.

"I wouldn't have it any other way," the captain said, glancing sidelong at him, as if she had known the outcome all along. She hadn't, of course. No one could have. But a part of him almost believed it so, and just when he needed that belief.

"Yes, ma'am," he said, already anticipating her next command, readying the landing thrusters.

"Helm is barely responding," Tuvok reported. "Power levels are down seventy-three percent. I believe we can still come close to our original destination, but it will not be possible to choose a proper landing sight."

"Let's just make it one we can walk away from," Janeway said, to enthusiastic nods from her shipmates.

The shuttle bucked, then rolled, then leveled slightly, only to fall abruptly again. Kim's gut floated up into his chest once more. He tried to ignore the feeling. He watched the viewscreen as the shuttle slipped through dense banks of black, ash-filled clouds. Then the ground seemed to leap up at them as they broke into the clear. A patchwork pattern of grasslands, cultivated fields, and dense forests lay below, stretching out to nearby hills and mountains in the east. Another mountain range was visible far to the south, where great plumes of smoke rose to fill the sky.

Kim fired the thrusters, correcting manually as best he could, while the others struggled to keep the ship's nose in position. With one final stomach-wrenching lurch, the shuttle pushed back, then settled down and hit the ground with a force that sent its three crew members sprawling.

"Everyone all right?" the captain asked as she and Tuvok picked themselves up off the deck yet again. One dim red light made the shuttle's interior vaguely visible.

Most of the instrument panels had gone dead, Kim noticed as he stood up and looked around him. He moved again to the main console, feeling a bruise on his lower ribs and another on his elbow. Then he began working, trying to determine what was off-line. "I'm okay, Captain," he said.

"I am unharmed as well, Captain," Tuvok said, "but it appears this shuttle will not fly again without considerable repairs. A separate crew will have to be sent down." He stood beside Kim, examining panels. "We have lost power, at least for the moment, but even if it can be restored it appears nearly everything is out."

"Including life-support," Kim said.

"And communications," Tuvok added.

Janeway nodded, her expression unreadable in the near-darkness. "Very well," she said. "Let's see if we can find out what's going on upstairs." The captain tapped her comm badge. "Janeway to *Voyager,* come in."

No response. Kim tried his own badge, then Tuvok, all to similar results.

"It is possible that interference from the planet's extreme magnetic field fluctuations is preventing the signal from getting through," Tuvok suggested.

"That has to be it, Captain," Kim interjected, trying to make himself useful. He was well aware that Tuvok and Janeway, between them, had more experience than he would likely accumulate in a lifetime. Still, neither of them ever made him feel that he was not a valued crewman, which only increased his determination to be just that.

"Cut off and shipwrecked," Janeway muttered, shaking her head gravely. Then her hands went to her hips, heralding a change in her mood. "What systems can you get to come back up?" she asked the Vulcan. "And how long will it take? That hope is all we've got going for us right now."

"I cannot guess at the time, but some repairs might be possible. I will make communications my priority."

"Understood. You'll stay here, then. See what you can do. Meanwhile, Mr. Kim and I are going to have a look around. Our landing was likely witnessed by someone, and I'd rather spot them before they spot us."

"I'd estimate we've landed just north of our target," Kim announced, recalling the last telemetry data he'd seen just before they touched down. He had gone over maps of the surface while waiting in the shuttle bay, and maps of this area in particular. The nearby village was one of the largest on this side of the planet. They had been aiming for a spot near there. For a moment, when they were still up in the clouds, he had worried they might land right on top of it.

"That also would put us only a few kilometers from the hills where the underground energy source was detected," Tuvok added.

"At least we're in the right neighborhood," Janeway remarked. "Not that it will do us a lot of good."

"Captain," Kim asked, thinking it pertinent to do so now, "do you think *Voyager* is under attack?"

"We have no way of knowing," Tuvok said.

"What I mean is, why would the Televek send their people aboard *Voyager* and then start shooting?"

"I think they were shooting only at the shuttle," Janeway said.

"But that doesn't make sense either."

"That's why we're here, Mr. Kim, to try to make sense of some of this. And that's what I intend to do. Phasers on stun," she directed him, checking her own weapon as she spoke. "I hope we won't have to use them. I don't want to make contact with the native population if we can avoid it. We have no reason to believe the Televek have."

"Aye, sir," Kim said, placing the hand phaser back on his belt. "I'm ready."

"Good." She pulled the manual release, and the shuttle's main hatch slowly opened. "Let's go."

CHAPTER
5

"BATTLE STATIONS, MR. ROLLINS!" CHAKOTAY SNAPPED as he rushed onto the bridge, the chief engineer right behind him. "Rearm photon torpedoes, prepare to fire on my command. Helm, prepare an evasive course."

Rollins stood at Tuvok's station touching keypads on the tactical control panel. "I would advise against firing, sir," he said. "We're too close to the target."

"He's right," B'Elanna told Chakotay from the engineering bay. "Without our shields we'd risk the chance of being caught in the backwash."

Chakotay looked from one to the other. "I know. Arm the torpedoes."

"The Televek are hailing us, Commander," Rollins announced.

"I'll bet they are."

"I knew they couldn't be trusted," Neelix said. He

had been lingering near the turbolift door. He walked up gingerly behind Chakotay, rubbing nervous hands together. "I did try to tell you."

Chakotay nodded, then fixed his gaze on the dark, angular shape of the Televek ship in the center of the main viewscreen. "Put them on," he said, adding, "This better be good."

"Why was a shuttle launched?" Gantel's slightly agitated voice immediately asked. "What were you trying to accomplish?"

"Why was it deliberately fired upon?" the commander countered tersely. "That shuttle represented no threat to you of any kind."

"Our weapons fire hit your shuttle quite by accident. It was intended as a warning, nothing more."

Chakotay frowned at this, and noticed his fists were clenched tightly against his outer thighs. He opened them, forcing himself to stretch his fingers. He doubted the Televek's aim was that bad. "A warning against what? The shuttle's mission was purely scientific, an attempt to gather more data. The planet's chaotic magnetic fields must be affecting your sensors, the same as ours. A mission to the surface was the only logical step."

"Apparently another . . . misunderstanding, Commander," the Televek's increasingly calm voice responded.

Chakotay balled his fists again. "You seem to have a lot of those."

"Only when we are uninformed."

"We have people aboard that shuttle!" Chakotay snapped.

"We regret any injuries, of course. It is quite possible there are survivors."

"Then I trust you won't mind if we send another shuttle down after our people," Chakotay replied. "Immediately."

"That will not be possible."

"Why not?" Paris said, nearly rising out of his seat at the helm.

"You can't expect us to leave them there!" B'Elanna injected.

Chakotay clenched his fists once more. "We intend to launch a rescue attempt. Do you intend to try to stop us?"

For a moment dead air filled the communication bands. Finally Gantel said, "There is much to explain. We are creating yet another misunderstanding, I think."

"Agreed," Chakotay said.

"Did Jonal and the others arrive safely?" Gantel asked then. "Have you spoken with them?"

"Yes," Chakotay said, still trying to control a sense of exasperation that threatened to overwhelm him. "And they seem to have almost as much trouble getting to the point as you do. Now, I want some answers."

"Of course, but first, may we speak to our advocates?"

"Right now?"

"Yes. I believe that may be the best way to proceed. Confusion serves no one. Direct communication serves best. They can help us both, I assure you."

"I can think of at least one other option," Chakotay told him, glancing first at Paris, then at Torres, aware even before he saw their faces that he was speaking for them as well.

"And if we obliterate each other, all is lost," Gantel

said. "In the interest of cooperation, and the well-being of those in the shuttle, you should summon our people."

"Very well. Mister Rollins, have our Drosary visitors brought directly to the bridge. They are to be kept under full security at all times."

"Commander," Rollins began, "if I may say so, sir, I don't see where that will help. In fact, it might confuse—"

"No, we are going to have this out, here and now," the commander replied. "Mr. Paris, maintain surface scans. Keep trying to find a way through that EM-field interference. If you get anything at all, speak up. That goes for everyone."

Chakotay paced silently as his orders were carried out. Within moments the three Drosary advocates stepped onto the bridge. Two armed security officers preceded them, while another two followed behind. As soon as the channel to the Televek was reopened, Jonal began a rapid discussion, which was quickly joined by Mila and Tassay. The content, however, was difficult to determine; it was as if they were speaking in a code.

Clearly, however, there was some disagreement or other, and it centered around *Voyager*—specifically, around "a class-nine joint venture," in Gantel's words.

"And what of the salvage?" Jonal asked.

"There can be no argument on this," Gantel replied.

"That was our original position," Tassay said.

"I have always advocated continuous evaluation," came Gantel's answer.

"Especially when it is most opportune," Mila said with what could only have been a touch of sarcasm.

"I can only recommend that we grant them the right of applied incentives," Jonal said emphatically. "Second tier, of course."

"How generous," Gantel replied, biting back. "I'm sure the first director will be pleased with that."

"And she will be more pleased, I suppose, with all of nothing," Mila chided, more sternly than Chakotay would have expected. Yet another long silence followed. The three Drosary stood calmly about, waiting patiently, as if they knew exactly what was to come.

"Agreed," Gantel said at last, "contingent on the first director's decisions, which are, we expect . . . imminent."

"Indeed," Tassay muttered, while the three of them exchanged a quick look, which Chakotay was inclined to read as a grimace.

"Sounds a lot like a family dispute," the commander remarked quietly, leaning toward his fellow crew members. The bridge officers exchanged glances, none of them terribly encouraging, Chakotay thought. "I'm beginning to wonder whether the Televek know what they're doing," he said, deciding a bit of cheerleading was in order.

"They know, Commander," Neelix said from between the command chairs, displaying his talent for never missing a word of any conversation he was within a parsec of. "Believe me, they do."

Thanks, Chakotay thought.

"I just hope *we* do," B'Elanna said broodingly.

"So do I," Paris confided.

Chakotay could only nod.

"Commander," Jonal said, after an exchange that seemed to have something to do with contingencies, followed by a brief farewell. "On behalf of our patrons we would like to renew our efforts to find avenues of cooperation and to allay our differences. We have additional information to share, which could benefit all concerned. We will begin by assuring you that if proper communications are maintained—something the three of us will see to directly, with your cooperation, of course—no further misfortunes need occur. The Televek were trying to prevent trouble, not start it, whether you believe that or not."

"That is true, Chakotay," Tassay said, moving closer to him now, looking at him with remarkably soulful eyes. "We must take one step back, I think, before we can move forward."

"First, the Televek are willing to be more flexible with regard to terms," Jonal said. This statement was accompanied by enthusiastic nods from the other two Drosary. "Second, they are prepared to coordinate efforts to locate your shuttlecraft on the planet's surface and, if possible, to communicate with any survivors. Ultimately it may even be possible to rescue the crew, but that is more complicated, as we will explain."

"Go right ahead," B'Elanna said coldly, barely beating Chakotay to it.

"Please," the commander said instead.

"We do not believe our warning phaser beam could have destroyed the shuttle, even though it made contact, as it was not of sufficient strength," Jonal said.

"The facts would tend to contradict you," Chakotay countered.

"The planet itself may be responsible for what happened," said Tassay.

"Why the planet?" Paris asked.

"That is key to what we must talk about," Mila answered. "You don't know what you are dealing with here. The Televek themselves have only begun to figure it out."

"In the meantime, they will power down their weapons once more, provided you will do the same," Jonal said soothingly, as though the idea was nothing more than a detail. "It is difficult to talk when the prospect of obliteration is only seconds away."

Chakotay stood considering, noticing how at ease these Drosary seemed to be once more, and then how Tassay was looking at him, concentrating on him, as if hungry for inspiration. Or, Chakotay mused, perhaps there was even more to it than that. "Understood," he said. "But you'll keep in mind that we tried this once before."

"Again, communication—"

"I know," Chakotay answered Jonal.

Tassay moved still closer to him, smiling now, which somehow seemed to make her entire presence warmer by a few degrees. Some part of him recognized the effect on another level, one he was trying to ignore. She was not an unattractive woman, but he simply had no time for personal relations at the moment, and he didn't see where she did, either. But the Drosary were aliens, complete with alien customs and ideals, something one couldn't lose sight of. It was possible they did not share his own aversion to mixing business with pleasure. Perhaps these Drosary were not only affable but capricious as well.

"We'll adjourn to the captain's ready room," he

said, thinking it best. "I have a lot more questions than answers, and I intend to start changing that ratio."

"An excellent suggestion," Jonal agreed.

"You too, Neelix," Chakotay said, which seemed to please the Talaxian not in the least. He wanted to be with Kes, of course, but right now she didn't need him as much as Chakotay did.

As the commander turned, he realized that Mila had drifted nearer to Paris and had already engaged him in a separate conversation. The commander cleared his throat loudly. Paris looked up and instantly caught the meaning of Chakotay's forbidding glare. The lieutenant stood up and took Mila gently by the arm, then turned her away from the helm station. "We wouldn't want you accidentally to touch anything," he said in explanation. "Why don't you go with the commander?"

"Oh, of course," Mila said, obviously somewhat embarrassed.

Everyone smiled.

They might all be spies, Chakotay thought. The question was whether or not it mattered. Either way, he intended to find out.

"Are you coming along?" Mila asked Paris.

"He is of more use to me out here," Chakotay said.

Mila looked remarkably childlike as she tipped her head. "Please, Commander, I insist. After all, your vessel, like our own, is at station-keeping. Do you not value Paris's opinions?"

Chakotay didn't like being squeezed, but then, he didn't like much of anything that was going on just now. What all this amounted to was another delay, and it wasn't worth that.

"Very well," he muttered, allowing the irritation to show in his voice. B'Elanna Torres stood not a meter from him, squarely between the Drosary and the ready room door with her arms folded in front of her. She would be the next one the Drosary wanted to come along. That was clear enough. "Is there anyone else you'd like to have join us?" the commander asked.

Mila looked directly at B'Elanna, then looked away. "No, this will be sufficient."

The look on B'Elanna's face could have soured Drindorian dragon's milk.

Chakotay shook his head, then threw up his hands. "Good," he said, glancing at B'Elanna as he brushed past her. "Someone has to get some work done around here."

"Commander, it's all right," Torres said as the ready room door slid open. "It's more than all right."

Chakotay paused and held her gaze for a moment. He had seen her this serious before—an overreaction in most people, but not in her, especially when lives were at stake. Just now he found her mood a comfort. He nodded to her and went inside.

As they gathered in the small, sparsely appointed ready room, Mila managed to get a smile out of Paris, who seemed clearly to be warming up to the beautiful young Drosary, a reaction that Chakotay had to admit was understandable, even under the circumstances. Tassay remained close by Chakotay's side as he stood in front of Janeway's desk and leaned back against it. The others settled on the large sofa on one side of the room. Tassay sat on the end nearer the commander.

"Where is your captain?" Jonal asked. "I had hoped to continue our discussion with her as well."

"She . . . has been detained a while longer. I have full authority to negotiate."

Jonal's expression did not change. "Very well, Commander."

"My first priority is to rescue the crew of our shuttlecraft," Chakotay said. "I think we should start there. The Televek apparently thought that in order to warn our people about something down there, it was worth endangering their lives. You were going to tell me what that something was."

No one said a word at first. Chakotay watched the Drosary for a moment, noting the silent communication that went on almost constantly among them. He sensed an earnestness about them now—a sincerity that seemed to transcend even this most awkward situation. He didn't trust the Televek, but he felt almost certain these three Drosary could be trusted to a point, that they were not malevolent in any case. Especially Tassay.

"The surface of Drenar Four is unapproachable," Jonal said then. "The Televek have tried. Your people would have failed to land there in any case."

Chakotay decided it was time to play bold with what facts he had and watch the Drosary's reactions. "You should know," he said, "that we have detected a substantial power source hidden several miles beneath the surface of the planet's main continent. We also think the Televek may already have a ship down there, in the same region. I trust you intend to explain these things as well."

"Ah, Commander," Jonal said, gently smiling, "my compliments to your ship and your crew. Perhaps some of your sensor technology would constitute worthy barter after all."

"Of course we can explain all that," Tassay reassured the commander.

"Then do," Chakotay prodded.

Jonal looked as if Chakotay had done him a favor—which was a welcome response, if not precisely what the commander had been expecting.

"Very well," Jonal said. "You see, despite every effort, the Televek have been unable to assist the population below. Landings and even close orbital passes are impossible due to an advanced planetary defense system. Anyone traveling too near the surface experiences attacks that result in massive systems failures. If the approach continues, the result is destruction. The power source you spoke of apparently has something to do with this defense system, so far as the Televek can determine."

"In fact, the Televek have already lost a ship in just that way," Mila said further. "The cruiser now in orbit was one of two. Daket, the commander of the other ship, felt certain that he could remodulate his shields in a manner that would allow safe penetration. Gantel did not agree. Finally Daket decided to make the attempt. His ship apparently crashed and has since been out of contact."

"And that's what your friends were trying to warn our shuttle about?" Paris asked, incredulous.

Mila put one slender hand on his forearm and nodded. "Truly it is," she said.

Paris frowned. "They couldn't just open a channel?"

"Gantel believed there wasn't time for a discussion," Tassay replied. "A warning shot seemed like the best choice."

"The Televek themselves have never encountered

any offensive or defensive system like this one," Jonal said. "It is intelligent, remarkably fast, and quite powerful. They even believe it may have come from some other part of the galaxy. Your part, perhaps, though you seem unfamiliar with it as well."

"That is true, at least so far," Chakotay conceded.

"We have another suggestion," Tassay said, practically in Chakotay's ear. He pulled away from her instinctively, putting a slight space between them. For now, at least, he told himself. "I'm still listening. What do you propose?"

"Applied incentives," Tassay said happily.

"I heard you mention that before," Paris said. "What is that all about?"

"Incentives are the lubricant of life," Mila explained. "They are utterly empowering, when properly exercised—something any Televek can tell you. And," she added, grinning fondly at Paris, "this holds true for nearly all political, business, and personal negotiations."

"Simply," Jonal said, "if *Voyager* could help the Televek analyze this remarkable defensive system, then disarm it, then both ships could work together to search for your shuttlecraft as well as for the missing Televek cruiser. Joint efforts could then be made to help the people of Drenar Four, as far as is practical."

"And for this, you would supply us with the repair components we need?" Chakotay said.

"Without any other exchange of equipment or Starfleet technologies?" Neelix pressed. "No phaser specs, that sort of thing?"

"Correct." Jonal seemed quite pleased with himself, as did his lovely companions.

Paris seemed almost as pleased as they were, but Chakotay was trying hard not to get too carried away. "What do the Televek get out of all this?" he asked.

Jonal shrugged, a very human gesture. "They would like to rescue their people just as you would yours, of course, but I will admit, Commander, that they wouldn't mind acquiring that Drenarian defensive system, or even some small part of it. It has, after all, defied their very best efforts so far."

"To that end, they might help repair your phasers, in whatever capacity you see fit, of course," Mila said serenely, "as long as the right salvage terms can be negotiated."

Paris looked at her. "Just what do you know about our phasers?"

Mila politely feigned a scoff. "The Televek are *very* good guessers. Your phasers are not currently powered up, nor were they during the recent shuttle mishap. Therefore, they are likely being repaired, as are so many of your other systems. You needn't confirm any of this, of course, if you prefer not to."

"A perceptive bunch, indeed," Neelix said quietly.

"If that were the case, why would the Televek have such a specific change of heart?" Chakotay asked. He sat still, eyes steady, waiting for the answer.

"Because they are convinced they will need your phasers," Tassay told him. She was sincere once more, her childish grin nearly gone. "Their hearts have nothing at all to do with it."

"Ah," Neelix said. "Now we're getting somewhere."

"You see, Commander," Jonal said, "they have had some time to consider the problem this situation poses, and they have come up with a plan. As I understand it, the defensive system's power levels are gradually dropping, and eventually free access to the surface will be available. But even if the surface can be reached, the power source and presumably the defense system's control center are both located in a cavern more than seven kilometers below the planet's surface. There seems to be no expeditious way of getting to it."

"There may be tunnels, or possibly a network of caves that lead down to the site," Paris suggested.

"And if there is not?" Jonal asked. "If the passageways have been sealed or hidden? Time may be short. As you already know, the planet is becoming very unstable."

"You mentioned a solution," Chakotay said.

Jonal nodded. "It has occurred to Gantel that if you could show the Televek how to improve their phaser efficiency to your ship's levels, it might be possible to use them to bore a hole that deep, and in rather good time. Short of that, you could simply use *Voyager*'s wonderful phasers to do the job, once they are repaired. Assuming they need repairs, of course."

All three of the Drosary were smiling. Chakotay had to admit it made sense. The transporters might be out for some time, and he wasn't about to tell the Televek about them. The devil would be in the details, but . . .

"I'll run the idea past my chief engineer, see if she thinks it can be done. As it happens, we do find ourselves in need of a replacement component for the phasers, an EPS flow regulator. It is something we can manufacture ourselves, but it will take considerable time and resources. If the Televek happened to have something comparable on hand—"

"Aren't you afraid of letting them in on all your secrets, Commander?" Neelix said, visibly concerned. "The captain said—"

"The component is a basic one," Chakotay said, speaking to everyone. "Very little information would be exchanged."

"Then you do see this offer as it is intended?" Mila said, hopeful.

"Yes. It would speed things up," Chakotay agreed. "And as you point out, the planet is unstable. Time is something our survivors may not have much of." He paused, still uncomfortable about discussing *Voyager*'s lack of firepower in such a tactically difficult situation. But this *did* seem like the only solution right now.

"I think I'm starting to like the idea as well," Paris said, smiling like the others.

"I'm inclined to think there is another catch somewhere," Neelix said, though his tone had softened.

"We are hiding nothing, Commander Chakotay," Tassay said. "Nothing at all."

"When will your people be ready to begin working with the Televek?" Jonal asked.

"My crew is ready now."

"Wonderful, and I'm sure you'll come to see this as a sensible decision," Jonal exclaimed to one and all. "And you must admit, it does sound like a first step toward a possible eventual sharing of more . . . unfamiliar information, does it not?"

Chakotay reminded himself of his discussions with Janeway and Tuvok, but this was the path that had been set before him, the only clear direction. There might not be another. "I cannot predict the future, but at present I think this limited agreement can be made," he said in answer.

"More than enough for now," Tassay said with enthusiasm, and Chakotay thought for a moment she might reach out and give him a hug.

Jonal was the first to stand. "We will inform Gantel at once."

"By all means," Chakotay said, rising too, leading everyone back out onto the bridge. Within moments contact with the Televek had been reestablished. Jonal explained everything perfectly. With very little discourse, the Televek agreed.

"But there may be a temporary . . . problem," Gantel said, addressing Chakotay. "I will need a moment. Can you stand by?"

"Of course," Chakotay said, more than a little curious. He stood at the center of the bridge for several moments. No one in the room said a word. Just as he was beginning to grow impatient, the Televek's voice sounded on the comm once more.

"As I suspected, a minor delay, Commander," Gantel began. "You must understand, the cruiser you see before you is not a merchant vessel, and we are not presently carrying in our inventory anything quite like the equipment you need. However, your needs, and of course ours, can still be met. You have my word as third director. I will explain in detail shortly. In the interim, you may of course transmit the specifications for your EPS flow regulator. In return, you will be sent all of the sensor data we have collected on Drenar Four. We will work from there."

"Shortly?" the commander repeated, skeptical.

"Very shortly."

"Very well."

"Good!" Tassay exclaimed, taking Chakotay's forearm gently in one hand.

"Can we get you something to eat or drink?" Paris asked, speaking to Mila at first. Then he looked up. "Any of you? I mean, this might take a while."

"Yes," Tassay said happily, "that would be wonderful."

"If you don't mind, of course," Jonal specified. Then he moved toward Chakotay and quietly took the commander briefly aside. "Is there any chance the captain could join us again?"

"I'll take you to our dining area," Chakotay said. "But I doubt Captain Janeway will be there. Unless she manages to free herself of her present duties."

Jonal shrugged somewhat dourly. "I see."

Chakotay gestured to the security guards as they left the bridge, indicating they should come along.

B'Elanna Torres hurried up the hallway on her way to the galley. She had put off eating anything for hours now, but hunger was beginning to take its toll. She needed a little something to stave off the jitters, something she could eat quickly. Repairs were proceeding, everyone was still leaping through hoops, trying to make some real progress, but she hated the thought of taking a break herself. Finally, though, her needs were beginning to affect her disposition.

She had a bowl of oatmeal in mind, or perhaps a cold sandwich. She'd long preferred human food to Klingon, just as she had always chosen to focus more on her human half than on her Klingon heritage. Most human dishes, like human beings themselves, were softer and easier to stomach. And in some cases quicker—a particular advantage just now.

She hesitated while the galley door slid open, then pushed her way inside.

"Torres, won't you join us?" Commander Chakotay said, waving her toward the long, shiny table where he sat with Lieutenant Paris, Neelix, Kes, and the three Drosary advocates.

Quite a crowd already, B'Elanna decided. They didn't need to make it any larger. And in any case, she was not thrilled with the idea of wasting a lot of time talking with creatures who didn't seem that interested in talking to her—and probably for good reason.

She still wasn't sure why, but she didn't like these Drosary no matter how she tried to rationalize the situation, and she was fairly certain they didn't like her, either. "I'm a little busy right now," she said. "I've only got a minute."

"Just for a moment, then," Chakotay said, to agreeable nods from the others. "I insist."

It wasn't an order. The commander was apparently just being cordial, for whatever reason. But that wasn't the point. She didn't want to tell him no. She decided it wouldn't hurt to ask Kes how she was doing in any case.

"Please, we would enjoy your company," Jonal said, waving much as Chakotay had done, getting it almost right. A change of heart, perhaps, B'Elanna thought, noting that even Neelix seemed to be enjoying the Drosary's company just now. But prudence had always been considered a valuable survival trait by nearly all species, B'Elanna thought, including both of hers.

"Let me grab a bite first," she said, lifting lids on pots, searching for breakfast, though she wasn't at all certain what meal the time of day required. She ended up with a bowl of something that was apparently hot cereal but was definitely not made of oats. She tasted it as she walked toward the table. The grain was palatable, a variety Neelix had helped find and gather several weeks ago on a planet very much like Drenar Four. You just needed to put a lot of sweetener on it, she decided. An awful lot.

"How's the arm?" she asked.

"Better, thanks," Kes replied. She grinned broadly. "We have an excellent medical staff."

"So I understand," B'Elanna said. She sat down and began to spoon the thick yellowish porridge into her mouth.

"The doctor can hardly manage without Kes," Neelix said proudly. "But he'll just have to manage for a little while longer."

"Your concern for one another is refreshing," Jonal said. "Even among different species."

"We have a great deal in common, it seems," Chakotay began.

B'Elanna looked up. "Who does?"

"Tassay and I. The Drosary and the Maquis. Our part of the galaxy and theirs." He smiled with genuine enthusiasm, something of a surprise to B'Elanna. "The Drosary have always desired a peaceful existence," he continued. "They would rather put their resources into building a colony, a better way of life, than fighting wars for governments they feel they have no part in. All that was taken away from them."

"One of the reasons we started our own colony," Tassay interjected, "was to escape the destruction of our culture, which goes back much further than my current homeworld's culture. The old ways, the old traditions, are all but gone now. All of our ancient customs are being lost."

Chakotay sat back and gazed warmly at her. "It seems we have even more in common than I thought."

"I ended up on that colony, where the Televek found us, for a very different reason, I'm afraid," Mila said, apparently addressing everyone, but looking mostly at Paris. "Personal reasons, I guess you could say."

"Tell me about them," Paris said, as sincere as B'Elanna had ever seen him.

Mila grew somber for a moment, thoughtful. Then she seemed to recover. "Very well. There was an accident on a small commercial space transport during a routine trip to one of my world's two moons. The ship was nearly lost, and many people died. I was the pilot. It was a systems failure, pure and simple—I was there, I know what happened—but that was never proven to the satisfaction of the review board. I lost my commission. I had a hard time living with the stigma, the stain, that followed me after that. Until I finally got far enough away."

"I . . . I do understand," Paris told her, taking her hand in his, gazing raptly at her. "Maybe too well." They seemed to have still more in common than Tassay and Chakotay, B'Elanna reflected, silently nodding as they both glanced toward her. They turned to each other again, and she watched Paris for a moment, watched him doting on Mila. Then she turned instead to Chakotay, who seemed to be paying a great deal of attention to Tassay at the moment.

It's enough to make anybody sick, B'Elanna told

herself, noticing she was not quite as hungry as she had been a moment ago.

"You seem upset," Jonal said to her, disturbing her speculations.

She looked at him. She was. "What makes you think so?"

"I can tell, that's all. Though it looks almost out of place on you."

No one had ever told her *that* before. "What do you mean by that?"

"You have many great responsibilities, I'm sure, but I am nearly as sure you have the means to meet them. You seem so . . . competent." His smile was soft, not the least acerbic, as she was sure hers would have been if she had been inclined to attempt one. She couldn't tell if he was being empathetic or diplomatic. Either way, she wasn't much in the mood. She shrugged. "It can get a little rough sometimes. Goes with the territory, I guess."

"You are different than many of the others."

"I'm only half human," she said, purposely glaring at him, "if that's okay with you."

"I assure you, it is. And I understand your reaction, I think, though you seem to be among very good people here. I admire this Federation of yours. You see, on my homeworld I too am something of a—a mixed breed, or half-breed, you might say. Mila and Tassay are as well. But the dominant society there has not yet risen above the ignorance that so often complicates such things."

"I . . . didn't know," B'Elanna said, somewhat stunned by the gentle man's words. "But for me, I think it's probably a little more complicated than that." She thought of how many times people had told her they understood what it was like to be B'Elanna Torres, how ridiculous she always thought they were. Though what she was doing right now was possibly worse. "Or maybe it isn't," she said. "Maybe I don't know."

"B'Elanna has had her share of successes as well as setbacks," Chakotay remarked.

"I'm sure we would all enjoy listening to you talk about them," Jonal told her. Mila and Tassay quickly agreed—Mila still holding Paris's hand while Tassay marveled at the tattoo over Chakotay's left eye.

"It's so nice to find beings who care about the lives of others the way you do," Kes said, smiling softly at the Drosary. "There is so much we can all learn from each other. So much I want to learn."

"The similarities do make the differences easier to understand," Neelix said, typically aiding Kes by any means available to him. Neelix and Kes had seemed largely content simply to observe the conversation until now. B'Elanna wasn't sure she liked the change.

"Sometimes there are things about others that we can never understand," she told Kes before glancing at Jonal.

"I suppose that's true," Kes said, "but working with the doctor has made me realize just how precious all life is and how easily it can be lost. It's wonderful to find people who embrace that same basic ideal."

"Isn't she remarkable," Neelix said. It was not a question. He grinned broadly at Kes and kissed her cheek. The sentiment seemed to carry all around the table. It stopped at B'Elanna Torres's chair.

Something about the Drosary still bothered her. She couldn't shake the uneasy, restless feeling the visitors seemed to inspire in her. Especially Jonal, despite the fact that she saw nothing at all wrong with him, specifically. Nothing dire, certainly . . .

It was the fault of her untrusting, unsociable Klingon side, she imagined; perhaps she wasn't unusually perceptive, just cursed.

She finished her porridge and stood up, regarding the others. In a way it was getting harder to dislike these strange visitors, and easier to understand why. If they got her the relay she wanted, with no new, unmentioned strings attached . . . well, maybe it would all work out.

Jonal gazed glowingly at her. She looked into his eyes and tried to smile, but something inside her churned. She tasted yellow cereal at the back of her throat.

"I—I have to get going," she sputtered, swallowing. Then she left them sitting there.

CHAPTER

6

JANEWAY STOOD AT THE EDGE OF A NEATLY CULTIVATED field, straddling a row of low, leafy orange plants bearing small round fruit that reminded her of young tomatoes. Bushier plants grew in alternate rows starting thirty meters to her right. Squash, she thought, or something very much like it. The crew of *Voyager* wouldn't get a chance to sample much of this produce, though. Everything in the field was dying.

Thick blackish-brown powder covered the land and all that grew from it to a depth of several inches. Rains had stiffened the early layers, but the soft dust on top led Janeway to believe it hadn't rained in a while. Someone had apparently been trying to keep the plants clean, the dust between the plants was deeper than the dust on them, but efforts seemed to be falling behind.

Kim plucked a small young fruit from the plant at his feet, brushed it off, and tucked it into the sample bag at his waist. He toed the plant and dislodged a thick cascade of dust and soot that tumbled from its stems and leaves. Clumps of the dark stuff still clung tenaciously to the plant.

"Definitely volcanic ash," Janeway said, reading its composition from her tricorder.

Kim held up his own tricorder and resumed scanning. "Most of it fairly recent, I'd say," he noted. "I'm surprised there's not more of it, judging by the activity in those mountains."

He pointed due south. A ridge of mighty peaks could be seen well in the distance, much like those just east of their current position, though more extensive. The southern mountains featured two great plumes of angry black smoke that rose seemingly to the top of the sky—the same clouds that the shuttle had flown through on its way down.

Janeway adjusted her tricorder from geologic scans back to the electromagnetic range. She instructed Kim to resume scanning for bioelectric and organic signatures in the direction of the largest village, nearer the eastern hills. As had been the case early on, the results were immediate.

"I'm reading multiple life signs, humanoid, and they're definitely on the move. They're approaching from the east, from the village, I'd say, Captain."

They had scanned this same group of people earlier. Few details could be discerned from such a distance, but they had assumed the party was headed toward the downed shuttle. Now that assumption seemed correct.

"Range?"

"Just under two kilometers."

"I don't think that's the only company we've got, either." Janeway turned slightly, allowing the tricorder to triangulate more accurately. "There. EM scan."

Kim recalibrated his own tricorder, waited, then slowly nodded. "These readings are definitely artificial. And they seem to coincide with the ferric metals readings we've been getting. I'd say it's the same source."

Janeway frowned. "So would I."

"I put the contact no more than a kilometer or so the other side of the village, near the hills."

"What would you say are the chances it's a Televek cruiser that's landed?"

"I'd say the chances are pretty good, Captain."

They stood staring out across the fields toward the forests beyond. A bristled carpet of tall, spindly trees, swaying gently in the warm morning breezes, covered the high ground as far as the eye could see. Crooked lines revealed the paths of mountain streams descending from distant peaks. This was high summer on Drenar Four's main continent, and one could not help but be impressed. It was a beautiful world if you looked under all the soot, and if you didn't mind that it was trying to pull itself apart.

"We'd better get out of the open, Captain," Kim said, adjusting his tricorder again, repeating his earlier scans. "Those people are moving at a good pace. They'll be emerging on the far side of these fields in just a few minutes."

"And they will no doubt find the shuttle after that.

We have to assume that's what they're looking for. And when they find it, I'd rather be outside watching than inside waiting. We may have to get Tuvok out of there, at least for the time being."

"What then?"

It was a straightforward, sensible question. She just didn't have a good answer. She placed one hand on the ensign's shoulder, gave him a gentle pat. "Don't worry, Mr. Kim. Whatever happens, I'm sure we'll keep busy."

They turned around and headed back the way they had come. The shuttle lay just beyond a knoll, toward the far side of an expansive grassy field. The field, one of many in this area, was surrounded by low, forested hills. Fields that had been left fallow, apparently. Janeway was fairly sure a stream ran by somewhere beyond the low bluff that stood just on the far side of the shuttle. They were probably going to need water, among other things, though she feared they might find only a flowing stream of mud.

"How are we doing?" she asked as they entered the shuttle's open hatch. They found Tuvok lying on his back, probing a web of circuitry under the navigation console. He had removed several of the access panels in the shuttle's forward control section, more in the rear cargo area.

"I am very close to restoring minimal power to some of the primary systems, including the computer and the sensors, both of which seem to be largely undamaged." He pushed back, then pulled himself up off the deck and moved toward another panel. "Mr. Kim, would you be so kind as to lend a hand?"

Kim nodded and went to Tuvok's side, then took

the probe from him and held it in position. Tuvok was apparently trying to use one section of conduit in place of another. Kim used the probe to fuse the connection. Tuvok stood up again suddenly and tapped the main console. "It looks good," Kim told him.

"Let's see what we've got," Janeway said.

At this, Kim withdrew the probe. Tuvok entered yet another command, and selected panels throughout the small ship suddenly flickered to life.

"Good work, Mr. Tuvok!" Janeway cried.

"A good beginning, but little else, I'm afraid," Tuvok said. "The rest of the repairs will take more time."

"Sensors will do for now. I want you to scan these coordinates." She held her tricorder up and let the Vulcan examine the readings. He nodded, then moved to the sensor panel and began working.

"We think it may be a ship, just as you suggested," Kim told Tuvok.

"We can't determine anything more, though," Janeway said. "Wreckage could easily read about the same, including those EM emissions, if someone left the lights on."

"Contact verified, Captain," Tuvok said after a moment. "I am reading what appears to be a fully operational Televek cruiser, very much like the one we encountered in orbit. I find no indication of damage of any kind, and power levels are consistent with those of its sister ship. I am also detecting considerable activity in the area surrounding the cruiser."

Janeway let out a sigh. "I knew they were up to something. I just wish I knew what it was."

"When we find out, I'll bet we won't like it," Kim said.

"Captain," Tuvok said, looking up at her, "the cruiser is also in close proximity to the underground energy source we detected from *Voyager*."

"How close?"

"Almost directly above it."

"Then they might be the ones who put it here," Kim suggested.

"Possible, but highly unlikely," Tuvok replied.

Janeway looked at him. "Why?"

"The cruiser and the energy source are separated by some seven miles of earth and rock, and I am reading no direct connection between the two points, physical, radiant or radio. Also, the underground energy source has a complex energy signature, including trace tetryon emissions, while the Televek cruiser is using a conventional matter-antimatter power source."

"So their signatures are entirely different from each other," Janeway said, considering. Tetryons were rare indeed. The Caretaker had produced similar emissions, but it had been extragalactic in nature. The Televek, most certainly, were not. "Any change in the readings from the underground energy source?" she asked, moving to Tuvok's side now, examining the data for herself.

Tuvok called up side-by-side displays of *Voyager*'s earlier reading and the shuttle's current scans. "The overall output of the power source is still exhibiting a continuous, steady drop. Present levels continue to spike downward, then recover, though for no apparent reason."

"The Televek might be draining it somehow,"

Janeway suggested, this time sparing Kim the task. "But maybe they're not taking the energy directly into their cruiser. A storage facility, perhaps. Scan for anything that might fit that description."

"I do not believe the Televek have the capability," Tuvok said as he made a fresh sensor sweep. He looked up after a moment. "No such facility has been detected, but I will continue to examine that possibility."

"Very well, Tuvok," Janeway told him. "But I think you are quite right about Televek capabilities. Which leaves us with plenty of possibilities, certainly. Clarification, however, seems in short supply." She grinned at the others; attempting to make light of their situation, at least for a moment. Only Kim grinned back.

"We have to go," she said with a sigh. "A party of Drenarians is headed this way. At least we think that's who they are. Shut everything down and lock up. I don't think the locals can do much more damage to the exterior. With luck, they'll nose around for a while, then move on. After they leave, we can come back and try to get communications working."

"Understood," Tuvok replied, already complying.

Once the hatch was sealed, they made their way up the face of the steep bluff, then hid among the thickly clustered trees that crowded its edge. The knoll east of the shuttle was just tall enough to block the captain's view of the fields beyond, but soon enough she saw thin puffs of gray smoke rising above the ridge. The approaching Drenarians were kicking up ash clouds, giving their position away. Janeway made a mental note to remember that.

It wasn't long before two dozen or more humanoid

individuals appeared. Even at a distance they seemed somewhat taller and huskier than most humans. As they descended the gentle slope and edged slowly, cautiously, toward the shuttle, Janeway noted that their features were crude and almost brutish. Thick, long, dark hair and heavy beards obscured the heads and faces of the males, and the few females didn't look much different, though their hair grew even longer. They wore sturdy handmade clothing, most of it apparently woven. Their shoes and packs, though, had clearly been made from animal skins.

With the last of them came three stout wooden wagons, small and two-wheeled, drawn by oxlike beasts that stood about complaisantly, chewing on the trampled, semiclean grassy tufts beneath their feet, as the caravan reached level ground and paused. The handful of individuals who appeared to be leading the way began to fan out, cautiously circling around the shuttlecraft, their bodies crouched low to the ground. They carried weapons, Janeway noticed now. Most held long, heavy knives that reminded her of ancient Roman short swords, but a few carried what appeared to be well-crafted, and probably quite deadly, crossbows.

Janeway began to wonder if these people hadn't been *given* some of their tools and technology, which seemed to postdate their lifestyle and brutish physiology considerably. It was possible the Televek had been here for quite some time.

When they completed their circle, the Drenarians held utterly still, as if they were waiting for something to happen, waiting for some kind of sign. Nothing moved. Even the breeze seemed to have died.

"Their actions tend to indicate that they are motivated by curiosity rather than hostility," Tuvok suggested.

"I agree," Janeway said. "That could be some kind of attack formation, but they don't look like a trained army. If they were, I don't think so many of them would have died the last time they tried this."

"The last time?" Kim asked.

"We have seen no deaths," Tuvok pointed out, still watching the Drenarians below. "To what are you referring?"

"I've seen these people before, in . . . in a dream. A vision, you might say. They died horribly. Phaser burns all over their bodies. Chakotay has seen them too. I suspect the Televek were responsible. Or will be. I have no way of knowing if, or when, those events took place."

The crouched Drenarians began inching closer to the shuttle now, drawing the circle smaller.

"But you suspect that what you saw has already happened?" Tuvok asked.

"I don't know, but it's certainly possible."

"If that is true, I am surprised they would come so near something like the shuttle," Tuvok said.

"So am I," Janeway replied. "They're either very brave and curious or utterly foolish."

One of the men had finally reached the shuttle. He used the tip of his knife to poke at its hull just aft of the port nacelle. When nothing happened, he struck the hull solidly, producing a metallic thrum that echoed across the field. He drew back, startled, a motion imitated by the others, but their trepidation lasted only a moment. As they all drew near again another male began trying to work the tip of his blade into the seam along the edge of the rear hatch.

"They don't waste any time, do they?" Kim noted.

"Remarkable," Tuvok said.

"They're clever, from what I can see," Janeway muttered. "I doubt they have the means to get inside. Still, they could conceivably do more damage if we let them poke around long enough."

"But if they *did* get inside . . ." Kim said.

Before anyone could say another word they heard the quake. A low, distant rumble at first, it grew rapidly, approaching from several directions at once as the ground beneath their feet began to twitch. The noise and the shaking seemed to build on each other as the quake rushed upward from the planet's crust, then swept through the bluff beneath their feet, knocking them to the ground.

"Grab on to something!" Janeway shouted, wrapping her arms around the smooth trunk of a stout young tree, pulling herself close to it as the growl of shaking earth became deafening. A hundred meters north of the shuttle the grasses abruptly heaved upward as a vast area of bedrock was pushed several meters skyward. An adjacent strip of land seemed to vanish entirely.

As Janeway watched the split in the earth travel still farther northward, racing toward the horizon, she felt thankful it had not come the other way and swallowed the shuttle whole. Below, the Drenarians were scrambling to gather together in the open. They huddled close to the waving grasses, watchful of developing dangers. So helpless, Janeway thought, and no doubt frightened. How could they understand what was happening to their world? As it was, with all the resources of *Voyager* at her disposal, she wasn't certain herself.

Suddenly Janeway felt the ground directly under her feet start to move. Behind her a series of loud, echoing cracks sounded as trees began to snap in half. Then the tree trunk she was clinging to began to rise.

"Head for open ground!" she commanded, updating her strategy, pointing to the Drenarians. There wasn't any choice. But as she tried to stand, the edge of the bluff jerked, then abruptly gave way. She saw Kim and Tuvok being thrown forward toward the field below.

She reached back toward the next closest tree as the earth disappeared from underneath her. Her hands came up empty. She felt herself falling, tumbling down the slope in a jumble of earth and roots and rocks. Sharp pain registered on her right side, and then her left leg turned underneath her. Abruptly her head slammed against something huge and hard, and she slipped quietly into darkness.

Captain Janeway was having a dream, though she was certain it was not her own. The acrid smell of hot sulfur and molten metals burned her nose and lungs; the smoke that curled and swirled from every direction made her eyes water. Blinking, then squinting, she found herself high up, and standing on a plateau only a few dozen meters from the edge of a great precipice. Far below and stretching out into the eerie distance lay a vast, glowing lake of molten lava. The steam and smoke and the high, arching cavern walls were illuminated for kilometers by the reddish glow of the lava lake, but more light came from behind her, bright light that radiated all around her, bringing stark detail to the entire plateau. As she turned, she was forced to raise her hand to block out the unnatural glare.

The plateau swept back to the nearest wall of the cavern, perhaps two hundred meters away. There, bathed in cool white light from dozens of fixtures set in the rock, and radiating light of its own, she saw an enormous machine unlike anything she had ever encountered.

Composed of thousands of glowing or darkened tubes all set in massive, curving banks of smooth metal, the components reminded Janeway of heat sinks coupled with scores of generators, though the scale was beyond her experience. Several of the tubes stretched from the plateau upward into the darkness of the cavern's ceiling. Still others twisted back into the cavern wall. Small, flat panels were scattered in wavelike patterns throughout the apparatus. Janeway tried to move toward the machine, but her feet would not cooperate.

Trapped, she thought, choking briefly, wondering how long she could survive in the heavily tainted atmosphere. What kind of dream is this? she wondered. Unless it wasn't any kind of dream at all. And if it wasn't, it occurred to her that death might be a real possibility here. She had never dreamed in such vivid colors before or wiped wet tears from her cheeks as the smoke continued to irritate her eyes, nor had she ever coughed so. No dream was this clear.

She closed her eyes, rubbing them against the sting. When she opened them again, she saw something pass by just over her shoulder, moving swiftly along the plateau's edge. She turned to follow it with her eyes, but only caught a glimpse of a tenuous figure, almost impossible to see in the strangely lit, heavily polluted air. Still, it reminded her of a similar apparition she had encountered once before, aboard *Voyager*. Another of Chakotay's visiting spirits . . . or hers.

She saw several figures now, each so vague she could barely be certain she was observing anything at all. Yet she could sense them, too. Near her. Almost a part of her. Then the dream began to fade away, replaced by growing darkness. She wondered if this was indeed the end. The ghosts had somehow brought her here, and the poisons in the air were killing her. Perhaps they didn't know, she thought. She found it impossible to believe that the ghosts would go to so much trouble, aboard *Voyager* and then here, simply to lure her to an elaborate death.

The darkness became nearly complete. She waited for pain, for panic, for anything, but nothing happened. Then, in a sudden fresh glow, the cavern dreams were replaced by a new image, that of a fantastic alien vessel, a ship several hundred times *Voyager*'s size, and completely unknown; in all her studies of countless Starfleet and alien records and in all her travels, she had seen nothing to compare with the ship that was now passing before her, blocking countless stars from view.

Composed mostly of smooth, curved sections, the ship glowed brightly in the night like Earth's own moon. It featured several towering assemblies of tubes not unlike those that made up much of the machine in the cave. She saw the ship passing star systems, countless numbers of them, traveling on for what must have been ages.

Then the ghost that had appeared to her in her

ready room was there again, drifting nearly formless in the dark as the alien vessel and its universe faded from view. The ghost called to her as it had before, communicating without words, telling her to come, telling her of its pain, and pleading with her . . . for help.

CHAPTER
7

GANTEL PACED THE FLOOR IN FRONT OF THE LAVISH, thickly upholstered chair that dominated the center of the cruiser's bridge. The chew stem he held between his teeth had turned ragged and lost all its flavor, and the subtle effects of its mildly euphoric chemical contents had long since worn off. He had another stem in his pocket, but he wanted to keep his edge just now, much as it pained him to admit it.

"Sit," his second associate, Triness, told him, making the request sound as much like a demand as possible. "You always think of something." She was the only one on the ship who would dare speak to Gantel in such a tone, at least where nonbusiness issues were concerned; he was constantly challenged during general commerce sessions, but that was only to be expected. Here he outranked everybody, and he seldom let anyone forget it.

"I will sit when I can do so with a favorable review in my hands," he said, pausing long enough to rake his long fingers through his great mane of thick white hair. "I will sit when my apparently overrated acquisitions director has something positive to tell me, instead of zero gain after zero gain."

"Daket deserves his rating, and you know it," Triness said, though she was apparently only defending the first associate on general grounds. "You want everything to go perfectly, of course, but even you cannot bend the universe to your will. And neither can Daket. He has been faced with many—"

"Unforeseen difficulties. I know."

"An associate in his position, I think, requires a certain—"

"Triness!" Gantel interrupted sharply, failing in his attempt to keep his voice level. "We are faced with an impending visit by First Director Shaale herself. I can grant Daket all the dispensations in the universe, but Shaale will require a great deal of me. I know the acquisitions team has . . . legitimate excuses, but Shaale never puts those two words together. In the meantime I have to make deals and apparently concessions with these Federation people, none of which makes good sense so far—unless we get results. But for the time being, I am dancing slow and dancing fast at the same time."

"I'd forgotten what a good dancer you are." Triness smiled curtly. "How long has it been since we danced? The last time was on Grelra Seven, I think, just after the revolt."

"Which revolt?"

It was a joke. Triness chuckled. "Why would anyone keep track?"

"I don't know," Gantel said, chuckling with her just a bit.

"You have been regional leader seven times, my dear," Triness cooed, playing the part of a doting mate, something she had never actually been. They were not lovers, though neither of them had yet ruled out that possibility.

Gantel eyed her warily. "What of it?"

"That buys a lot of dispensation."

"Ah, all true," Gantel said, preening. "Quite true."

"Even Shaale must take that into consideration."

Gantel sighed. "In a perfect universe. You won't mind if I worry just a little, all the same?"

"If you did not, you would not be a third director."

They both smiled. After sixteen missions together, they were becoming quite a team. He took as much comfort as he could from the thought, then turned again to the business at hand. "It's just so complicated. The assignment gets more demanding and less manageable by the minute. And I cannot decide whether these Federation people are a blessing or a curse. It would have been so much simpler if they had been relatively unarmed. Then we could have simply wiped them out."

"Simplify," Triness suggested, mostly in jest, "until you think of something."

Another joke, but Gantel suddenly saw a way to take this to heart. What he most wanted was a way to get these strange visitors out of the way, or better yet, entirely under control. But there were many ways to control others.

"I may have an answer," Gantel said, as the thought became fully formed in his mind, bringing with it a sense of relief. He always seemed to think of something. Always. He was simply reluctant to believe that circumstances would never change. "We will tell these Federation people the truth—or part of it, in any case. If we give them everything they want, more than likely we will not get what we want. But if we give them just enough, they might believe . . . just enough."

"They don't seem like the cooperative type to me," Triness said, understating the issue.

"Exactly. They're going to discover the first director's fleet soon enough, and that will complicate matters enormously. Unless . . ." He turned the thought over in his mind and noticed the most remarkable feature in the process. "Unless," he continued, "we tell them ahead of time, make it part of the deal, and involve them, to an extent. After all, once the fleet arrives, our options will multiply by many factors."

"That revelation must be handled correctly."

"Of course."

"And what will we have Jonal say we are doing about the components they have requested?"

"There are many such components among the holds of the first director's fleet, are there not?"

"Yes, but—"

"Well, then," Gantel said, smiling, "we will simply tell them the truth!"

"The truth?"

Gantel's smile broadened. "As any physician can tell you, even poison, in small doses, can sometimes be beneficial."

"I see." Triness tipped her head, a warm look of admiration on her face. "You know, I have always been attracted to the great contemporary artists." She glanced at the others on the bridge, all of whom quickly found ways to mind their own business. Then she rose, leaned close to Gantel, and kissed him on the cheek. "I'll get Jonal and the others on the comm," she said as she straightened up again. "But we will need to communicate our message very carefully."

Gantel nodded, satisfied. "That will be fine."

"I understand you have some additional news from the Televek," Chakotay said. He glanced at the others in the briefing room: Paris, Neelix, and Kes were seated to his left at the table, the Drosary to his right, while two security officers remained stationed at the door. He felt a pang of apprehension, but he tried his best to suppress it, at least until he had heard the advocates out.

"Yes, Commander, I must inform you that we have met with a small problem," Jonal said bleakly.

"More a minor delay, really," Tassay explained.

For a brief instant Chakotay let doubt fill his thoughts and, with it, a flicker of rage. Negotiations had barely gotten under way, yet already they were turning into a delicate tangle, and each effort to smooth the way seemed to create new ripples. What now? he wondered wearily. There were nearly two hundred people aboard *Voyager* who were waiting for results and whose future depended on what their commander did or didn't do, not to mention the fate of the captain and an unknown number of Drenarians on the planet below.

He took a deep breath. "And what is the nature of this, delay?"

Jonal folded both hands on the table in front of

him, presenting himself as an individual who was suddenly completely at ease. "To elaborate on what Gantel started to tell you earlier, the cruiser now in orbit is not a merchant vessel. In truth, they are carrying only enough spare parts and supplies to provide for their own minimum backup needs. Prudence requires they not compromise that status. The Televek neither expect nor desire further hostilities between your two peoples, but a systems failure aboard their vessel would leave them nearly defenseless—against you or any other threat that might arrive."

"That would be unacceptable under any circumstances, as I am sure you can imagine," Mila added.

"So you can't supply us with the phaser flow regulator," Paris said grimly, though as he glanced toward Mila, he smiled, affected by her look of concern. She had been clinging to Paris, just as Tassay seemed committed to following Chakotay around, as much as either man could allow. Neither of the women had been anything less than polite about it. In fact, the only ones aboard *Voyager* who weren't being thoroughly polite were Neelix and, to a lesser extent, B'Elanna Torres.

Chakotay fixed his eyes on Jonal. "But how can we help you if you can't help us?"

"Oh, I'm sure they have something in mind," Neelix said. "I just wonder if anyone around here is going to like it."

Chakotay found himself disposed to apologize for the short alien's behavior, but he fought the urge. Neelix, after all, was an authority on this sector and its people, if an eccentric one. All sensibilities aside, he could not be so easily dismissed, or censured.

"I think what Neelix means is that the Televek are a very resourceful people," Kes offered, not above smoothing feathers where her mate was concerned, and used to it.

"Then he knows them well enough," Tassay suggested.

Jonal smiled. "In fact, I am pleased to tell you that all will soon be well. The Televek have sent word to one of their merchant fleets, which was already bound for an area near this sector on quite another matter. The fleet contains several of the largest transports in the quadrant, and they are even now making their best speed toward our location. I am told your EPS regulator will be instantly obtained as soon as they arrive."

"Also, the transports and the other ships will be on hand in the event that at least some of the population of Drenar Four can be evacuated, assuming that becomes necessary," Mila said. "And of course to assist in any salvage operation we may be fortunate enough to undertake."

"They should arrive sometime tomorrow," Tassay assured the commander.

"That sounds reasonable to me," Paris said.

The door hissed open, and B'Elanna Torres entered the room. She immediately sat at the end of the table nearest the door, opposite Chakotay, visually acknowledging everyone, her expression serious.

"Meanwhile, we might discuss the details of our joint mission to disarm the planet's defensive system once everything is in place," Jonal continued, "so that salvage will be possible."

"In the interim, the Televek are still interested in your offer to share sensor specifications," Tassay said.

"It may help in our combined efforts to assess the situation on the planet."

"I can see to that," B'Elanna said. "If that's what you want, Commander." She fixed Chakotay with a pensive look that made him feel even more uneasy. Apparently her brief willingness to give the Drosary the benefit of the doubt had abated somewhat.

"It is," the commander told her. "But I will approve all transmissions, and I would like to review the data we have received from the Televek cruiser."

"Wonderful," Jonal said.

"Yes, especially for the Televek," Neelix remarked, rolling his eyes.

Kes squeezed his arm. "Neelix, please," she said.

"I'm sorry," he told her, "but if you ask me, these people have done nothing at all to earn our trust. Why should we give it to them just because they ask for it?"

"We are attempting to earn trust as we go," Jonal said, "for both sides."

"We have to try to work together," Chakotay said. "There are many lives at stake."

"Agreed, but the Televek themselves haven't even shown us their faces," Neelix pointed out. "And they seem conveniently unable to give us anything more substantial than rhetoric and sensor data."

"That is a fair observation," Torres said.

"You could lighten up a little," Paris told Torres, a concerned look on his face. "You know, the captain gave you her trust when you asked for it. And you, Neelix."

"That was because at the time she didn't know me very well," Neelix answered.

"My point exactly," Paris said.

Chakotay caught Kes using her hand to hide a grin.

"I think I'll agree with Neelix," B'Elanna said evenly.

"And I think we should get on with this," the commander said, scowling at the others. Then he tried a more affable expression as he turned to the Drosary. "Anything we can do that might expedite rescue efforts should be considered."

"Yes, please, that is the goal of this meeting," Tassay said, assisting Chakotay in that small way. She was a fine choice for an advocate, he thought, as were Jonal and Mila. Indeed, that choice spoke well of the Televek, even if Neelix and B'Elanna didn't.

"We are getting important data from the Televek, which I've been piecing together with our own," B'Elanna said. "At present there exists no safe means of approach to Drenar Four. The defensive system makes use of comparatively small, highly concentrated individual energy fields, which it directs toward any perceived threat."

"The cruiser the Televek lost reported multiple systems failures before contact was broken," Mila said.

"Unfortunately these fields your engineer describes are immune to phaser, photon, and other conventional weapon fire," Jonal said. "The Televek have also tried scrambling their frequencies with dampening fields, but to no effect."

"So the defensive fields work like an artificial immune system," Paris offered.

"Well put," Mila told him, to nods from Tassay and Jonal. Paris took the compliment well.

"He is just remarkable, isn't he?" B'Elanna said in a mocking tone, smiling at Mila in the same manner.

"But what I hear everyone saying is that there's nothing much we can do," Neelix said.

"We've already detected some of those fields moving about down there," Chakotay confirmed, trying to keep the discussion open. "They seem to be confined to the surface, at least for now."

"They are not always," Mila warned.

Jonal said, "If current trends in reductions at the main power source continue, the system should soon grow weak enough to eliminate the problem entirely. After that, rescue and salvage operations can be easily carried out."

"What do you mean by 'soon'?" Chakotay asked.

"We estimate two weeks."

"But the rate of the seismic activity down there is increasing so fast that we might not have that much time. This planet might be nothing but rubble by then."

"The Televek estimate they have nearly twice that long," Tassay assured him.

Chakotay took little comfort from this. No race, no technology he knew of, could predict the exact outcome of the kind of inexplicable violence that was occurring within Drenar Four. He was fairly certain that the aliens' guess was no better than anyone else's. Tomorrow the planet could decide to settle down and behave itself and stay quiet for a century—or it could turn itself into an asteroid field and take the captain and the others out with it. He shook his head.

"Paris, B'Elanna, this situation is unacceptable. I want some other options. See what else you can find out about those energy signatures. Put anyone you can spare on it. Work with the Televek wherever possible. We need access to the surface, and we need it now. Meanwhile, let's take another look at our computer models. I understand that one major quake and several smaller ones have occurred in the last few hours. Maybe we've learned something from them."

"An excellent suggestion, Commander," Jonal said graciously.

Paris and Torres acknowledged Chakotay, then got to their feet and started out the door. Mila rose to go with Paris, but Chakotay decided he had to draw the line.

"You three will remain with us," he told the advocates. "These officers have work to do, and there are certain security concerns, which I am sure you can understand."

Each of the Drosary quickly acquiesced. Chakotay wondered if, in their place, several of his own crew would have done the same.

"Commander, are you all right?" Tassay asked, interrupting his thoughts.

Probably not, he thought. He could only guess what his expression must be like; he made yet another effort to soften it before attempting to answer.

"Yes," he said. "I'm fine."

CHAPTER
8

THE CEILING SEEMED LOW, THE WALLS CLOSE, THOUGH there was not enough light in the room to allow further details to emerge. The smell of damp, smoke-permeated wood filled the air. Captain Janeway lay perfectly still, moving only her eyes, drawing slow, shallow breaths as consciousness grew more certain. She dared not try anything more; it hurt to blink, her head was throbbing so.

Now she began to notice noises coming from some-where beyond the darkened walls. Voices passed once, then again, and in between, she heard other sounds, a changing pattern of clatter that made little sense to her. When she was reasonably sure she was alone, she gently attempted to move her arms and legs, and found them to be in working order, though her left knee was sore. Next she tried to lift her head, and the pain exploded from within.

She let out a moan and pressed one hand to the top of her head. The welt was sizable and tender. She also felt dried blood but nothing fresh. It was coming back to her now—the shuttle, the Drenarians, the earthquake, and the fall. She checked her belt and found her tricorder and phaser still there.

Slowly she sat up and watched the world spin. She waited for it to stop, then got carefully to her feet. The ceiling was low; she had barely a foot of clearance. She reached toward the length of heavy cloth that covered a nearby window and pulled the curtain gently back, and light entered the room. She winced as her eyes reacted; she turned away from the window, looked about inside instead, and discovered she was in a log cabin much like those built hundreds of years ago on the American frontier. The furnishings—a table and a few chairs, a bed built along one wall, and a storage chest—were all simple and handmade, but neatly constructed. They featured hinges and braces of finely crafted metalwork. An oil lamp, unlit, rested on the table.

As she looked back toward the window, she noticed it had glass in it. She hadn't expected that. Outside she could see another cabin much like the one she was in. She folded the curtain flap under, which left a wedge of open window when she let go. Before she could do more, she heard voices outside, coming closer.

She steadied herself, one hand close to her phaser, as she heard the door latch move. She had no desire to demonstrate what the weapon could do—surely these people had been through enough already—but she was too weak to fight hand-to-hand, if it came to that.

When the door opened, the first one through it was Tuvok.

The Vulcan was followed closely by Kim. Then an older Drenarian male entered, neatly dressed in dark slacks and a long-sleeved tunic. The alien's clothing was clean and in good condition, but it looked nearly as old as he was. His hair was dark with a sprinkling of gray, and his face, unlike those of the other Drenarian men she had seen, was clean-shaven.

Up close the heavy head and facial features Janeway had observed earlier seemed less harsh, and she noticed a subtle hint of orange coloration in the wrinkles of the man's skin. Janeway felt the Drenarian's deep, dark eyes upon her as they faced each other, and she instinctively looked away, not certain why those eyes bothered her.

"Captain, you are well?" Tuvok asked, leaning forward to assess the damage to her head.

"I've been better," she said, waving him off.

"I would like you to meet a new friend of ours, Nan Loteth. Mr. Loteth, Captain Janeway."

She put out her hand, but the Drenarian only stared at it as if it were an unknown animal. Janeway withdrew the offer.

"They are not familiar," Tuvok explained.

"His people helped carry you back to their village after the earthquake," Kim said, sounding quite cheerful. "What's left of their village, that is. The quakes have knocked at least a third of it down, and a few sections have fallen straight into the ground. This section is relatively untouched, so far."

"But it may not be for long," Tuvok added.

Janeway looked up. "Explain."

"Since the last quake, according to Loteth, volcanic

activity to the south has actually decreased somewhat, but every aspect of this planet's behavior seems to be in flux," Tuvok reported. "At present the prevailing winds are from the northwest, which is why the rain of dust and ash in this area has ended locally, but if they should shift sufficiently it would be cause for concern."

"We've been waiting for you to come around," Kim said, something he apparently just had to get out. "Everyone has."

"They seem a most amiable people, Captain," Tuvok said, "and they have treated us with kindness. I have taken the liberty of explaining that we are here to help them."

"I'll bet they're impressed so far," Janeway replied, still reeling a bit, getting her sea legs.

Nan Loteth moved past them and went to the corner, where he poured something from an earthenware pitcher into a metal cup. "Drink," he said, his voice breathy but even. He handed the cup to Janeway.

"There isn't any lead in this, is there?" she asked, hesitating. Tuvok produced his tricorder and passed it over the cup, then shook his head. Janeway nodded. The water tasted awful. She drank it all.

"You aren't afraid of us?" Janeway asked the old man, recalling what she had seen in her first vision— if that scene had been real.

The Drenarian took the cup from her. "Of you, no."

"They claim they knew we were coming," Tuvok explained.

"They say they were told by the spirits in the hills, the spirits of their ancestors," Kim said.

"The ghosts," Janeway said.

"Apparently, Captain," Tuvok replied.

"I think I've met some of your ancestors myself," Janeway told Nan Loteth. "Twice, as a matter of fact. I'd like you to tell me more about them, if you don't mind."

The Drenarian nodded. "My people have always turned to the wisdom of those who have gone before, those we call the Jun-Tath. They protect us, comfort us, counsel us. Are you not guided in this world by those in the next?"

"Many of my people believe they are, though I have never personally known anyone to describe an encounter quite like the one I had," Janeway said. She described the ghostly entity she had seen in her ready room, and the dreams Chakotay had told her about, but stopped short of relating the dream—if it had been a dream—of her visit to the smoky cavern.

Nan Loteth seemed to understand completely. "We have been shown to you, and you have been shown to us," he said, wearing a gentle smile Janeway had thought his features incapable of. She decided there was a great deal to learn about these people, and despite the pain in her skull, she found herself eager to do so. Her unease had all but vanished.

She thought to say so, but hesitated as the earth began to shake perceptibly beneath her feet. A minor aftershock, only a fraction the intensity of the earlier quake. Still, it was more than enough to remind her that these people, whoever they were, were in danger of being lost to the universe forever. She looked in the Drenarian's eyes, and she was all but certain she could see this same thought reflected there.

"The Jun-Tath told us of the others, too," Nan

Loteth continued less easily, raising his voice somewhat. "Of a time when demons would descend from the skies, of the suffering of many, of the coming of the end of the world. When the others came in their great sky-boat, we knew in our hearts they were the demons we had seen in our visions. But some were not convinced. They had to be sure. They went to the clearing where the sky-boat rested, near the temple of Jaalett, and they watched. Nothing happened at first, but then the beings began leaving the boat for a time and returning."

"But no one made contact with them?" Janeway asked.

"No, our people stayed well away from them. When no one came out or went in for one full day, some of my people went closer. My own brother was among them."

Nan Loteth paused as the pain in his thoughts seemed to touch his face. Janeway remembered her first vision clearly enough. She waited for him to go on.

"When they were almost close enough to touch the sky-boat, burning light came in streams from the boat's hull and struck down all who stood there. Some say they heard the screams of the dying in the village itself."

"Phaser fire," Janeway confirmed, hearing her voice crack. She could feel the Drenarian's pain and fear. She had been there, after all. "I saw them, the bodies of your people. I wasn't sure it had really happened. I had hoped that . . ." She fell silent and stood just looking at Nan Loteth.

"That would seem to verify that the cruiser is at

least partially operational," Tuvok correctly noted. Janeway kept her attention on Nan Loteth.

"I went to the site," he continued. "A few of the men lay there still moving, some moaning, where they had fallen. Then the moaning stopped. The ones who had stayed back among the trees told us what had happened."

"You had to leave them there," Janeway said, nodding. "The bodies of the dead."

"We dared not go too close for fear we too would be burned."

"It was the only logical decision you could have made," Tuvok assured him.

"So you've stayed away since then?" Kim said, nodding in anticipation of the answer.

"No. We attacked the people of the boat from the trees at the edge of the clearing," the Drenarian said to everyone else's surprise, "but our weapons were of no use against them. We wounded a few of them, I think, but they set the forest ablaze, and we were forced to move away. After a time, we returned home. We thought they would come for us, and we have waited, ready to fight them however we can. So far they have stayed near the hills."

"And so much for the Televek's story about mounting a rescue expedition," Kim muttered darkly.

"We are not creatures of war, Captain," Nan Loteth said in a supplicating tone. "We have been at peace for five generations now. Our leaders have joined in a pact that has allowed us all to prosper. We do not have great armies to fight these demons. That is why the Jun-Tath have sent you to us."

"An interesting theory," Tuvok commented, his eyes wide.

"You still took quite a chance approaching our shuttle like that, after what the Televek—the demons—did to you," Janeway said. "Your vision of our landing must have been a very clear one."

"As was my own vision of you, Captain. And your two companions. That is why you were brought to my house. The Jun-Tath have chosen me to speak with you, I think. It is my great honor."

"And mine," Janeway reciprocated, trying out a smile of her own; it didn't hurt as much as she thought it might.

"Do you have anyone watching the sky-boat?" Tuvok asked.

"Yes, but few would survive an attack if it came." Nan Loteth sighed, and the lines in his face seemed to deepen. "Since the first attempt, a few of our bowmen have fired on the demons again, but now our arrows only bounce off their clothing."

"Light armor of some kind," Kim speculated.

"Your people are very brave, my friend," Janeway said, thinking of the Prime Directive, then trying not to, at least not for the moment. "And we intend to do whatever we can to help them stay that way. I promise you that."

Nan Loteth nodded, then turned and started out the door. The four of them made their way into a little yard between two houses where a flower garden now shriveled and died under ash and dust. Janeway could easily imagine how fine it all must have been. She noticed that the sun was low in the sky and that the shadows were growing long. The group moved on, around the corner and into the street.

From where they stood, the village seemed to go on

endlessly in all directions. They were only four houses from the nearby intersection that was shaped like a crow's foot. And the area was busy indeed. The smooth dirt streets were lined with houses and shops, many of them two stories high.

People walked in and out of numerous shops, and the Drenarians' now familiar beasts of burden pulled wagons loaded with goods and children down the center of each street. Again, Janeway was reminded of a frontier town—or perhaps an early American Indian village, she reflected, as she watched a woman pass by carrying a baby on her back in what could easily have passed for a papoose board.

Janeway watched a young man making his way toward them. He was carrying a stool and lighting oil lamps that hung on wooden poles. No moths gathered near his flames, nor did she note any other kind of insect. She had been stung and bitten on dozens of worlds like this one, but here insects were not a problem. This was not paradise, she realized. The planet's ecosystem was breaking down utterly, yet another indication of the Drenarians' grim situation.

A small crowd began to gather in front of Nan Loteth's house, their eyes wide under their heavy brows, to observe the strange new visitors. Their expressions were familiar enough to Janeway. She never ceased to be amazed by how similar most intelligent peoples were, not so much physiologically, but inside, in their hearts and minds, and how easily one could see that, even in the most alien eyes.

Janeway and her officers greeted the other Drenarians, then stood about for a long, awkward moment.

"You came from up there, from the night, just as the demons did." Nan Loteth pointed toward the sky. "The Jun-Tath have shown me this."

Janeway looked up. The stars had begun to appear and, with them, all three of the planet's moons, each one no more than a crescent. The smallest moon had just appeared over the big hills to the east and seemed to be chasing the others into the sky.

Janeway looked at Nan Loteth and saw the glow in his eyes suddenly dim.

"You do not answer," he said glumly.

"Yes," she said, nodding. "Yes, we came from the sky."

"Which star is yours?" he asked.

Janeway looked at him with mild surprise. It was one thing for a primitive people to imagine beings, perhaps gods or demons, descending from the sky or from mountaintops, or arriving from across the seas, from some far distant and unexplored part of their own world. Humanity's past was filled with gods of every manner and purpose—angels and spirits had filled mankind's mythical skies by day and by night—beings who controlled all the functions of the heavens from mountains and unseen worlds.

But that was not what Nan Loteth had said at all.

"What do you know of the stars?" she asked, regarding him more seriously now.

"I have seen them."

"What do you mean?" Janeway asked, glancing at Kim and Tuvok, both of whom seemed as fascinated as she was.

"Wait right here," Nan Loteth said, his eyes suddenly wide and full of excitement. "I will show you."

The old man disappeared back inside his cabin with a spry dash that made Janeway blink. She waited only a moment for his return.

"This is how I see," Nan Loteth exclaimed. He held in his hands a long, smooth wooden tube, which he gingerly handed to Janeway. She quickly recognized the device; it was composed of two tubes, one slightly smaller than the other, allowing it to slide in and out, thereby changing the overall tube length. A neatly cut glass disc had been fitted into either end of the tube.

"You look through it, like this," Nan Loteth explained, gently taking the tube back. He raised the device lengthwise toward the sky, then put the smaller end up to this right eye. Holding it steady, he aimed at the largest of the three moons, which had nearly reached its apex.

Janeway watched him with fresh regard.

"Look," he said excitedly. *"You* look." He handed the tube back to Janeway. She held it as he had and aimed it at the moon. Countless craters and stark mountain ranges leaped into focus as she gently slid the smaller tube out of the larger one, just a bit. The instrument was crude, but it was one Galileo himself would have been proud of.

"It is true, isn't it," Loteth said, "that the stars are suns, like our own sun? I have seen the other worlds in our sky, the ones that follow our world on its journey through the skies. They have moons, just like those." He waved at the three bright satellites crossing the darkened skies overhead.

"Quite remarkable," Tuvok said.

"Yes," Janeway agreed, now considering the Drenarian with fresh amazement.

"So you actually believe we might have come from one of the other worlds in this solar system?" Kim asked, equally surprised.

"No, I do not think so," Nan Loteth said.

Tuvok and Kim looked suddenly bewildered. "Most curious," the Vulcan said. "I would have thought—"

"No, Tuvok," Janeway said, watching Nan Loteth, "you don't understand. He doesn't think we're from his system, he believes we are from a world belonging to one of the other stars he sees."

"Yes," the Drenarian said, nodding, though his tone had grown more pensive. "Is . . . is it so?"

"I understand, Captain," Tuvok replied, now properly impressed.

"I do, too," Kim said.

For a long moment no one said another word, which apparently made Nan Loteth uncomfortable. "You must tell me," he said, almost pleading. "Many will not speak of this with me. They keep their children away. They say that beyond the sky there is only the realm of the gods. I have been told many times that, if I am fortunate, the Jun-Tath will one day heal my mind in a vision and I will cease to think such thoughts."

"That figures," Kim said, shaking his head.

Tuvok nodded. "I can well imagine how some of your contemporaries might feel that way."

"Then you think I sound like a fool, just as they do," the old man said, despondent now. He took the telescope back again, let it hang at his side, bowed his head. Then his eyes came up, peeking at Janeway puppylike from under that ridiculous brow. She couldn't help but smile at him.

"Now you think I am a joke," he said. "I am sorry."

"No, Nan Loteth. You do not sound like a fool, or a joke." She placed one hand gently on the arm that held the instrument. "You sound like a scientist."

"A . . . scientist?" the old man repeated.

"Yes. And a good one." Janeway turned and tugged gently at the Drenarian's arm, directing his attention toward the sky again. The heavens were half obscured by thick volcanic clouds, but where the winds had blown them clear the stars were multiplying as the darkness continued to deepen. "We are from a world much like yours, one that orbits a star, up there, just as yours does, but our star is much too far away for us to see from here. So far away, in fact, that we may never see it again. Though one day, perhaps, your people might find it."

Nan Loteth's breath had quickened. "How many stars are there? How many worlds?"

"Far too many to count."

The old man's mouth hung slightly open. "And what are these other worlds like?"

"Many are very much like your own," Janeway said.

The ground shook once more, another aftershock that did little more than rattle nerves and spook the draft animals along the street. Still, Janeway knew there would be more quakes like the one they had experienced at the shuttle, and if computer predictions held, they would grow in severity. Meanwhile, the wind might shift. . . .

As the tremor subsided, Nan Loteth asked Janeway to follow him up the street. "You need food," he said. "We haven't much, but what we do have is yours." He set off walking, leaving no one any choice. The rest of the crowd, more than three dozen strong now, came quietly along behind them, speaking only in whispers.

"Tuvok," Janeway said as they went, "Could the Televek have something to do with what is happening to this planet? Could the destruction be related to that anomalous underground power source, or to the Televek's attempts to get at it?"

"I doubt the Televek are capable of anything on that scale. However, I find it hard to believe that their arrival here during such a major geologic event is simply a coincidence."

Janeway nodded, then wondered if they were thinking along the same lines. "Can you explain?"

"I cannot. It is what I believe humans would call a . . . a hunch."

Janeway paused and stood looking at him. She and Tuvok had known each other for many years. He was as logical and staid as any Vulcan she had ever met, but sometimes, she had come to realize, he was capable of much more than that. "Mr. Tuvok," she said softly, "it would seem that I am starting to rub off on you."

"I would consider that a compliment, sir," Kim told the Vulcan, butting in before the other could respond.

Tuvok drew a long, contemplative breath. "Very well then, Mr. Kim, I will take your advice."

The walk continued past stables filled with animals and emitting a smell that seemed to change very little from one part of the galaxy to another. The next large building featured double doors flung wide. Peering in, Janeway saw what could only have been a blacksmith shop, judging by the bellows, three in all, that hung from the ceiling, with foot pedals rigged to work them. Two craftsmen were on hand, hammering at glowing bits of metal. Building spaceships, Janeway thought, which brought her right back to the situation at hand.

"Mr. Tuvok, would you agree, then, that the Televek's proximity to the underground power source is also not likely to be a coincidence?"

"Yes, but I remain doubtful that they control it, or that they have gained access to it. We have seen no evidence of that."

Janeway nodded. "Agreed."

"But they haven't given up trying," Kim said.

A woman, trailed by three children, moved cautiously to one side, allowing the strange aliens and the small mob that surrounded them to pass. No one seemed interested in blocking the way, yet no one panicked, either, which was something Janeway might have expected. She said as much to both her officers.

"I've never met a people quite like them," Tuvok agreed.

"Neither have I," Kim said with a wry grin, "but *Voyager* is my first mission, after all."

"We haven't forgotten," Janeway assured him.

"They are physiologically well behind mankind on an evolutionary scale," Tuvok said, "and yet they have inventions and ideas far ahead of anything early man was capable of, or the early ancestors of present-day Vulcans, for that matter."

"But the possibility still exists that they're being manipulated by some outside presence," Kim suggested.

"Perhaps," Tuvok said, "but I would suggest that they are simply very intelligent."

"An interesting theory, Mr. Tuvok," Janeway said,

finding the idea quite palatable. In man, just as with every advanced species mankind had encountered, the sudden emergence of intelligence as an evolutionary advantage, a key survival trait, had ultimately allowed those species to leap up the natural-selection ladder. With the Drenarians, things had simply gone a little faster than usual. Their first leaps had been nothing short of extraordinary, and their progress showed no signs of slowing down.

"Can you imagine Neanderthals developing villages and agriculture like this?" Kim said.

"The Drenarians are a remarkable people," Janeway agreed. "And as long as we're in it this far, I'll admit that I believe they are definitely worth saving. The trouble is, their own planet doesn't seem to agree."

"They may need protection as well, Captain," Tuvok said. "The Televek have left them alone until now, but there is no reason to believe they will continue to do so."

"Agreed. We may have to organize them somehow."

"Nan Loteth isn't one of their leaders," Kim explained, leaning toward the captain and away from the Drenarian just ahead of them, "although he does seem to be a respected citizen, a wise man of some kind."

"They have delegates who convene to form a governing council, which makes the laws and supports several regional chiefs," Tuvok said. "Nan Loteth, I believe, is one of the delegates."

"It reminds me of the Five Nations," Janeway said.

Tuvok looked at her. "I do not believe I am familiar."

"The Iroquois Confederation," Janeway said. "A self-governing Native American coalition of sorts. It guaranteed peace and cooperation over an entire region. The framers of the early American Constitution drew heavily upon the Indians' ideas."

"I'll bet Chakotay would have gotten a kick out of this conversation," Kim said.

"When we see him, we'll tell him about it," Janeway answered. "In the meantime, we have to find a way to make that possible. The Televek are the key. I'd like to go poke around their cruiser, see what kind of shape it's in, maybe get some idea just what they're up to."

"I can tell you that." Nan Loteth had apparently heard much of their conversation.

"Then tell us," Janeway prodded, "please."

"They want to steal the spirits of our ancestors. They have come for the Jun-Tath."

Tuvok cocked his head. "How do you know that?"

"I saw it in a vision. The spirits themselves have shown me. That is the most important reason for your being here, I think. You are not here for us alone. You are to help us save the Jun-Tath from the demons."

"But how could anyone steal a ghost?" Kim wondered.

"May I remind you, Ensign," Tuvok said, "that these particular ghosts show up on our tricorders, and that their EM signatures are virtually identical to those of the unidentified underground power source?"

"A source they seem inclined to cluster about, and which the Televek cruiser is presently practically on top of," Janeway added.

"So," Kim said, attempting to catch up, "you're saying that if the ghosts are somehow connected with the energy source, and if the Televek are after that source, then in effect they are after the ghosts."

"A logical assumption," Tuvok agreed.

Janeway nodded. "That's what I was thinking. Which is why we need to learn more about their plan and its progress so far." She faced Nan Loteth. "You must take us to the Televek demons' sky-boat," she said, "as soon as possible."

"Very well," came the Drenarian's answer, followed by a shrug. "But first you will eat."

They arrived just then at a merchant's stall. A tarp covered a street-facing table full of foods. A young female Drenarian stood on the other side, smiling. Janeway was handed something that reminded her very much of a sweet potato. She started to peel it, but the young woman minding the booth told her to leave the skin on.

"Its slight bitterness counters the sweetness," the woman explained. Then she handed over a bowl of brownish sauce thick with floating herbs, and waved them toward it. The captain dipped the tuber into the sauce and took a cautious bite, remembering the water. She was pleasantly surprised.

"Ah, good!" the Drenarian woman said when she saw Janeway's smile. She then gave the captain a small loaf of very dark bread into which large chunks of sweet fruit had been baked.

"Kim, remind me to have Neelix talk to these people," Janeway said, talking with her mouth full. Ensign Kim seemed to understand completely.

As she was washing the meal down with a sharp but palatable milky juice, a third tremor, much more violent than the others, rumbled up through the rock beneath their feet. It shook the landscape and rattled the booth's sturdy table, then rattled Janeway's teeth. This quake was felt more than seen. It was not as severe as the first one, but the tremors seemed to be coming closer together now. She put the empty juice cup down and turned to her host.

"These earthquakes represent a great danger," she told him, thinking it time. "They're the result of a larger problem, one you may not be entirely aware of. Your world is apparently re-forming itself, shifting internally due to forces we have not yet studied completely. We do believe this planet may eventually tear itself apart, and you with it, perhaps in a matter of weeks, or even days."

Nan Loteth's expression was grave, but he did not look shocked, and his nod told Janeway that she had underestimated him again.

"Something is wrong," he agreed. "Very wrong. The earthquakes and the volcanoes to the south, they are not right, not normal. There have been no stories of such disturbances for many, many generations. We have waited for the Jun-Tath to tell us what is happening and what to do, but they have not done so."

"How long has this activity been occurring?" Tuvok asked the Drenarian, already taking tricorder readings of the current tremor.

"For one full year, since the night of the third crescent."

Tuvok nodded. "And how many quakes were as severe as the one in which the captain was injured yesterday?"

"Many. I don't know the number, but they come more often now. We used to think the mountains would grow quiet again, and the earth would be still.

Now many fear it will only grow worse, as you say." He looked toward the east, to the angry, darkened sky.

"You mentioned a date," Janeway said, following his gaze, her thoughts just beginning to turn fully around. "The third crescent."

"A religious event of some kind?" Kim suggested.

"Perhaps," Nan Loteth said.

"You mean you don't know?" Janeway asked.

Nan Loteth looked skyward once more. "I know only what I have seen through my glass. The third crescent is like the other two, but smaller, and not so full of holes."

"Curious," Tuvok said.

Kim was still looking at the Drenarian. "What is?"

"The third moon," Janeway said, nodding to herself as she followed the Drenarian's gaze to the curved, pale sliver of light that continued to rise above the hills. "You're saying the earthquakes began when the third moon arrived."

"Soon after, yes," Nan Loteth replied.

"One year ago?" Tuvok asked.

"Yes. And I do not think they will stop until the wandering moon goes away again."

CHAPTER

9

CAPTAIN JANEWAY STOOD STUNNED BY THE REALIZATION, something she should have seen from the start. She could see, looking at him, that even Tuvok was embarrassed by his own lack of perception in this matter. Suddenly, however, the truth seemed obvious to both of them.

The two larger moons followed similar orbits around the planet, almost trailing each other across the sky when observed from the planet's surface, though in fact one had a much smaller orbit than the other, allowing it to appear to overtake the more distant moon from time to time. The third, slightly smaller, moon was at odds with the others, and no doubt with the planet itself.

When the brown dwarf star passed by the Drenar system it had certainly dislodged a number of planetary bodies, including Drenar's new third moon, which likely had been orbiting one of the system's large, outer gas giants at the time. Drenar Four had captured the moon as it traveled sunward, and the opposing tidal forces that had resulted from the pull of the three moons amounted to a celestial tug-of-war. A war the planet was about to lose.

If all three moons came close to lining up, as it now appeared they might, it would be a noteworthy event to say the least.

"The question is, how long have we got?" Kim wondered, seeing the implications clearly enough himself.

Tuvok stood with his tricorder open, playing at its small controls with deft fingers. "I am attempting to form an extrapolation," he said in answer.

"Please do," Janeway told him, content to wait. His knowledge in many areas was equal to her own, but being a Vulcan, he was unquestionably quicker. As the moments ticked past, however, she began to wonder.

Finally, with Kim looking strained, she said, "Is there a problem, Tuvok?"

"Yes, Captain. The patterns of magma movement beneath the crust have been occurring on a tremendous scale. However, their patterns are entirely unpredictable. In addition, the destabilization is increasing exponentially. There is no doubt that the planet will ultimately be destroyed by this process, probably in a matter of weeks, perhaps as few as two or three. But . . ."

Tuvok looked at Janeway and softly sighed, indicating that a bit of guesswork was involved in what was to come next. With Tuvok, however, you could dismiss nothing. He seldom went out on a limb, and when he did it was a short, stout one.

"Go on," she said.

"Considering the strength and frequency of the quakes, I believe it is possible that the planet's crust might rupture in a catastrophic manner much sooner than that—during the next full tide, to be precise, when the pull from the moons reaches maximum intensity. At that time, the combined fracturing and consequent erupting would reach a scale that could easily render the planet uninhabitable."

"They do look as if they're close to lining up, don't they?" Kim said, staring up at the night sky. Janeway nodded. The third crescent moon had risen higher now, and the first two moons were clearly drifting toward a common destination as well. Their projected orbits were easy enough to determine; even at a glance the prospects didn't look good.

"It is true, I think," Nan Loteth said, apparently grasping most of what they were saying. "The twin moons have always crossed once a year, and this year the crescent moon seems determined to join them."

"How long, Tuvok?" Janeway asked. She stood in front of him, holding her breath as he continued to work with the tricorder.

"Again, it is difficult to say. I will have to make some additional calculations. However, at present I estimate the next full lunar alignment will occur in . . ." Tuvok worked the keypad again, then shook his head.

"What is it?" Janeway asked.

"I wanted to be certain, Captain. The alignment should occur in approximately twenty-nine hours, seventeen minutes."

"That's what I was afraid of," Janeway said. She let her breath out, and felt an uncertain amount of her limited strength seep out with it. "That doesn't leave us much time."

"Captain," Kim said. He had flipped open his own tricorder upon hearing this last from Tuvok, and was busy scanning, apparently hopeful. "I've been monitoring the levels of magnetic interference, and I'm detecting the largest drop yet in this area. We might be able to get through to *Voyager* now."

"You are welcome to try, Mr. Kim," she said.

The ensign tapped at his comm badge. "Away team to *Voyager*. Kim to *Voyager*."

"Go ahead," a voice replied through the comm, though it was garbled and unidentifiable. Still, all three away team officers heard it clearly enough.

Janeway instantly tapped her own badge. "This is the captain."

"Rollins here, Captain. Are you all right?"

She could barely make out the words, could only hope that Rollins was having better luck on his end.

"Yes, we're fine," she said.

"We can't get to you," Rollins said. "A planetary defense system is keeping everyone out."

"What kind of system?" Tuvok inquired.

"Not now, Tuvok," the captain said. "Mr. Rollins, you have to listen to me carefully."

Quickly she told Rollins about the third moon and the coming lunar alignment, and what that apparently meant. "These people may only have a day," she said.

"Not to mention us," Kim added.

"Yes," Janeway acknowledged. "And it looks as though I was right about that second Televek cruiser."

She paused, getting the feeling that she was talking to herself. *"Voyager?"*

Nothing. Kim and Tuvok tried as well but got the same results.

"We've lost the signal again, Captain," Kim said apologetically, as if it were his fault.

"Damn! I wonder if they got any of that?" Janeway asked, not expecting an answer.

"It would appear there is little *Voyager* can do, even if they have received some of the information," Tuvok remarked. "At least for the time being."

"What was all that about a defense system?" Kim asked. "The only trouble we ran into was the Televek."

"It's possible that's exactly what our mysterious underground power source is doing here, and the transient energy readings we're picking up in the hills," Janeway said. "Though if that's the case, the defensive system doesn't seem to be working."

"Did the entity that visited you aboard *Voyager* seem like part of any defense system?" Tuvok asked.

"Not exactly, and if it is, it doesn't seem capable of defending these people against the Televek ship that landed. Still, the ghosts must be connected in some way."

They stood near the edge of the city now, looking down a wide, smooth promenade illuminated by starlight and moonbeams. Nan Loteth cleared his throat, the first time Janeway had heard him do that. She wondered if he'd picked the habit up from one of them.

"So what do we do now?" Kim asked gingerly.

"In the absence of alternatives, I recommend we

follow our plan to investigate the Televek presence here," Tuvok said.

"The temple of Jaalett is nearly half a day's walk along this road," Nan Loteth said. "If we leave tonight, we will be there before morning."

"We'll go there soon, but not right now," Janeway said. Then she faced Nan Loteth. "First, I'd like to get back to our shuttlecraft and make another attempt to get our communications equipment working so we can contact our friends in our other sky-boat. They need to know about the moons, and especially about that Televek ship near your temple. Our friends may be in more danger than we are. There's no telling what our friend Gantel and his advocates are doing."

Nan Loteth nodded vigorously. "I will send men from the village with you. I have been told that the demons have visited your sky-boat already and may still be there. You will need good warriors to protect you."

"That makes sense; the demons must have witnessed our landing," Janeway said. "But you must listen to me, Nan Loteth. I don't want any more of your people getting killed. Don't worry about us. We can protect ourselves. We will go alone, for now. When we return, you may take us to your temple so that we can see the demon ship for ourselves."

"If the Televek have been there for a while, they may have gained access to the shuttle's interior by now," Kim speculated.

"A logical concern," Tuvok agreed.

"If they are inside our shuttle," Janeway remarked, looking from one officer to the other, "they are just going to have to leave."

"When will you go?" Nan Loteth asked.

Janeway took a deep breath. "Now," she said, seeing no point in delaying their departure. She was exhausted, and she wanted nothing more than to stay here for a few days, but at that instant yet another aftershock rumbled beneath her feet, reminding her that for now, rest was not possible.

The three of them set out walking toward the edge of the village, moving out of earshot, waving goodbye.

Gantel ran his hands through his hair in mild exasperation. "That is rather bad news," he said, purposely understating the gravity of the situation as he received the communication. It would be too easy to get excited and upset, and that wouldn't accomplish anything. "Do you think their ship received the transmission?"

"There is a strong possibility they did," Triness said sadly. "But it couldn't have been very readable, and we were able to correct for it within minutes. I doubt a substantive exchange was made. The only thing we got from the message was information about the three moons. I for one am surprised it has taken these Federation people this long to figure that out, if indeed they have. They are a pathetic bunch, I think."

"Always the optimist," Gantel told her, but then, that was one reason he liked having her around. Hers was a bothersome job, in its own way, but one she didn't seem to mind.

"They know the shuttle crew is alive, in any case."

"We gave them reason to hope that was true," Triness pointed out.

"Is there a chance that *Voyager*'s sensors could have picked up anything we wouldn't want them picking up?"

"No," Triness said. "The breach was along a very narrow microwave band."

"A definite consolation. Is Daket having any luck locating the landing party? Or has he as many excuses for failing at that as he has for his failure to obtain access to the power source?"

"One of his teams has located the shuttle. We think the occupants may have been taken into a Drenarian village."

"Leave them there, then. For now. We can destroy the village later on and be done with all of them."

"Precisely what Daket was thinking." Triness grinned.

Gantel sat contemplating the situation. There was nothing he could do now but wait and see what the starship commander would do next, if anything. Over the years the third director had gotten very good at waiting for favorable developments, and his patience had been rewarded often enough. He could only hope for similar results this time—preferably *before* First Director Shaale arrived and was forced to intervene. Better to ask for the fleet's assistance with regard to specific plans and obvious results than to go begging for help in apparent desperation. He wanted that lovely Federation starship to be a gift to Shaale, not a burdensome military consideration, at the very least.

He looked at the strange vessel that filled the main viewscreen. Soon, he thought. Soon enough . . .

"At least we know they're alive!" Chakotay said, rushing onto the bridge, then huddling over the tactical station, crowding Rollins out of the way. "Computer, repeat the last message from the away team."

The ship's computer complied. Chakotay listened intently, straining to make out the words that came through, words twisted and muddied by a thick ocean of interference.

"Let me see if I can clean that up a bit, Commander," Rollins offered. Chakotay lent a hand. They played the message back again and again, adjusting the filters each time, then using the computer to enhance the results.

"That's as good as we're going to get it," the ensign said finally.

Chakotay heaved a deep sigh. The message wasn't that clear, and it got worse the farther they tried to go, right up to the point at which the signal was lost altogether. Several things, though, were clear: the third moon was new, the coming lunar alignment was causing the earthquakes and magma eruptions, and the tidal forces now building might cause the planet literally to come apart.

"How long until the lunar alignment?" Chakotay wondered aloud, tapping at the console to engage the computer in the task of answering his question. He waited. He didn't like the answer. The other timetables facing him ran through his mind, and he began to feel very uncomfortable. He checked the figures one more time to be certain.

"Commander . . ." Rollins began, seeing the answer too. Then his voice trailed off as he realized the implications.

"Mr. Rollins, you have the conn," Chakotay said, practically lunging away from the console. He headed straight toward the turbolift. "If you need me I'll be in engineering."

"I already have a job!" B'Elanna Torres snapped, moving from one console to the next, leaving her commander standing there.

Chakotay frowned as he glanced to either side. Numerous engineering personnel worked feverishly at every station, occasionally calling out to one another, while others came and went in a constant procession. He went after the chief engineer, who had momentarily settled near the power transfer conduits leading to the dilithium housing.

"Well, I've got another job for you," he said.

"How many people do you think I am?"

"What's your status right now?" Chakotay asked, brushing past her question.

Torres made a sound somewhere in her throat, which Chakotay was sure owed little to her human side. She tossed her fallen bangs back out of her eyes and looked at him. "We're making progress," she said with a firm nod. Her features relaxed just a little bit, an indication she truly meant what she said. "Slow, but sure."

"I've got something I want you to hear," Chakotay said. Most of the crew knew there had been a message from the captain, but he knew B'Elanna hadn't had a chance to listen to it yet. He ordered the computer to repeat the best version of the message. B'Elanna played it several times.

"What do you expect me to do?" she asked skeptically.

Chakotay was sure, just by the look she was giving him, that she already had a pretty good idea.

"You tell me," he said.

She looked straight past him with a cold, distant stare, one that his years with her had taught him meant her mind was operating at hyperspeed, which was exactly the result he had hoped for. The best way to approach B'Elanna Torres was not to barge in, ordering her to produce results. Better to tell her you had a question, one that no one else could answer. What she lacked in discipline she made up for in determination and brains.

She looked down suddenly and began pacing the floor. After a moment she raised her eyes and focused them again. She made her way straight to the main engineering console and began playing her fingers across the keypad panels. On one of the screens before her a simulation appeared; it began to change as B'Elanna reworked the mathematics. Then she shook her head in frustration.

"What are you thinking?" Chakotay asked, quietly drawing up beside her. "What's wrong?"

"The way I see it, our only option is to reconfigure the main deflector to project a subspace field, which can be wrapped around each moon in succession and used to help *Voyager* move them. Similar attempts have been tried before with Galaxy-class ships. It's exactly like trying to push a boulder up a hill. In this case, however, the boulder is too big and the hill is too steep, so we'll have to use the subspace field to make the boulder temporarily lighter. We'd never be able to alter the course of any of these moons significantly, but if we can move each moon a little, the accumulative effect might be enough to ease their destructive alignment. We'll just be postponing the inevitable, but we can postpone it for quite a while."

Chakotay couldn't help giving her a broad grin. A little time was all they needed. "How long can we postpone the disaster?"

"Weeks, decades, maybe centuries. I don't know. The calculations are incredibly complex. It'll take hours."

"We don't have hours," Chakotay reminded her.

"In any case, we need the warp engines back on-line before we can even consider the attempt. No warp engines, no subspace fields. And they'll have to be reconfigured to do the job. They won't be available as ship's drives."

"Understood."

"And we don't have any time to waste, I'd say," B'Elanna added.

Chakotay let his smile broaden. "I thought I already had you working on it."

"Yes, sir," Torres said after a momentary pause. She frowned coldly. "Anything else?"

"I'm sure there is. I just haven't thought of it yet."

B'Elanna began to growl.

Chakotay stepped back once. "That's the B'Elanna I'm so crazy about," he said, nodding to her. He turned and made a hasty exit, thinking it best. B'Elanna made no attempt to stop him.

When Chakotay arrived back on the bridge the three Drosary visitors and their security detachment were waiting for him as ordered. He quickly explained the facts about the lunar alignment and what he intended to do about it. "We don't know if we'll be successful in the attempt, but we do think we can at least buy the planet and everyone on it some time.

Perhaps, with the help of the Televek, we can do even better than that."

"Remarkable," Jonal replied, seeming genuinely impressed. "You and your people are a source of constant amazement!"

"Agreed," Tassay said, sidling up to Chakotay once more, apparently pleased to be back in his presence. Mila had already fetched up next to Paris and seemed amused at something the lieutenant had just said. Chakotay was sure he didn't need to know what it was.

"Of course I will speak of this with Gantel at once," Jonal said. "Can you transmit whatever calculations and projections you might have?"

"Of course. I'll see to it right away. Mister Paris. Have Torres transfer all pertinent data to the Televek, whatever we've got. Mister Stephens," he added, speaking to the young ensign who had taken Kim's place at Ops. "Open a channel."

Jonal explained the idea to Gantel quickly enough. No reply was immediately forthcoming, but finally Gantel agreed that it was a commendable concept, after which he repeated many of the same things about human resourcefulness that Jonal had said. But there was something different about Gantel's reaction. Chakotay had come to know the Televek's voice, that being his only means of identifying the commander, and he thought Gantel sounded mildly incredulous. In a moment, however, that attitude seemed to change.

Once the upload transmission had been completed, Jonal and Gantel continued to talk for a few moments, and Chakotay wasn't sure he liked what he heard. The trouble was, he couldn't understand much of it. They seemed to be speaking in circles, using numerous metaphors and similes. There were direct references to continued cooperation and communication, and a repeated endorsement of the plan to move the moons, but a certain pessimism clearly existed. "I am sorry," Gantel said. "This is something they will simply have to accept."

"As you say," Jonal replied. He turned to Chakotay once more. He did not appear grim, but neither was he jubilant, not by a long shot. "I regret to inform you, Commander, that the Televek will be unable personally to assist you in your valiant efforts at this time—efforts they do support in principle."

Chakotay was having trouble believing what he was hearing. "What is the problem?"

"There are two, actually. While the Televek are of course familiar with warp field manipulation techniques, the cruiser now in orbit does not have the control capability such an endeavor would require."

"Couldn't modifications be made?" Paris asked. "Perhaps our own engineers could help."

"Not quickly enough, and, as I'm sure you understand, Gantel does not want your technicians working aboard his ship. At least not yet."

"You said there were two reasons," Chakotay reminded the advocate.

"Yes. You see, Commander, the Televek are convinced that the continuing drop in the energy levels of the plant's defense system are directly related to the seismic activity. This is based on records gathered from previous encounters with the planet, which date back several decades. Therefore, it is possible that if the seismic process were somehow to be interrupted, or even slowed, the defense system might not be recoverable."

"But stopping the quakes would put everyone out of danger!" Paris exclaimed, rising out of his chair, examining all three alien visitors with suddenly wary eyes.

"Yes and no," Mila told him, bending slightly to bring her own very serious face close to his. "With the system revitalized, you would still not be able to get down to the surface to rescue your away team or any of the indigenous populations, perhaps not ever. And your own people, and any Televek survivors, would not be able to get back into orbit, whether their ships were functional or not. All of them would be trapped on Drenar Four indefinitely."

"But at this rate they might all be dead by the time we can safely get to them," Paris said.

"Or they might not be," Tassay replied.

"If it turned out that way, we'd just have to find a way to defeat the planet's defenses," Chakotay said, trying to sort things out.

"Easily proposed, but difficult to do," Jonal replied. "The Televek have tried, and they are not the first. But you haven't heard me out. When the other ships in the rescue fleet arrive, it is entirely possible that, working together, you and they could find a means. Also, depending on how much time the planet itself has left, some of those arriving ships might be able to assist in the attempt to realign the moons."

Chakotay considered this for a moment. It made sense, especially from the aliens' point of view. He just didn't like it very much. There were far too many "ifs" and "buts." On the other hand, none of the facts seemed to be in his favor just now. And none of the options seemed workable.

"We do understand how you must feel, I assure you," Tassay insisted, then waited for Chakotay's response, sincere as could be, the commander noted. His training and, perhaps more importantly, his experience had taught him never to completely trust anyone, not even the Federation, and yet he found himself doing just that where Tassay was concerned. He decided to try and keep her at a distance, at least for the time being. The whole idea bothered him more than a little. The Drosary had earned his trust so far, he thought, and he believed he had earned theirs. He wasn't sure he could necessarily say the same of the Televek, who were the ones he was ultimately dealing with—a point he thought it best to keep clearly in mind.

"Very well, but I trust the Televek won't object if we go ahead and begin trying in the meantime. We're not even sure the attempt is plausible."

The Drosary turned to one another and mumbled for a brief moment. Then Jonal looked up. "Of course not, Commander. We will inform Gantel. I'm sure he will understand, just as you do."

"Of course," Chakotay said, drawing three quiet Drosary smiles. He noticed that Paris had calmed considerably and was now standing nearly face to face with Mila; an aura of chemistry hung about them. Chakotay cleared his throat loudly. "Who is minding your station, Mister Paris?"

Chakotay heard the turbolift door hiss open. He turned in time to witness B'Elanna's brisk entrance onto the bridge. As before, she headed straight to the engineering station, barely glancing at the others on the bridge. Her eyes never met those of the Drosary— or anyone else, for that matter—though Chakotay noticed she managed to frown rather heavily.

"Sorry, sir," Paris said as he sat down hastily and began a quick review. Mila stepped back a bit.

B'Elanna tapped at her consoles, then turned abruptly to face the commander. "Would you like my report?" she asked, looking past him to the three advocates with what Chakotay read as a mild flash of venom.

"Of course I would like your report, Lieutenant," Chakotay told her. She still clearly had a problem with the aliens, for which he really didn't see any basis. Not yet, anyway. He made a mental note to have a word with her.

"What about . . . them, sir?" she asked, nodding at the Drosary.

"Would you rather we spoke in the captain's ready room?" Chakotay offered rather curtly.

B'Elanna didn't hesitate. "I would."

"Very well." Chakotay bit the words off as he started across the bridge. He took a deep breath and calmed himself somewhat as the ready room door slid aside. He turned, then waited for the door to close behind B'Elanna.

"It's not like they're transmitting everything we say," he told B'Elanna. "We're controlling that, and frankly so are they. They've been very helpful, at least to a point, and I'd say—"

"Do you want my report or not?" she interrupted, standing less than a meter from him.

Chakotay reminded himself of her Klingon temper, her ongoing struggle to control that part of herself, and his desire to give her the chance to do so. He saw her mixed heritage as one of her greatest strengths and had always tried to encourage her to accept herself as she was, just as he had. Of course, her more aggressive nature could get out of hand. He didn't understand her animosity toward the Drosary, something he thought had diminished since their talk in the mess hall, but he didn't think confronting her over it would do anyone any good right now. He nodded.

"I have the warp engines back on line."

Chakotay felt a sudden swell of enthusiasm. "That's *very* good news, B'Elanna," he said, trying to maintain a proper measure of composure. "What about the main deflector dish?"

"That was one of the first things we were able to repair. It wasn't damaged very badly. I'm a little concerned about the engines, though. They aren't exactly specification ready."

"What can you give us?"

"Sixty percent, maybe. And I can't guarantee how long that will last, or if it will be enough."

"I know a way to find out," Chakotay said.

B'Elanna nodded. "The computer is still working out the calculations, but we should be ready to attempt diverting the first moon in about an hour. I suggest we try the smallest moon first."

"That's also the one closest to us."

She nodded again. "It's up to you."

"I agree." He raised an eyebrow. "Completely. And thank you, Lieutenant. We'll begin as soon as you're ready. I'll have Paris get right on it as well. Anything else?"

She just looked at him, hands fidgeting at waist

level as she stood there. "No, sir, I guess not," she said.

He didn't believe her. "I think you should give our guests another chance, B'Elanna." Chakotay stepped toward her, stood just in front of her. "There is nothing inherently wrong with people getting along. Or are you worried about the captain and Kim, or—"

"If you want to get this show on the road, you're going to have to let me go back to work," B'Elanna said evenly.

Chakotay sighed. "That's it?"

"Yes, sir."

"Very well. Dismissed."

The door slid open again as the two of them moved toward it. B'Elanna lingered for a moment in the opening, looking out onto the bridge. Mila and Tassay had gathered around Paris for an amicable chat. Jonal was standing near the captain's chair having a casual conversation with four other members of the bridge crew. Their small group suddenly chuckled at something Jonal had said, and then the banter quickly resumed.

Then Tassay looked up toward the ready room. She smiled and started toward Chakotay as soon as she spotted him. B'Elanna turned and stepped back into the ready room, clutching Chakotay's sleeve as she did so and pulling him back inside. She let the door hiss shut again.

"Don't you see it?" she said in a peppery tone, glaring at him.

"See what?"

"We have possibly hostile aliens on the bridge, in a tactical situation."

"The situation is unusual, but in effect the Drosary are ambassadors, so their presence is not unprecedented by any means," Chakotay said, considering. "Under the circumstances—"

"But *everybody* likes them. Jonal is the life of the party, Mila is practically sitting in Paris's lap, Tassay can't wait to see you—for God's sake, if she had a tail it would wag!"

"You just don't know her as well as I do."

"But you just met her!"

"She has quite a story to tell, B'Elanna," Chakotay said, trying again. "Her people do. She comes from a very large, extended family. They have a great respect for all life, for their creator and the gifts he has given them. She says that, in their own way, the Televek have always had a similar philosophy. They are terribly misunderstood by most peoples, especially in regard to their business dealings. They believe that by selling comparable goods to both sides in a conflict they are in effect preventing either side from gaining an unfair advantage, thereby often preventing slaughter. They've made enemies because of this, and it's made them overly cautious, but—"

"I guess I'm just a little too impressed, Chakotay. Did it ever occur to you that they also can make twice as much profit that way?"

"Yes, of course. But you're still not seeing the situation from their side. I am at least trying to."

"You think I don't see them clearly? I watch them, Commander, the way they talk and act, the way you and everyone else around here acts when they are around, and I don't know why, but I keep getting this urge to rip them in half."

"Then get over it, Lieutenant. Soon enough, if we

cooperate with them, work with them a little, we will have the captain and the others back, and we'll also have our phasers back in working order. We might even save a race of people who alone are probably worth all of this trouble, maybe more. Then we'll be on our way, and so will the Televek."

"I see. Sounds sweet."

They faced each other in silence for a moment. Chakotay didn't want it left like this. He knew there was more he wanted to say. And he couldn't say for sure she wasn't right.

"You are key to so much of this," he finally added. "You have to work with them. As chief engineer, you could at least try to keep an open mind."

She closed her eyes, then opened them and looked up at him again. "Maybe things just aren't happening soon enough."

"I know, but they will. This is your Klingon blood talking, I think. I'm not saying you shouldn't listen to it; we both know it will always be a part of you, that you need it, but . . . maybe you should try listening to your human side, for now."

B'Elanna took a breath. "My human side feels the same way," she said. "And, Commander, since you are acting as captain, you could also try to keep an open mind."

She turned away. This time when the door opened onto the bridge, she stepped through and kept going. Chakotay watched her leave, then found Tassay standing there, waiting for him to come toward her. She was lovely, and highly skilled as a negotiator, and very, very friendly. It was almost too good to be true. . . .

CHAPTER
10

AN INDIRECT APPROACH SEEMED WISEST. JANEWAY LED the way around the south end of the Drenarians' extensive planted fields, following a line of trees and brush that bordered the field. Finally the three of them drew within sight of the knoll where the shuttle had landed. They crouched lower among the bushes, using them for cover. Ash and soot had covered them from head to toe, blending them in with their surroundings almost completely. Nan Loteth had given them lengths of cloth to tie bandanalike over their noses and mouths, which helped them to breathe. These had proven quite effective.

Janeway's first concern was that any Televek present might have infrared sensing equipment trained on them. Tuvok kept watch with his tricorder. He ran a fresh scan, and decided that, so far at least, they had apparently not been detected. Kim continued scanning the planet itself. Earthquakes were often preceded by a sudden jerk that was easily detectable. That wasn't much, but some warning, at least, would be helpful.

The morning sun was already growing uncomfortably hot, and their brisk, obstacle-fraught hike had made them sweat, causing ash to cling to their skin. The cool shade provided by the trees felt good, as did the gentle breeze.

When they neared the site, they dropped down into a shallow ravine, keeping their heads low. As they drew up approximately parallel with the shuttle's location, Janeway dropped down on all fours, then waited while Tuvok and Kim did the same. Then they crawled up and forward through the thick, natural hedge.

From here the shuttle was plainly visible just over one hundred meters away. It appeared largely untouched, though the main hatch had clearly been opened, and just as they had feared, the shuttle was now well guarded. Half a dozen figures clad in black-and-white uniforms stood about, visually scanning their surroundings. At this distance details were difficult to discern. Still, Janeway was sure, as she shaded her eyes with one open hand, that she could see long white hair peeking out from under their squat helmets. Televek, certainly. Or Drosary. Or whatever they were calling themselves this morning.

"Captain," Tuvok said, raising his tricorder and tapping at it once more, "the bioscans of the Televek guarding our shuttle are precisely the same as those of the Drosary advocates aboard *Voyager.*"

"You read my mind, Mr. Tuvok."

The Vulcan tipped his head toward her. "I have done no such thing, Captain."

"Then I guess we just think alike."

"I'm getting the same readings, Captain," Kim said, duplicating Tuvok's scans. "Doesn't this mean that we've been had?"

"That is the only logical explanation," Janeway said.

Tuvok looked at her. "Captain—"

"I know," Janeway said, grinning. "I read your mind." She turned toward the shuttle again. "This also means that everything Gantel and his advocates told us was a lie," she muttered. "At least we have to assume as much. Which means that three Televek are up there on my ship right now, lying to Chakotay. And we don't know exactly what they're up to. We must make contact with *Voyager* again at any cost."

"There are probably more Televek inside the shuttle as well," Tuvok pointed out. "In all, too many to attempt a frontal assault."

"If the main hatch is blocked, we'll just have to think of something else," Janeway said, looking around, seeing no easy approach. Each of the Televek was holding a stubby energy rifle, and the sentinels were spaced fairly evenly around the shuttle. Thick, knee-high grass covered the ground between the tree line and the shuttle, but it would not provide any real cover.

"Any trace of sensor equipment in use?" she asked Tuvok.

"I continue to find none, Captain," Tuvok said, holding his open tricorder out again, moving it gently from side to side.

"They don't need sensors," Kim said. "With all that open ground we'll never get close without drawing their fire."

"Agreed, Captain," Tuvok said. "I am scanning several bodies in the grass, all approximately twenty meters from the shuttle. They are almost certainly Drenarian."

"Nan Loteth's people," Janeway concluded.

"I'll bet they never knew what hit them," Kim said.

Janeway briefly envisioned the scene, energy beams striking unprotected flesh from well beyond the range of the Drenarians' primitive weapons. She shook the image off, but as she peered out into the tall, soot-covered grasses, she could see several dark shapes. The three officers observed a long moment of silence. Nothing changed in the field.

Janeway looked out to her left, eyeing the bluff where she had fallen the day before. A large part of hillside had fallen away during the last big quake, but the newer edge was rather like the old. She had an idea. She didn't like the variables, but there wasn't time to worry about that.

"We'll have to split up. Tuvok, I want you to stand by here. Try to get a little closer if you can, but keep your head down. And keep your face covered, so you won't choke on the dust. Don't risk being seen. Kim and I are going to work our way up there and attempt to draw some of those guards away from the shuttlecraft. If that strategy works, the rest will be up to you."

Tuvok briefly appraised the situation, then nodded. "I understand, Captain."

"Good. If you're able to get aboard, I want you to

get communications working first. Contact the ship, tell them what we know. After that, if possible, see if you can get the transporter operational."

"Captain, even if I am able to do so, I doubt we will be able to transport anyone up to *Voyager*'s high orbit," Tuvok said. "The same magnetic fields that are hampering our communicator signals might well distort the transporter beam."

"I know," Janeway said. "And you're right, but I may have something else in mind. Don't worry, I'm not holding you to any promises."

Tuvok gazed out at his target. "Very well, I will do my best."

Janeway touched Tuvok's shoulder, stopping him as he instantly prepared to belly-crawl out beyond the tree line. "I know you will," she said. "And we both know we have to try to make this work. But not at the expense of one of my best officers."

The Vulcan turned to her for a moment. "That would be an unfortunate waste." His expression did not change. She didn't expect it would. Janeway nodded and let him go.

They watched Tuvok inch his way out through the grass. Then Janeway slid back, signaling Kim to follow, and the two of them headed toward the higher ground.

"On my mark." Chakotay watched from the captain's chair as the smallest of the three moons drew nearer, filling the main viewscreen. The maneuver had required only a minor course correction; Drenar's newest moon was in an orbit only slightly higher than *Voyager*'s had been.

The three Drosary stood clustered to his left, well out of the way, exactly where the commander had asked them to stand. He had stopped short of removing them from the bridge entirely, at least for now, but he didn't mind keeping them in check. Still, they had complied with his requests without the slightest incident, saying they completely understood. Chakotay took this as another sign that he was largely right about them, and that B'Elanna was overreacting.

As *Voyager* slowly closed the distance, using only a fraction of the impulse engines' output, the details of the moon became more clearly visible. The surface was unusually smooth.

"Moving to optimum position," Paris said, alternating his attention between his console and the main screen. "Things must have been pretty quiet wherever this moon used to be," he added, observing the moon as Chakotay did.

"Ice may have covered its surface," Chakotay suggested. "That would have evaporated as the moon traveled sunward."

"Like a giant comet," Paris suggested. "Must have had one hell of a tail."

"We should be able to detect its debris trail without too much trouble," Chakotay said.

"If you two are through sight-seeing," B'Elanna said over the comm, "we are ready down here."

"Good," Chakotay answered. "Mr. Paris, engage the warp engines. Mr. Rollins, activate the main deflector."

The commander stood up and moved to Ops, where Ensign Stephens kept watch in place of Kim. Over the ensign's shoulder he watched the monitor displaying the warp field, a misshapen bubble that reached out from the starship's bow and bumped into the giant moon, which was hundreds of times *Voyager*'s size. The bubble slowly spread out until it touched nearly a third of the satellite's surface.

"That's all we've got," B'Elanna said.

Chakotay nodded. "Impulse power, Mr. Paris. Easy does it."

For several minutes everyone remained in place, fully engaged in silent station-keeping. Then: "I show movement, Commander," Stephens sang out, to the sound of relieved sighs from one and all.

"Warp engines are holding at sixty-three percent," Paris reported.

"All three graviton polarity generators on-line and operating within acceptable limits," B'Elanna added.

"Good work, Torres," Chakotay told her.

"Rollins will have to keep compensating for the moon's density variations manually," she responded. "I'll keep a watch on things down here. Meanwhile, if you don't mind, I'd like to get back to being all those other miracle workers you think I am. Torres out."

It would be hours before they were through with just this moon, then they had to see what they could do about the others. After that, they might have to go back and work on this one again. Even by their best estimates, it would be some time before any significant effect was felt below on the planet. But for the first time since *Voyager* had entered orbit around Drenar Four, Chakotay felt that they were getting somewhere.

He looked up again, willing the moon to move. "Progress, Mr. Rollins?"

"Point zero zero three percent, sir."

"Very well. Steady as she goes."

Janeway experienced a sense of foreboding as she approached the edge of the bluff. The top of her head still ached from the last time she'd been here. She edged forward with extra caution until she and Kim were in good positions, hidden behind the dense trees, some of which had recently fallen into one another. She could see Tuvok from here, a dark shape in the tall grass still at least fifty meters from the shuttle-craft. None of the Televek seemed to have spotted him yet. She knew their ignorance wouldn't last long.

She drew her hand phaser. "On stun," she said as Kim drew his. She took aim. "Ready . . . fire."

Twin bright phaser beams flickered toward the shuttle, and two of the Televek guards dropped instantly. Janeway fired again as the others scurried for cover. One of them fired back, a wild shot that found only air. Kim managed to drop another guard before the opportunity was lost. Janeway's second shot missed. All the remaining Televek were behind the shuttle now, and all of them began firing back. This time the shots were much closer.

"Reset," Janeway said. She put her phaser on full, then fired again, aiming high, letting the beam strike a large spike of rock just beyond the shuttle and causing the rock to explode. Kim chose a young tree ten meters to the left. It burst open when the heat of the beam seared its trunk. Smoke and steam curled from the split pieces.

"Now let's send them an invitation," Janeway said.

She stood up and fired once more, making sure she was seen. Kim grimly did the same. Much of the dust that had covered their clothing had fallen off. On the ridge, against the drab forest background, the two officers made an excellent target. The Televek immediately tried to fire on their position, but Janeway had already turned and leaped out of the way. Kim followed.

A little too close, Janeway thought, though she didn't let her opinion show. She signaled Kim, and they moved back from the edge and waited, silent. Soon enough they heard the Televek guards coming out of hiding, firing preemptive shots at the trees where Janeway and Kim had just been, then moving toward the bluff. She heard them calling to one another as they climbed up the loose hillside.

"Let's not make it too easy for them, Mr. Kim. You go, that way." He did as he was told. When the first Televek peeked over the edge, Janeway fired. She aimed and hit a fallen tree, a warning shot that landed just inches from the Televek's head, then turned again and sprinted deeper into the forested area. Kim was just ahead of her now. She was catching up, but she could hear the Televek right behind her, also catching up. Her plan was working—perhaps a little too well.

Tuvok raised his head up far enough to get a clear view. He held there, carefully watching the shuttle. He saw only one Televek remaining, crouched in a defensive position behind the starboard nacelle, concentrating on the tumbled-down hill as the guard's comrades scrambled up the loose dirt and fought their way over the top. They all disappeared, chasing the captain and Kim. Tuvok dropped back down and began to crawl more quickly, though he was careful not to kick up too much dust.

A few meters ahead he reached the dead Drenarians, who had probably been killed the night before, Tuvok surmised. They lay stiff and cold, their waxen faces oblivious to the heat of the midday sun. He crawled past them, toward the shuttle, keeping a steady eye on the one remaining guard.

The position of the guard and the open hatch forced him to circle the shuttle so as to use the ship itself for cover. When he finally reached the hull he was near the bow. He set his phaser on stun, then rose, stepped around the bow, and fired, taking the partially hidden guard completely by surprise. The guard slumped silently to the ground. Tuvok rushed on, past the nacelle, certain there was no time to waste. He paused beside the hatch, then took a deep breath and charged in through the opening.

Another helmetless Televek stood tinkering at the main control panel, apparently hurrying to get some particular task accomplished. He was holding a blunt energy weapon in one hand while he attempted to use some type of probe with the other. When he looked up, Tuvok fired.

Tuvok moved forward, stepping over the Televek's still form, and began examining the work the intruder had been doing. A number of circuits had been patched or rerouted.

"Thank you for your assistance," the Vulcan said out loud, nodding to the figure at his feet. "You have saved me a good deal of time."

He put away his phaser and dragged the Televek just outside the shuttle. Then he slipped back inside, activated the emergency lighting system, and manually closed the hatch, sealing it shut. Tuvok needed only a moment to appraise the situation. The Televek's repairs, apparently intended to restore main power, had indeed been helpful, but much work remained to be done. He wasted no time in getting to it.

CHAPTER 11

GANTEL SAT QUIETLY IN HIS VAST SUITE—VAST FOR A battle cruiser, certainly—gazing wistfully at the baubles that filled every shelf, every corner, and much of the wall space. Even the chairs and tables were the finest available; the dining set was the prize among them, an antique older than some stars, or nearly so. His wardrobe was the match of any director's, tenth level on up, with the possible exception of Shaale herself.

But his life had many such amenities. He dined on the finest cuisine, foods prepared by a chef he had personally abducted from a Torthesian resort nearly nine years ago, and worth the effort, make no mistake. His collection of music—a passion considered curious by many Televek, but one he indulged nonetheless—was unequaled anywhere, so far as he knew, and would surpass even that high mark once he acquired the music libraries of the Federation starship *Voyager*.

Still, as his eyes came to rest on the set of exotically crafted, painstakingly hand-painted Pollian vases, neatly arranged from small to large, his mind sought to digress into a pool of swirling, self-indulgent doubt. For a moment, but for just a moment, he did not resist.

It was the goal of any civilized creature to obtain position, power, and wealth, and he had done so by doing what few Televek dared: he had taken some big risks; he had taken the important chances, despite what that tended to do to his stomach, and only when he had thought the time was right. It was a question of both want and need, as far as Gantel was concerned. When you wanted something badly enough, you needed to find a way to acquire it. And he had.

His success had cost him, though—three mates, so far, some gastrointestinal therapy, and a short list of enemies he had spent some years keeping an eye on. But all that was to be expected. And it had been worth the risk. Hadn't it . . . ?

An old friend had once told him that there came a time in every director's life, and even in every associate's, when absolutely ridiculous questions would arise to plunder the sanity of the mind. Questions like "What is the meaning of life?"

All this, Gantel thought as he looked past the priceless vases to the jeweled Awakening Day ceremonial chalice, something from his own world, then on to more of his belongings. But the temptation was to imagine there might be another meaning. A deeper, more spiritual one.

He had always laughed at such idiocy. Failings

could be traced to mistakes, successes to adroitness. And enough successes piled one on top of the other constituted fulfillment. But then what? . . .

Gantel blinked. One needed to be drunk, or at least getting there, in order to ponder such topics, and he simply couldn't indulge himself to that extent right now. Not with so much going on at once, so many variables, so many ways for something to go wrong and leave a blight the size of Drenar Four itself on his otherwise splendid career.

His instincts told him to make a deal with himself, sell himself a purely adequate bill of tried philosophical goods, just as every other Televek did, the same package his own parents had promoted. And the truth was, Gantel had very good instincts. No one could deny that.

He stood up and slowly crossed the room, where he paused to examine the contents of a case filled with hand weapons, ancient sharp-edged instruments he could only imagine trying actually to use in hand-to-hand combat. The idea was incredible, in fact. He could only imagine what the wounds would look like, what a death like that might be like. He thought of it often, in fact.

At the far wall a curved shard of burned metal rested on a shelf, kept in place by three transparent pins. The piece, a meter long and roughly twice as wide as Gantel's own head, was jagged on all but one edge. It had been part of the armor used to protect the Vanolens' massive primary space habitat. And it had been impenetrable, a problem the Thaitifa, in their quest to rule the Vanolens, had come to Gantel to solve.

Briefly, Gantel had fretted over his decision. The

Vanolens were a glorious people. Their civilization had been around for millions of years. Even longer than the Televek themselves. Artisans at heart, the lot of them. And their cities in space were simply remarkable. He had spent some time there in his youth, listening to music, and he still remembered the name of one particularly alluring windwhyle player he'd met at the East Ocean Symphonic Review, and the many talents she embodied.

Gantel had been only a third associate then, and the stars knew there were more than enough eager associates of every rank scrambling to climb up one more rung on the ladder of success. But as luck would have it—though to this day he had never admitted that luck had anything to do with it—he had come into possession of a phase-shifted payload device capable of delivering any obtainable warhead to any programmable point inside virtually any fixed defensive barrier.

In the end, of course, he had sold the delivery system to the Thaitifa, and they had used it to great effect against the Vanolens. The sale was what mattered, after all, not the ones who had died, not even the real estate that had been obliterated, and in the end he had been able to find comfort in that belief—that and the fact that the Thaitifa had paid the most ridiculous price imaginable, a boon that by itself had propelled Gantel to first associate at his next evaluation.

It had been the right choice. And in any case, if he hadn't closed the deal, some other associate would have, sooner or later.

His one true regret was that the delivery units he

had sold the Thaitifa were the only ones he'd had on hand. Before he was able to obtain more, the Garn, from whom he had purchased the weapons—a race of methane-breathing quadrupeds who, during negotiations, had given new meaning to words like "challenging" and "awkward"—had managed to lose the war they were fighting, and lose it in a big way. There had been nothing left but ashes by the time Gantel got around to going back.

With a sigh Gantel meandered back across the room and, from one of the taps over the microbar, drew an icy glass of berry juice—a blend selected from nine different worlds, a combination of flavors to please any palate. He drank it all. It tasted wonderful. He was coming out of the dark pool now, exorcising his doubt, feeling better.

He had met with failure more than once along the way, the price of taking chances, but throughout his celebrated career Gantel had managed to find a way to cover up his worst setbacks, usually by placing most of the blame on someone else; and to be sure he had closed on many a marginal deal, snatched breakthroughs from the jaws of calamity, fooled the sharpest opponents into trusting him completely, and turned the needs and suffering of others into opportunity and profit many times over.

Drenar Four was no exception, he told himself, setting his glass down. *"Enta sa tnoai,"* he said out loud, quoting in the ancient tongue: "Seize the deal."

He focused once more on the situation at hand. The cruiser's shields had been repaired, and Gantel was relatively certain that the Federation ship's photon torpedoes could not collapse them, at least not in a first volley. And without any shields of its own, the Federation vessel would not survive long enough to fire many rounds. Triness would see to that.

Jonal and the others were doing a fair job under the circumstances; they were as capable a team as any he had fielded in some time. The trouble was, like most Televek, Gantel hated to rely on others, an instinct the Televek had retained since prehistoric times. But civilization, and success itself, usually required the delegation of responsibility. A director, certainly, must direct.

Moreover, his plan to feign assistance, though certainly risky, was a good one; it had been working famously, and should continue to do so.

Although this new wrinkle, moving the moons around to alleviate the tectonic pressures within the planet, had the potential to pose some nasty complications. Still, though, he doubted the visitors had the time or the resources to make any real difference. They would be finished as soon as he said so. All he had to do was keep things from getting any more convoluted, keep the risk factors from escalating, until the rest of the plan could be—

"We have the first director on our extended scans," Triness said, her voice nearly as melodic as the strains of a Vanolen windwhyle to his ears. And indeed she spoke mostly welcome words. He wasn't looking forward to First Director Shaale's arrival, but unless something went incredibly wrong—something he had resolved not to think about, at least not constantly— the rest of the week promised to turn out very well indeed.

Gantel drew a second glass of juice with a sigh of

imposed satisfaction. He marveled at the color and the tantalizing aroma; then he set the glass back down. He wasn't thirsty anymore. And his stomach didn't feel quite well.

"Very good," he said, gathering up his director's dress coat, shrugging the weight of it onto his shoulders. "I'll be up in a moment."

Chakotay watched the viewscreen fill up with moon. The first phase of their efforts had gone well indeed. Though the process was akin to watching water evaporate, the first moon's trajectory had been measurably altered. The second moon's movement would be much less impressive, and the strain on the warp engines as the deflector was again activated was sure to worsen.

But B'Elanna insisted that what little *Voyager* was beginning to accomplish was within the desired parameters, and she hadn't advised calling the mission off—not yet, anyway. Chakotay took her word on all of it. Nearly impossible feats of precise engineering under extreme duress were the sort of thing she was good at; he'd staked his life on that more than once.

He rose from the captain's chair, then returned once more to the ops station where he had been standing for much of the past few hours, peering over Ensign Stephens's shoulder. The whole thing was theory. They couldn't be sure that their effort would have a large enough effect to ease the violent turbulence within the planet, or whether the benefits, even if they succeeded, would come in time. But it made sense to try, if only to help ease the sense of helplessness that Chakotay knew the crew felt.

"Commander," Paris said, "extreme long-range sensors are picking up several vessels. They appear to be on a direct course toward the Drenar system."

"Those are certainly the Televek transport and supply ships we told you about," Jonal said, drawing up beside the Commander at Ops. The Drosary glanced at the panel where the sensor information was displayed and smiled, first at the ensign, then at Chakotay. "Just as promised, help is on the way."

"You will all be quite pleased when the Televek vessels arrive," Tassay said as she and Mila joined the others. "They will help bring our problems, and those of the people below, to an acceptable solution. And when all of that is finished, before we go our separate ways, there will be time for some of us to get to know some of you a little bit . . . better, perhaps."

Chakotay found her looking only at him as she spoke this last. Looking into him, it seemed. And he felt for a moment as if he were staring deeply into some part of her as well.

"I certainly hope so," Mila said, strolling back toward Paris's station, running one fingertip lightly across the back of his neck. He seemed to weather the assault well enough.

"You are a wonderfully skilled pilot," she told him. "I'll bet you're the best your Starfleet has to offer."

"You don't have to tell him that," Chakotay remarked. "Just ask him, and he'll be glad to tell you."

"I was a good pilot, too," Mila said, slightly more serious. "One day I will be again, and I will demonstrate my skill."

Paris looked up at her, his expression softer than any that Chakotay was used to seeing. "I believe you," he said. "And I think you'll get your chance, just as I have."

Chakotay turned at the sound of the turbolift door opening behind him. Lieutenant Torres stepped onto the bridge and stopped in mid-stride. Her eyes narrowed, and she pursed her lips. Chakotay followed her gaze to Paris and Mila, who were engaged together in what was becoming a special moment. Mila bent over, her nose nearly touching the lieutenant's as he raised his face to hers. They whispered briefly to each other, grinning frivolously.

When Chakotay looked back, he found B'Elanna still rigid, fists clenched at her sides, only she was looking at him now. He felt Tassay behind him then, her warm breath on the back of his neck. One of her hands gently touched his side. "I hope things work out perfectly," she said softly, "for all of us."

Chakotay felt a little chill, and perhaps he also felt guilty, as if he'd just been caught in a lie. He gently brushed Tassay's hand aside. "You have something to report, Lieutenant?" he asked Torres, hearing his voice crack as he spoke. He cleared his throat and waited. The answer seemed to take a while.

"Not right now," Torres said stiffly.

"Then why are you on the bridge?" Chakotay asked, feeling slightly annoyed. After all, she wasn't helping anyone just standing there casting a dark mood over the bridge. At least, he didn't want to think she was helping . . .

Again she paused. "Just checking the image on the main screen," she said. Which made no sense. It wasn't any different from the monitor screens in engineering.

"Checking for what?"

"It's a long story, I guess," she answered. "It's just . . ." She looked away from the screen, looked at everyone on the bridge.

"Just what?"

B'Elanna let a look of sad frustration cross her features for just an instant, very different from the strict expression she had brought in with her. "I have a lot to do right now. Duties. You understand, or at least I think you do. I know you used to." She spun on her heel and tromped back toward the lift door.

"Where are you going?" Chakotay asked.

"I'll be in Engineering," she said, "doing what needs to be done." And then she was gone.

Chakotay stood silently contemplating B'Elanna's last words. He could hear Tassay trying to talk to him again, continuing the same conversation, as if nothing had happened. "I have such plans," she continued. Something about taking a shuttle through the rest of the Drenar system in a couple of days to do some sight-seeing. He was trying very hard not to listen.

"Commander," Rollins said, "those ships are approaching optimal sensor range. I'm scanning now."

"Excellent," Jonal said, moving toward Rollins in the tactical bay as the ensign worked at his consoles. The Drosary stepped closer and attempted to look down at the readings, but Rollins waved him off as if he were a fly buzzing too close.

"Those are definitely Televek reactor signatures," Rollins reported.

"They are such punctual people, these Televek," Tassay said, her voice loud in Chakotay's ear.

"And nearly as friendly as we are," Mila told Paris, again nose to nose.

"Commander," Rollins said then, looking up, wide-eyed. "This is odd. They don't look much like transports or supply ships. Any of them. I'm trying to verify tonnage, configuration, and energy curves, but as far as I can tell, those ships are all identical to that—"

Jonal wrapped his arm around Rollins's neck, cutting him off in mid-sentence. At almost the same instant Mila wrapped an arm around Paris's neck and tightened it, nearly lifting him out of his seat. Chakotay tried to move, but he felt hands grabbing him, reining him in. Before he could utter a sound, Tassay had one hand over his face, an arm firmly around his middle. She bent him backward far enough to immobilize him, nearly far enough to break his back, and held him fast.

"We'll have to take control ahead of schedule!" Jonal shouted. Chakotay watched as Mila forced Paris to one side, then used her free hand to tap rapidly at the helm panel. The ship lurched once, hard to port, then again, to starboard, shuddering as the force rippled through the hull and deck plates. Then *Voyager* came to a full stop. Jonal held Rollins aside and worked the tactical controls. In a moment he looked up at the other Drosary. "We are secure at the moment."

Chakotay tried to struggle, but that effort quickly proved pointless. The two security guards stationed on the bridge were of little use at the moment as well. Even as Jonal, Mila, and Tassay performed their tasks, they held their captives so as to shield themselves against the guards' drawn phasers.

Chakotay was amazed at the strength the Drosary

possessed; it was even more remarkable than their well-defined physiques would suggest. He was helpless against her hold, as were the others.

"What do you want?" he managed, though his words came out garbled under the pressure of Tassay's hand.

"We want all of you to remain perfectly still, or we will snap the necks of these officers one by one," Jonal replied. He turned to Chakotay. "Tell your officers to do as I say."

Chakotay said nothing at all. He couldn't give these people that kind of freedom; he wouldn't.

Jonal asked again, but the commander kept still. "Very well, then, they will do what you say," Jonal said angrily after only a slight hesitation. "Have your guards put down their weapons. Then I want the bridge sealed off."

The difference was subtle. Simon says, more or less. But Chakotay thought this was something he could try to work with. "Seal the doors," he told Stephens, who quickly complied. He told the guards to comply as well.

"A good start," Jonal said. "Seal the conduits, too. I want the computer to begin continuous scans of all areas surrounding the bridge. We don't want anyone breaking in through a wall somewhere. Tell the computer to do that, or Tassay will kill you. Once that happens, you will be replaced by another bridge officer, who will die in turn, until I get what I want."

"Very well," Chakotay said, giving the commands. There wasn't anything else he could do just yet.

"Doors and conduits are sealed, scans are in place," Stephens reported after a moment.

"Now change the bridge computer control authorization code so that no one can surprise us," Jonal ordered, grinning slightly. "Change it to accept my voice, my name."

"I can't do that," Chakotay muttered.

"Then I will kill you, and that one," Tassay said, nodding toward Stephens. Her voice sounded different, cold.

Chakotay grudgingly nodded, and once again the ensign complied. "Computer, transfer all controls, authorization code alpha-fine, abacrom-dexter, six, four, zero, nine, one. Copy voice authorization." Chakotay looked to Jonal, who nodded and spoke his name. The computer confirmed the transfer.

Jonal seemed to worry over the tactical console for a moment after that, tapping at it sporadically. Then he straightened, his expression one of mild satisfaction.

Chakotay made an effort to straighten as well, but Tassay seemed disinclined to allow it. She had her other hand around his throat now, but she wasn't squeezing very hard.

"I'll bet you don't even think I'm cute," he said to her. When she made no reply, he added, "I thought we were just starting to get somewhere. I had a little country house with a white picket fence all picked out."

Tassay adjusted her grip. "I don't know what you're talking about."

"I know you don't," Chakotay said.

"Open a channel to Gantel," Mila told Jonal, apparently anxious.

Jonal nodded silently, then worked at the console.

"Done!" he shouted the moment contact was established, obviously pleased with himself. Suddenly the screen was no longer filled with the planet's smallest moon.

"We have a visual," Stephens said as the fact became evident. The face on the screen was that of a male who could have easily been Jonal's brother. The room in the background was well lit and decorated with colorful tapestries. Several other figures stood about, apparently attending the communication. They all looked much the same. The women could have been Mila and Tassay's sisters.

"You're all Televek," Paris said, stating the obvious, squirming to no avail.

"So it would seem," Chakotay muttered.

"Gantel," Jonal said, acknowledging the image on the screen. "The bridge is secured. We are in control of the ship."

Gantel's expression didn't change. "Already?"

"There was no choice. They are fairly bright, as you know. They were about to scan Shaale's fleet. They would have figured the situation out."

"That is what I like about you, Jonal, your ability to adapt. It is just as well. Our pods are ready. The teams have been assembled. We can begin launching almost immediately. You haven't damaged anything valuable, have you?"

"Of course not."

"So you are pirates," Chakotay said.

"Oh, we are much more than that, and you, my friend, are a fool," Mila replied. She jerked Paris off the floor to punctuate the statement, and to still his struggling body. "All of you are fools. No wonder you wandered so far from home and got lost."

"I liked Jonal's opinion better," Paris muttered.

"Whatever, it still doesn't change the fact that they have some very impressive technology," an impatient Gantel said from the screen. "Most of which we will find quite valuable, I am certain. Jonal, do you intend to stand there like that until we relieve you?"

"No, of course not," Jonal replied. He turned to Chakotay. "Commander, tell all of your people to move toward the forward area of the bridge, between the helm and the main screen. They won't be needed for a while, and we can keep a better eye on them there. We will tend to all stations. Your only task now is to wait quietly."

"And after you've stripped *Voyager* of whatever you want, what will you do then?" Chakotay asked, as the bridge crew began to comply. "What happens to us?"

"They'll either kill us, or leave us here to die," Paris said bitterly.

"We have no intention of stripping your vessel," the Televek commander answered from the screen again. "I plan to take the whole vessel home! After we've finished using it to help retrieve our salvage from the planet, of course."

"Do you have any intention of helping those people down there?" Chakotay asked, his tone implying he already knew the answer.

"We are interested in the defensive system that protects them," Gantel said. "We have no need of the Drenarians, nor do we need any of you. The most obvious solution is to escort all of you down to the planet, once we've disarmed the system. Then we'll let the universe decide your fate."

"Leave all our troubles behind," Jonal said, smiling at Chakotay.

"It is amazing that so primitive a race could create such a ship," Tassay remarked.

"Indeed," Mila said.

"Such a windfall," Gantel agreed.

"We aren't so primitive," Paris said. "What makes you think you're any better?"

"Oh, but we are better, and we are right," Jonal said, letting go of Rollins and motioning him to join the others, who were nearly all gathered in front of the viewscreen now. Mila let go of Paris, who moved slowly away from her. Finally Tassay let Chakotay go as well. Jonal and Mila collected two discarded phasers and trained them on the crew.

"You are barbarians, thieves, and liars," Chakotay said in response.

"Not at all, Commander," Jonal said. "You see, we represent a leap in evolution far beyond what any one aboard *Voyager* could boast. Our instincts are empathic. They no longer alert us to primitive dangers long vanished from our way of life. We react instead to other intelligent beings' minds, to their psyches, their most immutable characteristics. This facilitates familiarity and, with practice, manipulation."

"So now we're buddies," Stephens said, shaking his head.

"You knew exactly which buttons to push with each one of us, in order to win our trust," Paris said.

Jonal nodded. "Once we had spent a little time with you, yes."

"You're salesmen," Chakotay said grimly. "Natural born salesmen."

"Sure," Paris moaned. "And we bought a lemon."

"Nine lemons, if you count the cruiser in orbit with

us," Rollins said. "The other eight are approaching at warp eight, according to the last sensor data I saw."

"We are well adapted to survival in an advanced social environment," Mila said, looking straight at Paris again. "While you are still better suited to life in an armed camp set in some wilderness outback."

"I'd like to take you out into the wilderness," Paris told her, smiling sickly at her.

"You still find me attractive, don't you?" Mila cooed, smiling back. "I knew you did."

"I find you repulsive," Paris said, suddenly glaring at her. "But I would like to do something primitive to you, like break your neck."

"I should silence you right now!" Mila shouted at him.

"I see no reason not to," Gantel said from the screen. "None of them will survive in any case."

Mila's grin returned, but her expression was filled with malice now. She glanced at her two companions, who quietly nodded to her.

"How can you call yourselves advanced and still have so little regard for life?" Chakotay challenged them.

"We have exceptional regard for life, Commander," Jonal said. "Our own."

"I won't let you kill him," Chakotay said bitterly, stepping forward, all but blocking Mila's shot.

"You will once you are dead," Tassay said, taking the phaser from Jonal and aiming it at the commander.

Mila raised her arm and aimed her weapon as well. Jonal frowned. "Get on with it."

"Very well," Mila answered.

But with that all three Televek suddenly began to change into pillars of sparkling matter. They cried out in hollow, echoing voices as they disappeared from the bridge in a fading cloud of transporter particles.

Cheers burst from the lips of every officer present.

Chakotay turned to Stephens and made a quick hand motion, two fingers drawn across his throat.

Stephens reached the ops station in three leaps and complied. The main screen went blank. He looked up, panting. "Transmission terminated, Commander."

"Unlock everything," Chakotay told him. He took another breath. "Computer, release all controls, authorization code alpha-fine, abacrom-dexter, six, four, zero, nine, two."

"Control status, normal," the computer replied.

"Chakotay to transporter room!" the commander shouted, slapping hard at his comm badge. "How—"

"The aliens are in custody and headed for the brig, Commander, and Lt. Torres is on her way up to see you right now," the transporter officer replied. An instant later Lieutenant Torres stepped once more onto the bridge.

"Torres!" Chakotay said, holding both hands out toward her, grinning. "B'Elanna!"

"It is me," she kidded. She smiled back, purposely demure, as she met him halfway and returned his embrace. He let her go almost at once.

"It seems Neelix wasn't the only one in this part of the galaxy who'd never seen a transporter before," she told him.

"I bet they'll never forget it," Chakotay replied.

Torres smiled at the others. "I suppose they left without even saying good-bye."

"As a matter of fact, they were just about to," Paris

told her as he reclaimed his station. "Thanks," he said, when B'Elanna looked at him.

"I'm just glad they're gone," Rollins added as he began working to restore normal control.

"Yes," Chakotay said less enthusiastically, looking up at the blank screen, well aware of what was out there. "But I'm afraid most of them haven't gone very far."

CHAPTER
12

GANTEL LEANED FORWARD IN HIS CHAIR, OPENED HIS mouth—and found no words appropriate to the occasion. A splendid series of curses came to mind, but by then it was too late even to curse. The Federation ship had broken contact. He uttered the obscenities under his breath for his own benefit. Then he turned to his crew.

"I've never seen anything like that!" Triness said, an unfamiliar touch of nervousness in her voice. "It is as if my own eyes—"

"That's why I want to see it again," Gantel said. "Run the last few minutes of transmission back. We need another look. Have the computer analyze the images."

They watched again as Jonal, Mila, and Tassay vanished from sight and the screen went black. The computer was of no immediate help.

"It looks as though they were vaporized somehow," Triness said as the cruiser began to come about. Her eyes narrowed as she and Gantel stared at the blank screen. "Yet no weapon was used, at least not by anyone on their bridge."

"None we know of," Gantel said. His gaze drifted, until he sat looking at his feet, staring at as fine a pair of K'Heplian leather boots as had ever walked a deck. This was the kind of situation that could go either way. Boon or bust. With the fleet due to arrive in no time, whatever he did next would make the difference between risk and ruin. The problem was, no hint of a solution seemed willing to present itself.

But he couldn't just stay here, doing nothing.

"Range to target?" Gantel shouted.

"Four hundred thousand kilometers," the helmsman said.

"Close to one hundred thousand immediately."

The screen lit up again with a view of near space. The planet's smallest moon filled most of the field, but a minute spot could be seen crossing its equinox, moving into the light. The moon began to grow as the cruiser drew forward.

"Whatever they did, they must have done it from a remote location," the navigation officer said, taking her chances by speaking out of turn. "So the technology may have control limitations." Her comment was met with nods all around.

"Still, imagine the power such a device would give an aggressor," Triness said.

"Imagine the price it would command!" Gantel exclaimed.

"More than enough to make up for the loss of the envoys," Triness suggested.

Gantel nodded agreement. "And a hundred like them."

Then Triness seemed to come to some fresh perspective. She looked at Gantel as if he had changed color.

"What is it?" he asked.

"At the moment," she said, her eyes drifting back toward the main viewer, "I am most concerned about . . . the range of the weapon."

Gantel considered this briefly. He had to agree. They were already getting very close to the Federation ship. "It's range must be limited, or they would have used it against us by now. What is our present distance?"

"One hundred fifty and closing."

"All stop."

"Agreed, the device must have a short range," Triness said.

"Or," Gantel suggested, "they were saving it. Keeping it a secret until they needed to use it."

"Indeed," Triness said, her lips pursed in speculation.

Gantel leaned forward to peer at the Federation ship. "This must be done right. Whatever this device is, it must be ours. I want to present it to Shaale myself."

That was the key, of course. The kind of bold maneuver that would put him in very good stead with the first director, perhaps even earn him a special commission. But more importantly, he would, if he handled the deal correctly, retain the distribution rights to the device. And if the stars were on his side, the distribution profits would be in addition to whatever windfall came from the recovery of the defensive system on Drenar Four. Overall, this would be the most successful, most profitable mission in memory—*anyone's* memory, so far as Gantel knew! Surely that possibility was worth the risk, a thousand times over.

The Federation ship was apparently a treasure trove of technological wonders. Even if nothing of value proved recoverable from the planet itself, the capture of *Voyager,* intact, meant Gantel would succeed. The hard part, of course, would be doing just that.

"Have they raised their shields yet?"

"No," Triness reported. "Their shields must still be down. I have raised ours."

"Very well, let's get a little closer."

"I didn't know the transporters were functioning again," Chakotay said, as he watched the Televek approach. The cruiser came to an abrupt halt, maintaining a little more distance than earlier.

B'Elanna shrugged. "They weren't, until . . . well until just a couple of minutes ago. I was trying to tell you we were close when I came up here the last time."

"Why didn't you?"

"Everyone seemed a little . . . preoccupied."

"I guess we did at that," Chakotay said, an intended note of apology in his voice.

"Anyway," Torres went on, "when the ship lurched both ways and came to full stop I had a pretty good idea what was going on, and who was behind it. When the bridge was suddenly isolated, I knew."

"You were completely right about them," Chakotay said. "You knew all along, didn't you?"

"My Klingon blood, I guess." She looked at him and smiled. "And my human heart."

Chakotay couldn't help but smile back. Torres often came to him for guidance, yet this time he had been the one in need. He looked at her with subtle admiration. He wanted to say something, but a simple thank-you would not have sufficed. "B'Elanna," he said, "who we are is sometimes our greatest weakness, but it also can be our greatest strength."

The lieutenant said nothing for a moment, but Chakotay knew even before she nodded that she understood.

"Commander," Stephens said, indicating the main viewscreen. "The Televek are trying to hail us again."

"I'll bet they're not too happy," Paris said.

"I'll bet their friends in that fleet of cruisers heading our way won't be very happy when they get here, either," Rollins added.

Chakotay frowned. "Any change in the planet's status?"

"It's churning in the continental region again, Commander," Ensign Stephens reported crisply. "Major eruptions from numerous active volcanoes, and quakes everywhere, offshore as well."

"How bad?"

"I can't get a clear enough reading, but I think this is the worst we've seen since our arrival."

Chakotay stood utterly silent as he considered his next move. He took a deep breath. "Go to red alert. Target weapons. Transporter room, can you get a fix on the away team?"

"I've been trying, sir," Hoffman said over the comm. "I've located three signals that I think may be them, but I've been unable to make a positive ID, and I can't get a good lock. We're still fighting an ocean of interference down there. Those could be Drenarians, or even Televek for all I know. I'm sorry, Commander."

"Understood. Mr. Rollins, you have the bridge. Keep those photon torpedoes trained on that cruiser. I'll be in the transporter room. B'Elanna," he added wryly, already headed off the bridge, "get back to work."

The turbolift door closed just in time.

Drenar Four was coming apart. Tuvok felt the quake approaching, but he was ill prepared for the violence it contained when it fully arrived. Even after bracing himself, feet apart, hands pressed against the console and bulkhead, he was quickly knocked away from all supportive surfaces, then thrown down to the hard deck. He crept along the moving floor, eyes unable to focus as the vibrations increased further still.

The ground beneath the shuttle heaved, tossing him upward. He tried to stay as limp as possible, aware that nothing quite facilitated the breaking of bones like rigid muscles, but the first impact point proved to be the side of his head. Which, fortunately, did not give very much. He watched the deck charge up to greet him yet again. Then the shaking returned.

A brief quieting of the shock waves allowed him to distinguish between up and down. He ached in numerous places, but nothing hurt enough to suggest a critical injury. Getting his wind back, he scrambled straight under the main console just in front of the pilot's chair, the only place inside the shuttle where he thought he might stand a chance of wedging himself in firmly enough to stay put.

A second series of shock waves arrived, more brutal than any Tuvok had ever experienced, but this time he did not take flight. He felt the entire shuttle move once more, bouncing its way perhaps a meter or two to the west. Then it held, shaking with the rest of the world but tipping up sharply at the bow, as if pointing toward the heavens from which it had descended. A moment later the shaking suddenly stopped, leaving an all-encompassing silence inside the small compartment.

Tuvok slowly extracted himself from his twisted position on the floor and tried to stand up. One knee cracked and made him wince. His head swam for a moment, and he felt a sizable shoulder bruise announce itself as he tried to lift his arms. All in all, however, as he attempted to work the worst of the kinks out, he considered himself fortunate. He turned toward the main console and tried to bring up the power. Everything was out again.

Back to basics, he thought. It took several minutes to find the ruptured feed, and several more to patch it back together. Next he made use of the probe the Televek had supplied, a crude but effective instrument. Within minutes he had restored power to half of the systems on the shuttle. But as he moved on to his first priority, the communications system, he realized there was no hope of repairing it. That entire section of the console was split in two, from the instrument panel to the deck, and many of its components had been ruined.

Tuvok let a long, grim, illogical sigh seep out before

he took a fresh breath and turned to his second challenge: the transporter system. The damage to this portion of the main control panel was minimal, but he couldn't get the controls to respond, leading him to suspect trouble with the transporter itself. He started toward the stern of the shuttle, clinging to anything he could find in order to keep from tumbling straight into the rear hatch. Beginning just moments from now there would be a series of aftershocks, if not another full quake. He expected things would only get worse. And the Televek might return at any moment. Time was short.

Tuvok saw no logic in pessimistic speculation, but he could not help acknowledging the grim status of the mission, and his aspect of it in particular.

Then he set aside his doubts, quickly and efficiently. "I will work faster," he said out loud, as if Drenar Four itself could hear. He censored himself, then executed a controlled tumble into the aft compartment. He went to work precisely where he landed.

Phaser fire lit up the darkened woods and sent clouds of burning bark and hissing splinters into the air as errant shots struck the trunks of trees. Janeway and Kim stopped running momentarily to return fire, and to watch the pursuing Televek dive for cover. They stayed pinned down for only a moment.

Slowly, first one, then another of the aliens began to turn out in a flanking maneuver, crawling for the most part, heads down. The undergrowth was just thick enough so that Janeway couldn't get a clear shot. Finally she signaled Kim to fall back again, the only thing they could do to avoid getting caught in Televek crossfire.

Once they had scurried far enough away to risk it, they stood nearly upright, then ran as fast as the tangle of green and brown would allow. The footing grew especially treacherous in places. Janeway was stepping over a small boulder and glancing over her shoulder when she heard Kim shout into her ear.

In almost the same instant she felt him hit her hard in the side, tackle style, knocking her off her feet. She lay there, face in the dirt for an instant, then got her arms under her and lifted her head up. She heaved air into her empty lungs, filling them back up. As she shook off the daze from the fall, she understood.

The earth here was split, partly a result of the natural roll of the landscape, though in this place there was clear evidence of recent changes brought about by the quakes. A great chasm cut through the forest from left to right; it was no more than two meters wide but too deep and too shadowed to allow sight to penetrate. Turned around, checking for their pursuers, Janeway had nearly stumbled into it. Kim had been more observant and had acted quickly. He had saved her life.

"Thanks," she said.

Kim's grin was feeble but sincere. "You're welcome, Captain."

"We'll have to jump over it," she said. After allowing Kim to help her to her feet, she collected her hand phaser, and then they both stood back a few paces and broke into another sprint. They cleared the empty distance easily enough, but no sooner had they rolled up and gotten to their feet than they were forced to drop as the heat of a phaser beam passed between them. The Televek had found them again.

"Keep moving," Janeway snapped, starting off

once more. "Fire over your shoulder. Watch where you're—"

Before she could finish, the ground began to rumble. Then it shook with an all too familiar tremor. Janeway grabbed the nearest tree only to find it suddenly being uprooted as a fresh, jagged fissure appeared from nowhere, crossing the forest floor right beneath her, racing to join the one they had just jumped across. She heard Kim yelling to her again.

"I know!" she shouted, letting go, leaping backward. The underbrush dug at her back when she landed. This time, though, it was she who helped Kim to his feet as the tremors momentarily subsided—but did not end. A fresh wave was already beginning.

Janeway glanced back. She could see two of the Televek getting up, looking for their quarry as they got their bearings again. One of them spotted the two Federation uniforms right away.

"They're still coming," she said, tugging at Kim's silt-covered uniform sleeve.

"So we're still going," he replied, wasting no time in complying. As they leaped the new ravine, the quakes reintensified, sending the far edge of the gap straight up half a meter, just as they landed on it. They rose with the land, shins bruised, momentum carrying them forward, and tumbled helplessly down the other side, then down again as they reached a wide natural gully.

Janeway saw Kim trying to grab ahold of the trees and scrub; she was already trying to do the same, but the intensifying shock waves emanating from beneath them made every target a moving one. The world was shaking and undulating like a storm-tossed sea.

Both officers plunged downward until a pair of

massive fallen trees blocked their path. As they slammed into the smooth bark, the quake abruptly ended, as if a great hand had reached out and stilled all motion.

"Captain, are you still all right?" Kim asked, groaning heavily as he spoke the words, trying to get up again. He closed both eyes and flinched as he attempted to straighten his back; then he moaned again.

"I think so," Janeway answered, making a face she thought nearly matched Kim's as she tried to get her own legs underneath her. Winds were building now, shifting, as if a great storm was approaching, but the thickening gray clouds that filled the sky were not from any weather system, Janeway was certain of that. Soon volcanic ash would begin to fall from them, blanketing everything, eventually smothering all the life in this region, even if the world itself managed to survive.

"Maybe those Televek fell into that new crevice," Kim said wistfully. As his words joined the gusting winds they were made mute by another phaser blast. Kim cried out, then fell, clutching his right leg.

"You're hit!" Janeway shouted, snatching at the ensign's uniform. She raised her weapon and fired in the direction of the attack without looking up, concerned primarily with Kim's condition, and with getting him to cover. The apex where the fallen trees crossed stood more than three meters tall, and the trees themselves were nearly that thick as well.

Janeway managed to move along the massive trunk of one fallen tree, pulling Kim with her until they reached a spot where the trunk was only a meter high. Here Janeway propped Kim up, then heaved him over the tree bole. She fired again, then scrambled over the trunk after him. She got the ensign sitting up, then poked her head up enough to find a target, and fired over the top of the trunk. She was forced to duck again as several Televek weapons fired back.

Great chunks of wood were torn away as the phaser blasts gouged them out. Bits and pieces of wood and bark showered down on Janeway and Kim. They huddled still lower. "How is it?" she asked, trying to examine the phaser burn.

"I don't think they've finished me yet, but it doesn't feel very good," he confessed. The young officer seemed lucid enough, if less than chipper. He was holding his leg still, taking deep breaths, and looking up at her as if this was somehow his own fault.

"I didn't ask you to play human shield for me," she told him. "But I appreciate the gesture."

Kim smiled at this, nearly erasing the lines of pain from his face for just a moment. Janeway recognized the consequences of the sudden lull in incoming fire. She rose up slightly and fired back once more, trying to find real targets this time. The Televek were lying along the upper edge of the gully, but she couldn't tell exactly where. It didn't matter; she was certain they wouldn't stay put for long.

She saw two heads pop up, and then two energy weapons fired. She decided to duck rather than take a shot, instincts screaming, and found it had been the right decision as the part of the tree trunk vanished in a wet hail of steaming, exploding tree fibers exactly where her face had been.

"These trees will be vapor in a few minutes," she said. "Do you think you can still walk?"

Kim tried to move the injured leg. She watched as pain turned his features into twisted disarray. She checked her own phaser and noted that the charge was nearly depleted. Kim's weapon would have more charge, but not much more.

"Our situation doesn't look good, does it, Captain?" Kim wheezed, trying to get comfortable, though that was clearly impossible. Janeway knew that he relied upon her for courage and guidance at least as much as any other member of her crew. She wanted to tell him she had a plan, that they would get out of this mess, that everything was going to be all right, but as she thought the situation over, she decided that Kim deserved to hear it straight.

Another round of phaser fire landed, burning so much of the tree trunk away that they were forced to move more than half a meter to one side. She looked at him as they settled again. She had all the rhetoric memorized, especially the part about all of the cadets knowing when they joined the Academy that they might one day be called to put their lives on the line, but that speech wouldn't suffice either. She had given most of her life to Starfleet, but she couldn't go out quoting dogma.

"Kim, I want you to know—"

"Captain!" Kim shouted, staring past her.

An unnatural ringing sounded in her ear, and a bright glowing cloud assaulted her eyes as she turned around. The sudden mixture of alarm and revelation that followed nearly caused her to cry out. Then she watched Tuvok materialize just inches from her. He wore one of the shuttle's transporter armbands on his left arm and carried two identical bands and a tricorder in his hands.

"Captain," the Vulcan said, standing up, looking down at her.

"Duck!" she yelled, yanking hard at his sleeve as a Televek beam seared the air a hand's breadth away from his head. He crouched beside her.

"Thank you, Captain."

"You're quite welcome. I take it you've been busy."

"I wish I had better news to report," he conceded. "I am afraid shuttle communications are completely disabled. But as you can see, I was able to get the transporter working."

"I knew you'd come through, Tuvok," Kim said, making a face that passed for cheerful.

"However," Tuvok continued, his sullen look growing more so, "it is not working very well."

Shots burned into the trees once more. Janeway picked up Kim's hand phaser, then nodded toward the Televek on the crest of the hill. Tuvok drew his weapon from his waist, and they both rose up and opened fire. Even before they had dropped back down, a fresh salvo of return fire arrived from their left flank, vaporizing the trunk of a sapling not half a meter behind the three officers. Janeway and Tuvok both took aim and fired a continuous burst at the point of origin. Janeway's phaser went dead. She put it on her belt and started using Kim's weapon. "This one won't last long," she told the lieutenant.

"Then I am just in time," Tuvok said, putting one of the bands around Kim's upper arm. "I suggest we move Mr. Kim to safety first."

"Agreed," Janeway said, helping him fasten the band.

"I was unable to provide the transporter with sustained minimal operating power, so I activated the system using an automated pulse power curve, which repeats itself every four minutes. There was no other choice. When the curve peaks, the pulse provides enough energy to transport one person. That is how I was able to join you."

Janeway nodded, impressed with what Tuvok had accomplished in so short a time, and understanding his logic completely. She was already preparing for contingencies. "When is the next power peak?"

Tuvok examined his tricorder. "In exactly fifteen seconds."

"Good. Kim goes first, then you, then me."

"I guess I'll be seeing you guys around, then," Kim said, attempting another grin.

Janeway winked at him, then silently put on the last armband. Tuvok concentrated on the tricorder. He tapped in the command, then sent it. Four seconds later Kim dematerialized and was gone.

"Keep firing, Mr. Tuvok, and stay down," Janeway ordered. "You have the left flank; I'll take the hill."

They fired several shots, then moved farther down along the massive, battered tree trunks. Janeway checked her weapon. Only a small charge remained. Another shot flashed, biting into bark just above Tuvok's head, this time from their right flank.

Janeway fired two parallel bursts at a dark glimmer of movement, and a figure pulled farther back into cover behind the trees. She thought she might have hit her target, but there was no way to tell.

"One minute, eleven seconds," Tuvok reported. "Captain, I do not see how you can hope to fend the Televek off by yourself for another ten minutes."

"You're going to leave me your phaser, aren't you?" Janeway asked. There followed a brief pause. A gentle tremor shook the earth. Another phaser shot seared into hardwood just inches away.

Tuvok looked at her, his features calm. "Indeed, I insist, Captain."

Vulcan humor was subtle, but Janeway was a fan.

The attack had quieted for a moment. They used the opportunity to return fire in three directions. Then they ducked down once more and waited.

"Ten seconds," Tuvok said. She gave him the go-ahead. He nodded grimly. "Five seconds," he said. "Three." He keyed the tricorder and sent the command. Nothing happened.

Janeway mouthed a silent curse. "What's wrong?"

"It would seem that there is not enough power. My initial calculations were correct. However, the condition of the transporter and the number of variables—"

The tree trunk shattered, sending Janeway and Tuvok backward in a fresh shower of splinters and pulp. Janeway found herself lying on her back, looking up at the trees as they waved in the building winds beneath clouds of smoke and ash. She felt the ground start to shake again, harder still. An aftershock, or another full quake. She tried to sit up, discovered Tuvok doing the same beside her.

They looked up the hill together, their eyes drawn to the four Televek rushing down on their position. Janeway could hear more footfalls from their left flank.

"If we remain perfectly still and offer no resistance, they may decide not to shoot us," Tuvok said almost too calmly, a perfectly logical assumption.

"I wouldn't count on it," Janeway said.

Janeway watched the closest Televek raise his weapon and take aim as he stumbled toward her. Then the forest blurred, and disappeared.

CHAPTER
13

DAKET STOOD BESIDE HIS CRUISER, LEANING ON A flanged section of the hull, catching his breath. He'd been in the woods with one of his teams, going over scores of unremarkable ground echo readings, killing time while he waited for Tolif's team at the downed shuttle to report in. Then the latest round of quakes had shaken the forest hard enough to bring trees crashing down and send the bedrock heaving up.

Daket was still young and agile, thank the stars, and probably just plain lucky, he guessed. After all that he'd been through, he was still here, still alive and well. He was destined to collide with greatness one day, he had no doubt of that, but at times like these he wondered whether the universe clearly understood that fact.

Somehow he'd managed to sprint into the clearing before the second, even more violent quakes had hit.

For a time he worried that the end might well be at hand for all of them, that this absurd planet might have come to claim them, but this second round of tremors had finally subsided like the others.

Temporarily . . .

The clearing around the cruiser had remained fairly stable, and the cruiser itself had come through the experience unharmed, but Daket knew that was part luck as well, and he didn't trust to luck. The quakes were getting worse, and the next one might spell disaster. All of which only made his current set of dilemmas that much more convoluted.

Not one single member of this team wanted to die here, and Daket would not hold on to his status as a director for long if the others decided they could not trust him in that regard. And neither could he blame them. Indeed, in their position, he would have been plotting exactly what he knew they were plotting.

Not that he was willing to die, either. He had been certain from the outset that the risks on this mission would be unacceptable. Daket didn't like to take chances. He never did, in fact, unless he was forced to do so. Which was the case at present, of course. His was a difficult position.

Despite the intensive foot searches and scanning operations his teams had been carrying out for days now, he had been unable to discover an access route to the exotic, and doubtless extremely valuable power source that lay several kilometers below his feet. Nor had he learned much more about his elusive target. In short, his mission was a complete failure.

He had managed in his reports, however, to describe his team's efforts and circumstances in a truly superlative light, as would any proper associate, or director, so as to make himself and his crew seem utterly commendable. The trick, certainly, was to report all of the positives and omit all of the negatives—nothing every bottom-fed manager and assistant in the sector didn't do. But Daket liked to think he was especially good at it, and he thought he had proven that fact on Drenar Four.

Even that small success seemed threatened now, however. The problems were being compounded. It wasn't just the dead ends, the earthquakes, the volcanoes, the injuries, or the endless complaining that Gantel and his people incessantly poured down on him from their stable orbit—it was the new aliens now. They weren't content with troubling Gantel, apparently.

"Find their shuttle!" the third director had said. "Be certain there were no survivors," he'd said. "Then repair their shuttle and we will take it with us," he'd said.

It had all sounded simple enough.

Nothing had worked out that way.

The small craft from the Federation starship had landed, not crashed. Not only had this left the ship intact, but several armed and able survivors had emerged as well. And before Tolif's team could reach the site, the Drenarians had taken the visitors to their village. Their town was no fortress, certainly, but a great amount of time and manpower would have been required in order to extract the Drenarians' new guests.

The alternative, unfortunately, was to live with the threat these *Voyager* people posed. That was unacceptable as well, but it had so far been less risky than the other option.

"We have them under close surveillance," Daket had several times reported to Gantel. "Each breath they take is being counted."

The aliens had been somewhere in the village, after all, and that was close enough. But even before the following dawn Daket had been presented with yet another troubling report from one of his scouts: a small party that included the shuttle crew had left the village, heading back in the direction of the downed ship.

The team Daket had in place at the shuttle had been ready for the imminent return of the visitors. Daket could only hope his people would be able to dispose of the intruders quickly when they arrived, and that the whole process would not cause too great a delay. After all, playing tag with the landing party was not his primary task—or even his secondary goal, for that matter.

"I am seeing to the work on the shuttle personally," he had since told Gantel, even though he didn't quite know where the little vessel was. He'd told Gantel he was seeing to the ground echo work personally, too, and the grid search teams, and the energy source evaluations, and whatever else Gantel asked about. That was, of course, what Gantel wanted to hear. And that was the important thing.

"The third director is hailing you," a voice from the bridge said over Daket's belt communicator.

"You will explain that at the moment I am in the field inspecting the extensive damage to our operations caused by the last round of quakes, that lives and equipment are being lost, but we are coping. Tell him I will contact him shortly."

"Yes, Daket."

The comm went silent. No one on the bridge knew he was standing just outside the ship.

Daket looked up to skies clouded with volcanic smoke and ash. Time was running out. He had a growing urge to tell Gantel that this mission was entirely senseless, that he and his crew had waited long enough, done all they could, risked too much already. That it was time to go. The presence of those who had landed in the shuttle and that of their friends in orbit didn't matter one way or the other, as far as Daket was concerned, especially with the first director on her way here. He was almost certain Gantel would agree if he were down here instead of up there. But Daket was as certain that saying so would only get him into more trouble than he knew how to get out of.

And he didn't want to risk that.

Gantel kept insisting that Daket hold on and keep working until Shaale and the fleet arrived. "We must appear to be fighting against failure, exploring every option right up until the last."

And he was right, of course. Gantel hadn't gotten to be a third director by misreading his opportunities. Or by going easy on those directly beneath him, as Daket had discovered times enough.

It wasn't that Daket's excuses weren't good ones—they were classic—it was just that Gantel did not want to hear any of them. Which left Daket at a considerable loss. Rules were not rules anymore, it seemed.

Daket looked about the grassy clearing. His teams were beginning to come and go in regular patterns again, setting up new probes and going out to take readings on the ones already deployed. It was possible the quakes would reveal underground passageways, or even create them, though Daket didn't think anyone on this planet was quite that lucky. At least not anyone working with him. And probably not even Gantel.

He checked the time. He hadn't gotten a report from the team at the shuttlecraft in several hours, which was unacceptable to begin with. Moreover, that was quite probably what Gantel wanted to know about. Tolif, who was in charge of that bunch, was a competent fellow, and usually quite punctual. Daket shook his head. He had endured enough difficulties for one day, and nearly been crushed by falling timbers on top of all that.

"I don't need this," he said out loud, to the planet itself, and to the filthy skies above, as he pushed off and headed back into the cruiser. "And I certainly don't deserve it." He headed straight for the bridge.

"Still no word from Tolif?" he asked, though he was quite sure he would have been told.

"None," said Tatel, the young female associate on duty. She had only joined the crew on this trip. Daket hardly knew a thing about her, and that suited him just fine.

"Try to raise them again. What was their status at last contact?"

"Progress was being made. I have a report."

Daket looked at the screen at his command station. Tolif's notes were thorough, but they offered nothing promising. Nothing at all. The shuttle systems were badly damaged, and getting them back on line was proving to be a difficult task. An update had been promised, but it hadn't come. Worst case, they had all died in the recent round of quakes. Daket shook his head; it would be difficult to put a positive spin on that.

"Very well," Daket said gravely, shrugging his shoulders. "Did Gantel say what he wanted?"

"There have been some developments in orbit, I believe."

Which meant nothing good, certainly, Daket decided. Any developments in orbit would have little effect on his end of operations, unless time or circumstances had necessitated a change in plans.

Unless—could he dare hope?—they were finally going to leave this broken-up, boiling pit of a planet. Daket couldn't imagine what grim task Gantel might have in mind, but anything would be better than sitting here. Almost anything, surely. He ordered Tatel to make contact.

"Wait," Tatel said, leaning forward, working at her controls. "I have a response from Tolif and his team."

Daket looked up, his eyes wide. "Yes?"

After a pause that seemed endless, the associate sat back and made a decidedly sour face. "It . . ." she began, "I'm afraid it isn't good news."

Janeway felt a surge of relief as *Voyager*'s transporter room appeared before her eyes. She felt a second, smaller comfort as Chakotay and a pair of security officers lowered their weapons and grinned at her like so many children. She turned and found Tuvok standing beside her.

"Take Ensign Kim to sickbay," Chakotay said, signaling the security officers to help Kim as Janeway stepped off the transporter pad. "Did we interrupt something?" he asked, glancing at the weapons in the others' hands.

"A most welcome interruption," Janeway assured the commander.

"I would agree," Tuvok added.

"Next time," Chakotay told the captain, retaining his grin, "don't stay away so long."

"I'll try not to. And by the way, the next time the spirits move you, remind me to pay closer attention."

"Yes, sir. And may I say, you look terrible?"

Janeway glanced down at herself. She was still covered with dirt and ash, much of it now caked with sweat, and her uniform was torn on both sleeves and at one knee. Tuvok looked only slightly better. She nodded. "Thank you," she said. She moved toward the door, waited for it to slide away, then headed out at a brisk pace. Chakotay fell into step along side her.

"What's our status?" she asked.

"Where do you want me to start?" Chakotay said, though it was not a question. "We figured out what you meant in the message you sent, then we did some calculations. The lunar alignment will spell catastrophe for the planet. And a lot sooner than anyone expected."

"I'm not surprised," Janeway said, letting go of any last hope that she might be wrong. "Go on."

"Torres worked out a plan to move the moons a little at a time, one by one, using a projected warp field and *Voyager*'s impulse engines. We estimate the collective effect will be enough to prevent precise alignment from occurring. We've already begun the effort. We've completed the work on the first moon, and we're ready to move on to the second."

"Your statement would indicate that you have the warp engines back on-line," Tuvok said.

"Yes. And the transporter, as you know. And all thanks to B'Elanna. I was getting to that." The commander's smile rather resembled that of a father relating his daughter's latest achievement. Janeway almost envied him that status. The young, often volatile lieutenant had been forced upon Janeway by her new first officer when the Maquis and Federation crews had been thrown together, but B'Elanna was turning out to be every bit the prodigy Chakotay had insisted she was. And she was certainly earning her keep this day.

"I'll have to thank her personally for that last one," Janeway said with a slight shudder. "Truth is, we were in a pretty bad way down there."

"I estimate we had a five percent chance for survival," Tuvok added.

"You are a comfort," Janeway quipped.

"Thank you, Captain," Tuvok said, "but I fail to see how you could find such a statement comforting."

"There's just something about you, Tuvok," Chakotay murmured.

"Lieutenant Torres has mentioned that to me on several occasions," Tuvok said. "I do not understand it, but I am pleased by it."

They slipped into a turbolift as the door opened. "Bridge," Janeway commanded. She slapped at her comm badge. "Captain to Sickbay. How is Ensign Kim?"

"He is doing very well at the moment," the holographic doctor replied, sounding almost cheerful. The doctor seemed to enjoy clear-cut emergency medical procedures, as opposed to day-to-day minor aches and pains he ordinarily had to deal with. He had, after all, been programmed for the former, not the latter. Overall, though, Janeway had few complaints. For a hologram, the doctor had a remarkable variety of abilities, and together he and Kes, his talented protégée, seemed to meet *Voyager*'s every medical need.

"Is he in pain?" Janeway asked.

"No, Captain. I've begun healing most of the damage, and I'll give him something to make him rest. He'll be as good as new in a couple of days. Should I expect to see more wounded?" The doctor sounded almost too cheerful now.

"That is a very good question. I'll let you know when I have an answer. Janeway out."

"Our three visitors were all Televek, of course," Chakotay continued. "We believe nearly everything they said was a lie. A little while ago they attempted to take over the ship. They failed thanks to B'Elanna Torres."

"Where are they now?" Tuvok asked.

"In the brig."

"Good," Janeway said. "I'd like to have a talk with them."

"We have another problem," Chakotay went on. "Long-range sensors have confirmed a fleet of Televek ships headed toward this system at near warp eight. We were led to believe they were rescue and support ships, but we now suspect they are battle cruisers. The Televek seem interested only in acquiring this planet's defensive system, which primarily consists of that underground power source we've been monitoring."

"Our information would seem to agree," Tuvok said.

"They have a ship down there, too," Janeway said. "Another cruiser, just like the one in orbit."

The door opened, and the three of them rushed onto the bridge, Chakotay in the lead.

"Commander," Rollins yelped from the tactical station.

"What is it?" Janeway said, right behind him.

"Captain, we've got problems. The Televek have raised their shields again and aimed their weapons. They've been trying to hail us, but we've been stalling. It doesn't seem to be working. Gantel saw his people vanish from our bridge."

"Vanish?" Janeway asked, one eyebrow raised.

Chakotay nodded grimly.

"Welcome back, Captain," Paris said, obviously pleased to see her in one piece again.

"Thank you, Mr. Paris. Continue red alert. What is our weapons status?"

"Photons armed and ready," Paris replied. "Phasers are still inoperative."

"Captain," Stephens said from behind the consoles at the operations station, "the Televek are still hailing us. They are demanding—"

"Very well." Janeway trained her eyes on the main screen. The Televek cruiser hung in the distance. She placed her hands firmly on her hips. "Open a channel, Mr. Stephens. I am good and ready for this."

"Gantel," Triness said, obviously a bit unnerved, "First Director Shaale's adjunct is signaling. They require a report."

No one among the crew had ever served directly under the first director—even Gantel had only met her once—and her imminent arrival did no one's nerves a service.

"Tell them we are honored, of course," Gantel said. "And a report will be forthcoming."

"When? They will ask."

Gantel glared at Triness. He needed an answer. The trouble was, he didn't have one. "Soon."

"Very well," Triness said, clearly forlorn.

The first director's timing was a perfect disaster. Everything was going wrong at once, and nothing very right was happening to balance out the negatives. Gantel felt a slight panic welling up inside him, felt despair clawing at his throat until—

No! he told himself, getting a grip.

He immediately turned the panic into brutal rage, a talent that had stood him in good stead over the years, especially in times like these. If you went after everyone else, and did it loudly enough and fiercely enough, sometimes you could soar above the very worse crisis. Often you could lay enough blame to avoid personal injury. At the very least, you could gain a degree of satisfaction.

There was nothing left for it.

"What's the problem with Daket?" he bellowed at the bridge crew.

"We have him on the comm now, Director," Triness answered, obviously pleased with her sudden good fortune of timing.

"Put him through!"

"Director," Daket said, his face filling the screen, his expression one of practiced but shallow confidence. "My team surprised the intruders when they returned to their shuttle. They chased the aliens relentlessly through the woods, wounding several of them on the run, even as yet another life-threatening round of quakes—"

"Yes, and what became of the visitors?" Gantel demanded, not interested in the details at the moment.

Daket looked pallid now, deathly so. "They . . . they vanished."

Gantel shook his head. "I know what you mean. I've just seen it for myself. Jonal and the others . . ."

"Then they are all dead?" Daket said.

"Perhaps, though I don't know for certain. What is your status?"

"Ah, of course. My status. In fact, throughout the painstaking process of—"

"Daket, Shaale will be here soon. Give me the bottom line. You don't have a thing, do you?"

"Correct," Daket admitted after a pause.

"Very well. Prepare to leave the surface, but wait until you get my order. We are going to deliver a worthy gift to the first director when she arrives, you and I, one that might make up for some of our . . . setbacks. If we cannot immediately meet our first goal, we must concentrate on our second, the starship itself."

With Daket's nod Gantel touched a pad on his own small instrument panel, canceling the signal. He only hoped Daket would be of some use if the need arose. Daket was the sort who wouldn't take a chance if his life depended on it. Gantel could hardly blame him at the moment.

"Prepare for battle," he commanded the bridge crew. "Shields at maximum. Helm, steady ahead. Prepare to fire on my command." Gantel waited as the two ships drew slightly nearer each other. The way he saw it, he had only one chance: attempt to disable *Voyager* without completely destroying her, then board her and take over the controls. At that point he could simply eliminate whatever crew had survived the attack.

He would then present whatever was left of the craft to Shaale. With luck, those wonderfully powerful phaser systems would survive the action, along with the remarkable vanishing device, and he could still salvage this whole operation, right under the first director's nose. Too good to be true, no doubt, but it sounded infinitely better than the alternatives.

Gantel straightened himself in his chair and took a breath. "Triness, hail the Federation vessel."

Tuvok moved to assume the tactical station, eliciting a look of welcome relief from Rollins. The Vulcan's fingers moved only briefly; then he looked to Janeway and nodded.

"Commander Gantel on-screen," Stephens said.

The face of the Televek commander appeared just as Janeway had expected it might. A face Janeway was seeing for the first time, yet one she felt she had seen many times before. Gantel did not look pleased.

"What have you done with my people?" he demanded immediately, almost as if nothing else worth discussing had occurred.

"They are being held for crimes against the Federation," Janeway said. "I'll decide what to do with them."

"You have no right to hold them or to judge them!"

"We have every right. They lied to us, threatened my people, and attempted to seize my ship. But the crimes your emissaries have committed pale in comparison to those your people on the planet below are guilty of. I've been to the surface, Gantel. I know about the other ship, and about your assassins."

Gantel fumed. "I won't discuss that."

"I think you will."

"You are an insolent fool, Captain!" Gantel roared, leaning forward until his image filled the entire viewscreen. Janeway got the impression he didn't act this way often, though he seemed to have a flair for histrionics.

"I am beginning to think at least one of us is a fool," she said.

Gantel stared at her. "You have no business here, yet you feel you have the right to make rules for others and apply them at will. I must inform you that you do not. And you have few options in any case. If you attempt to fire on us, or if you try to leave orbit, we will destroy you. That is something I wish to avoid, but occasionally it is necessary to accept one loss in order to prevent two."

"Your own people are aboard my ship," Janeway reminded him. "And they're going to stay here for a while."

"Their families will be compensated," Gantel said flatly. "You have lost, Captain. One way or another, your ship, or whatever is left of it, will be boarded and taken from you. We hope to take *Voyager* intact, thus sparing the lives of your crew, but if we have no alternatives, so be it."

"Captain," a breathless voice hissed from just behind Janeway's left ear. She glanced back to find Lieutenant Torres standing there, chest heaving as she tried to catch her breath. She had apparently been running. Janeway hadn't even heard the lift door opening. She turned her head slightly. "Yes?"

B'Elanna nodded toward the face on the screen.

"Gantel, one moment, please," Janeway told the Televek commander.

"Do not cut me off, Captain," Gantel protested. "Not again. You are in no position to—"

Janeway signaled Stephens, and the comm went silent.

"I've been monitoring things from Engineering," B'Elanna said. "I didn't want to use the comm."

"Yes, yes," Janeway asked impatiently, "what is it?"

"I suggest you try the shields, Captain."

Janeway reached out and took B'Elanna by both arms. "Shields?"

Torres's earnest expression was softened by a modest grin as she nodded. "Shields, Captain."

"Lieutenant," Janeway joked, shaking her head as her own smile broadened, "remind me to make you my chief engineer one of these days." With that she spun half around again and faced the screen. "Mr. Tuvok, shields up!"

The face on the screen had darkened suddenly. As Gantel listened to someone on his bridge, a silent vow seemed to emanate from his tightening lips, something Janeway could not decipher.

"Mr. Stephens, reopen that channel."

"Open, sir."

"Gantel, you won't mind if we don't go quietly," Janeway told him. Abruptly, the image on the screen was gone.

"Hail the surface. Get me Daket!"

"Yes, Director," Triness replied.

Gantel could see his career dissolving before his eyes as his carefully laid plans fell to pieces. One way or another, though, the Federation ship and its captain were going to solve his problems. At the very least, they would cease to be one, shields or no shields.

"Tell Daket I need him up here at once. We are engaging the Federation ship."

With this order too, Triness complied. After a moment she nodded.

Gantel stared unblinking at the ship on his screen. Then he stood up and pounded the little console in front of his chair with his fist. He would catch *Voyager* in a cross fire if he had to, but he didn't want to wait for that. "Very well. Open fire."

CHAPTER
14

Daket eased himself back into the comfort of his chair on the bridge and received the message with a mixture of trepidation and relief. He was being ordered back into orbit, finally, and probably not a moment too soon, given the rapidly deteriorating condition of the planet—another round of aftershocks had rattled the cruiser only moments ago. But with the first director's fleet still several light-years out, and with Daket's mission here anything but complete, the order made only one kind of sense.

"Did they describe the tactical situation in detail?" he asked Tatel.

"Not specifically, but the message was unusually brief, and they did not wait for a reply. I've been monitoring communications between Gantel and the Federation vessel. They were discontinued just a short time ago. Gantel's cruiser is now moving into what must be an attack position, though he is keeping his distance."

Daket didn't like the sound of that. "Get everyone back here immediately. Prepare for departure. The field personnel are not to go back for anything. Equipment that cannot be carried in one trip is to be left behind."

Daket waited nervously as his orders were conveyed to his crews both on and off the cruiser. No matter what efforts were made it would take at least half an hour to get packed and powered up. It had actually taken longer than that during the drills they had conducted, but of course everyone had known they weren't really getting out of here at that time. This was not a drill.

And there was at least one positive aspect to this dilemma: Tolif and the rest of his remarkably incompetent team at the Federation shuttle would never make it back in time.

"Daket," Tatel said, turning away from her consoles, a flicker of poorly concealed distress in her eyes.

"What now?" Daket asked.

"I'm reading engines and weapons—"

She stopped as she glanced back at her instruments.

"I am listening," Daket reminded her.

"I'm receiving another message. Gantel is attacking *Voyager*."

"Put it on my monitor."

Daket looked at the screen that rose from the floor just to the right and front of his command chair.

"I am detecting weapons fire," Tatel said.

"I see it." Daket heaved himself up out of his chair.

The way he saw it, one of two things was about to happen: either Gantel, bold and irrational as ever, would be destroyed by the Federation ship, leaving Daket in command of the entire mission—or Daket's own timely arrival in orbit would be a deciding factor in the success of whatever unfortunate engagement Gantel had gotten himself into. Either possibility would, under the impending scrutiny of First Director Shaale, likely lead to Daket's promotion to director, and all with an extremely limited amount of risk and effort on his part. A promotion that he felt was long overdue. He just had to be careful. *Extremely* careful.

In either case, he couldn't wait to get off Drenar Four and back into space, even if it was only to get shot at.

"Initiate emergency departure procedures. We'll have to leave a few people behind."

Tatel looked up, and Daket had trouble reading her expression. The stress was getting to her, he thought, like everyone else.

"What are you waiting for?"

"Nothing," Tatel said. She went quickly to work.

"Televek weapons powering up. Targeting beams detected. They are firing," Tuvok announced from the tactical bay. A single bright energy beam signaled the attack. Then a second, different volley erupted from the cruiser, quite unlike anything Janeway had ever experienced. A continuous string of blue-white cluster-style bursts streamed out of the attacking ship's lower hull; they reached *Voyager* almost instantly, and their rapid impact was quickly felt.

"Report," she ordered.

"They are using a photonic pulse weapon of some kind," Tuvok said. "The individual pulses are not very intense, but in great numbers their impact is formidable."

"Shield integrity is holding, levels dropping slightly. Down fourteen percent," B'Elanna Torres said from the bridge's engineering bay.

"How long before the shields collapse?"

"If the Televek can maintain this level of attack," Torres said, "I estimate shield collapse will occur in four minutes, twenty-seven seconds."

"Give or take," Janeway heard Paris say under his breath. She nodded to herself. The pulses and energy beams continued to pound the shields, shaking *Voyager* with their impact and sending shock waves through the hull and deck, making the ship ring like a giant bell. Janeway wasn't sure the crew would last as long as the shields.

Gantel was leaving her no choice. "Ready photon torpedoes."

"Forward photons armed and ready," Tuvok answered.

"We have to make these torpedoes count," Janeway said. "They're all we've got right now, and we can't get any replacements. We can't afford to waste a single one."

"I have every intention of making them count," Tuvok said, looking up, somewhat perplexed.

"Range two hundred thousand, target locked," Paris said.

"Shields down thirty-seven percent," Tuvok dutifully reported.

Janeway held her breath, nodded. "Fire one."

"Torpedo away," Tuvok said as he touched his panel. The loud echo of the weapon as it fired sounded throughout the ship. Janeway watched as the first salvo reached the cruiser and vanished in a fierce white flash.

"The Televek's forward shields have collapsed," Tuvok said, his voice a monotone now. "They are trying to rebuild them."

"Open a channel," Janeway said. "Tell them to stand down or be destroyed." She turned to Chakotay. "Without our shields, they must have thought they could take us out quickly," Janeway speculated.

"But they must have detected our shields when they went up."

"And they must have assumed they could knock them out again without much trouble. Let's see what they'll do now."

Chakotay nodded. "I wouldn't care to guess."

"No response to our hails, Captain," Stephens said.

For the moment hostilities had ceased. No one on the bridge spoke a word as all eyes watched the main screen. Then both Televek weapons opened fire again, just as before. *Voyager's* lights dimmed momentarily, then brightened somewhat as the shields absorbed the initial impact.

"Evasive maneuvers, Mr. Paris," Janeway responded.

"Captain," B'Elanna said, "we can't keep this up forever. The shields are down nearly fifty percent and dropping. Unless we start rerouting power from vital systems, they're not going to protect us much longer."

"Televek forward shields are building up again,

Captain," Tuvok said. "Twenty-three percent and climbing."

"Captain, enough is enough," Chakotay said.

Janeway eyed the main screen with cold resolve, then nodded in agreement. "Target two," she said. "Fire two."

Tuvok touched his panel once more. "Number two away."

Almost instantly the second torpedo crossed the distance between the ships. It penetrated the Televek's partial shields and detonated, spilling most of the blast inward, where it struck the cruiser directly. The impact caused a massive rupture in the cruiser's hull. Gases and debris poured from the opening, leaving a trail as the ship veered off. It exploded in a violent fireball a second later. A huge cloud of debris and vapor particles began to spread out through space, continuing the orbit the ship had been maintaining.

"Apparently the Televek underestimated the strength of our torpedoes," Chakotay suggested.

"I guess so," Paris said.

To his credit, Janeway noticed, Paris wore no smile at all. She looked around the bridge, saw similarly solemn faces looking back. If there had been another way, she would have taken it, and she was certain that the entire crew knew that.

"Captain!" Neelix said, his voice thin and excited, as he hurried off the turbolift, Kes trailing close behind him. "We saw the whole thing on the monitors. Splendid! Splendid job! I knew all along those Televek weren't to be trusted."

"I think we all agree you were right," Janeway conceded.

"He often is," Kes said with a smile.

"It's good to see you up and around, Kes," the captain said.

"Thank you, Captain," Kes replied.

"She does look remarkably well, doesn't she?" Neelix remarked.

"Captain," Ensign Stephens said, intently examining one of the ops panels. "I have located the shuttle on the planet's surface. Clear as can be. It just . . . it just appeared."

"That Televek cruiser may have been making the magnetic field interference seem much worse than it is," Chakotay suggested.

"Agreed," Tuvok said, looking down at his own displays. "We are scanning clearly now."

"Run a full sensor sweep of the area around the central power source," Janeway said. "Look for anything we might have missed, anything that might help us. And get a fix on that second cruiser down there. If they lied about everything else, they would have lied about its condition as well, which is what I've suspected since we spotted it."

She waited while Tuvok ran his scans. There was no sign of a liftoff as yet, but the Televek vessel's power source was active and levels were rising, indicating possible preparation for one. Considerable activity was taking place in and around the site; warm bodies and equipment were being moved toward the cruiser.

"Looks like we may be getting some more company up here," Chakotay said. He examined the readings over Janeway's shoulder as he joined her and Stephens at Ops.

"We don't have much time, either way," Janeway

said, half talking to herself. She looked at Chakotay. "Gantel had no intention of helping the Drenarians on the planet. And neither do his friends in the second ship. If anyone is going to do anything for those people, it will have to be us."

"And it'll have to be now," Neelix agreed, his lightly spotted brow forming a dark line over his small eyes. "We've still got an entire Televek war fleet breathing down our necks."

"There just isn't time to finish diverting the moons," Chakotay said. "I don't want to abandon the effort any more than you do, but—"

"I know." Janeway placed her fist loosely against her lips and cast her gaze downward, trying to concentrate. There was a way. Like pieces of a puzzle, one she should be able to assemble, the answer was in her head somewhere, just around a corner. This she knew. She just needed to gather all of the pieces. . . .

"We're missing something," she said, turning to the others. "We must be."

"What we're missing is our best chance to get out of here," Neelix suggested. "Captain, it never was your responsibility to protect or assist these Drenarians in the first place. I can appreciate your compassion—I feel the same way—but sometimes, when you've done all you can do and it just isn't enough, the only alternative is to accept that fact."

"I think he may be right about that, too, Captain," Kes said gently. "Your people are so willing to help wherever and whenever help is needed, to do whatever needs to be done. I've seen it again and again. It's one reason why I'm so glad to be here, learning from you. But I've also learned that even the best doctor loses a patient sometimes. It's the will of the gods, perhaps, or it's just their time. You can't hold yourself responsible."

Janeway didn't have a good argument at the moment. She felt numb. "We're talking about losing an entire world. And a most remarkable people. You haven't met them, Kes. They are worth saving, a fact that seems lost on the Televek. I don't want to give up."

"If I may, Captain, numbers of individuals do not make the Prime Directive any less valid or logical," Tuvok said.

"Captain, why don't you just beam up as many Drenarians as you can, then leave before it's too late?" Neelix suggested.

"Yes," Kes agreed. "You could save dozens that way."

"I've thought of that," Janeway said, "and we may be left with no other choice, but I'm reluctant to let it come to that. And we have another consideration: if we tried to flee on the impulse engines we'd be sitting ducks. We would have to reconfigure the warp drive first. I'm not sure we have the time, and I *am* sure that would mean abandoning any hope of lunar realignment. And I don't know of any other way to stop the planet's destruction."

"If we didn't have a fleet of cruisers closing in on us, you could keep trying to move those moons," Neelix said. "But we do, Captain. There isn't anything you can do about that."

"I have to agree," Chakotay said thoughtfully. "We can't fight them all off with just a few torpedoes."

"Or with the shields already half depleted," Torres added. "We'd be no match for so many ships even under ideal conditions."

Janeway felt her uncertainty turn into something firm and determined in her gut. If she let *Voyager* be destroyed, she would be helping no one, but the idea of running away, of letting so many perish . . .

A flicker of an idea tickled the back of her mind. She looked up, trying to think clearly, trailing after her thoughts so as not to lose them. "Mr. Neelix, what was it you just said, about being responsible for protecting these people?" Janeway stepped down and walked slowly across the bridge to the captain's chair. Then she turned, still sorting things out, beginning to get somewhere.

Chakotay looked at her. "What is it, Captain?"

"Whose responsibility is it to protect the Drenarians?" she asked. "I mean, if *we* can't protect them, who can?"

"No one," Neelix said.

"I guess it would be whoever built the planetary defense system," Paris offered.

"Yes," Janeway said, looking at him, "but whoever that was is gone now. The defensive system, however, is still here. And that must be the key."

"It would seem the system is faltering, Captain," Tuvok said. "And we do not know enough about it to address that particular problem in the time remaining."

"But that's just it, Tuvok," Janeway said, growing more excited, seeing the solution more clearly as she turned and paced just behind Paris's back. "I think I may know what's wrong, thanks to something I saw in a dream." She stopped and faced Chakotay. "Something the ghosts showed me."

"Captain," Neelix said, "what Tuvok said, about there not being enough time, well—"

"And if I'm right, I can think of only one way to fix it." She spun half about once more. "Lieutenant Torres."

"Yes, Captain."

"I'll need a shielded antimatter container fitted with a detonator. I want it charged and ready for transport as soon as possible. And two antigravity floaters. How soon can you supply them?"

B'Elanna shrugged. "In about five minutes, Captain."

"Good. Meet me in the transporter room in six minutes." She paused again, still finishing the idea in her mind. "Mr. Tuvok, have the transporter room get a fix on that underground power source everyone is so interested in. There is a plateau down there, at the western end, I think. Have them locate it. I want to get as close to ground zero as possible."

"What do you plan to do, Captain?" Paris asked, staring at her. "Blowing yourself up won't help." His expression was one of intense concern.

"I'm going to try to recharge that defense system's batteries. I'm not sure it will work, but I know I have to try, and I think we have just enough time."

"You'll need someone to go with you," Paris volunteered, rising out of his chair.

"No, I'll go," Chakotay said. "If anything goes wrong, Paris can get the ship to safety as quick as anyone." He looked hard at Janeway. "I stayed behind the last time. This time I'm going."

"What if you succeed, and that defense system decides to come after us?" Neelix hastily asked. "As Tuvok said, we don't know enough about it."

"The captain may know more than you think," Chakotay said.

"You'll have to trust me, Neelix," Janeway told the Talaxian, who silently nodded in return.

Chakotay stood beside the captain, pressing her for a response to his request to accompany her.

Janeway sighed audibly. She didn't like the idea, but she didn't hate it enough to deny Chakotay his wish. She had gotten to know the commander well enough to recognize the look in his eye. He was a Maquis, after all, and they seemed to have a preference for being in the thick of things. Besides, if her plan didn't work, the rest might not matter anyway. "Very well," she said. "Let's go."

"The Federation ship launched a photon weapon of some type at Gantel's cruiser. A direct hit," Tatel said, anxiously watching her tactical panels while maintaining contact with Triness, her counterpart on the bridge of Gantel's ship. "The cruiser has lost its forward shields."

"Impressive, for a single strike," Daket said, managing at least to sound self-assured. "Small wonder Gantel is so interested in acquiring that ship."

"I have downloaded a report on the Federation's secret weapon," Tatel added.

Daket was already somewhat familiar with this—a secret technology that somehow had allowed these Federation people to make their enemies, Gantel's emissaries, vanish into thin air without any visible actuators or support apparatus. Capturing such a device was indeed a most enticing prospect, as long as the would-be captor did not become a victim.

"Transfer the report to my console. I'd like to read it," he said. At least, I'd like to try, Daket thought, not certain he would get the chance.

"You have it," Tatel said. She went back to scanning her screens again, and listening to communications from orbit. She frowned suddenly, an unusual public expression for any Televek.

Daket didn't like the look of it. "What?" he prodded.

"Gantel is planning to continue the attack. They are rebuilding their forward shields, transferring power." She paused, apparently waiting.

"What now?" Daket asked, certain he wanted to know, though increasingly certain he would not like what he heard.

"They've opened fire again. *Voyager's* shields are weakening. Gantel believes that if he can deplete them another ten percent, they will collapse. If he waits, they may be able to recover, or outmaneuver the attempt. The Federation ship is apparently quite agile. Gantel has stated—"

Tatel went silent. She held still for a moment, staring down; then she played her fingers once more over the panels before her. After a few seconds her hands rose, then hovered in the air just above the console, as if she feared what it might do.

"Report, Associate," Daket insisted.

"We have lost contact with Gantel's ship," she said, turning away from her controls. "They must have taken damage." She was looking at Daket with eyes full of pain and . . . remorse, perhaps, which was clearly misplaced.

A character flaw, he decided. As if she could have done something. As if they mattered more than she did, Daket mused, scoffing at the idea. Already he was getting to know her too well, perhaps. A replacement would be best, when they got back home.

"Check your instruments," he told her.

"Functioning normally."

"Then their communications must have been knocked out."

"No," Tatel said, slowly shaking her head.

When she said nothing else, Gantel asked: "What do you mean, no?"

"I mean they're gone. No readings, no telemetry, nothing on sensors. Only the Federation ship is showing up."

She looked worse now; Daket was sure he had never seen such an alien expression on a Televek face before. Tatel wasn't quite right, he decided. Able, efficient, loyal, but not right. This was no time for futile laments. Everything had just changed. It was time to act, to address the facts. The prospect of disaster was real, something Daket was already having trouble dealing with.

He felt every muscle in his body growing tense, a condition he had been fighting, a minor battle he had lost. Nothing compared to Gantel's, of course.

At least not yet.

"If there is a positive spin to be put on any of this," Daket told the bridge crew, stating only the obvious, "I would be interested in knowing what it is. How long before we can lift off?"

"Three minutes. Most of our personnel have returned. We have only—"

Daket cut Tatel off. He had decided pretense was largely useless at this point. "Anyone who has not returned in three minutes . . . will wait here. Time has run out. The fleet will arrive in less than an hour. We will be on hand to greet Shaale."

With luck—something that seemed to be in short

supply this day—Daket would learn precisely what had befallen Gantel's vessel, so that he could avoid that same fate. Or he could simply stay out of harm's way until the fleet arrived, which was clearly the more attractive option, provided he could make it work.

In any case he couldn't just stay on the surface. If the earthquakes didn't destroy him, Shaale would see his career destroyed. He could have no defense for such inaction. He'd accomplished next to nothing, which was hardly an excuse for continuing to do so. Gantel's unfortunate end meant there was no one to help, and no one on whom to shift the blame—but it also meant that if anything good did come of this mission, Daket was in a position to take most of the credit for it. A delicate and risky position, to say the least, which did nothing for the throbbing in his head or the burning sensation in his stomach, but an opportunity nonetheless. A beginning . . . or an end.

"Two minutes," Tatel said.

Daket felt his chest tighten. "I know," he said. "I know."

The place looked much as it had in the dream, but the differences were immediately apparent. Everywhere, Janeway could see signs of deterioration in the great underground cavern. She stood with Chakotay in what might have been the exact spot her consciousness had occupied when she had visited here before, and as she breathed, she was reminded of the stark reality of this place. The smell of smoke and sulfur made each breath difficult, though oddly, it was not as bad as she had perceived the same air to be during the vision.

The machine was every bit as massive and remarkable as she remembered, but it had been damaged in numerous places. Dozens of tubes had been broken or crushed by falling rock. The entire plateau was littered with rubble, Janeway noticed, as she let go of the package they had brought along, leaving Chakotay to tend it. She turned slowly in a circle while Chakotay steadied the antimatter container. Large sections of the cavern walls had been sheered away, collapsing into piles of debris; some of them had even tumbled over and into parts of the machine. In those places, the bright tubes had gone dim, or completely dark.

The walls themselves were marked by massive cracks that ran from the roof of the cavern to the floor of the plateau, or beyond it and over the edge, reaching toward the great abyss below. Some of the cracks were clearly very deep.

Janeway realized that Chakotay had been silently following her gaze, seeing all of this for the first time. And they could see quite well. Not only the machine itself, but also the dozens of fixtures surrounding it radiated light. They combined to form a small subterranean sun. But in the vast region beyond the plateau the darkness gathered quickly, concealing the distance entirely.

"It's a natural cavern," Chakotay said softly.

"I believe so," Janeway said.

"Nature can be a powerful creative force."

In the silence between their words a low rumble could be heard, a sound that came from deep beneath their feet and reverberated in the chasm all around them. "It also can destroy what it creates," Janeway said, just as the mild aftershock sent a small cascade of rock and gravel tumbling down a wall somewhere beyond their sight, out in the darkness. She turned again toward the cavern wall behind them. "There," she told Chakotay. "That's what all the fuss is about."

"I've never seen anything quite like it," he said, steadying the antimatter container. "It looks so simple in a way." He squinted at the machine. "Was it in this condition in your vision?"

"No. It's been damaged, but that isn't all that's wrong with it. That isn't why we've been reading such erratic and continuously fading power levels. At least I don't think so. There's another factor. That way," she said, nodding in the other direction.

Chakotay stared at the wall of glowing tubes for a moment longer, then he turned and grasped his side of the antigravity unit. They started slowly toward the edge of the plateau, keeping the container between them, careful of their footing. When they were less than fifty meters from the edge, Janeway paused and pointed.

"That's it," she said. "Down there."

She hadn't seen this in a vision, not exactly, but she had known, somehow, what she would find if she came here. The ghosts had wanted her to come here; it was something she knew she had to do. This close, and with their eyes adjusting further to the dimming light beyond their position, more detail emerged.

The mighty ocean of glowing molten lava that had boiled for kilometers below the cliff had grown cool and dark. A lava dome had formed there, containing the fires of the planet's heart. Fires that had burned here for ages.

Janeway let the antimatter container hover again, let Chakotay steady it, while she pulled her tricorder free and flipped it open. She scanned, rotating in a full circle, switching band widths. After a moment she looked up. "I had to be sure," she said.

"Of what?" Chakotay asked, the perfect audience.

"The defense system, the machine, it uses geothermal energy as a power source. It's virtually unlimited unless something cuts off the flow of lava."

"Like an earthquake?"

"Or several dozen of them. I suspected something like this when Nan Loteth told us that the volcanoes to the south were new."

"So you think that when the crust shifted, part of the lava flow was redirected away from here," Chakotay said.

"Exactly. Apparently this pool never completely drained, but it cooled enough to allow a dry dome to form over the top of it." She examined the tricorder readings again, confirming her hunch as best she could. "Subsequent quakes have returned much of the flow to this area, as far as I can tell, but it's trapped under the lava dome. If we can open a big enough hole in the dome, let the lava underneath it come up, I think it might return . . ."

Janeway fell silent as a sudden wave of dizziness nearly toppled her. She felt herself stumble forward, toward the edge. Then her eyes saw nothing, yet her head was filled with images. She faced the ghosts again, many of them this time. They seemed to be crowding all around her, pressing nearer, whispering all at once. Their messages were jumbled. But slowly, clearer impressions emerged. As before, no words were spoken, but Janeway understood. Her perspective had changed. She wasn't in the cavern anymore, but on the surface, in an area just outside the village, a place she somehow recognized, even though she was certain she had never been there before.

Anguish filled her heart as she went with the ghosts to this place. They took her through the trees, past the bodies of numerous dead Drenarians. Abruptly they emerged into a clearing, the place where Nan Loteth had told her the second Televek cruiser had landed. But as they broke out of the woods the reason for the ghosts' great concern became apparent. Winds swept the grasses and nearby branches as the cruiser boosted itself off the ground, rising skyward, fully operational, as Janeway had expected. It rotated until it was nose up. Then it slipped away through the clouds and was gone.

A small band of Televek ran into the clearing from the far trees just after the ship had vanished. They stood yelling and waving at the clouds in anger. Janeway had no idea why they were not aboard. And at first she had no idea why the ghosts would be upset by the Televek's departure from a field littered with dead Drenarians. Surely they knew what the Televek had been after, just as the villagers did. She tried to communicate this to them but she had no means. She could only gaze up at the shrinking hole in the clouds, made by the cruiser, at the sky beyond.

Then she remembered *Voyager;* the ghosts seemed to want this image in her mind. They pushed it aside momentarily to show her what could not have been a memory of her own: an external view of the ascending cruiser achieving orbit. Then she saw *Voyager* again, following a moon, orbiting Drenar Four. Alone. The images did not change for several seconds, until the second Televek cruiser appeared yet again, moving up into a high orbit above the planet, seeking an intercept course with *Voyager*.

The ghosts pressed suddenly inward, closer to Janeway's mind. *Sorrow,* she thought—that was the only word she could use to describe what she felt from them now. They were terribly . . . sorry.

Sorry they were so weak; sorry they could not help the Drenarians; sorry they were helpless to do anything to help *Voyager*—to help by doing something specific, Janeway sensed, though she received no clue as to what that was.

"That is why I've come," she said out loud, not certain whether she had actually spoken. But she thought she heard the sound of her voice echoing around her as the last word left her lips, heard it with her ears.

The visions faded from her mind, and she was once more standing in the mammoth cavern. She looked at Chakotay and found a darkened, worried expression on his face. He steadied himself, looking dizzy for an instant, then better.

"You saw it too?" she asked.

"Yes. We don't have any time to waste."

Janeway nodded, and they crossed the distance to the edge of the plateau.

"This would be an unfortunate time for one of those big quakes to occur," Chakotay said, as they stood only inches from the drop.

Janeway nodded, remembering her earlier fall. When she leaned forward and peered over the edge, she could see the dark lava dome below, but not clearly. "The detonation should occur just above the surface in order to produce the maximum effect. I want the biggest hole I can get."

"Agreed," Chakotay said, leaning forward next to her. "I wouldn't want to have to do this twice."

"Any guess as to the distance?"

Chakotay frowned. "I'd say it's about six hundred meters."

"That's where I'd put it, too."

"I'll set the floaters at minimum negative buoyancy. Drenar Four's gravity is about ninety-seven percent earth normal, so that should allow the container to drop at about two meters per second.

Janeway ran the numbers in her head. "We'll set the timer at four and a half minutes. Ready?"

Chakotay nodded. Both of them went to work. As Chakotay finished with the second floater, Janeway activated the timer. They stood up and held their breath, then they both pushed. The container drifted free of the plateau and slowly began to descend.

Janeway tapped her comm badge. "Transporter room, this is the captain. Beam us up."

There was no response.

CHAPTER
15

DAKET HAD OPTED TO WAIT UNTIL THE ENERGY LEVELS OF the planetary defense system dropped again, a decision that would cost him additional moments. But weighed against the possibility of an attack, he felt he'd made the only sane decision; the ferocity of the planet's ghostly defenders was legendary. It wasn't worth the risk.

He would never know, of course, if his trepidation had been justified, but as he watched the sensor images of the Federation ship grow, watched the planet display itself fully on the main viewscreen, visual proof that his cruiser had safely achieved a low orbit, he thought the evidence was clearly on his side.

An uneventful ascent, Daket mused. The very best kind.

What happened next would likely be anything but.

He had glanced at the report on the remarkable Federation weapon that made Jonal and the others disappear. Gantel had no doubt intended to seize *Voyager* more or less in one piece, had been playing for time, looking for an angle. Then he'd gone to the edge of sanity and attacked, alone. Unfortunately, his plan had backfired.

Daket also noted that Gantel had been keeping his distance from his target during the entire engagement, no doubt concerned about the range of *Voyager*'s exotic secret weapon, something that also concerned Daket. Perhaps the device had been used against Gantel after all? Daket could only hope he would not directly find that out.

"We are closing," Tatel said. "Shields at maximum."

"Maintain a distance of two hundred thousand kilometers from the target."

"Yes, Daket, but at that range our weapons' energy levels will drop approximately three-tenths of a percent per—"

"I am aware of that, but the distance will be a problem for them as well, I presume. I plan to use this mutual disadvantage to my advantage." Daket paused, smiling to himself. He wondered if even Gantel could have maintained such presence of mind under so much duress. He didn't think so. "That should put them within range of all our weapons," he went on, "while leaving a comfortable margin for safety."

Or error, Daket thought. He didn't have to destroy the Federation ship, after all; he just had to make a valiant effort and keep the crew more or less occupied until the fleet arrived. The result would be adequate for his purposes, and to do more would be foolish, as Gantel had so brilliantly demonstrated.

Daket took a breath. "Target weapons. Transfer all shield power to the forward shields and then keep the bow straight on. If they fire their photon weapons we will attempt to maneuver away from the torpedoes, or target it with our dispersion beams and destroy it. But if we take a direct strike, I want to face it with enough shields to withstand the blast. If nothing else, we can learn from Gantel's mistakes."

Several seconds passed while the cruiser's position was corrected and the shields were restructured. Directly Tatel turned to Daket and grinned slightly, nodding.

Daket grinned back. "Commence firing when ready."

"Commence firing," Tatel said to the fourth associate manning the weapons station, a young man who had a natural flair for accuracy—something Daket was counting on in no small measure.

The pulse cannon and forward phasers lit up the darkness of space between the vessels. In the distance a sphere of sparkling energy suddenly glowed to life, surrounding the Federation ship, evidence that her shields were attempting to absorb and deflect the assault. Now, Daket thought—wishing he were close enough to use his finely honed senses to determine better what the commander of that ship might do next—now it begins. He leaned forward, resting both elbows on the small console before him. He placed his hands just under his chin and began watching his opponent, waiting for . . . anything.

"Second cruiser is moving to a high matching orbit," Rollins stated, again at Ops, while Tuvok took command. "They will be within targeting range in less than a minute."

"Which means we're moving into their weapons' range as well," Lieutenant Tom Paris said. That meant *Voyager* might have to move away from her current position and well out of transporter range, something no one wanted right now. He couldn't imagine what was taking the captain and Chakotay so long. They should have signaled by now.

Tuvok moved away from the ops bay where he had been reviewing the power allocation with Ensign Stephens. He made his way quickly to the captain's chair and neatly seated himself. Neelix and Kes remained silent. The two of them stood just beside Tuvok, hovering at the back of the bridge's lower level, hand in hand. Neelix had urged Kes to go to *Voyager*'s sickbay, where the details of what was happening would not directly affect her, but she was not needed there now, and she had insisted on staying here.

"Maintain red alert," Tuvok said. "Prepare for evasive maneuvers."

"Aye, sir," Paris answered, "but—"

"Cruiser closing to two hundred thousand kilometers," Rollins said. "Their weapons systems are powered up, and they have raised shields."

"On-screen," Tuvok said. "Mr. Paris, bring us about. Mr. Rollins, arm forward photons."

"Tuvok," B'Elanna said, looking up from the engineering station displays. "I recommend we avoid another firefight if possible. Our shields will not withstand another encounter like the one we just had."

Paris couldn't resist giving her a sidelong look. That wasn't the kind of statement B'Elanna was known for, and she knew as well as he did what the alternatives meant. Paris took that as a bad sign.

"I appreciate the advice, Lieutenant," Tuvok replied, "but that may not be an option."

"Lieutenant," Rollins said, "the cruiser is now within range, but they're no longer closing. They're holding position, matching orbits with us."

"I think you should listen to B'Elanna," Neelix said. "We may be able to come back around."

His expression was not one of fear, Paris decided, but of concern. Neelix had never been burdened by the need to make command decisions of the sort that Tuvok now faced, but he had managed to survive on his own in this part of the galaxy for many years, and he had exhibited no lack of loyalty—either to Kes or to the captain and crew of *Voyager*. It was not self-preservation that motivated him now; it was group preservation. Paris didn't have a problem with that.

"I'm reading a substantial power buildup in their forward shields," Rollins added, "but . . ."

Tuvok looked up. "Yes?"

"The energy matrix pattern isn't familiar."

Tuvok stood up again and moved to the aft area of the bridge's upper level. He stepped into the tactical station bay and stood over Rollins's shoulder, examining the data for himself.

"Lieutenant Torres, what would you make of this?" He reached past Rollins to work the short-range sensor controls; then he tapped once more, and the data appeared on a screen at the engineering station. B'Elanna quickly analyzed it.

"They're using an overlay pattern of some kind," she said after just a moment. "They appear to be loading their forward shields by systematically depleting all the others."

"Then they have made a foolish mistake," Neelix said. "We can attack them from behind."

"We can't maneuver fast enough for that," Paris told him.

"Agreed," Tuvok said. "It is logical to assume that this commander is aware of the fate of the first cruiser, and is determined to compensate. Their shields are apparently quite sophisticated. I believe they are attempting to provide an adequate defense against our photon torpedoes."

"They're still reinforcing, layering their forward shields," B'Elanna continued, looking down, her fingers working the controls. "If they can keep the bow facing our attacks, I think they can hold us off for quite a while."

"Which is probably why they aren't getting too close," Paris guessed.

"Agreed," Tuvok said.

"And by maintaining distance," B'Elanna added, "they can fire their energy weapons at us while maximizing their chances of avoiding a direct torpedo hit."

Tuvok came as close to frowning as a Vulcan could. "Helm, hold position until I say otherwise. Mr. Rollins, try hailing the cruiser. I would like to attempt negotiations one more time. I cannot believe such a successful race would abandon all reason when given an opportunity to—"

"They are firing," Stephens said.

"Confirmed," said Rollins. "Photon pulse and phaser fire."

"Believe it, Mr. Tuvok," Neelix moaned.

His words were punctuated by a series of shock waves that pounded *Voyager* with a nearly deafening roar—an experience with which the entire crew was already too familiar.

"Commander!" Stephens said, shouting after Tuvok as he headed back toward the bridge's lower level, stumbling slightly on the shuddering deck.

"The captain is hailing. They're ready to beam up."

Tuvok whirled about, stood absolutely still for a moment. He nodded to Stephens. "Put her on," he said. Then he raised his voice to shout over the din permeating the ship. "Captain, we are under attack. We will not be able to drop our shields in order to beam you up. I will attempt to move the ship out of danger, then return for you at the earliest—"

"I'm afraid we won't be here when you get back," Janeway said anxiously. "The detonation timer is set, and we can't get to it. In about four minutes, nothing is going to matter to us anymore."

"Shields down to fifty-three percent," B'Elanna dutifully reported. Paris could hear the frustration in her voice, could see it on her face. He knew exactly how she felt.

"Helm," Tuvok said, "evasive maneuvers."

Paris didn't like the sound of that. "We can't just leave the captain," he said pleadingly, but he prepared to comply nonetheless. He saw no alternative, but neither could he accept the prospect of abandoning Janeway.

"I would prefer to retrieve the captain and Mr.

Chakotay if at all possible," Tuvok said. "But we cannot remain here, and we cannot drop our shields."

"Tuvok's right," Chakotay said, his voice just loud enough to be heard. "There's nothing you can do for us."

"Maybe there is," Paris said, looking at the main viewscreen, at the nearest moon still displayed there. "I may have an idea." His fingers began working the helm controls. "It just might work, if there's time."

"Whatever it is," Janeway responded in a level voice, "this would be a very good time to try it."

Paris looked to Tuvok. The Vulcan nodded, a blanket go-ahead. Paris engaged the impulse engines. The small moon on the screen began to grow larger again, then began to move to port. The pounding ceased as *Voyager* evaded the barrage of weapons fire.

"The Televek cruiser is pursuing, maintaining distance," Rollins said. "They are retargeting."

"Three minutes, Mr. Paris," Janeway said from below the planet's surface. "How is it going?"

"Hold on, Captain," Paris said. Sweat was gathering on his brow, beginning to seep into his eyes. He blinked sharply and fought the urge to take his hands away from the controls. "We've got plenty of time."

"Bridge to Engineering," Tuvok said, just as the Televek weapons found *Voyager* once again. Paris glanced up and saw the Vulcan watching the moon now. He understood, Paris thought. He understood completely.

"Engineering," Lieutenant Carey responded.

"Mr. Carey, you will go at once to the transporter room, where you will personally stand by for immediate beam-up of the captain and Commander Chakotay."

"Yes, sir," Carey answered. "I'm on my way." He signed off immediately.

"We'll only have a moment," Paris said.

Tuvok nodded. "Lieutenant Torres, prepare to drop the shields on my command. How long will it take to raise them again?"

"They're taking quite a beating. It'll take at least a minute and a half, unless . . ."

Paris glanced back to B'Elanna. She was looking from one bridge officer to the next, intense awareness in her narrowed eyes. "Nothing. I'll be ready," she said. She turned back to her station and went to work.

Paris did the same. The maneuver wasn't a terribly tricky one, at least not ordinarily; he simply had to put *Voyager* into orbit around the moon. But they would only have half an orbit during which the moon would be between *Voyager* and the Televek cruiser—when *Voyager* was on the planet-facing side of the moon. They wouldn't have time to try again, and their speed was much too high right now. Braking would have to be absolutely precise.

No matter, Paris told himself. He would deal with that.

"One minute and thirty seconds," Chakotay said from the planet's depths, his voice still as calm as a Vulcan's.

"We are hurrying, Commander," Tuvok answered calmly, though he seemed as close to showing angst as Paris believed him capable. Paris was aware that for a Vulcan, that serene demeanor came naturally, a characteristic of the species; Chakotay's nearly inhuman emotional control seemed to come from another source. The two of them and Captain Janeway were an inspiration to one another, Paris had noted, often drawing from each other's strengths. They were an inspiration to him as well.

He waited until the last possible moment, until Stephens verified that the moon had begun to pass directly between the two ships; then he reversed the impulse engines and made one final course correction. *Voyager* slowed just enough to allow the moon's gentle gravitation pull to capture her, if only for a moment, and swing her around toward the planet.

"All clear," Rollins stated, sounding breathless.

"Lieutenant Torres," Tuvok said.

B'Elanna nodded. "Shields down."

Tuvok raised his voice. "Bridge to Carey. Beam them up—now."

"We don't have a good lock, Lieutenant," Ensign Carey replied. "We're at just over 41,000 kilometers from the planet's surface, that's at the extreme limits of our transporter range."

Tuvok rocked back on his heels and wrinkled his brow—in an almost human expression, Paris thought. "I suggest you try anyway," he said tersely. "That is why I called you."

"Yes, sir. Engaging—now."

"Fifty seconds," Chakotay's voice informed the bridge. "How is it going?"

"Boosting to maximum gain," Carey said. "Transferring all available power. Recalibrating the targeting scanners. Mr. Tuvok, we have a coordinate lock. It's not perfect, but it might do."

Paris watched the moon spinning beneath them on the main viewscreen, then falling away behind them. The assumption was that the Televek ship would follow them around the back of the moon. The risk was that the cruiser would instead double back, and be waiting when *Voyager* emerged on the moon's planet-facing side. He didn't see them so far.

"Fifteen seconds," Janeway said. "If anyone's interested."

"Transporter room," Tuvok said. "Please report!"

Lieutenant Carey's voice came back quickly. "Bridge, we are engaging now."

Janeway stared at the towering underground walls, and the hardened ocean of lava that stretched out before her. She wouldn't die alone, but that was little comfort. She glanced down, eyeing the time readout on her tricorder: fifteen seconds, fourteen. "It wasn't supposed to work out like this," she said.

Chakotay looked at her. "I know. Don't give up," he said, following her gaze. "We've still got . . . six seconds."

Janeway started to speak, but the words froze on her lips as she and Chakotay dematerialized. "Five," she said, as she found herself standing on *Voyager*'s transporter pad.

"We've got them!" Carey shouted.

"Captain," Tuvok's voice said from the intercom, "you are needed on the bridge."

Janeway still held her tricorder in her hand. She glanced down: two . . . one . . . zero. "Bridge, are you reading anything on the planet?"

"We are registering detonation, Captain," Stephens responded.

"Thank you." Janeway closed her eyes and took a slow, deep breath. In the ancient cavern beneath the surface of Drenar Four the antimatter explosion had ruptured the lava dome, allowing hot magma to flow back up, reforming the molten underground lake. No instruments told Janeway this was so. She just knew. She looked at Chakotay and saw the same certainty reflected in his eyes. She couldn't help returning his mild grin of satisfaction.

"We'll be right there," Chakotay said. He turned to Carey. "Beam us directly to the bridge."

Janeway cleared her throat as the bridge appeared all around her and her first officer. They were greeted by a chorus of welcomes.

"Mr. Paris," Janeway said, still allowing herself a soft smile, "that was nice work. All of you," she added, looking about.

"The shields are on line," B'Elanna said half a moment after that. "I've got them up to sixty percent, but I can't do much better than that."

"Very well," Janeway acknowledged.

"What have you done about our friends in the second cruiser?" Chakotay asked.

"Oh, they're right behind us," Paris answered. "Or coming around to flank us."

Tuvok bowed his head in a semiformal greeting. "We will know in approximately twenty seconds," he said.

"Understood," Janeway said, taking to her chair. "Look sharp, everyone."

"Photons?" Chakotay asked Tuvok as the Vulcan returned to his post at the tactical station, relieving Rollins.

"Armed and ready," Tuvok said. "But they may not do us any good. The cruiser has reinforced its forward shields, an effort that we believe will prove quite effective. And they are keeping their distance. I estimate they will be able to survive several direct photon detonations, if they are unable to avoid them altogether."

"I certainly don't intend to throw any torpedoes away," Janeway said. "We'll have to think of something else."

"No sign of the Televek, Lieutenant," Stephens said. On the screen the moon had nearly vanished from sight. Black space filled much of their field of vision; the crescent of the planet itself filled the rest.

"You sure they're right behind us?" Chakotay asked.

"Confirmed," Tuvok said, working his console. "I have the cruiser on sensors now. They are just leaving lunar orbit, following our trail precisely."

"Are we still within range of their weapons?"

The ship lurched, then shook as the Televek answered Janeway's question.

"Evasive maneuvers, Mr. Paris," Janeway ordered. "Buy us some time."

"They seem curiously intent on simply following us around," Tuvok said, cocking his head.

"Explain," Janeway said.

"Their energy weapons lose power and accuracy over distance, yet they do not advance for a maximum assault, presumably because their fleet will arrive shortly. I believe that 'buying time,' as you say, is precisely what they are attempting to do."

"So, unlike Gantel, this Televek commander is in no hurry to be a hero," Janeway mused, as the thrum of weapon fire contacting the shields ceased momentarily, further testimony to Paris's skill as a pilot. The respite would be a short one, she was certain of that.

"We could leave a trail of mines behind us," Paris

suggested, still working the helm controls, "and use approximate settings on the timers."

"I suspect they would detect and destroy explosive devices of that type," Tuvok said. "Their shield and sensor technologies have been demonstrated to be as advanced as our own."

"What about another antimatter container?" Chakotay suggested. "Properly shielded, they wouldn't scan anything like explosives, only the EM fields."

"We'd need an external detonator, and they would be able to detect that," Janeway said.

"If we had phasers, we could just leave a container behind, then detonate it from *Voyager* when the Televek got close enough," Paris replied.

"But we do not have phasers, Lieutenant," Tuvok said. "Therefore, we cannot—"

"No, *we* don't have phasers," B'Elanna said, stepping away from her station, leaning on the upper level railing, "but the Televek do."

The ship shook as another Televek shot landed. "We are all aware of that, Lieutenant," Neelix said.

"Neelix!" Janeway said, causing the Talaxian to step back slightly, nearer Kes. B'Elanna's expression was one of intense concentration as Janeway turned to face her. "What are you getting at, Torres?"

"We could use a class-one subspace probe. Replace most of the instrument package with a shielded antimatter container. That wouldn't do any good against their reinforced forward shields, but I'm guessing they can't reconfigure any faster than we can, which gives us some time. More than enough, I think."

Janeway took one step closer, her eyes locked with

B'Elanna's. "If we program the probe to follow the ion trail from their impulse engines . . ."

"It just might get close enough," B'Elanna finished.

"Captain," Tuvok said, clearly catching on, "it should be possible to modify the probe to radiate a deceptive energy pattern, one that mimics those of a message buoy."

"Make them think it isn't dangerous," B'Elanna said, backing up the idea.

"That might buy us a little extra time," Janeway agreed.

"But won't they see us launch the probe?" Kes asked.

"Yes, unless . . ." Paris said slowly, allowing the thought to form behind his darting eyes.

"Unless?" Janeway prodded.

"Well," Paris said, shrugging, "they followed us around one moon. They just might follow us around another. Once more around the horn?"

Janeway felt a twinge of satisfaction as all the pieces of the plan seemed to gather. "How long before the rest of the Televek fleet arrives?"

"Approximately twenty-one minutes," Tuvok answered.

"At this rate, our shields will be gone by then," B'Elanna reminded everyone.

Janeway nodded. She looked at the main screen once more, at the second moon coming into view in the distance, larger than the one they were leaving behind. "Mr. Paris, lay in a course for that moon. Take us around it. B'Elanna, ready that probe."

Voyager shook as the pursuing Televek cruiser found her again with full weapons fire. Lieutenant Torres sprang from her station, remarkably sure-footed under the circumstances, and sprinted off the bridge.

"They're going around behind the second moon," Tatel reported. "Do we follow?"

"Yes, of course, but continue to maintain distance," Daket said. "They are an unusually resourceful lot, a lesson many of our colleagues have already paid dearly to learn." Daket sat back, waiting out the maneuver. He planned to have his own last lessons taught to him at a great price by one of the lovely and talented aquatic masseurs of Troevsta Prime.

"The Federation ship has entered a shallow lunar orbit," Tatel announced a moment later. "Matching now."

Daket watched the small, sunlit white dot that was *Voyager* go dark and disappear behind the great looming moon just ahead. Out of sight. Out of range. It didn't matter. He could play the game for another few minutes, which was all he needed to do. He had already begun to relax, telling himself that the worst was over, and the best, by his estimation, was coming very shortly.

"Orbit acquired."

"Be prepared for any sort of surprise," Daket cautioned.

Tatel nodded. "Their ion trail is steady. They have yet to deviate from their projected course and speed."

Daket took subtle comfort in that. It was short-lived. A proximity alarm sounded softly from several consoles. Daket tapped at his panels, studying the displays. He found what he was looking for, a very small contact directly below the cruiser, rising, moving steadily into a low lunar orbit. "Analysis."

"It appears to be a probe of some kind, sublight, compact, unarmed," Tatel said. "Is there any record of probes associated with Drenar Four's defensive system?" Daket asked.

"Checking now," Tatel responded. They waited while computer file data was searched. Nothing turned up.

"The probe is rising directly off our stern," Tatel said, obviously growing somewhat concerned. "Closing to one hundred thousand meters. It is emitting a beacon signal of some kind. The frequency doesn't match anything in the computer."

"A beacon?" Daket said.

"It poses no immediate threat," Tatel went on. "It isn't even scanning us. Nonetheless, I recommend we begin reconfiguring the rear shields."

"That would take too long, and if the probe is from *Voyager,* that may be exactly what their captain wants us to do. A trick designed to make us vulnerable to their attack. They must be desperate by now, and they are nearly out of time."

Tatel was silent now. She hadn't thought of that.

Daket smiled to himself, then leaned back in his chair. This was not the time to start taking chances. He felt a mild glow of satisfaction, and he did not intend to let it go cold just yet. He would be hailed as a hero and promoted, and he would grow rich if anything at all came of this mission. Another few minutes of outwitting these Federation interlopers and it would all come his way.

Tatel squirmed in her seat. "The probe is closing on us."

Daket nodded affably. "Let's not take any chances. Use the aft phasers to destroy it. Now."

"Targeting probe," Tatel said.

"On-screen."

The probe appeared as a negligible dot on the aft viewscreen.

"Firing."

The cruiser's thin energy beam touched the point in space that was the probe. A blindingly brilliant white flash filled the screen, and a chill shook Daket's body. He opened his mouth to scream. He didn't get the chance.

CHAPTER
16

IN THE AFT VIEW DISPLAYED ON THE MAIN BRIDGE SCREEN Janeway could see the halo of the antimatter explosion, a bright white glow that blossomed, then faded somewhere just beyond the moon's horizon. "Report," she said, fighting a tightness in her throat.

"Massive damage to aft portions of the cruiser," Tuvok said. "Their shields have collapsed, main power is apparently off-line, propulsion systems inoperative."

"Excellent, Captain!" Neelix declared. "It seems you've blown their backside off."

"I believe I said that," Tuvok remarked.

Janeway nodded, then took a breath. "Survivors?"

"I am reading life signs in the ship's forward segments, but not many," Tuvok answered. "Life support is failing."

"We can't just leave them," Janeway said. "Mr.

Paris, bring us around again. Tuvok, prepare an away team."

"Are you sure they're worth saving, Captain?" Neelix asked, his voice taking on a suddenly serious tone. "I get the feeling they would sell their own children if the deal looked good enough."

"That's a bit harsh, don't you think?" Janeway asked.

"If I may, Captain," Paris said, "they would never go back for us," Paris said.

Janeway looked at him. It wasn't a joke, not coming from Tom. He knew what it was like to have others give up on you, then to have someone pull you back. She tried to smile. "I'd like to think they might," she said. "There are always a few good apples in the barrel, Mr. Paris. I've had to believe that."

"I'd like to believe that, too," Kes said, leaving an earnest silence in the air.

"Yes, sir," Paris said. "I just meant—"

"I know." Janeway tapped her comm badge. "Captain to Sickbay."

"Yes, Captain," the doctor responded.

"You may have some new business in a few minutes."

"We're ready down here, Captain," the holographic doctor said, "despite the fact that this is the first attempt anyone has made since we arrived in this system to inform me about what's going on. Can I assume these new patients will be members of our crew?"

"No. Televek, actually."

"Of . . . course," the doctor said after a pause. "You know, that really is the sort of thing that makes a difference to medical personnel."

Janeway glanced at Chakotay, found him hiding a chuckle behind one hand. The doctor was right of course, that was the hell of it. "Understood," she said.

"We're approaching the cruiser's position again, Captain," Paris announced. "We should match orbits in approximately—"

"Captain," Tuvok said, his fingers responding to a warning klaxon that sounded almost in concert with his words. "The Televek fleet is dropping out of warp, entering the Drenar system."

Daket pulled himself up to a sitting position. He rested there a moment, trying to breathe, choking instead. Dim emergency lighting cast everything in purplish-blue as he looked about the bridge. Every control panel he could see had gone dark. The engines had been lost; he was sure of that. How they had managed to escape complete annihilation he could not imagine, but he did not intend to spend time questioning that small bit of good fortune.

He tried to stand and found that the effort produced intense pain. Glancing at his right leg, he saw a wound just below the knee caused by a tangle of flying metal. He looked more carefully about the bridge, straining to make out details. He saw enough movement to tell him that most of the bridge crew had survived, but they were not on their feet, and the bridge itself was ruined.

"Tatel!" he shouted, gagging on the air as he tried to refill his lungs. The smoke was nearly invisible in the surrounding twilight, but it was thick, he decided. And possibly toxic. There was no way to know for certain.

"Here," Tatel said, a slim figure rising and stumbling toward him.

Daket realized the deck was pitched to starboard several degrees. "How bad is the damage?"

"I don't know," she said, choking the words out. "Every system is off-line, including life-support. And we're leaking air. I can hear it."

"No positives there," Daket moaned, shaking his head.

"We must assume that much of the stern is destroyed, along with the landing bays. I don't think there is anyone alive beyond section three. My concern is that the ship might break up."

"We have to get out of here," Daket groaned.

"We should be able to reach the forward emergency pods," Tatel offered. "Can you move?" She was looking down at his leg.

"I'll have to," Daket said, gritting his teeth. If they could actually reach the pods, and if they could get aboard before the cruiser broke up, and if the pods would launch, and if the Federation ship did not attack the pods and destroy them as soon as they were launched—which was precisely what a Televek commander would do, what Daket himself would likely do, he thought grimly, all things being equal—if all that happened, it would constitute the first thing that had actually gone well during this entire venture. . . .

The other four members of the bridge crew were limping or crawling away now, following Daket's overheard advice. As they began to move, a deafening groan issued from the cruiser's ruptured hull, metal tearing at metal. The sound was felt as well as heard. Daket hastily tried to scramble up as the others around him vanished through the bridge's forward hatchway, scurrying toward the pods. The pain in his leg stopped him cold.

He winced and eased himself back down, listening to the bulkheads twisting apart. When he looked up, he saw Tatel coming back toward him. The groaning had stopped, if only for a moment.

"I will help you," Tatel said, reaching down, grabbing Daket's large frame beneath his arms, and hoisting him up. She was apparently stronger than she looked.

Daket said nothing, but he did not object. In fact, he was quite grateful for the assistance as they made their way through the open doorway into the corridor beyond, then began to navigate the fallen beams and rubble and smoke. For the life of him, though, he could not figure Tatel's angle, her motivation, for such a foolish act of bravery. But then, not everyone had commercial command potential, something Daket himself had always known he possessed. It followed that in order for him to be "more," someone else clearly had to be . . . "less." Not all Televek were created equal, after all. And in any case, he suspected Tatel wasn't quite right. As she pulled him into one of the pods Daket decided Tatel was simply a technically proficient but hopelessly provincial fool.

"Put a full tactical display of the Televek fleet on-screen," Janeway said. "Include our position. How long before they're on top of us?"

"Approximately two minutes, eleven seconds," Tuvok replied.

"Captain," Kes said, her expression making her seem to have lived all of life in the last few moments,

"I think you should listen to Neelix now. Your only alternative may be to leave."

An obvious statement, Janeway thought, but after so much, having no choice left but to abandon Drenar Four was a hard thing to accept. She could only assume that Kes knew this, and knew as well that, coming from her, the words would be easier to hear; Janeway could see it in the young Ocampa's eyes.

"Bridge to Engineering," Janeway said loudly. "Lieutenant Torres."

"Yes, Captain."

"How long will it take to reconfigure the warp drives?"

"At least fifteen minutes." Torres was silent for a moment, as if she had lost her breath. "And that's if we don't run into problems," she added finally. They both knew that would not be enough time.

"Get right on it," Janeway said. "Do the best you can."

"Our problems are about to be compounded," Paris said, glancing up at the main screen, "unless we get moving."

"Agreed," Janeway said. Paris was carrying out orders, bringing *Voyager* around the nearby moon once again, just approaching the position of the cruiser that had paced them here. Paris would find the derelict, or he would do whatever he could to take *Voyager* to safety. The problem with the latter was that no safe place existed. The combined Televek fleet could outgun and outmaneuver *Voyager* many times over, rendering any tactical attempts to hide behind planets or moons quite hopeless. Yet if they lingered here, *Voyager*'s future would certainly consist of only minutes.

"Abandon the rescue attempt," she said at last. "Helm, plot a course toward the outer gas giants. Mr. Stephens, try hailing the Televek fleet. With a little luck, I may be able to buy us some time."

"The Televek are not responding," Stephens said after only a moment. "The fleet continues to approach at nearly full impulse."

Tuvok said, "Their heading will bring them directly to us. I estimate they will intercept in fifty-nine seconds."

"If we leave the system without warp capability we'll be sitting ducks," Chakotay said.

"And if we stay, they'll cut us off," Janeway muttered. She looked up at the screen as the image changed to real space, magnified many times. At least a dozen ships could be seen now, small shining dots like tiny stars against the black night of space. She stood up and stepped forward. There were words that needed to be said to the crew, both Starfleet and Maquis, men and women who had truly begun to work together and hope together. She had always thought there would be time to say them. It wasn't working out that way.

"Arm the photons and transfer all available power to the shields, including life-support. We won't fire unless they do, but I want to be ready." She looked around her, found Chakotay looking back. "We won't go quietly," she said. "I promise you."

He returned a silent, solemn nod.

"Captain," Tuvok said, his voice raised above his usual Vulcan monotone. "I am detecting multiple energy readings from the planet. Similar to previous contacts, but stronger." He paused. "Much stronger. I'm also reading a massive buildup—"

"In the cavern!" Janeway said, eyes wide as she spun one-half turn to face the tactical bay. "How many individual readings?"

"Dozens, and all of the contacts appear to be headed toward space."

"Put it up," Janeway ordered.

The tactical display Tuvok had been monitoring appeared on the main screen. All eyes watched as a cloud of energy bursts swept up from the planet's surface. They rushed past *Voyager*'s position in an instant, then continued out into space.

"Projected course?" Janeway asked.

Tuvok paused, verifying. "They appear to be on an intercept course toward the Televek fleet. Their individual power levels are continuing to rise to extraordinary levels."

Janeway narrowed her gaze and watched the ghosts cross the screen, watched the Televek fleet bearing down on them, nearly arrived at Drenar Four, close to *Voyager*'s own position now. "I'll just bet they are," she murmured, nodding to herself.

"The energy beings are attacking," Stephens said.

"So it would seem," Chakotay replied.

"The Televek do appear to be under attack," Tuvok said. "Though the nature of the attack is not clear. No weapons have been fired by the energy entities. The Televek are firing, but their weapons are having no verifiable effect."

Chakotay raised his eyebrows. "How do you know the fleet is under attack?"

"The Televek are having . . . technical difficulties. They are experiencing an extraordinary number of system overloads and failures."

"I've got their ship-to-ship communications," Stephens said.

"Let's hear it," Janeway said.

The speaker suddenly erupted in a jumble of voices and background noise. Most of the noise sounded like a series of small explosions. Fire control and massive outages seemed to be of utmost importance to most of the voices being heard.

"It sounds as if entire consoles are shorting out, catching fire," Chakotay said.

"Sensor and audio data indicate that all of the Televek ships are having similar problems," Tuvok said. "The Televek continue to attempt counterattacks, but I have observed no effect on their targets."

"That's because they're only chasing ghosts," Chakotay said with a grin. He looked to the captain.

"Our ghosts, Commander." Janeway smiled back.

The audio confusion was suddenly interrupted by a thundering voice, a female voice. "Withdraw!" the Televek commander shouted.

"I have a visual," Stephens reported.

Janeway nodded to him.

The woman's face appeared on the screen, a Televek not like unlike the others, though she was far older than anyone Janeway had encountered so far, and clearly she had wealth and stature beyond the dreams of most. The bridge of her ship was like the court of a queen, gaudily upholstered and decorated with tapestries, glittering fixtures and fine, scrolled metal arches; her mantled uniform was exquisite in design and color—bright colors, Janeway noted, as if the whole of the universe was supposed to notice her.

"Try to open a channel, Mr. Stephens," Janeway

said, as she watched and listened to the Televek commander shouting in a frantic, yet somehow utterly authoritative voice. A cold intensity gleamed in her narrowed green eyes. Heads would roll, Janeway thought. One way or another.

"Captain," Tuvok said, "two of the cruisers have lost all power. Life pods are being launched. The first of those are at present being collected by neighboring vessels. Several of the other cruisers appear to be maintaining minimal power and control, but I am also showing massive systems failures on the lead ship. A reactor core containment failure is imminent."

Janeway was still watching the woman who had threatened to cast doom on them all. "Any luck with that hail?"

Stephens shook his head. "They're not responding, Captain."

"I didn't think she would."

"It is too late in any case," Tuvok said. The image of the Televek commander, Shaale—if Jonal had told her the right name—suddenly vanished, replaced by a view of space. To one side of the screen a brilliant multicolored flash suddenly lit the heavens.

"The lead cruiser has been destroyed," Tuvok finished. "I am not reading any survivors."

"I'm picking up a hailing signal from just off our starboard," Stephens said.

"Confirm two contacts," Tuvok added. "They are Televek pods. They must have come from the damaged cruiser we left orbiting the near moon."

"They're signaling their fleet that they're coming, Captain," Stephens added.

"How many life signs?" Janeway asked.

Tuvok studied his console. "Eleven in one pod, six in the other."

"Good." Janeway tapped her comm badge. "Bridge to transporter room. I want you to beam Jonal, Mila, and Tassay onto the second of those two pods. Tuvok will transfer the coordinates."

"Aye, sir," came the transporter chief's reply.

"Are you just letting them go?" Chakotay asked.

Janeway sighed. "I'm not going to keep them in our brig for the next seventy years." She held his gaze for a moment. "Comments, Commander?"

Chakotay shrugged agreeably. "Not a one, Captain."

"Transporter room reports all three prisoners beamed aboard the second pod," Tuvok announced.

"Good," Janeway said, knitting her fingers together behind her back. "Mr. Tuvok, I'd like you to put the tactical display back up on the main screen."

As the image appeared, it was clear that the surviving Televek ships were turning, heading away. Two hulks remained, drifting not far from the debris that marked the place where Shaale's vessel had been.

"Bridge to Engineering."

"Torres here, Captain."

"Belay that warp drive reconfiguration order. We've still got moons to move, and it looks as if we just might get the chance."

Janeway turned to Chakotay and saw a stark, wide-eyed look suddenly cross his face. He gasped as his breath seemed to catch in his throat. She tried to reach for him, but suddenly she couldn't see him anymore, and the ghosts were with her.

* * *

Voices filled Janeway's mind, but they were not all the voices of ghosts. Among them were the frightened, astonished voices of more than one hundred forty men and women, the entire crew of *Voyager*. All together, somehow, somewhere, they touched one another in the gentlest way. Then the ghosts began to speak to everyone at once.

There were no words, just as before; it was more a sense, an essence, a tacit meaning. This time, however, there were no visions of suffering, no attacks, no fear, no omens of catastrophes to come, no dead. Just a notion that could only be translated into words like "thank you" . . . "the children" . . . "thank you" . . .

The children were the Drenarians, Janeway thought, sure of it. But the people of Drenar Four were not the children of the ghosts, and the ghosts were not their ancestors. The reality was better than that.

Yet even as those thoughts came to her, the images in her mind—in the mind of everyone on board—suddenly changed. She saw something of the great consciousness that had sent the ghosts, the presence that had spoken to her and to Chakotay, and that spoke to the others now.

At their first entry into the alien stream of consciousness a blizzard of perceptions overwhelmed the crew, bits and pieces of galaxies and worlds and peoples, information that came in emotional as well as visual form. But the stream quickly narrowed and became an image only Janeway recognized, that of a fantastic alien vessel, a ship several hundred times *Voyager*'s size . . . passing before her eyes, blocking countless stars from view. . . .

CHAPTER
17

LIEUTENANT TORRES WAITED PATIENTLY TO BE ADDRESSED while Janeway listened to the reports of the other officers gathered at the briefing room table. *Voyager* was almost back to normal.

"We're ready to get under way, Captain," B'Elanna said in turn. "We have nearly full warp capability, and full impulse." With Drenar Four's three moons finally moved into their projected positions she had at last been able to reconfigure the warp drives. She had even managed to get a small repair crew down to the planet to retrieve *Voyager*'s damaged shuttlecraft.

And according to preliminary data, the planet itself had already begun to quiet, though this change was measurable only by using *Voyager*'s sensors; it would be weeks before the Drenarians noticed a real difference. But it would be enough of a difference, B'Elanna thought, quite pleased with the notion.

"Thank you, Lieutenant," Janeway said. "A good job, all of you."

"How soon will we be leaving?" Neelix said, the first time he had spoken this morning.

"Soon enough," Janeway told him. "Why are you in such a hurry?"

Neelix looked slightly miffed. "I'm not, Captain. I simply wanted to mention that before we go, we ought to take one of your shuttlecraft over to those abandoned Televek cruisers and do a little . . . poking around, for inventory's sake."

Janeway and Chakotay looked at each other, then both of them turned toward B'Elanna.

"Agreed," B'Elanna said. "After all, they did say those ships might have the kinds of parts we need. Maybe that was the one thing they were telling the truth about."

"Neelix," Janeway said with a smile, "I'm going to take you up on that. Paris, lay in a course to those abandoned ships. We'll beam over. Commander," she told Chakotay, "and B'Elanna, make a list. We're going shopping!"

Within minutes *Voyager* stood alongside one of the silent, drifting Televek cruisers. A moment later Captain Janeway, Chakotay, Paris, and Lieutenant Torres materialized in a darkened corridor, handheld lights revealing smooth, unadorned walls. "Chakotay and I will take the bridge,"

Janeway said. "You two know what you have to do. Keep in touch."

They split up, each pair making their way, listening to their own heavy footfalls echo in the otherwise utterly still air—stale air, Janeway noted, thick with the smell of burned circuitry and uncertain chemicals. And cold. Interior temperatures were falling steadily. Janeway could already see her own breath. Life-support had been eliminated along with everything else when the ghosts had attacked.

Guided by Rollins on *Voyager*'s bridge, Janeway found the Televek bridge quickly enough. She and Chakotay went to work at once, looking over the various systems, attempting to determine the extent of the damage.

"We aren't going to get main power on-line," Chakotay said. He was crouched at one of the five compact console clusters that made up most of the bridge. "The primary feeds are melted, along with all contiguous components."

So they weren't going to be able to analyze or test any Televek technologies—not right away, in any case—but as Janeway examined what she guessed must be the tactical and weapons control center, she saw that it hardly mattered. She stood up and let out a deep sigh. "Even if we could route power in here somehow, everything is ruined. The destruction was quite thorough."

Chakotay stood up as well. He nodded, a gesture barely noted in the reflected glow of his flash beam on the panels to either side.

Janeway tapped her comm badge once more. "Torres, Paris, we've got nothing in here. Are you having any luck?"

"Negative, Captain," B'Elanna replied. "Engineering is completely useless. Everything is burned beyond repair. Some of it is still smoldering. The ship's fire-control systems must have begun to function for a short time before the power went dead. Otherwise, I don't think we'd be standing here right now."

"Captain," Tuvok's voice interrupted.

Janeway tapped her badge once more. "Go ahead."

"I am scanning what appears to be a sizable storage area very near the engineering and weapons sections of the cruiser. But the entire section is well shielded. Direct transport inside will not be possible. Subsequent scans indicate a similar room aboard the other derelict. Also, those same scans have turned up very little in terms of stockpiles or supplies, other than ship's stores, and equipment in use."

"You'd expect more, wouldn't you?" Janeway said sardonically.

"Yes, Captain. If the Televek are indeed arms and technology merchants, and if they are routinely as cautious as we have been led to believe, then it is logical to assume they would take the precaution of carrying valuable merchandise in just such an area."

"Acknowledged. Janeway to Torres. Did you get that?"

"Yes, Captain."

"I want both of you to meet us in the corridor near that storage facility at once."

"We're on our way, Captain," Paris replied.

The away team met at where two hallways intersected. They found themselves facing a large double hatchway composed of two-inch-thick terminium. Both B'Elanna and Chakotay looked the entry system over carefully before offering Janeway a mutual shrug.

"It's locked," the Commander noted.

"And without power to anything, we can't bypass the seal," B'Elanna said. "We're going to have to do this another way."

"Agreed," Janeway said. Janeway gave both officers the go-ahead. All three of them stood back as Janeway tapped at her badge. "Transporter room, we're going to need a Type III phaser compression rifle, immediately."

A moment later the rifle materialized on the deck at Chakotay's feet. The commander picked the weapon up and set it to maximum, then held it in both hands at waist level. He waited while the others looked away, then fired point-blank at the center of the doors. One full burst was enough.

"Take care that you don't get burned," Janeway warned as the four of them stepped forward, their faces warm from the heat of the phaser, and used their hands to push the big doors aside. They slid open easily. Paris was the first one through the entryway. Janeway raised her light with his to scan the room. She could hardly believe her eyes.

The room was immense and filled to every corner with dozens of containers, large and small. But without opening a single one it was clear what most of them contained. Diagrams had been attached to the cartons, all of them depicting hardware and components, from EPS conduits and regulators and graviton generators to phaser emitters. And in between the many stacks and rows of crates, on open pallets and protected by clear covering, there rested larger equipment meant for heavy excavation and assault. The Televek had come prepared for some serious digging and a no-contest perimeter defense.

"I can tell you right now," B'Elanna said, striding up to a short stack of crates, the end cap of an aisle formed by dozens of crates, all slightly larger. "We've got that EPS regulator we need, and about seven more, right here."

She laid her hand on one of the crates and seemed

to trace the surface with her fingers, then she looked back at the others and smiled. "They're a little different from ours," she added, turning again to the diagram on the crate's exterior, examining it more closely. "But I think this'll work."

"Janeway to *Voyager*. We're going to need an engineering team over here right away. We've got a big job for them."

B'Elanna started tapping at the nearest crate's keypad while the others headed into the stacks.

The rest of the away team, led by Lieutenant Carey, arrived moments later and went straight to work, cataloging first, opening crates when necessary, then reviewing the data they had collected with one of the two engineering officers. Six hours later Lieutenant Torres pronounced them finished.

Not only would the storeroom provide the EPS unit they needed to bring the phasers back, but one large crate held a precious bonus—a pair of warp-capable tactical probes roughly the size of *Voyager*'s photon torpedoes. B'Elanna examined the find and decided that the entire guidance and instrument mechanism would have to be gutted, but the units could be converted to resupply *Voyager*'s limited stores.

And there was more—a considerable collection of components and hand weapons, no doubt on both ships, all for the taking, but many of them would have served little purpose aboard *Voyager,* and it was not immediately clear what some of the others were for. Moreover, *Voyager*'s own storage capacity was severely limited. In the end, choices had to be made. The second cruiser was largely left alone.

As Janeway sat in the captain's chair reviewing the

final list of procurements, she found she had few complaints.

"That will be all for now," she said, adding a satisfied smile as she handed the PADD back to B'Elanna. She placed both palms flat on the arms of the chair and gazed at the main screen, which was filled with a view of Drenar Four and the stars beyond. "Prepare to get under way," she told the bridge crew.

"Are you planning to visit the Drenarians again before we leave?" Chakotay asked from his own chair, just to Janeway's left.

"No," she said. "We've gone over the line as it is. I think the Prime Directive has been bludgeoned enough for now, current arguments notwithstanding."

"Of course, Captain," Chakotay said wryly.

Janeway looked at him. "Haven't we already had this conversation?"

"Several times," Paris remarked, eyes steady ahead.

"It remains a question that has no definitive answer," Tuvok said. "We cannot be sure how much of the Drenarians' current civilization is the result of the ghosts, or the being or beings who created the ghosts. Therefore, one cannot truly say whether or not we acted irresponsibly when we attempted to avert their destruction."

"I have some idea," Janeway said, looking first at him, then at the others. They waited quietly for her to go on. She took a deep breath. "It's something I learned in the visions I had—or was given. I've had some time to collect my thoughts, and I've got my theories. The Drenarians are convinced that a very ancient god visited them, and that before it left, it opened their hearts and minds to the spirits of their own ancestors. I believe the dying god who passed this way ages ago was actually an alien being possessed of remarkable technology, a being composed of pure energy, perhaps, possibly from another galaxy. What all of you saw, in the vision we all shared, was a glimpse of its spacecraft."

"Yes, Captain," Tuvok said. "It would be illogical to assume anything else."

"Agreed," Chakotay said simply.

"What made the alien travel to the surface of Drenar Four I can't begin to know, but it spent time among the local inhabitants and grew quite fond of them, of their remarkable civilization; perhaps it was even impressed, as I was, by their natural prowess. But either the alien was dying or it implied that it was, and the Drenarians did everything they could to make its final days as satisfactory and fulfilling as possible—little more than gestures to the alien, certainly, but well received, I believe."

"So before it left, the alien created the ghosts to help protect these people," Chakotay concluded.

"Yes," Janeway said. "It built a sort of fence around the planet, but one that would blend with their own culture, without compromising it any more than necessary."

"Like the Caretaker," Paris said, making the connection. "It wanted to protect the race it had found, though for a different reason."

"It could even have been the second Caretaker," Chakotay said offhandedly, as if the idea seemed almost too possible.

"Maybe, but I didn't see that in any of my visions," Janeway said. "We may never know."

"Then in essence we did precisely what that alien did," Tuvok suggested. "We protected the Drenarians while interfering with their culture as little as possible."

"Yes, I'd say so," Chakotay replied, nodding mostly to himself.

"They have lost a certain innocence now, though, haven't they?" Janeway said, rather melancholy. She looked up to find the others staring back at her, obviously concerned—about her, she knew, but not just her. "But they've lost none of their promise, I think," she added.

"Present, or future," Tuvok said.

Janeway acknowledged him with a nod. "Thank you, Mr. Tuvok."

"It *was* right, to help them," Chakotay said, his expression almost pensive. "We couldn't have just walked away."

"You can only live one day at a time," Janeway conceded grimly. Then she let a smile find her lips.

"Take us out of here, Mister Paris."

The smile tightened.

"Take us home."

8   13   14   28   35